THE ENDURING LEGACY

AN AGRIPUNK STORY

THE MARTINIERE LEGACY BOOK FOUR

JOYCE REYNOLDS-WARD

1 / RETURN OF THE PRODIGAL SON

RUBY

Ruby Barkley scowled as she held up one of her favorite nice winter sweaters, a green cashmere that she had splurged on three years ago. Was this going to work for her first official Family functions in Paris, as the Matriarch of the Martinieres? Or was it too worn and shabby? Could she get away with wearing it over one of her nice snap-button Western shirts?

Trying to figure these things out was *hard*, damn it. She had *some* appropriate clothing, but those were mostly for official and/or formal gatherings, or summer business casual dress. The jeans and Western snap-button shirts she regularly wore around her Double R Ranch and for other occasions were too informal even for at-home in Paris, she suspected.

And she *definitely* didn't want to come off as a hick hayseed rancher. It wasn't just Paris. It was a change in how she did business as well. Paris was the beginning of an entirely new life. She had been dancing around this realization ever since Gabe had become *The Martiniere* in October. And now, with the big Martiniere Family Christmas celebration bearing down upon them—

A huge sigh from her husband distracted her. Ruby put the sweater down, glad to think about something besides appropriate wear for *this new life* for at least a few minutes.

"What's wrong, Gabe?"

Gabriel Martiniere looked up, face solemn. He sat at the end of their bed, gazing at his interlocked fingers.

"Oh, nothing."

She sat next to him. "That sigh didn't sound like it was nothing. Damn it, Gabe. You promised to stop hiding things from me. What's wrong?"

Gabe shook his head, a smile quickly twitching his lips before fading. "You caught me, Ruby." He sighed again, but softer. "It's —it's just become real for me. This is the first Family Christmas I've been to since my testimony against the Group thirty years ago. And I'm returning as *The Martiniere*. Not the rebel I used to be." He waved a hand. "All that's happened until now hasn't hit me like this. *I'm The Martiniere.* I have the authority—and the responsibility."

Ruby absorbed this information silently, putting her arm around Gabe and giving him a squeeze. When they were here in Northeastern Oregon, either at her Double R Ranch or Gabe's Moondance Ranch near Pendleton, it was easy to forget that Gabe—once a flat-broke saddle bronc rider on the run—was now one of the richest and most powerful men in the world. The Martiniere, head not only of the interlocking structures that formally made up the Martiniere Family—with a capital F, always—but of the Family's privately held conglomerate, the Martiniere Group.

"I'm quaking in my boots, myself," she said finally. "I don't have the right clothing, and I've never done anything like this. Two weeks in Paris. Yeah, some of it is business, but you know what really scares me? Will I measure up to everyday clothing and manners? I don't have the right casual wear, and as the Matriarch, I know I can't come across as a hick hayseed rodeo queen."

Gabe's grandmother Donna had dropped the title of Matriarch of the Martinieres on Ruby when Gabe and Ruby had remarried a few short months ago. Besides providing Ruby with the authority to manipulate Martiniere mind control programming, being the Matriarch gave her power over the Family structures, including advisory boards of assorted charities and nonprofits that she was still learning about. And that was in addition to her duties for the ranch and the businesses that she ran in collaboration with Gabe.

Gabe laughed softly and slid his arm around Ruby, pulling her close. "Clothing can be remedied pretty quickly in Paris, Ruby."

Ruby rolled her eyes. "Duh, damn it. I should have been thinking about that. Too accustomed to not having money. Another attitude I have to work on."

"It takes getting used to. I'm—" he hesitated, frowning thoughtfully. "After thirty years away from the Family, there's still some things I'm readjusting to. Even though my marriage to Rachel brought me into some money, that went away after her death. And her money was—nothing—compared to the resources we have now."

"Yeah," she said slowly. Her encounters with Gabe's second wife Rachel had been brief, and tied to Brandon, Ruby and Gabe's now-adult son from their first marriage. But it still hurt to know that there had been someone else Gabe had loved enough to marry. And mourn, when she died. Still mourned, at times.

Gabe hugged her, then kissed her temple. "I'm sorry. I shouldn't bring her up."

"Rachel gave you and Brandon joy, and she wasn't the one who broke us up," Ruby said tartly. "Her memory has a place in our lives."

Have to be fair. Rachel loved both Gabe and Brandon. Was a good stepmother to Bran. Even though—

Ruby still remembered the pain when she learned that Gabe was remarrying.

At least it wasn't Mariah Meyers.

"Oh, Ruby." Gabe kissed her again. "In any case, I'm planning to do some shopping, because I need to upgrade my wardrobe. I'd say pack light, with plans to invest in high-quality winter business and casual attire in Paris."

"Fussing about clothes is silly, next to your worries."

"Your concerns aren't silly. Just new experiences for you—and I'm not that worried, really. It's just—I suddenly realized that thirty years ago, the last time I was in Paris for Christmas, I showed up late, and between Serg and Piotr; Kendra and Scott and some of the other cousins, I was shambling, staggering drunk for the whole three weeks I was there. When I wasn't fighting with Philip and Joseph. This time is going to be so different."

Gabe had originally thought Philip was his uncle, until his grandmother revealed just before he and Ruby remarried that Philip was his father. Philip was the former Martiniere, with a legacy of corruption and exploitation that Ruby, Gabe, and their allies inside the Family were only starting to ferret out.

Joseph had been Gabe's cousin and Philip's adopted son, now dead as well.

Ruby leaned into Gabe, providing comfort through contact.

He continued after a significant pause. "It's the contrast. If it hadn't been for my allies dragging me out to get drunk back then, things could have gotten pretty ugly. Philip and I nearly got into several fistfights, as it were." He shivered. "And honestly? If I had started beating on him, it wouldn't have stopped until he was dead. If he hadn't locked me down with mind control vocal tones and killed me first, that is. It was too damned close for comfort at times. One or the other of us would have died. It was just that bad. My first Christmas here at the Double R, rough as it was, was still pleasant by comparison."

"Oh, Gabe."

Gabe exhaled. "I haven't missed that experience."

"And then there's going to be wondering who's on our side and who isn't."

"Mmm, that's always been part of Family life. Factions forming and breaking. Except for our closest kin, and even that's not guaranteed." Gabe rubbed his face. "I keep being struck by the difference. Thirty years. Coming back as the Martiniere, not simply a high-level heir. That's going to be different. Starting with the accommodations. Before, I had a junior suite. Now we're in the penthouse's primary suite."

"Penthouse? Junior suite?" Ruby's voice screeched out of control.

Just *how big* was the Martiniere mansion in Paris? Big enough to hold at least fifty or more family members easily during the holidays, from the way both Gabe and his sister—originally thought his cousin—Justine talked.

Ruby hadn't had time to discuss their housing with Gabe after he told her he would take care of it, and she trusted him to advise her of any special considerations. Her life had become even more hectic over the past six weeks. Brandon and Kris getting married; Kris's difficult pregnancy.

Ruby and Gabe's adopted son Mikey, Philip's five-year-old clone, had contracted strep throat after Thanksgiving, and given his fragile health, that had been an issue.

Work. Setting the spring release dates for new versions of the biobots both strictly hers and those she shared with Gabe and their business partner, plus Gabe's microbials. Since Gabe was buried in Martiniere business connected to the change in leadership for both the Group and the Family, Ruby was managing those distribution agreements, plus orders and plans for expanding their labs.

And at the same time handling a miserably sick five-year-old and advising a nervous son about his pregnant wife. While Charlie Thompson was an excellent ranch manager and they were in winter mode, she still needed to keep track of events on the Double R.

That initial flood of work tied to the biobots had diminished to a manageable level, only requiring a couple of hours a day to check in as she hired subordinates. And, fortunately, Mikey was pretty good about keeping himself entertained. Almost too good—if anything, Ruby had to keep an eye on him to ensure he wasn't concealing how bad he felt.

She hoped—probably futile, but a woman could dream—that Paris was a chance to take a holiday from business. Gabe *had* promised that this would be their belated honeymoon, but Ruby knew their businesses too damn well to imagine that they could completely get away from work. Even in Paris. *Especially* in Paris, with Gabe's responsibilities as the Martiniere.

Gabe nodded. "Yes. We're in the penthouse. Have our own primary suite. I invited Brandon and Kris; Justine and Donald; and Donna-gran to stay with us, in the junior penthouse suites."

"Oh." She could handle seeing their son Brandon and his wife Kris, Gabe's sister Justine and her ex-husband Donald, and his grandmother Donna in a casual setting. Justine and Donna had stayed at the Double R and Moondance, already knew Ruby and how she did things. Ruby still didn't understand the dynamics between Justine and Donald, but they seemed to be amiable, and the two were a couple at Family functions, ever since Gabe had become the Martiniere.

So we see Donald and Justine together in a Martiniere setting, both public and private. That will be interesting.

When those two had first come to the Double R last summer, they had been much more lovey-dovey than they still were in public. Something was happening there. Ruby just didn't know what.

"The penthouse is private, for the Martiniere and his chosen family members. Has its own kitchen and cleaning staff. Secure entrance. Secure locks on each suite in the penthouse."

Ruby raised her brows at that. "Are things that difficult?"

"The reasons for the layout are based on Family history over more than four centuries. Not just me and Philip, or Philip and his brothers." Gabe nuzzled her temple and cheek once more. "But it also allows for privacy and a chance to relax."

"Now *that* sounds promising," Ruby said. She turned her head just enough to capture Gabe's lips in a long, lingering kiss.

"Temptress," Gabe murmured against her lips.

"Always," she purred back, as his hands slid under her turtleneck and they flopped onto the bed.

———

It was a long flight from the Double R to Paris even on a private jet, one of the fleet maintained by Justine. Before landing in Paris, Gabe, Ruby, and Mikey changed from the sweats they had traveled in to more formal attire—slacks, collared shirt and tie with a jacket for Gabe and Mikey, a skirt suit for Ruby, and good overcoats for all three of them.

"Here's what to expect," Gabe said. "Mikey, listen close, because you are part of this." He rubbed his face and continued. "When we arrive at the house, there *will* be a reception. The whole damn Family in residence by then. I'm not sure what my uncle Gerard has in mind—I asked him to keep it simple because we are jet-lagged. No food or formal reception—we'll eat once we go to the penthouse. It will be a good excuse to break free sooner. But it's not just my return to his house after thirty years. I'm returning as the Martiniere."

"And all of us need to go through it?" Ruby glanced over at Mikey. His face had gone tight and pale. He chewed on his lower lip. "Mikey's really tired."

"The initial greeting, yes. It will be carefully choreographed. First us, then Brandon and Kris, then Justine and Donald. The Martiniere and his close family. There will be photographs."

"It sounds like a royal function," she said.

"Don't kid yourself—if France had gone back to a monarchy while Philip was alive, he'd have been agitating to become king, in spite of his US passport. As Martinieres, we descend from

Charles the Ninth through a cadet branch connected to his illegitimate son, Charles de Valois. Plus occasional marriages to junior Bourbons." Gabe fixed Mikey with a stern look. "Philip took that ancestry much more seriously than he should have. It fueled his ambitions to become the dictator of the United States."

Mikey nodded, his face mirroring Gabe's solemn expression. Gabe smiled and ruffled Mikey's hair, then straightened it out.

"The cyborg brothers will be there, Mikey, and they'll take care of you. You won't have to do much besides the initial greetings and photographs."

Mikey didn't look quite as scared after Gabe mentioned his former protectors.

"But where am I staying?" he asked.

"You'll be in the penthouse, with us. The brothers are serving as our personal protection, so they'll be in and out."

Ruby contemplated that. She was still adjusting to this new life, not just the money but the other parts of being a Martiniere.

"Meanwhile," Gabe concluded as the plane descended. "Just remember this. I'm proud of you. You are *my family*, and to hell with anyone who has a problem with any member of it."

His face took on that stern expression that Ruby was beginning to recognize as being *The Martiniere Has Spoken.*

New to her—like so much of the Martiniere life.

Ruby couldn't help stifling a yawn as they rode through Paris, cobblestones and pavement glimmering damp under streetlights. While she had napped during their flight, she was still tired. Mikey slumped against her side. He had fallen asleep shortly after they got into the SUV.

They slowed to turn through a stone archway as iron gates swung open, and drove into an enclosed courtyard. Ruby glanced around at the imposing structure that *surrounded* them.

It was just like the castles she had seen in photographs, except—no moat. And it was in the middle of Paris.

So fucking big.

"Welcome to the Hôtel Martiniere," Gabe said, his voice oddly tight as Mikey jerked awake.

"Is this all—?" she asked in a very small voice.

"Yes," Gabe said, pointing to a well-lighted entrance. "We go in there, and the penthouse is in that portion. But all of this?" He waved a hand. "Yes." He pointed to the wing on their right. "I was born in Los Angeles. But I spent my first seven years there, before we returned to LA. My late sister Louisa was born here."

"Wow," Mikey whispered, his eyes wide.

The passenger door opened next to Mikey, and a woman wearing a uniform with a long, gray overcoat and white gloves held out her hand. Mikey pushed close to Ruby, his slight body tensing.

Ruby gently kissed the top of his head. "It's all right, Mikey. Give her your hand." She glanced at the woman. "Be patient with him, please," she said in French. "He's shy with strangers. Also, his French is minimal."

The woman smiled at Mikey. "I am just helping you out of the vehicle so that you don't fall, little one," she said softly, in heavily accented English.

Mikey hesitantly extended his hand to rest it on her white glove. Then he stood carefully. He slipped on the running board as he stepped down, and the woman caught him, steadying Mikey until he stood straight on the ground. Then she turned back to offer a hand to Ruby, and finally Gabe.

"Mikey," Gabe said once he was out of the SUV. "I need to take Ruby's left hand. You can take my free hand or hers. Your choice."

Mikey pressed in close to Ruby and took her right hand.

Doors slammed behind them. Ruby glanced back to see Brandon and Kris, her pregnancy showing under her heavy coat, and the cyborged brothers, who had flown over with them. More doors thumping, and Justine stepped out of her SUV, accompanied by Donald.

Gabe turned slightly to look at the others as they lined up.

"Here we go," he said. "Everyone ready for the presentation of the new Martiniere and his close family?"

"Yes," Ruby said.

Mikey nodded.

"As ready as I'll ever be," Brandon said, his voice tight.

"Easier than you expect," Justine said. "Relax."

"That's what you think, Tine. You've not been away as long as I have," Gabe muttered as he faced forward. "All right. Let's do this."

Uniformed security staff standing alongside the red carpet leading to the double front doors bowed to Ruby and Gabe as they passed by. When they approached the doors, two of the staff opened them. Ruby briefly wondered if they were indentured or free. No way to tell with gloved hands and high collars. The Martiniere trefoil indenture brand could be either on the webbing between thumb and index finger of the person's right hand, or on the neck. Hand meant temporary. Neck meant permanent. Neither would be visible in the uniforms staff wore.

Gabe nodded at the staff as his hand tensed on Ruby's. He straightened up, imperceptibly an inch taller, his face tightening and falling into stern lines. Ruby followed suit.

On her other side, Mikey clenched her hand almost as snugly as Gabe did.

This is it.

The real meaning of becoming a Martiniere.

Butterflies danced in her gut. And this was somehow more daunting to face than Grand Entry at the Pendleton Round-Up. Riding barrels at the National Finals. Making formal sales presentations to a large group of investors. She really *had* married into nobility, even though they no longer claimed any titles.

Before they stepped inside, Gabe released Ruby's hand, slipping his arm under her elbow, then taking hold of her hand again as he raised their arms, displaying the emerald Martiniere mind control command ring that served as her wedding band. Another Family tradition. If she ran a finger over the emerald, then she could issue commands to any mind-conditioned Martiniere or Martiniere indentured servant—and be obeyed. A ring worn only by certain wives of the Martiniere—and it had been hidden in Gabe's possession for years.

Gabe's uncle Gerard met them. "Gabriel. Welcome home."

Gabe inclined his head. "Thank you, Gerard."

Breathe, Ruby, she told herself as she looked beyond Gabe and Gerard to the mass of people waiting to see them.

Gerard greeted Brandon and Kris. Then he guided them to Mikey's side, and placed Justine next to Gabe, Donald on the far side of Justine. Staff stepped forward and Gabe helped Ruby and Mikey out of their overcoats, then removed his. He slipped his arm back under hers as Mikey clenched hard on her other hand, pushing close to Ruby's side.

Gerard stepped forward and clapped his hands.

"Family," Gerard said, in French. Ruby listened closely. She'd been cramming and updating her college French over the past few weeks for survival's sake. "May I introduce the new Martiniere and his close kin. Gabriel Marcus Martiniere, son of Philip. His wife, Ruby Marie Barkley, the new Matriarch. Their adopted son, Michael. Their son Brandon, the Martiniere-in-waiting, and his wife Krista. Gabriel's sister Justine and her former husband, Donald Atwood."

Gerard bowed low to Gabe. The mass of people beyond him bowed or curtsied, deeper than Gerard. Gabe inhaled sharply, his hand and arm tensing even more on Ruby's.

So many faces.

And they all seemed to be questioning, demanding.

When Gabe spoke, his voice was steady and calm, unwavering, as if he wasn't gripping Ruby's hand as hard as he could to keep from trembling.

"Family," he said, in English. "I thank you all for this welcome. My family and I are grateful for this honor. It's a quite different reception from when I was here last, thirty years ago, and my everlasting thanks go to those of you who supported me and made me your Martiniere." He paused, repeating what he had just said in French before switching back to English. "I appreciate your presence. But it has been a long flight from Oregon. Michael has been ill and Brandon's wife is expecting their first child."

Some of the elders amongst the mass of people shifted their attention to Brandon and Kris, growing approval and pleasure softening their expressions.

"They in particular need time to rest," Gabe continued. "I ask that we save the formalities for Christmas dinner and keep our introductions informal." Another repeat in French, then continuing in English. "As many of you know, my dear Ruby and I have recently remarried, and this is the first opportunity we have had for a honeymoon. I ask for your indulgence during my first Christmas as the Martiniere. We will be withdrawing more than you might expect otherwise, and I request that we treat tonight as an informal gathering."

The crowd burst into applause even before Gabe repeated his words in French, tight faces softening into smiles.

How much of the French is simply formality?

Mikey pushed closer to Ruby.

"Let our revelries begin. May our holiday be peaceful and without conflict. I will conduct limited business, of course, but for this gathering—" He eased his hand free and wrapped his arm around Ruby, turning her slightly to give her a big kiss. "This is our belated honeymoon."

More applause, and laughter. Ruby grinned at Gabe, then looked down at Mikey. His face was pinched and drawn.

"I think we'd better give Mikey a break after the photographs," she said softly to Gabe, as photographers now pushed in front of the rest of the Family.

Gabe nodded. "Bran, if you and Kris want to take Mikey and go to the penthouse once the photos are done, that would be a really good idea. There's supposed to be a cold supper waiting for us."

"I'm good with that," Brandon said.

"Gerard—?" Gabe asked.

"I'll escort them upstairs," Gerard said. "You do remember—"

"I'm not likely to forget the way to the penthouse," Gabe said dryly. "Even if it has been thirty years since I got hauled up there for an ass-chewing by Philip."

Once Brandon, Kris, and Mikey followed Gerard up the stairs, followed by the cyborged brothers, Justine moved to stand next to Ruby while Donald stepped away to speak to other Family members.

The Family approached in smaller groups. Ruby recognized some faces from her quick trip to Europe during October to drum up support for Gabe's bid to depose Philip. Some had attended their wedding, and still others had made the trek to Moondance for the meeting which confirmed Gabe as the Martiniere. As they came forward, Justine whispered to Ruby how they were connected to Gabe.

"There's going to be problems with Adrien and Vincent," Justine muttered to Ruby, nodding toward two middle-aged men who hung back, once most of the Family had greeted them and introduced themselves to Ruby.

"I'm not surprised," Ruby whispered back. She had already encountered the two during her previous trip to Europe. Both men had grilled her intensely about Gabe's intentions. Vincent was Gerard's younger son and Adrien the younger son of Gabe's aunt Madeline.

Justine rolled her eyes. "Younger sons. A problem for the Family over centuries."

"This isn't the 1600s."

"That's what you think."

"Ladies." Gabe's voice was soft but firm. "Not the place."

"All *right*, Gabie," Justine snarked in response, smirking.

Gabe's hand was tighter on Ruby's than ever. "Enough, Justine," she said quietly.

Her sister-in-law glanced at them, and didn't say any more.

At last, it was done. Gabe put his arm around Ruby. "That's all for tonight," he said firmly. "We are tired and hungry. More tomorrow."

Justine and Donald remained behind with the other Family members as Gabe propelled Ruby through the gathered crowd and up the stairs, the firm pressure on her back only easing after they had climbed a couple of flights and were on a landing out of sight from below. Then he dropped his arm from her back and leaned against the railing.

"Are you all right?" Ruby asked. His face was its normal color, so…not a health problem?

But Gabe had already experienced one heart attack, nine years ago, at age forty-eight.

Ruby vividly remembered Brandon's frantic call from Moondance when it happened. He had planned to go to a science fiction convention with Gabe and Rachel that weekend.

—Mom. Dad's in the hospital, in Pendleton, and they're talking about possible transport to Portland. I'm—oh God, Mom. Sixteen-year-old Brandon's voice had quavered over the comm.

Oh shit, had been her first thought. *What's happened now?*

—What is it, Bran?

—Heart attack. They won't tell me anything more than that. And Rachel—she's having a hard time. Freaking out. I drove her to the hospital. She can't stop crying. I have to support her. And we still have fields to plant. Oh God, Ma, he just collapsed after he called me to dinner. Said something about avenging him. What is that all about?

—I don't know.

She had steadied Brandon, given him suggestions about handling Rachel, told him to take what time was needed to help

Gabe and Rachel, and then not heard any more details until she and Gabe were together again.

Now, she wished that she had pushed further at the time, perhaps even called Gabe to ask *what the hell did you mean when you asked Brandon to avenge you?*

Not that Gabe could have told her anything, locked down as he had been, thanks to mind control.

And heart problems shouldn't be an issue these days, because of the anti-aging serum they'd been given.

Five years grace.

After five years—the lifetime of the serum, supposedly—health issues could be a worry. But Ruby was concerned, all the same. That same serum hadn't prevented cardiac problems in Gabe's grandmother Donna, and Gabe had dealt with many more health challenges than Donna.

Gabe rubbed his face and exhaled. "I just need a moment, Rubes." He looked up and gave her a faint smile. "It's not my heart. I promise." He pushed off the railing and reached for her again, taking her into his arms, nuzzling that area between her neck and shoulder that he sought when he desired solace.

They stood together for a few moments. Then Gabe straightened up. "Yeah. First appearance at Family Christmas as the Martiniere. Now that it's over, I'm feeling one hell of an adrenaline crash on top of jet lag. It'll be better after this." He smiled at Ruby. "I'm absolutely starving." He pulled away, but took her left hand as they climbed up the stairs.

"Not surprising. You didn't eat much today."

"Old habits. I never ate a lot during Christmas until you and I got together. If I knew there was a likelihood that I'd have my control words used on me, I wouldn't eat much, to minimize the risk of puking or soiling myself. Because sometimes things were just that bad." He grimaced. "Like what happened during my testimony. Philip got a psychotropic to me that augmented the effects of my control words. When his attorney used those words in the courtroom, the results were—pretty damn embarrassing.

Even though something like that happening was *extremely* unlikely to happen tonight, even though all of that programming is *gone*, old concerns die hard."

She tightened her hand on his. "I'm sorry."

Gabe shrugged and glanced around. "I have a lot of things to adjust to yet. Especially being the prodigal son, after being in exile so long." They stopped at the head of the stairs and he raised her hand to his lips. "And I am so, so very grateful to have you at my side, my love. So very damn grateful."

That sharp, piercing gaze of his smoldered as Gabe straightened up with a slow smile, his eyes fixed on her, sending a frisson of delight through her body.

They say that power's an aphrodisiac, but I've never really needed that with Gabe.

Ruby smirked at him.

Then again, perhaps she had always sensed the power lying underneath his façade, back when he appeared to be just an impoverished bronc rider on the run from indenture.

"The two of us together, Gabe," she said softly. "Side by side, we can deal with just about anything. Even now."

He exhaled. "*Especially* now." He pulled her close and they kissed. "Mmm."

"Food first," she said. "Then a shower, and—we'll see, hmm?"

"I'm going to hold you to that," he said.

Ruby laughed as Gabe opened the door to the penthouse.

She could get used to this life, she supposed.

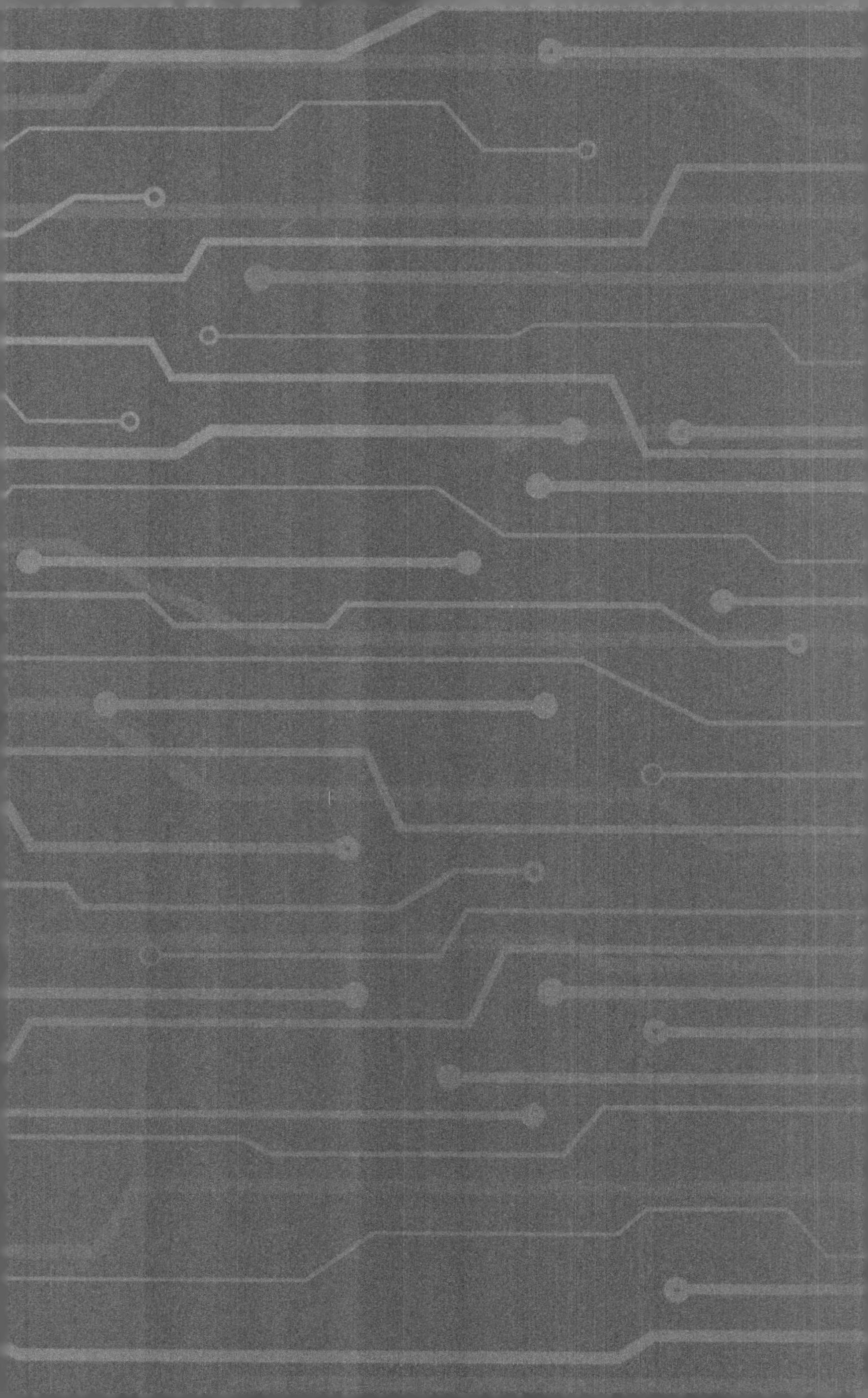

GABE

The conversation he squelched between Ruby and Justine about *younger sons* during the night of their arrival continued to haunt Gabe two days later, as he dealt with the aftermath of their first full day in Paris. Indentureds controlled by Adrien attempted to abduct Ruby while shopping. His beloved handled them, but…it shouldn't have happened.

Those indentureds were of a class that should not have been exported from the US, much less still be active. *Specifically* of the type that Gabe demanded be deprogrammed and released once he became the Martiniere. Uncovering the details revealed the degree to which Adrien had been manipulated by Philip.

Younger sons. Problems. And they were his concern, as the Martiniere. How many other disaffected younger sons within the Family did he have to deal with, besides Adrien and Vincent? And why weren't more of the Family's younger members here, for Family Christmas? Had traditions changed?

Gabe didn't think so. Ending traditions was *not* something that Philip did. *He* was the rebel, not Philip.

And as for Vincent and Adrien—well, he *had* dealt with them.

Vincent was easily handled by transferring him to cousin Arthur's division, getting him away from his older brother David's supervision in Gerard's division. A simple case of sibling rivalry.

But Adrien. A problem without a solution within the Family. And while Vincent was happy with the prospect of a change in roles, and might settle into working with Arthur and his son Charles, Adrien reminded Gabe too damn much of Philip in his drive for power and control.

Could he have done something different with Adrien other than turn him over to the authorities? Gabe wrestled with that issue as he dealt with Martiniere business the morning of their second day in Paris.

He had missed so much of the Family dynamics while in exile. *Was* this a younger son issue, like Justine had hinted? He needed to have a long talk with his sister. After all, she had informally been their father's enforcer—to what degree, Gabe still didn't know, and wasn't sure he wanted to know. They were still reconstructing their relationship.

And yet. He had promised Ruby and Mikey that they would have *fun*. Managing this issue wasn't going to go away with one morning's effort. He could work straight through Christmas, and it wouldn't solve the problem that he visualized emerging.

Gabe sighed. He shared his uncle Gerard's office, sitting at Gerard's big desk while his uncle took a smaller one in the corner. Not the routine that Philip had maintained, from what Gabe remembered—but unlike the days of Philip, the penthouse had no free space for meetings, because his family took up all the rooms. Nor did he feel inclined to drag Family leaders up to the penthouse to bask in his glory, as Philip had done. The Martiniere Group was a business, damn it, and he was going to manage it like one. Not as his own personal fief and springboard to greater power, like Philip. And he sure as hell wasn't going to direct the Family in that manner, either.

"That is a heavy sigh, Gabriel," Gerard said, in French.

"I knew things were bad," Gabe said, continuing in French. "Family members were coming to me even before Ruby and I remarried and I became the Martiniere." He waved his right hand. "Lower-level family members. And then there's this business with Adrien and Vincent—what should I know about things that have been happening with the high-level heirs?"

Gerard heaved a sigh of his own. "This talk is best held with others present."

Gabe rubbed his chin. "Then let's get it over with. I can already feel Ruby eying me with her arms crossed and her toe tapping. I'm sure she's ready to relax and wants me to be done with business. This *is* supposed to be our honeymoon."

Gerard laughed. "Your Ruby is quite the woman, Gabriel. I would not cross her, either. Formidable even before she became the Matriarch, or at least that is the impression I got from Arthur, Piotr, and Paul."

Gabe nodded. Cousins Arthur and Paul had met Ruby when Justine had taken her to the Real Truthers fundraising banquet where Philip had received the party's nomination for President. And Piotr...Gabe would give good money to figure out where Cousin Piotr encountered Ruby. Unless Serg had been talking to his father.

Then again, Piotr met Brandon as a ten-year-old, when Bran had been clumsily programmed by one of Philip's agents, and Piotr removed the programming. It wouldn't surprise Gabe that Piotr found a means to discreetly encounter Brandon's mother at some point after that. After all, Brandon was a potential Martiniere-in-waiting, and Piotr would want to know more about his background. Ruby hadn't mentioned meeting Piotr, but she was sufficiently visible over the years that it wouldn't be difficult for his sneaky elder cousin to find a means to observe her in action.

"The stupidest belief I ever held when I was on the run was thinking that Ruby couldn't hold her own within the Family," he said softly. "But I was afraid of what Philip would do to her and Brandon…." His voice trailed off.

He would never willingly call that man his father. *Saul* was his father. *Philip* was his sperm donor.

Gerard's face tightened. "You were right to fear what Philip could have done to Ruby and Brandon, Gabriel." He paused. "And that is very close to what we need to discuss. Give me a moment and I will call the others in."

As Gerard sent out the message to the Family leaders staying at the Hôtel Martiniere, Gabe poured himself more coffee.

"I think this meeting might best be held in the library," Gerard said.

Gabe nodded and followed his uncle down the hallway. The library. Traditional and mandatory retreat for the men of the Family after formal dinners, when Gerard would dispense whisky, cognac, and cigars. Then they would be subjected to one of Philip's rants about the failings of Family leaders.

This was still mid-morning, though. Did Gerard mean to pour alcohol for this discussion? If so….

Gerard gestured toward the big chair that had always been Philip's as they entered. "Your seat, Martiniere."

"This feels—weird," Gabe said softly in English, as he settled into the big chair.

Gerard raised his brows. "You look like you belong there, Gabriel."

"Memories. I suppose it's time to start making new ones."

"Especially with *this* discussion," Gerard said, continuing in English. "Whisky? Cognac?"

"I think whisky for this talk."

So it is one of those *discussions. Damn it.*

Gabe's gut tightened as Arthur and his son Charles filed in, followed by Paul, Ken, Piotr, and Christopher. Pierre Durand, Adrien's elder brother. Others. Gerard's elder son David and Brandon entered together, last of all, laughing at something Brandon had said.

A good sign.

But Bran always did well mixing with others—part of his past job in media.

Gerard pointed to the smaller chair next to Gabe's. "The seat for the Martiniere-in-waiting."

Brandon eyed Gabe. He nodded.

Gerard set the glass of whisky on the table next to Gabe before he closed the door. "Cognac or whisky?" he asked Brandon.

Brandon raised his brows, looking at Gabe.

"I'm drinking whisky," Gabe said. "Along with my coffee."

"Then the same for me," Brandon said.

Silence ruled, except for Gerard's careful questions as he dispensed the liquor. Gabe sipped his coffee, waiting. Remembering the routines.

"I don't intend for this to be as formal as past gatherings of this sort," he said finally, in English, once Gerard settled into his seat. "But I have been away for thirty years. Things have happened within the Family that I am not completely aware of, and that I need to know." He exhaled. "Furthermore, I have no fucking desire to rule either the Family or the Group with the same damn stranglehold that Philip did for all those years, with the exception of my edict about indentured workers. We're all competent, and I respect what you do."

He paused, noticing the degree to which faces and bodies relaxed.

"However, we have a problem," he said. "Ever since I revealed myself, I've had a number of appeals from lower-level Family members for help, because they opposed Philip. There appears to be a certain degree of dissatisfaction within the Family ranks, both personally and within the Group." He sipped his whisky. "One thing concerns me, as I review files and look around to see who is and isn't here. Why are so few high-level heirs present for our Christmas gathering? Our numbers are about half of what I thought they would be. Does this reflect disapproval of me as the Martiniere—or does it illustrate another problem within the Family?"

Significant glances.

Arthur sighed. "Martiniere, those you see here today are the survivors of several Family purges."

"What happened to them?" God, he wanted to toss that damned whisky down his throat after hearing that.

Damn you, Philip.

And Artie wasn't usually this formal, even in these gatherings. Calling him *Martiniere,* instead of *Gabe* or *Gabriel?*

This is bad. Oh, this has to be bad.

"Some are dead," Piotr said. "Others institutionalized. Still others disowned."

Gabe's fingers tightened on his whisky.

What the hell.

He tossed it down his throat after all.

"So that's why there are so few heirs Brandon's age." Gerard approached with the whisky bottle and Gabe held his glass out. "So few my age. How the hell did Philip pull that off?"

"Accidents, or so we've been told," Christopher said. "I sent my children into hiding to keep them from Philip."

"Hiding?" Gabe sipped his whisky. Gerard had given him a generous pour.

So this session is going to be that fucking awful, damn it.

"Alice and Ben grew up with my wife's relatives in Australia, under assumed names," Christopher answered. "My sister Kendra and her family were attacked and tortured by alleged pirates twenty years ago, in the Caribbean. No survivors."

Gabe winced. His uncle Peter, Christopher's father, had been one of Philip's first victims, even before the man Gabe called *father,* Philip's older twin, Saul. Cousin Kendra helped Justine escape from Philip, and was part of the early resistance to Philip's tyranny within the Family.

To hear that Kendra was amongst the fallen—damn it, not fair, not fair at all.

"My children established their homes in Switzerland," David said. "Again, under assumed names."

"Any others?" Gabe asked.

"Everyone has a story," Gerard said. "Your disappearance was a warning to us. Many of our children and grandchildren have not been raised within the Family, to protect them from Philip."

"Then let's hear it." Gabe braced himself with another sip.

Gabe listened as each man recited the litany of hidden, lost, and relocated heirs. Dead. Placed in Martiniere Group branches located in countries distant from Europe and North America, under assumed names. Disappeared—with unknown fates, just as he had been. Some institutionalized. Some forced into indenture, their records and identities lost.

Ten high-level Martiniere heirs gone, either to death, institutionalization, or indenture, their estates folded into Philip's. Ten more hidden, waiting for the outcome of the latest power struggle. Two generations—his and Brandon's—diminished by the losses. And those were just the *high-level* heirs. The decimation was worse amongst the less powerful family members.

Gabe rubbed his face, thinking.

Wrong, so damned fucking wrong.

All things considered, after hearing this news, Adrien and Vincent *should* have been holding higher, more responsible positions within the Family and the Group than they did, especially given the shortage of other heirs. This meant that there were many more non-Family members in Group leadership positions than he realized.

A good thing or a bad thing?

He wouldn't know until he had each and every division leader checked out. At least a certain percentage of them would be devoted to Philip—he was certain of that. Not every follower of Philip would have resigned or fled after his death. And enough of them would be just sneaky and discreet enough to stay hidden—God, how many of them were members of that damned cult of the Electric Born, that Philip had created? He knew too damn much about the Electric Born from his days with Alvarez Armory.

Gabe dropped his hand and took another sip of whisky, shuddering at the memory of what one branch of the Electric Born had done to Rafe Alvarez, his brother-in-law from his second marriage. They had butchered Rafe like they would a cow or hog. Gabe *hoped* that Rafe died before the worst of that happened, but he suspected that poor Rafe had been sedated and alive for part of it.

None of that branch of the Electric Born survived. He made sure of that, one of the few times Gabe gave free rein to the rage in his blood, killing freely like Philip would have. Oh, that was one bloody mess. But the Heaven's Reach commune that tortured Rafe was just one of many similar compounds that Philip established in North America.

And in other places?

Gabe didn't know—and the reality was that he knew less than he should.

"We have to fix this situation," he said finally, breaking the silence. "We have two problems. First, the lost and hidden heirs. Second, the constraints on Family members who *have* remained active within the Group, but not advanced in their positions. It's one thing to have fewer Family members in leadership positions because we don't have competent people. It's another to have younger members—sons and daughters alike—frustrated and engaged in problematic behaviors because there's no paths within the Group for them to prove themselves."

"Philip did not encourage dissension or initiative except amongst his favorites," Paul said. "And, frankly—I refused to expose my children other than Lucien to his tender mercies."

"I don't blame you," Gabe said. "I have too many memories of drinking my way through this holiday to keep from hurting too badly, should Philip decide to use my control words to render me helpless while he beat me."

"All of us here have been subjected to Philip's rages," David said. "It was the price for accepting Family and Group leadership. And even when my father forbade Philip from beating people here—Philip found other means to hurt everyone."

"Well, that era is *over*," Gabe said. "It's probably too late for this year, but I want the word to go out. I want to recruit qualified Family members for leadership roles in the Group. Bring forth your hidden family—men and women alike. Recommend lower-level heirs if needed." He studied the Family heads in front of him. "The strength of the Martiniere Group has always rested in the diverse abilities of our Family members. I refuse to believe that our strength is fading—because if it has, then there is no reason for us to be a privately held company. We might as well take the Group public and bring in fresh ideas."

He allowed himself a sardonic smile at the intake of breath from that last statement. Only Christopher and those around him, from the British Family, didn't react. Chris half-smiled at that statement.

Need to find out what that's all about.

Too much he still didn't know, and Chris *had been* a leader in one attempt to overthrow Philip. No time to investigate that until now—and it was surprising that Chris was still alive. That spoke to his ability to maneuver.

"I want reports from each of you about the status of those missing high-level heirs from your branches of the Family," Gabe continued. "I want to know who is legitimately institutionalized, and who isn't. Which ones got forced into indenture. Those whose fates we don't know—yet. Brandon."

"Yes?"

"You're good at tracking indentureds, and you have the connections within the indentured freedom groups. I want you and Kris to find and release those Martinieres who have been forced into indenture. No matter what level heir they are. They'll be excellent advisors for the process of phasing out indenture within the Group."

His son's lips tightened—indenture was the fate that Philip had intended for him, after all. "I will." Brandon glanced over at Charles. "Charles, if possible, I'd like to borrow Vincent for this job. I think he'll be good at it."

"Good." Gabe eyed the others. "The other thing. I don't want just your sons and brothers. I want your wives, daughters and sisters. We've been a patriarchy too damn long. Justine should have been able to depose Philip and shut down Joseph when they went off the rails years ago. But because of our damn Family structures, she couldn't. And now we're in a position where we can't afford the luxury of exclusively male leadership. We *need* our women, now more than ever."

It wasn't only Justine who had been harmed by this policy. His aunts Madeline and Jeannette were brilliant. But only Madeline's sons, Pierre and Adrien, held positions in the Group, and Adrien was a mess, unqualified and power-hungry.

Jeannette's son, Marc Legarde, worked for a Group competitor.

And then there was Donna-gran—as the Matriarch, she possessed power within the Family. But the structures had kept her from challenging Philip effectively. Heaven forbid that she could have stepped up as Martiniere after her husband Louis's death, even though she would have performed that job superbly.

Chris smiled at Gabe, a full, non-ironic smile this time. His daughter, Alice, was highly recommended by Brandon as a potential division leader, along with David's daughter Juliette, Gerard's granddaughter. Alice and Juliette were two of Brandon's peers that Gabe knew about.

"Will our family members be safe?" Cousin Pierre asked, a skeptical tone in his voice.

"I'm *not* Philip," Gabe said. He eyed the men sitting in front of him. "And if it makes people more comfortable to meet with me elsewhere, I am prepared for that. Brandon's residence, Moondance Ranch, is large enough to hold small Family gatherings, and will be my official base in North America. I will be traveling to Los Angeles to deal with situations at the Group headquarters there—but for Family matters, I'd prefer that we use Moondance."

He *had* promised Ruby that only the closest Family members would come to her Double R Ranch. And Rachel *had* originally designed Moondance to be an executive retreat. Moondance was meant to be a corporate showcase. He and Rachel hadn't managed to do it during her lifetime—but now, it would serve as the Martiniere base in North America. Get everything away from Los Angeles and Philip's former base there. Eventually.

"Are there any more questions?" he asked.

Thoughtful silence.

"I am prepared to talk with people on an individual basis throughout the holiday," he continued. "But I mean what I say. I have no desire to recreate what has been the norm for both the Family and the Group over the past forty-five years, since Philip became the Martiniere. I have pleasant childhood memories of happy Family gatherings, before Saul's death. I fully intend to restore that era—if I can, in the time that my health leaves for me." He drained his whisky. "That's all. Go forth and enjoy the holiday."

He remained seated as the others rose, finishing their drinks and murmuring softly, too softly for Gabe to hear what they were saying.

"They're still skittish," Brandon leaned over to say quietly.

"2014 to 2059," Gabe said. "Forty-five years under Philip's not-so-tender mercies." He shook his head. "That will take a while to erase."

"That's the impression I've gotten," Brandon said, as David and Charles approached. "Dad. I'll handle things from here. Mom's waiting, and you look tired."

"I'm sure she is," Gabe murmured.

Gabe listened when his son told him to rest. Bran knew Gabe's limits, better than he did sometimes. He got up and took both glass and cup to the sideboard, where Gerard and Piotr stood.

"I'm going back upstairs to spend time with Ruby," he told them. "Just message me if anyone wants to talk privately. Let the others know that I'm available, all right?"

Gerard smiled. "I am not going to be the one standing between you and your honeymoon with Ruby."

Piotr chuckled. "I am not going to offend your dear wife. She packs a punch."

Gabe made a note to himself to ask Cousin Piotr about *exactly when* he met Ruby.

Later. He wanted to spend time with Ruby.

No. Not *wanted*. He *needed* to spend time with Ruby after this meeting.

He needed time with his warrior wife—the perfect companion for who he was now.

RUBY AND DONNA-GRAN WERE DISCUSSING MIKEY WHEN GABE slipped into the penthouse.

"Ruby?" he called, to alert her to his presence.

"In here," she said.

He glanced, and saw that she already held a glass of wine. Good.

"I'm going to change and get some wine," he said.

He went to their private suite. Gerard apparently redecorated the whole damn penthouse after Philip's death, which meant few resonances from past years came back to haunt Gabe.

He owed his uncle a *lot* for doing that. He needed to thank Gerard privately, perhaps offer some compensation from his own funds, because this had to be a rush job and quite expensive. It wasn't just paint. There was a change in décor that reflected what Gabe used to like—a more contemporary design than Philip ever would have tolerated. Not the Western decor at the Double R or Moondance that he preferred these days, but it still was pleasant, and more reflective of the European location.

Two lives these days, Gabriel, two lives.

He wouldn't give up the ranch life. Nor deny how he had lived over the past thirty years. And if the Family didn't like it— too bad. He was *The Martiniere.*

Gabe hung up his suit jacket and tie, kicked off his loafers, and pulled on a sweater and slippers. Less formal, finally, though not as casual as he would be back home at the Double R. Then he went back out to join Ruby and Donna-gran.

After sipping on a glass of wine and chatting a little, he checked on Mikey. His adopted son—*father's clone*—lay on the floor in his room in one of the junior suites, playing with some old metal cars that Ruby resurrected from the Double R's attic— possibly inherited from her uncles, or even her grandfather. Brandon had played with them as a child, too, and remembered each one fondly when he hung out with Mikey. The paint was long worn off, so they weren't collectables. But they worked as toys.

"You doing okay?" Gabe dropped on the floor next to Mikey. The young clone responded best to adults who placed themselves at his level. He still had intense PTSD from being Philip's blood donor. Plus whatever else Philip did to him. Mikey didn't like adults towering over him, and Gabe didn't blame the kid one bit.

It was no consolation that Philip had been as cruel to his clones—*himself*—as he had been to his children. If not more so.

Did he ever care for any of us, even Justine? Or were we all just tools for Philip to manipulate as he saw fit?

He *still* could not comprehend why the man who was his sperm donor had hated him so much. That first night in Philip's house after the plane crash, reeling from the shock of losing his entire family—and Philip yelling at Gabe about not sitting up straight at the dinner table, then beating the crap out of him for breaking into tears. Even though he had been yanked away from a hard day of physical training at Northview Military Academy and clobbered with the news about his parents and sister dying in that plane crash, the headmaster trying to be gentle while Philip glowered disapprovingly at him—that horrific first week with Philip as his guardian—

Gabe shook his head.

That was then. This is now. Philip's dead and I'm the Martiniere. I won.

Or did I?

"Uh-huh." Mikey sat up and scrunched over next to Gabe. "Tired."

"Maybe you ought to crawl into bed and take a nap."

"Wanted to wait for you." Mikey gulped and buried his head in Gabe's side. "Kinda scared."

"Scared? Why?"

Mikey had been afraid yesterday after they scrambled security to deal with the attack on Ruby. His experiences in Philip's hands had left the young clone hypervigilant and watchful. But Mikey usually recovered quickly from these episodes. He wouldn't carry the worry over into the next day. His resilience astounded Gabe at times, more like Mikey was his own son rather than the clone of his biofather.

Then again, *his* resilience had to come from somewhere.

"Something doesn't feel right," Mikey whispered.

"Oh? The other kids?" Gabe didn't *think* that little kids would be *that* aware of Mikey's status as Philip's clone.

"No," Mikey said. He shivered. "Just something I feel. Like I've been here before, but it wasn't like this. Darker. More like downstairs. Lots of goldy stuff."

That sent a corresponding chill down Gabe's spine. Cloning wasn't *supposed* to carry cellular memories. But Mikey and his twelve predecessors were prototypes, something that wasn't *supposed* to be capable of existing. One of Philip's greatest creations—and deepest secrets.

"That *was* what this place used to look like," Gabe said slowly. "But things have changed. Not as dark. Not as goldy."

"Oh." He felt Mikey relax against him a little bit.

Damn it. Another thing to think about.

Cellular memories?

Then again, maybe Mikey had seen pictures someplace.

"Why don't you hop into bed and I'll sit with you a bit. I plan to go for a walk in a little while. Want to join me and Ruby?"

"Yeah."

"Then why don't you nap? Get some rest first."

Mikey stood up and crawled into bed, grabbing his stable of stuffies close. Gabe tucked him in, stroking Mikey's forehead over and over to soothe him into sleep. Mikey had that stray strand of black hair that hung like a comma over his forehead.

Just like Philip's. And his. And Brandon's.

Gabe pushed it back to join the rest of Mikey's hair.

Mikey closed his eyes under Gabe's touch. It didn't take long before his breath came smooth and easy, asleep. Gabe tiptoed out.

Ruby was alone in the living area when he entered. He sat next to her and took another sip of wine. She snuggled up close to him and he put his arm around her shoulders.

"I have to watch out for bad habits," he said. "Already had two glasses of whisky. This has to be it until we get back from walking. Mikey's taking a nap now."

"Something's bothering him."

"Somehow, he remembers what this place looked like before."

Ruby frowned. "Philip never brought him here—did he?"

"Gerard and the Family would have known about Mikey if Philip had. I have to wonder about cellular memories."

"God. *Another* thing."

"Yeah. It's more likely that he's come across a picture from before, not that. I told him that what he remembers was what this penthouse looked like before, but not now. That seemed to settle him. But we'll have to think about it." Another deep, hard exhale.

"Tough meeting?"

"Heads of Family." He shook his head. "Rubes, the situation within the Family is worse than I thought, and I have to deal with it as quickly as possible to build trust. Ten high-level heirs missing. They may be dead, may be institutionalized—may be indentured. Ten more in hiding, waiting to see what I end up doing as the Martiniere. The Heads of Family dumped it all on me this morning."

"Oh *God*. So that's why you had the drinks."

"Major family purges. It's worse than I thought," he repeated. "And all of the Heads of Family report being brutalized." He shivered. "I know far too well what that was like. Forty-five years. Two generations, mine and Bran's, just—left in shreds. Shattered." Gabe waved his glass—carefully, so he wouldn't spill it. "How the hell do I fix all of this?"

"One step at a time, my dear. Bit by bit, piece by piece," Ruby said. She set down her glass, eased his glass from his fingers to place it next to hers, then took Gabe's head in her hands. "And I am here, at your side, to help you do it."

She kissed his forehead, then his eyelids, and finally his lips.

"Ah, Ruby," Gabe sighed. "My love. My Matriarch."

"My Martiniere," she whispered, before kissing him harder than before.

He focused on kissing his beloved *properly*.

She chuckled against his lips. "I think we'd better go to our private space before we scandalize someone."

He chuckled back, then swept her up in his arms.

Oh God, what would he do without Ruby?

Damn it, he should have realized she was his warrior wife years ago.

No one came to the penthouse that day. But Gabe received several furtive messages over the next two days, requesting a private audience before the Family Christmas Eve Dinner.

Gabe saw them in the Martiniere's private suite, not the public area shared by the other close family members. Another break from Philip's traditions. And he insisted that Ruby be a part of it as well—an additional change. Ruby's presence seemed to soften the tension in those meetings, especially as word spread and wives accompanied their husbands.

Brandon, Kris, Donald, and Vincent took over Gerard's office to track down those Family members who had disappeared into indenture, Brandon occasionally relaying news when Gabe and Ruby met with particular family members.

Justine and Donna-gran held their own interviews with the Family women, collecting names to put forth for leadership roles.

The cyborg brothers kept Mikey engaged. They had been his protectors and guardians throughout his short life, had cared for him when he was in Philip's hands. He was safest with them. And, as more Family members petitioned for private audiences, Mikey's presence diminished yet another source of tension, because they brought their young children along as well. He played with the assorted young cousins, and seemed to relax more around other children than he had before.

An unexpected asset, both for them and for Mikey. And definitely a change from Philip's era.

Finally, it was Christmas Eve day. The house had slowly filled up after that meeting with the Heads of Family. Gabe and Ruby greeted all of them on arrival, frequently hearing *we hadn't planned to come, then our Head of Family called to say it was safe.*

Even better, instead of the tense silence he remembered from thirty years ago, Gabe heard children playing as he went about the house.

Christmas *was* best with children, after all.

Gerard pulled Gabe aside about midday. "I am very glad that

I had the parlor decorated with the Christmas tree this year. Gabriel. Thank you for what you have done so far. Not everyone is here, but there are many more Family members present than I have seen in years."

"It's a start, at least. I'm still appalled by what I'm hearing." He shook his head. "I knew things were bad. I didn't know they were this bad. I just—I wasn't in a position to act sooner. Locked down solid until something tied to getting the G9 virus knocked all of that programming loose. Piotr told me years ago that it would take Philip or Donna-gran to free me from it. We tried."

"Nobody is blaming you. Piotr and Serg made it known that you had been immobilized, and that it would take years for you to work your way free. I am glad that you found a means to do it." Gerard smiled. "I am also simply grateful that the old mansion is full of joyful noise again. That I lived to see it. Thank you, Gabriel."

"You're welcome. But I still wish you would accept repayment for the work you put into remodeling the penthouse."

"It was the least I could do in return for you and Ruby finally releasing us from Philip and Joseph's oppression." Gerard gestured with both hands. "The joy in this house is more than enough repayment."

Gabe decreed that instead of Midnight Mass, he and Ruby were going to an early Mass for children because of Mikey, and that Family Dinner would be held afterwards. He whispered guidance to Ruby, Brandon, Kris, and Mikey during the service —surprised that even after his long absence from church, he still knew the rituals.

Belief was not a part of Gabe's life—not since his first family's funeral Mass, and his subsequent experiences under Philip's custody. But pro forma attendance was expected of the Martiniere, and this was yet another means of healing within the predominantly Catholic Family. Philip hadn't attended Mass for years, adhering to evangelical Protestantism tailored toward the Electric Born cult he had been developing as part of his striving for political power.

They returned from the Mass to splendid smells from the great dining room. Ruby wore the Martiniere heirloom emeralds along with her gorgeous, sea-green, wedding dress and Gabe the copy of what had been his favorite formal morning dress suit, black with a gold-patterned black brocade waistcoat and gold cravat. Ruby sat at one end of the table, Mikey, Kris, Donna-gran, and Justine near her, and Gabe at the other end, with Brandon and Gerard.

Tradition.

And while he might roll his eyes in private at some of the old Family traditions, his instincts told him that tradition was desperately needed as part of the Family's healing process.

So they ate. And ate. And ate.

And toasted.

Gabe felt slightly lightheaded when he rose at the end, but not the head-pounding agony of past Family Christmases, when he had been drinking to hold back pain. He wasn't certain if it was alcohol, or the general giddy joy that permeated this Family Christmas.

"I would like to offer a toast to our Matriarch," he said in English, swiftly repeating in French. "Ruby. The love of my life. I would not be standing here without Ruby's help and ongoing support. Even after the years of separation, she has always held my heart. I give thanks every day that she allowed me back into her life. To Ruby Marie Barkley, the best damn rodeo queen in the world, and my beloved wife."

"To Ruby," the Family chorused.

Gabe drained his champagne. "Bran, you have the box?" he murmured.

"Right here." Brandon handed Gabe the box from Cartier. Gabe smirked as he walked toward Ruby.

"And now, I want to present my beloved with a much-deserved present and token of my love." He set the box in front of Ruby.

"Gabe?" Her voice quavered.

"Go ahead," he said softly.

Ruby gasped as she opened it, to reveal the tiara he had commissioned for her. "I—I—this is so much—"

"You deserve a crown from me," Gabe said softly.

"I—I—I—"

He had so rarely seen Ruby rendered speechless like this.

The tiara had a central brilliant-cut emerald, ringed by pearls and citrines and set in gold. The Martiniere colors. Four heart-shaped rubies were placed at the emerald's cardinal points, top, bottom, and sides. Gabe delicately lifted it.

"Stand up," he said.

She rose, her eyes fixed on him. Gabe carefully eased it onto her head—a perfect fit. He'd gotten the measurements from her favorite felt hat that she had worn to the AgSuperhero.

"Now I've put rubies as well as emeralds on my Ruby."

She blinked at him, tears glimmering in her eyes as the Family broke into applause. Gabe pulled her close and kissed her, hard and long.

"Gabe, you shouldn't have," she whispered. "The expense—"

"I *should* have done this years ago," he murmured. "I should have said *fuck you* to Philip from the beginning, revealed myself, and collected my income so that I could have bought many more beautiful things for you. You've earned this crown many times over, and this is nothing. A trifle. You are the queen of my heart, and, by God, I am going to make things right for what time we have left together."

Ruby sniffled, tears trickling down her cheeks. He brushed them away, then kissed her again.

Then he straightened up and took her arm. "So shall we hand out presents now?"

More applause.

He and Ruby led the Family into the adjoining parlor, where stacks of presents had been accumulating as Family members arrived.

It felt right.

But if anyone had told him a year ago that he would be *here*, with Ruby, he wouldn't have believed it.

Perhaps he could cause as rapid a change within the Family and the Group.

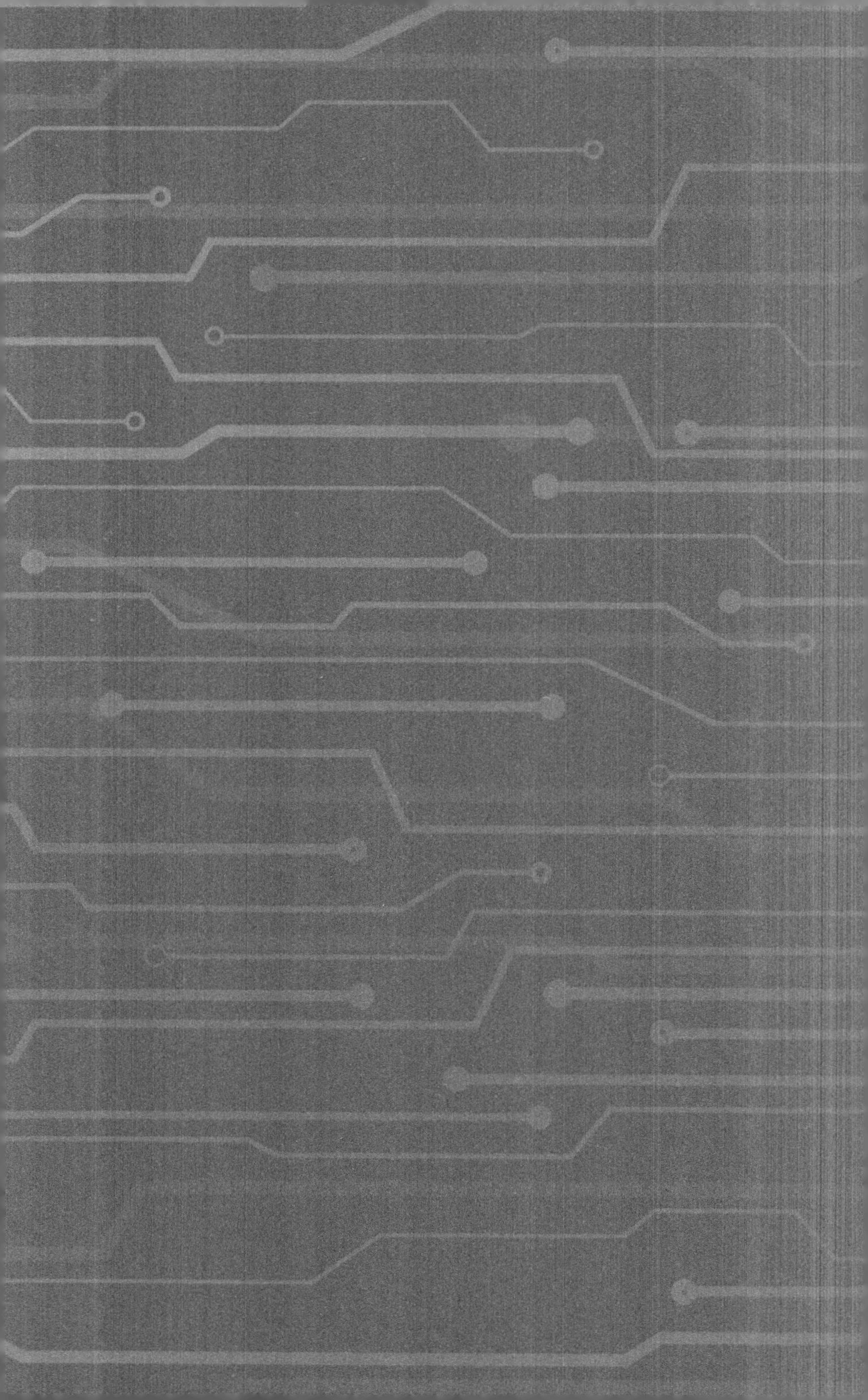

RUBY

Amongst the other social events of Ruby's first Family Christmas was a dance. A renewal of a tradition that Gabe's parents—*God, it's confusing between Saul and Philip; which man do I call Gabe's father?*—supported, but Philip let lapse. Gabe brought up the notion at Christmas breakfast, to an enthusiastic reception.

The first obstacle was that most of the Family members on site already had commitments for New Year's Eve. But—something on the 30th—

"The old dances were quite the galas." Gabe half-smiled, as a handful of Family members reviewed both electronic and hard copy files in Gerard's office on the afternoon of Christmas Day, to prepare for the party. "Can't do the big gala thing on such short notice this year, but do you suppose we could pull it off on New Year's Eve proper next year, Gerard?"

"We might need to keep it on the 30th," Gerard said. "Scheduling. But if you'd like to revive the tradition for next year—"

"I think it would be an excellent idea." Gabe eyed Brandon. "As long as you're willing to keep it up after me."

"A big party? Of course, Dad!" Brandon smirked at Gabe.

Ruby rolled her eyes at them—father and son hadn't met a party that they *didn't* enjoy—and went back to studying old pictures of past galas.

Once upon a time, the Martiniere New Year's Gala *had* been quite the affair. Donna-gran on the arm of her husband Louis Martiniere, the then-Martiniere. Saul and Angelica, during Saul's tenure as the Martiniere. Then-Martiniere Charles's wife Eloise even managed to hold a scaled-down Gala in her London exile during World War II, while Charles was at war.

"Why did Philip cancel the Gala?" Ruby asked. "After all, it kept going during the World Wars."

Donna-gran sniffed from her corner, where she was reviewing past records. "Because my poor damned megalomaniac fool of a son couldn't compete with his older brother, and didn't like the fancy affairs. He condemned anything big and splashy that was fun." She sighed. "And dancing probably reminded Philip of Angelica. I don't think he ever got over Angelica choosing Saul over him."

Awkward silence filled Gerard's office.

Then Gabe coughed. "I think this year has to be just Family. But next year—yes. If we have enough time to pull it off—I don't care if it's the 30th or the 31st, let's relaunch the Martiniere Gala. For this year, though—let's have some fun. It has been one hell of a year. Costume, formal dress, casual dress—doesn't matter. All ages."

"We won't be able to provide live music this year. Too short a lead time," Justine said thoughtfully.

"We didn't have live music when Ruby and I remarried," Gabe said. "I'm all right with that. And since this is Ruby and my delayed honeymoon, I want some input into the music."

Justine rolled her eyes. "More Willie Nelson, Gabie?"

"At least *some*," Gabe insisted. "Strauss waltzes, yes. A mix of more recent music, yes. But we're gonna have some Willie, at least early on before us old folks get tired and sneak off to bed."

And with that, the party planning gained momentum.

———

"CAN I GO TO THE PARTY?" MIKEY ASKED AS RUBY AND GABE tucked him into bed.

Ruby arched a brow at Gabe. It had only been two hours since they finished that meeting. Word must have been flying around the house. It surprised her how quickly information spread within the vastness of the Hôtel Martiniere.

And we don't even have the household of earlier eras.

She could just imagine what it must have been like when the house was constantly full of assorted family members and their servants.

Gabe laughed. "Of course, Mikey! Especially this year. Next year will be more formal, but this year is just for fun. Wear something you want to play in."

"Jeans and one of my nice ranch shirts?" Mikey's voice quavered a little. He was good about dressing up for various occasions, but Ruby got the impression that he was ready to go back home, to the quiet and informality of the Double R.

"And your boots as well, if that's what you want to wear." Gabe's voice softened. "Missing the ranch?"

Mikey nodded. "And horses. And Charlie's dogs. Hey, can I have a puppy?"

Ruby winced, remembering how Gabe had insisted that infant Brandon have a puppy during the early days of their first marriage. Three dogs later...once Gabe started acquiring dogs, puppies tended to follow him home. She suspected it wouldn't be different now. It was surprising that puppies *hadn't* made an appearance yet.

Gabe smirked. "Soon, Mikey, soon. For both the puppies and going home."

"Pupp*ies*?" Ruby raised her brows at Gabe. "Plural?"

"We'll get to that eventually." Gabe evaded her glare. "But

yes, Mikey. Whatever you're comfortable wearing for the party, as long as it's not your pajamas, all right?"

"No way!" Mikey snorted.

Gabe laughed. "Some people like wearing pajamas to events."

Mikey made a face and turned onto his side, pulling his stuffies tight to him. Gabe stroked Mikey's forehead.

Gabe stood up and Ruby ducked in to kiss Mikey's forehead. Then they left.

"So Mikey's going western. What are you wearing?" she asked Gabe.

He smirked at her. "*I* think it's time the Family started adjusting to the notion that the Martiniere and the Matriarch are ranchers in the US West."

"But we didn't bring—"

"Oh yes we did," Gabe said. "Your good Lucchese boots. My Noconas. Those matching 1950s-era replica Scully shirts you got us—the black with red rose embroidery. Nice dress jeans, and *yes*, I'll iron them for us. My Sweets Rodeo Saddle Bronc Champion buckle and your Miss Rodeo Oregon buckle."

"You planned this," she accused.

"I hoped for a possibility." As they went into their private suite, he pulled her close for a kiss. "And even though I'm now the Martiniere, I'm still a rebel at heart."

Ruby laughed and buried her head in Gabe's chest.

Like Mikey, she was tiring of the high society life. Dressing up in clothing she was familiar with for one big Family event was a relief.

***

"Ready?" Gabe asked after they dressed for the party.

Ruby checked the fit of her tiara. She wore the silver earrings that went with the lucky locket tucked under her shirt. All she really needed now was a hat—but Gabe hadn't brought those.

Hat carriers would have given it away.

It was clear he meant this to be a surprise for her as well as the Family.

"I'm ready to show the Family how shitkickers party."

She studied her husband. All Gabe needed was a hat to finish off his ensemble—he wore a silk maroon glad rag tucked around his neck that matched the embroidered roses on his black snap-button shirt. While Gabe always looked good in his bespoke suits (*oh God, especially that one black morning suit*), the old-style Western shirt better accented his once-more-lean, lithe figure, in her opinion. Couple that with well-fitted and pressed jeans, the silver belt buckle, the pointed-toed Nocona boots; subtract the lines in his face, and even at fifty-seven he still looked like the wandering saddle bronc rider who had caught her interest all those years ago.

Just a more affluent version.

Gabe threw his head back in a full laugh. Then he kissed her.

"Aw, Rubes. The woman of my heart." He slid his arm around her waist. "Let's collect the others."

Brandon and Kris, Justine and Donald, Donna-gran, and Mikey, along with the cyborg brothers Carl and Frederick, waited for them in the main living area. Ruby raised her brows as she saw they wore jeans and snap-button shirts.

"You scripted this," she accused Gabe.

"Actually, *I* did," Brandon said.

Ruby shook her head. "You Martiniere men. All right. Let's party."

They processed down the stairs. The sliding doors which separated the dining room and the grand parlor from the entrance foyer were both open, turning the space into a ballroom. Family members milled about, even though the music hadn't started yet. Mikey ran to join a group of younger cousins playing in one corner.

"The Martiniere is here—let the music begin!" Gerard announced.

A Strauss waltz—*The Blue Danube? Something else?*—played. Gabe swept Ruby into his arms and they waltzed. Other Family members joined them. Ruby kept her focus on Gabe, even as she exchanged pleasantries with Family members between dances. Those smoldering dark eyes, that grin that made her heart leap —no, *that* hadn't changed. Even after heartbreak and divorce, he still was the man who won her heart so many years ago as Gabe Ramirez, a broke ranch hand and saddle bronc rider.

Willie Nelson followed Strauss and Gabe smirked. They shifted from straight waltz to Western Swing. Then it was back to a traditional waltz.

She lost track of time between dances, stopping to eat and drink, and checking on Mikey. Almost like the Grange dances back home, except...*in Paris.* At one point Kris took Mikey upstairs. Brandon danced with Ruby before joining Kris. Gabe and Justine danced, while Ruby sat with Donald. He was pale with a faint sweaty sheen, and Ruby wondered if he was all right. Justine had mentioned that Donald had a chronic health condition, but never went into detail about it.

"Whew." Gabe dropped into the open seat by Ruby, throwing his arm around her shoulders while Justine sat next to Donald. "Old man's getting tired, but I do want a couple more rounds with my darling. Just have to wait for the right set of songs." He smirked at her. "It's a bit tamer than what we used to do, for certain. Getting old."

Ruby laughed softly and snuggled into him as they watched the dancers.

"This was a good idea, Gabe," Donald said. "Everything I've heard and seen about what you've done this Christmas. Many small things that have made a big difference."

"I wanted to make this a happy time," Gabe said. "The Family needs it." He paused, as if to say more, but then grinned as the opening notes of "Blue Eyes Crying in the Rain" played. "And here's our set, Rubes. Let's give 'em a real taste of good dancing."

Ruby grinned as well. Her husband had always been a good dancer—and now she knew it came in part from having a ballerina for a mother. Someday she hoped to see clips of Angelica dancing. She had found reviews but so far, no actual footage.

"Blue Eyes" segued into "Whiskey River," "Mammas Don't Let Your Babies Grow Up to Be Cowboys," and then, finally, the haunting strains of "My Heroes Have Always Been Cowboys." The look in Gabe's eyes warned her that he wanted to *make this one big*, even before he extended his arm to swing her.

"Let's leave 'em with a real show," he murmured. This had been one of their signature songs at the rodeo and Grange dances.

Ruby followed Gabe's lead through slow, delicate spins, swings, and twirls separated by close embraces. They flowed together, like they had all those years ago when they were young and wild on the local rodeo circuit, rodeoing their break from hard work on the Double R.

A second chance. We got a second chance.

A year ago, if anyone had told Ruby that she would be dancing with Gabe, once again his wife, and now a member of one of the most powerful families in the world, she wouldn't have believed it.

A fairytale come true; one she hadn't even known was even a possibility for rancher Ruby Barkley. Dancing with Gabe *here*, at the Hôtel Martiniere in Paris, just like they were at a rodeo dance, suddenly slammed the reality home.

Ruby was damned sure going to make the most of it.

Their eyes didn't leave each other as they danced their love. Gabe dipped her for the final notes, then kissed Ruby hard.

Applause startled Ruby out of the semi-trance the dance had evoked in her, and she realized they were alone on the floor, the rest of the Family watching them.

Gabe threw a two-finger salute. "And that's a good night for us," he intoned. "Have fun and stay safe, folks. See you all tomorrow."

Ruby held back her giggles until they were safely a couple of flights up the stairs, because Gabe's vocal tones sounded *so much* like a rodeo announcer with that *good night*. Gabe snickered along with her. They stopped at the next landing and he kissed her again, soft at first, then more insistent.

"You are going to scandalize the Family," she whispered against his lips.

"I don't care," he murmured back. "I'm no fucking prig like Philip. Saul deeply loved my mother—and showed it. Daily. Here and at home. It's time the Family was reminded of what a Martiniere capable of loving his wife and family looks like." He kissed her some more. "I am proud of my redheaded rodeo queen. My Matriarch. My greatest love."

JANUARY, *2060*

DANCING PROVED TO BE A GOOD METAPHOR FOR 2060.

Ruby's days seemed to be filled with dancing on the edge of problems, juggling business and family and her responsibilities as the Matriarch.

That included supervising the new nonprofit, the Indentured Recovery Project. Its purpose was to help former indentureds transition back to regular life and work, or fund support for those people too damaged to function in everyday society.

Most of the time, their staff handled the cases.

But there were some that needed higher-up intervention—usually the worst and most challenging.

Ruby *thought* she had seen everything before, given her meth-head parents, her father's shiftless family, and her knowledge about poverty in Thunder County and Northeastern Oregon.

She had not.

TOO MUCH, TOO MUCH, TOO MUCH.

Ruby fought back sobs as she careened through the kitchen and onto the back porch. Wind and snow raged outside as a miserably cold and wet late-January blizzard howled outside. She yanked on her insulated overalls, her insulated boots, her winter jacket, heavy gloves, and a hat, still struggling with tears.

Storm or no, she had to get out. Had to get away from the images burned on her brain from today's review of the latest IRP difficult case.

As she slammed out the door and into the storm, Ruby thought she heard Gabe calling, but she didn't turn back. Now that she was outside where Gabe—and most importantly, Mikey—couldn't hear her, Ruby let herself cry as she staggered against the wind, toward the horse pasture. She slipped through the gate and searched for the herd, not wanting to call them in this storm. Even if they could hear her. She was sobbing too hard to yell, anyway.

The horse herd stood in the lee of the cottonwoods lining the irrigation ditch, tails to the wind, standing over the remnants of the morning hay drop that hadn't been eaten or blown away. Ruby made her way toward them, trudging through the foot of snow. She *needed* her horses right now.

She scratched noses as she went through the herd, until she reached the palomino mare Legacy, great-granddaughter of Ruby's old rodeo and barrel racing mount Sunshine. Legacy nuzzled Ruby as she buried her head in Legacy's neck.

How could people do something like what she had just read and seen? *How?*

Ruby didn't know how long she stood there, her arms around Legacy's neck, shaking with sobs. Then Gabe gently eased her away from Legacy.

"Rubes. What's wrong?"

She gulped. "I want to resurrect your damned father and kill him all over again, very slowly and painfully. Multiple times."

"IRP?" he asked. "A bad case?"

She nodded, still sniffling. "Have you ever heard of Heaven's Reach, Gabe?"

He went still, his face tight and hard, eyes dead as he stared at her. "Who? For God's sake, Ruby, who the hell survived that nightmare?"

"You know about it, then?"

"Unfortunately, yes. Who from Heaven's Reach?"

Another shuddering gulp. "A man named Doug Gates." The pictures she'd been trying to banish came back, too damned vividly. She choked. "He—he informed Alvarez Armory—oh God, Gabe, was that one of your actions?"

Gabe nodded, his mouth thin and tight. "Gates was supposed to be protected. God damn it, *they were supposed to get him the fuck out of there!* God damn my father-in-law Hernan. God damn my brother-in-law Rick. The fuckers. I knew I should have let Serg take care of Gates. *I knew it.* But I was promised otherwise, trusted local authorities who said they'd work with Hernan and Rick to keep Gates safe, when I should have fucking known better, of course Philip—*fuck.*"

"They took his arms and his legs." She couldn't stop sobbing, couldn't stop talking. "Hacked them off at elbows and knees with an axe. Castrated him. It's a cut and dried case but I had to approve the expense and find housing, and all the treatments—"

"Shh. Shh." He pulled her close. "I'll take care of this one, Rubes. Personally. Not the IRP."

"But do you have the time? There's a fuck of a lot of paperwork on this one, because he's in really bad shape."

"I'll *make* the fucking time. I owe it to Gates. He was Alvarez Armory's insider in Heaven's Reach." Gabe gently guided her from the herd and toward the pasture gate, his arm holding her tight as she kept sobbing. "If I'd known—fuck. Heaven's Reach was a fucking nightmare, Ruby. Members brainwashed six ways from forever, worshiped Philip and Joseph as gods. Part of that God damned Electric Born cult my thrice-cursed sperm donor created. Heaven's Reach started as a commune that took over the town of North Fork, up near the Canadian border. It was supposed to be just another one of those actions where the Armory came in and kicked out the intruders." They went through the gate. Gabe guided Ruby toward the barn. "Tell you more in here."

"Mikey?"

Gabe nodded. "He doesn't need to hear this. It's—entirely possible he came from a Heaven's Reach lab."

"Oh God. How bad is it?" Going inside the stable was a relief from the wind-blown snow. They sat on her old tack trunk. The wind rattled the rafters but the barn was snug enough.

"It's fucking bad, Ruby. The worst thing that happened when I was part of Alvarez Armory." He shuddered. "Besides possibly being the source of Philip's cloning projects, Heaven's Reach was a den of vipers. Damn near literally. Philip experimented with weaponizing them. There was a potion called the Kiss. One person took the dose. Then any physical contact with another person left their target malleable to all sorts of mind control. They used it on Rafe Alvarez. My favorite brother-in-law, the man who was the closest damn thing I ever had to a brother." Gabe closed his eyes for a moment and shook his head. "Then they wiped out all but a handful of that unit of the Armory. I'll— give you the file on the Kiss. You'd better know about it. Just in case some element of those fuckers are still around. You need to know the defenses."

"Oh."

"Philip sent the video of Rafe's killing to Rafe's father Hernan. Who called me, blamed me for Rafe's death. Swore I'd never get another penny of his money. He did not cut Rachel off —thank God for that, or I would have been further in debt for her cancer treatments. But we were both severed from social contact with the Alvarez family after Rafe's funeral, and they took Rachel's body away from me when she died from the G9, while I was still down sick from it."

"Aw, fuck, Gabe. That's awful."

He nodded. "*I* was the reason that Rachel didn't have any contact with her family for the last three years of her life. She only had me and Brandon, and her quilting friends. She even talked about meeting you so that you could share Brandon's early days with her. Erica—her mother—never tried to reach out. They knew damned good and well that Rachel's cancer had returned. But—" he exhaled hard. "I don't know what conversations passed between her and her father. I do know that she chose me over her family. Not that they were good about staying in contact when her cancer returned. Rafe—Rafe was the only one who checked in with us. He told me that they had been the same way when she had cancer before." Gabe rubbed his face. "The Alvarezes were *not quite* as messed up as the Martinieres. Barely."

"That's still pretty fucked up."

Gabe nodded. "Anyway. Heaven's Reach. I called Serg, and Brandon—Bran knew Rafe well. Vygotsky Security and what was left of the Armory took care of those evil people. Gates wanted to stay. I should have insisted he go with Serg."

"Was—was it as bad as my records say?"

"If they're quoting Gates, every bit of it is true."

"They were cannibals?"

He nodded. "Part of how they refined the Kiss. Eat the flesh of those they used it on—though near as I can tell, they didn't do that to Rafe. We didn't do all the killing. We caught the women who administered the Kiss to Rafe and his group leaders. The men of Heaven's Reach murdered the women in a suicide assault, and those who didn't fight it out with us killed themselves as well. Oh, it was one damn bloody mess, Ruby." Gabe grimaced.

Ruby buried her head in her hands.

Too much. Too much. Too much.

"Rubes," he said softly. "Are we all right? Or is this—"

She raised her head. His brows furrowed, not in anger but with worry.

"Are we all right?" His voice quavered. "Yes, I led mercenary actions when I was part of Alvarez Armory. I killed people. You knew that I've killed people. The men who attacked us that first Christmas."

"They killed my friend Britt. They would have killed us."

"Necessary. But God, Rubes, I swear that those I killed as part of the Armory were much the same."

She gulped. "I killed my father and then your cousin Joseph. I'm not much better."

"Necessary. Your father would have killed you. Joey tried to kill me."

Another gulp. She buried her head in his chest. He held her tight. They sat together for a while, as the storm shook the rafters.

"Come on," Gabe said finally. "It's damn cold out here, and while Beck's at the house, Mikey's gonna be wondering where we've gotten ourselves to. Let's warm up before we do evening chores, all right?"

"All right." She coughed. "Sorry to be—"

"You have nothing to be sorry about. I'm the one who should be sorry," Gabe said, as they got up. "If it wasn't for my damned sperm donor—you would never have needed to know about something like Heaven's Reach. Are you sure you're up to continuing with the Indentured Recovery Project?"

"I am." She coughed again. "I am," she said more firmly this time. "It's my job as the Matriarch. I have to lead."

"You don't *have* to do a damned thing if you don't want to. And if it's too damned much, *tell me.*"

Ruby shook her head. "I'm not dumping this work on you. You already have enough to handle. Normally I can deal with—rough situations. This was just—"

"All right," he said.

They climbed the steps to the back porch, stomping the snow off of their boots, then began the process of shedding their outdoor clothing.

Before they went inside, Gabe took her in his arms again. "Just promise me this, Ruby. Next time, when it gets to be too much? *Come to me.* Don't go tearing outside bawling like that without a word. You scared the shit out of me. I didn't know what the hell was wrong, but I knew it was bad."

"You said *when*, not *if*. Are there going to be more stories like Gates popping up?"

"God, I hope not. But—damn, I don't know. Just please. Come to me when you get overwhelmed. I need to know that. No matter what I'm doing. Interrupt me. You're my highest priority. All right?"

"I will," she promised.

"Good." He rested his forehead against hers. "I know I'm a fine one to talk to you about *keeping stuff inside*, thanks to my bad habit of keeping secrets. But hon, you do it too. Not as much. Different things. Still. Don't lock your emotions away from me because you don't want to load me down. I promise to do better on my part. We're in this—together."

She nodded. He kissed her again, and they went inside.

THAT EVENING, AFTER DOING CHORES AND EATING DINNER, THEY danced in the living room. Mikey watched them from the nest of pillows and blankets he had accumulated on the couch, his new heeler puppy, Smudge, tucked in with him. The fire roared high in the wood stove. While the shabby but comfortable ranch house living room was nothing like the ballroom in the Hôtel Martiniere, it was still roomy enough for several couples to dance.

They waltzed to a mix of classical waltzes and Willie Nelson, blowing off the nervous energy from the day by focusing on each other and their movements to the music.

Soon enough, a night of dancing became their traditional means of coping with the tough days.

"It almost seems obscene to dance in the face of tragedy," Ruby said after both of them had experienced a rough day and they were dancing again. "Isn't dancing for celebration?"

Gabe was silent for a few beats as he spun her, then took her back into his arms.

"Saul and my mother would frequently dance together after difficult days—oh, I had those figured out at a very early age. But one or the other of them would cue up the music—it depended on who felt the need. Saul liked Strauss. Mother— when I heard *Swan Lake*, I knew she'd had a tough day."

"But dancing only to relieve stress? Seems gloomy in some respects."

"Oh no." Gabe spun her again. "Remember. Philip Martiniere may have been my sperm donor, but Saul Martiniere raised me for my first twelve years. And I am the son of Angelica Ramirez Martiniere, who once aspired to achieving a prima ballerina position with the New York City Ballet, before she broke her ankle. Saul loved dance, not just as art to watch but as something to do. I grew up with dance during my formative years. And I am grateful that I have a partner with whom I can remember to dance, and who inspires me to have many reasons to dance. Joy. Sorrow. We should have danced more when we were younger. It might have made a difference." He leaned in close to kiss her neck. "We need to dance more now."

What could she say to that?

Besides, once Ruby thought about it, her grandparents had danced in this very same living room. For the same reason?

Possibly.

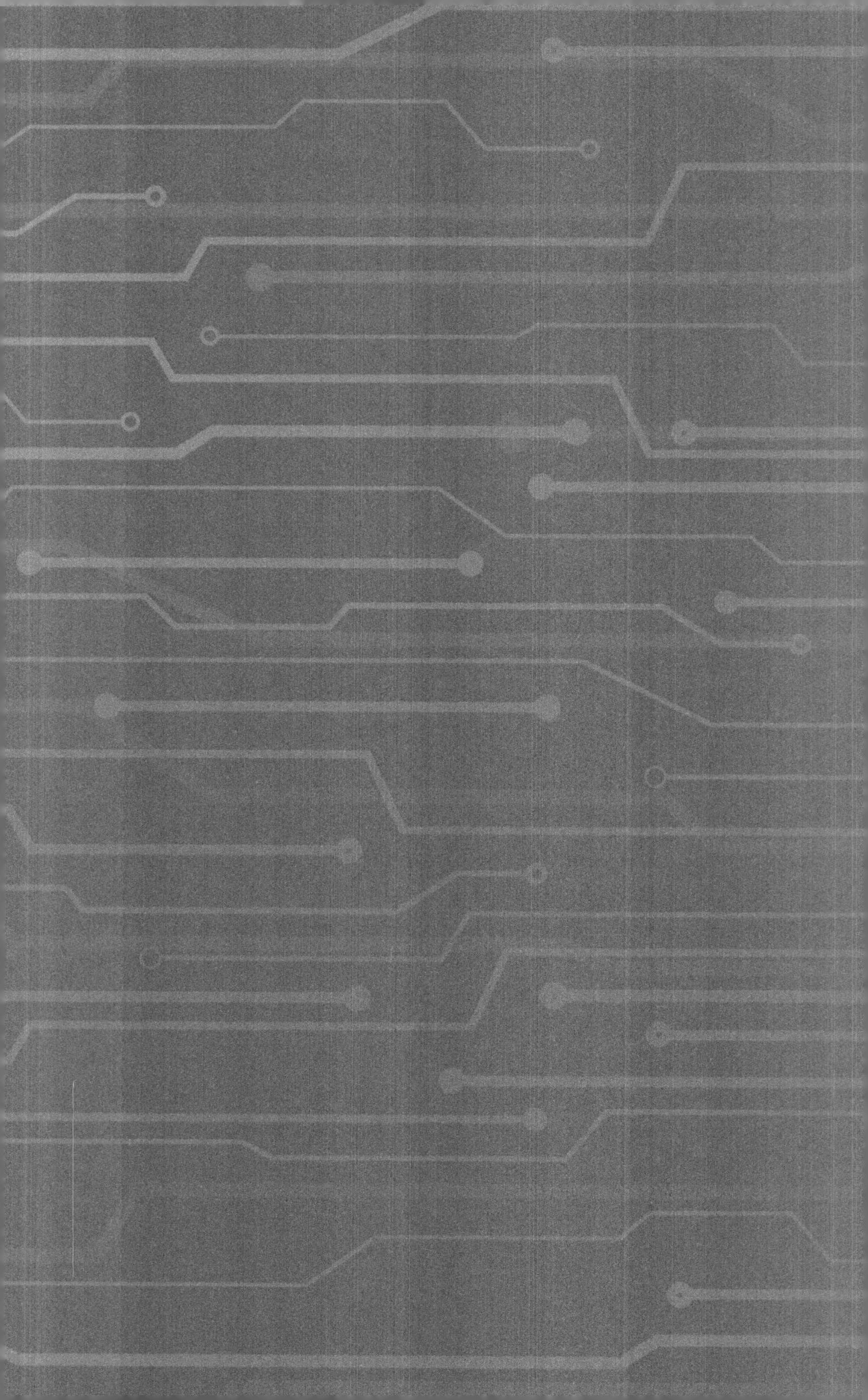

GABE

THREE WEEKS BACK AT THE DOUBLE R AFTER FAMILY CHRISTMAS, and then a flight to Los Angeles with Brandon to finally organize the setup at the Martiniere Group headquarters. Eliot McNaughton, First Secretary of External Affairs, performed admirably after Philip's death, taking on the leadership of both Internal and External Affairs (*and just why in hell was the Group organized like that? History? It was bizarre and totally unlike any past experience Gabe had with corporate structures outside of the Group*). Justine lent a hand covering things at headquarters from her secretive position as Director of Security—but it was time that Gabe and Brandon went to LA to take care of business.

Gabe tapped his fingers on his armrest. Brandon looked up from his comp projection—editing one of the 'casts that he and Kris were putting out about the problems with indenture.

"Doing all right, Dad?"

"I don't like flying, especially without your mother," Gabe grumbled. Flying brought back memories of being twelve years old at the funeral Mass for his family, his back aching from the first of Philip's beatings.

Brandon nodded. "Got it. Can you hold off on the tapping, please? Need to finish this edit, and it bleeds over." He turned back to his work.

Gabe sighed and stilled his fingers, lacing them together so he wouldn't start tapping the armrest again. He should be reviewing certain Group records, but—he wanted to think about what lay ahead of them. He needed to deal with some very touchy subjects that he had been avoiding for several months, ever since he had become the Martiniere.

His primary concern was his growing awareness that Justine's role in the Group was more significant than he first realized. Her work was in the areas of External Affairs and security, no connections to Heaven's Reach or the Electric Born. As near as Gabe could discern, ties to those damned subgroups were restricted to her brother Joey and to an earlier Internal Affairs First Secretary, Greg Hallock.

But his sister—how compromised was she? Gabe had little doubt about her loyalty to him as the Martiniere. However, she was Philip's Director of Security for fifteen years. Lots of whispers about her being Philip's enforcer, reinforced by things he read since he became the Martiniere. And then there was her stint as First Secretary, External Affairs, years ago, about the time she divorced Donald. Was she enmeshed in something that might cause him problems? That might end up being problematic as he set about fixing things within the Group?

A big question—and he had been avoiding dealing with it. He and Justine were building a new relationship, based on being siblings instead of cousins.

But there were other dynamics as well. He wanted to take care of these questions away from Ruby—she and Justine were close. And this was something he didn't want to bring up with Brandon just yet, either, because Justine and Brandon were also close, and that was a necessary linkage.

Gabe sighed. Better to handle it *now* rather than later.

Another issue, one he *could* discuss with Brandon when his

son had a free moment. The Los Angeles headquarters.

If Gabe had his druthers, he would completely eliminate the Group's LA headquarters. Decentralize the whole damned thing. Not move it to Pendleton—the thought was tempting, but there was just no support present for the labs. No structures. That move would require building support structures from the ground up, and that was simply a waste of funds—even before the consequences caused by asking people to relocate.

They needed to find a new location for a corporate headquarters. But where?

However, that sort of reform was a low priority. He planned to encourage decentralizing—something Justine already did, at least until her Chicago condo caught fire. But security could be that flexible. Labs, not so much.

Then there was the fact that he intended to hand over the title of Martiniere to Brandon in a few years. He couldn't do it all himself, much less create a mess for Bran to fix.

"You got a moment, Bran?" he asked when his son looked up and stretched.

"Sure. I'm done with this segment. What are you thinking about?"

"I'm still of a mind to decentralize the Group, move the headquarters out of LA, along with as many other functions as possible. But that's a big job. I won't be able to finish it in under five years. Especially the labs."

"I'm not wild about the labs being in LA." Bran shrugged. "It means regular monitoring trips there. But moving them to Pendleton, absent another jump in temperatures, or a catastrophe scenario, is simply unworkable right now."

"Agreed." Gabe rubbed his face. "All the same, we need to start creating alternatives—something my damned sperm donor refused to consider. You've seen the meteorological projections. The cost to maintain those labs in that location rises exponentially. Even with alternative energy sources on site. It's bad enough now, but it'll be worse in ten years."

"Pendleton doesn't fare much better. It gets *hot* there." Brandon stroked his goatee, pursing his lips.

Gabe rolled his eyes. "I *know* that. How many years did I operate Moondance, and just how far is it from Pendleton?"

"I know, I know." Brandon paused. "It's a Group-wide consideration. We got lucky in the late '20s with that brief volcanic-caused cooling. I've been talking it over with David and Chris. They've been working on contingency plans which include the eventual relocation of everything out of LA."

Gerard had handed over leadership of the French subsidiaries under his control to his son David at Family Christmas. Chris had ascended to leadership of the British branch years ago, when he was still in his thirties. David's daughter Juliette and Chris's daughter Alice were their nominated successors—which happened after Gabe's speeches at Family Christmas about the need for diversity.

New ideas. Change within the Family. A break from forty-five years of his damned sperm donor's iron grasp on how the Group and Family did things, and his insistence that they follow the traditions of Salic Law.

"I've asked McNaughton to initiate a search for new headquarters locations," Gabe said. "A slow transition."

"I agree," Brandon said. "Let me finish up this next segment. I'll be available to talk then."

Gabe sighed and leaned back, looking out the window, thinking again about how much he hated flying, especially when Ruby remained behind.

No choice right now, though. Uprooting Mikey or leaving him with Kris wasn't the best of ideas at the moment. Mikey had developed a cold after Family Christmas, and staying home was best for him.

Gabe also wasn't certain just how much time Mikey had spent in and around the Los Angeles labs, which might be a trigger for him.

They still hadn't identified where Mikey had been created.

LA, or a Heaven's Reach facility?

Too damned many unknowns. Including climate futures.

MCNAUGHTON, FORTUNATELY, WASN'T ONE FOR ELABORATE greeting ceremonies. Justine was already with him when Gabe and Brandon arrived. She and McNaughton had been lovers after her divorce from Donald, and Gabe wondered to what degree her resumed relationship with Donald affected their interactions.

If at all.

He didn't detect any tension between Justine and McNaughton as they gave him and Brandon a quick tour of headquarters. The biggest change from what Gabe remembered was the degree to which Justine had taken over the lower floors for security management and training. Apparently, the previous Internal Affairs First Secretary, Raven Deschamps, had already started decentralizing some of their operations, more than Gabe realized. Philip hadn't had time to roll back Deschamps's actions when he took over Internal Affairs following Deschamps's death in 2058.

Otherwise, the place had hardly changed over the past thirty years, from when he worked at the labs nearby and reported to headquarters. Gabe tensed as they went to the top floor, where Philip's office suite—now his—was located.

"I'd like you to relocate to the top floor," he said to Justine as the elevator rose. "Unless you have strategic reasons for being on the tenth floor."

"The tenth floor is convenient for training purposes. And I have a mostly empty office on the top floor. But now that I don't need to avoid Joey or our father—" she shrugged. "It really doesn't matter where I'm based."

The elevator stopped. Gabe stepped out first, followed by the others, tensing in preparation for a flood of memories.

To his surprise, the reception desk was streamlined and automated. McNaughton noticed his startle.

"Raven convinced Philip to set up automated reception," he said. "One of the last things Raven completed before his death."

As they walked down the hallway to his office, Gabe noted that one of the suites had Justine's name on it.

"So that's your show office?" he asked.

A glance between Justine and McNaughton. "Eliot and Raven understood why I preferred the tenth floor. This—" she waved her hand at the door as they passed by. "—was mostly for Daddy-damned-dearest's sensibilities. It isn't as secure as my tenth-floor office. Nor is it as big. Tenth floor has my personal workout space, and it allows me to remind folks of my priorities with regard to conditioning and training."

Philip's office—now *his*—was next door to Justine's, a big corner suite.

"Joseph took over Raven's old office after Raven's death," McNaughton said. "Corner plus. I didn't know for certain what you two wanted to do, so I split the difference. You're in this corner; Brandon's in the other. I'm down the other hallway. Interior offices are primarily support staff and records, along with staff lunchroom and security support."

Gabe nodded. Still a lot of wasted space. He took a deep breath, then opened the door to his office, steeling himself against possible Philip resonances.

Instead, to his relief, this area was also modified. The dark oak paneling with mahogany and gilt accents that had been Philip's preferences were gone in favor of white walls and pine or bamboo furnishings, with beige or light green cloth. It was much brighter than he remembered these offices being.

A young Hispanic woman sat behind the desk. She rose and bowed.

"I am Corina Ruiz, your headquarters executive assistant if you don't already have one selected," she said. "I've been working with Justine and Eliot to facilitate your transition into these offices."

Gabe bowed in return. "Thank you for your work, Ms. Ruiz. We'll talk later, but I plan to use your services."

"She's been cleared," Justine added. "Former indentured." A faint smile twitched her lips. "Applications to be your assistant in the Los Angeles office were *quite* competitive, Gabie, especially amongst those clerical indentureds who were freed by your orders. I hope you don't mind that I took this action."

"I appreciate what you have done for us, Mr. Martiniere," Ruiz said softly.

Gabe nodded. He glanced around the outer office. Ruby and the Double R staff served as his assistants on the ranch, but he definitely needed someone competent here. "Tine, thanks. If I can't trust *you* to hire someone reliable—"

Who had been in charge of redecorating—Justine or Ruiz? *Redecorating* appeared to be a common theme throughout the Family and the Group, an apparent attempt to purge all memories of Philip.

Or was this just a normal part of the leadership transition?

He opened the door to his inner office, hesitating in the doorway. Bigger than the office spaces at the Double R or Moondance —to be expected. All the same, he didn't feel comfortable taking that first step inside.

God damn it, you're the Martiniere. This is your space. Not Philip's.

But even scolding himself didn't get rid of his hesitancy. Too much conditioning in his younger years.

"I'll get Brandon set up in his office," McNaughton said. A welcome if brief distraction.

"Thank you." Gabe turned. "Ms. Ruiz, I'll talk to you in a few minutes and we'll discuss my preferences. Right now, I want to meet with my sister."

"Calling me on the carpet, hmm?" Justine said wryly. He picked up on the slight tension in her voice.

"No. Just needing to meet with you." *And probably a bit of asking for accountability, but no need to make a big deal of it.* Another thought occurred to him. "McNaughton. Before you leave—I'm not certain if you, Ms. Ruiz, or Justine will handle this, but my wife also needs office space next door for when she comes to LA, along with a play and study area for our adopted son. I'd like that space for Michael to be privately accessible for both Ruby and me, no outside entry except from our offices."

"That can easily be done," McNaughton said. "Brandon, do you want a similar setup for your wife?"

"Studio space as well as office space, because we will still be making 'casts," Brandon said. "Dad, I'll take care of setting things up for Mom, Mikey, and Kris. Eliot, I'll have a similar need for Kris. Our first child is due at the end of May. Let's talk. Justine, I'm assuming you handled the hiring of my assistant as well?"

"Yes," she said. "Do you want a second one for Kris—same for Ruby?"

"I'll check with Ruby to see if she wants an assistant."

Having an assistant to coordinate things here in LA might be a solution for the heavy emotional workload that the Indentured Recovery Project was putting on Ruby. He turned back to the office—now *his*, not Philip's, tensing once again in anticipation.

He exhaled with relief as he eyed the room in more detail. Plain. Not much décor here, definitely nothing of Philip's remaining. A computer cube on the desk. A big, comfortable chair with an ottoman he could pull in behind the desk if he wanted to elevate his feet, identical to the one he had in his Double R office. Similar chairs for others to use. Couch, sleek and minimalist in light green with a glass and chrome coffee table in front of it. Credenza made of bamboo, probably containing liquor and bar supplies. The desk was pine with a glass top and chrome trim, understated rather than chunky and imposing.

Gabe walked in and looked around. Several framed pictures

on the wall. Him on his favorite saddle bronc, Skydancer. Ruby on her old barrel horse Sunshine, wearing her Miss Rodeo Oregon regalia for a Grand Entry run-in. Him, Ruby, and Jeff Swait standing with hands clasped and raised high in front of the studio crowd, after winning the AgSuperhero eleven months ago. The close family picture from this past Christmas, his first one as the Martiniere.

He studied their expressions in this portrait. Ruby was radiant, Mikey frightened, Brandon triumphant, Kris worried, Donald and Justine with faint smiles, and his face—quizzical was the best term that Gabe could think of to describe it.

"I didn't want to leave the walls completely barren," Justine said. "And I thought you'd appreciate those pictures."

"Thank you." He crossed the room and sat in his chair, gesturing to Justine to take one of the others.

"So why do I feel like I'm under the microscope?" Justine glanced around. "This place still has resonances of our damned father. Even with all the changes."

"You spent a lot more time in this office than I ever did." Gabe exhaled slowly, steepleing his fingertips together. "And that's the part I want to know more about."

Her face tightened. "There was a lot more going on than I think you realize."

"Then tell me." He kept his voice soft, tapping his index fingers against his chin. "You've shown by your actions that you were never one of Philip's lackeys, or at least that you were never part of his agendas. But you have held responsible positions within the Group, at a high level. A deeper involvement than I ever suspected or knew, until I started reviewing records. At the end, you were considered to be Philip's enforcer." He paused. "How did all this happen, Tine? Given what I knew about your relationship with our father when I dropped out of sight, it's completely unexpected."

Justine grimaced. "The Family required my involvement, Gabriel. Both times."

Oh. Oh.

The words hung between them. Gabe shivered.

The Family required it.

Unlike him, Justine might have separated herself from their father—but she had *not* walked away from the Family. Like he had.

"Tell me more," he said finally.

She exhaled, looking not at him but beyond him. "The first time, our fucking father showed up at a horse show. Requested that we meet more formally, to discuss me taking a *logistics position.*" Sarcasm tinged her voice. "I told Donald, and he contacted Serg and Kendra. The next thing I knew, Gerard, Kendra, Piotr, Serg, and Donald's mother Barbie showed up at the barn on my return to Mist Knoll, our residence at the time. A very hush-hush meeting—and I learned that the Board had rejected Joey as a potential Martiniere-in-waiting. The Board demanded that Daddy-damned-dearest put me in an equivalent position. Uncle Gerry was very nice about it—but I was given no choice but to accept our father's offer. By the Family, not him."

"Hmm."

Interesting, very interesting.

"That *logistics position* turned out to be First Secretary of External Affairs," Justine said bitterly. "At the same time, Donald became very ill. Taking that position brought about my divorce. And it ended very dramatically, when I learned too damned much about what Daddy-fucking-dearest was doing with his Electric Born cult."

"I'm sorry, Tine."

Now she looked at him. "I could have used your presence, Gabie. I really could have." The hurt in her voice made him ache. "If you had been available, then the Family would have turned to you. Not me. I could have been with Donald full time, when he really needed *me.*"

"From what I've seen, you did an excellent job as First Secretary," he said.

Justine's lips tightened even more. "Gabriel, I was just *twenty-one years old* when that happened. I had a sick husband, who encouraged me to follow through, and hid how ill he was until *after* I signed the contract and couldn't walk away without triggering a pile of consequences." She exhaled, and sagged slightly in her chair. "While I was angry at you, I also knew that you'd made many sacrifices to save me. It was my turn to pay back all those—you, Serg, Piotr, Gerry, Donald, Kendra—who helped me get away from our damned father." Her chin raised slightly. "The Board set me as a watchdog on our father. Until I made a major mistake when digging into the Electric Born records, I performed that job—very well."

"I'm surprised he agreed to making you First Secretary of External Affairs."

"I'd had my hysterectomy by then." Grim voice now. "Daddy-damned-dearest was most explicit that my lack of female reproductive organs partially qualified me, although, since I had the unfortunate fate of being born female, with two X chromosomes instead of XY, I could never ascend to the full position of Martiniere, much less Martiniere-in-waiting."

"I'm sorry," he said.

"He threw it in my face many times." Her expression softened. "And the second time around, when I became Director of Security, the reasoning from the Family was very much the same, only delivered by Piotr once he emerged from a long period underground. The Board required it. And, by that point, I had decided that there were only two people qualified to be our father's successor. You—or me."

Gabe raised his brows at that.

Justine tightened her lips again and nodded. "And then I made another mistake." She waved one hand. "It's not material to this discussion. But I spent too damned many years under *his* thumb as a result." Now she steepled her fingers, mirroring his posture. "Any more questions?"

"I have quite a few of them, especially after my discussion

with the Heads of Families at Christmas about the degree to which our damned father decimated any competition." He sighed. "But that's going to be an ongoing conversation—too long for one meeting. How the hell did you survive, Tine?"

Justine exhaled. "In a nutshell, Donald. And the fact that I discovered a vulnerability in Eliot. I protected Eliot; Eliot protected me. Donald, Eliot, and Nick were all key players."

Nick? Who's Nick?

Another player Gabe didn't know about. One of her boyfriends post-divorce?

Justine continued. "But much of it was scrambling and sheer good luck. Serg working undercover within the Group during one incident that could have gone bad for me, among other things."

"You survived."

She shrugged. "For some reason, our damned father pulled his punches when it came to me. He *knew* Joey was a fuckup, and for some crazy reason, he'd tolerate my sass. Even if he wouldn't make me the Martiniere-in-waiting. He just couldn't go that far, but—" She shook her head. "He brought me in as Director of Security because he was being blackmailed by Greg Hallock. Eliminating Hallock earned me the title of being Daddy-poo's enforcer. But Daddy-fucking-dearest also told me that I was the only one—perhaps you as well—who wouldn't destroy the Group in the process of deposing him."

Gabe snorted. "You managed to survive, nonetheless."

"In part because he found a lever to keep me under control." She laughed bitterly. "Little did he know how desperate I was just before you reappeared. It took constant support from Donald to keep me from activating Donald's Little Divorce Present to the Martinieres and tearing it all down, during 2058."

"Wow. It was that bad." Gabe eyed Justine, remembering the skinny, tense, jittery woman she had been almost a year ago. His sister had actually gained weight during the past year, and while she was watchful, she lacked that sharp edge she had possessed while their father was alive.

Another victim of our damned father. But she had the guts to face him head-on.

"Yes. The main reason I stayed, and didn't invoke Donald's program? What activating Donald's Little Divorce Present would have done to the innocents in the Family. It would have wrecked the financial support for those who had done no wrong. I did what I could to protect people, Gabie, especially when I worked as Director of Security. I kept Piotr and Serg from being destroyed, and others." Justine looked down, then back up. "I wasn't perfect. But the Family would have been much more reduced if I hadn't been Director of Security these past few years. I kept looking for my opportunity, hoping that maybe you could come back. If not—I was fully prepared to fight my way into becoming the Martiniere myself."

"I believe you." Gabe rubbed his face. "And I need you to remain as Director of Security—if you'll keep it." He sensed there was much more below the surface, but—this was sufficient. For now.

"Of course."

"You're welcome." Gabe studied his hands. "Final thing. Personal, a favor the Martiniere is asking the Director of Security to handle. There was a captain in Philip's guard. He may not remain within the Group."

He could trust his sister in her role as Director of Security to handle this particular situation.

"And?"

Gabe tightened his lips. "He not only beat the crap out of me when our damned father programmed me so I couldn't even say who I really was—but he brutalized Brandon when Bran was little. I never got his name. But if he still works for the Group—I want him out of here. Preferably with extreme prejudice."

Justine raised her brows. "What the *fuck*, Gabriel?"

"After Philip beat the crap out of me and introduced more

nanos into my system so that I was severely locked down, that man continued to whale on me. Left me with internal injuries and broken ribs. And what he did to Bran—" He winced. "Bran was just ten years old. That, more than anything, is why I'd happily see that man gone."

"When did that happen?" Justine scowled.

"Me? Just before the divorce from Ruby. April 1, 2036. Brandon—September-October of 2043." Gabe let himself bare his teeth slightly. "I beat the crap out of that man in return, after Brandon. I can't find his name in the records, but *I want him gone*. If he's not already dead, hopefully from what I did to him."

"If he's not in the records, that probably means he was part of the Electric Born. Daddy-fucking-dearest brought in a lot of personal security from those fuckers, and those would be the sort of jobs they'd handle."

Gabe leaned his head against the back of his chair. "This is such a fucking mess, Tine. It really is."

"Yes." Her voice was flat, noncommittal.

"While personally I'd *like* to be a part of the reckoning for that man, realistically, I shouldn't be."

"Agreed." That grim tone in her voice again. "You can't afford that sort of vengeance-taking as the Martiniere, not with what you're trying to do for the Group and the Family. I'll take care of it, Gabriel."

Gabriel instead of *Gabie*. That, the suddenly hard set of her face, and the tone were all reminiscent of their father. Gabe stifled a shudder. He was seeing Justine as the enforcer. *His* enforcer now, not Philip's.

On the other hand, I also have moments like that as well, for the same sort of realities.

All the same, he softened his voice. "That's pretty much it. I want to tour the labs, but that can wait until tomorrow. I expect that to take most of the day."

He wanted to pry more information from Justine about her

connection with McNaughton, but this was most likely enough for now.

Justine's expression eased in return. She got up, and paused. "I'm setting up dinner plans for tonight. Eliot and Nick, Donald, you, me, Brandon. It'll be at the house. A chance for you to know Eliot and Nick."

"That sounds good." He and Brandon were staying at Justine's oceanfront house for the duration of their time in Los Angeles. Gabe supposed that sooner or later, he'd need to set up his own residence here—then again, he'd not had the opportunity to examine her compound just yet. Staying there might be the best option.

And dinner would be an excellent opportunity to learn more about the connection between his sister and McNaughton. Especially with Donald present. He needed to know if there would be problems from that direction.

"Oh, can you send Ms. Ruiz in?" he asked. "Thank you for finding her."

She grinned at him. "Corina is very good at what she does, Gabie. She's not security, but I don't think you need that." Justine hesitated. "She was Raven's personal assistant while she was still indentured, and he had the highest regard for her. Was planning to buy her contract before he died; left her enough money to buy herself free and set herself up for life. Our damned father was an absolute ass to her. Eliot found her a spot in External Affairs to get away from him. Be—gentle with Corina to start with, all right?"

"I'll keep that in mind." He was glad for the warning. Given Justine's past history working with indentured women and championing women's reproductive rights, he wasn't surprised by her actions.

And Deschamps wanting to buy her contract? Poor woman was probably still in mourning, because Gabe was pretty damned sure that meant they were lovers. Even though that went against all HR regulations—Ruiz must be someone pretty special, for a strict rule-follower like Deschamps to disregard protocol to this extreme.

He needed to be extra careful with her, then.

It wasn't the Double R, but Gabe was grateful that the heat and smog had eased off at Justine's house so that they could gather outdoors for dinner. Not that he wanted to eat outside at the Double R in January other than a quick sandwich during all-day ranch chores. Januarys in Northeastern Oregon were *cold*. Los Angeles was nothing like it.

Gabe shed tie and suit jacket, unbuttoned the collar and top two buttons of his shirt, and removed cuff links to roll his sleeves up before joining the others on the deck overlooking the ocean. Now he sprawled in a lounge chair, mojito in hand, savoring the slight breeze. Somehow that drink felt more appropriate in this setting than his usual whisky. Watching the sun set over the ocean brought back childhood memories—the good ones, for once. The days when Saul, his mother Angelica, and his little sister Louisa were still alive, and they lived in a house on a cliff overlooking the ocean.

Back when he still thought Philip was his uncle, not his biological father, and Saul had been Papa. Not his biological uncle.

Justine's deck was very much like the one at his childhood home. When Gabe leaned his head back and closed his eyes, he could almost imagine himself in that long-ago era. It was a delightful antidote to the intense day he had spent getting things organized, with too damned many flashbacks to the bad years. And a contrast to the memories from his teens.

No bad memories by the ocean.

Gabe turned his face to the soft zephyr, enjoying its gentle brush on his face.

Who now owned his childhood home? Or had it survived

landslides and wildfires? If he bought property here, it would be oceanfront. Someplace like this. Maybe he *should* look for his old home.

Or perhaps just plan on sharing this compound with Justine. It appeared to have plenty of space. He'd look around and talk to her. After all, he didn't *intend* to stay here forever. Just a week or so every month, as long as he was the Martiniere. Ruby and Mikey might appreciate spending time near the ocean. But nothing permanent, nothing forever. LA had ceased being *home* many years ago. *Home* was Northeastern Oregon, most particularly the Double R.

"You look relaxed," Brandon said quietly.

Gabe opened his eyes. "Memories," he said. "Before my family died, I lived in a place very much like this. It was—the good time of my childhood."

"Was that why you and Rachel spent so much time on the water?"

Gabe nodded. Rachel. His gentle wife, not his warrior wife. His second wife's upbringing was very similar to his when it came to material things, only in San Diego, not Los Angeles. And while Hernan and Erica Alvarez were—well, he wasn't going to think poorly of the dead—they had not been vicious to Rachel as a child. Not like Philip had been to his children—and his clones.

Except for Joey, who wasn't even his own.

But then, even though Joey was Philip's nephew, not his son, he'd been just like Philip.

"Pretty much. Your mother didn't have that same background, except for Thunder Lake. Not the same at all."

Brandon snorted. "I should say not." His water and beach experience as a kid was primarily with Thunder Lake, and occasional excursions on the Columbia and Puget Sound with Gabe and Rachel.

"A place like this comes with concerns," Justine said. She sat upright in Donald's lap, taking a break from supervising dinner preparations. Donald's arms wrapped loosely around her waist.

"Earthquake. Fire. Landslide." Her mouth quirked. "But it's worth it for evenings like this."

"Better than the islands?" Donald asked.

Justine gave him a knowing look, one brow raised with a slight smirk. "Solitaire Island is gone. I do enjoy Nameless, in part because I can stand it year-round. It has seasons, and I don't need to worry about hurricanes."

Nameless?

Gabe had visited Solitaire, the Caribbean island owned by Donald's mother, shortly after Justine married Donald. Nameless must be Donald's island residence, somewhere off of the coast of British Columbia. Both Justine and Donald were vague about its specific location.

"Nameless is nice," said Nick. He and McNaughton sat close together, not quite touching. Justine had welcomed both men warmly, as had Donald. Gabe now recognized Nick as another man who had been part of Justine's publicly identified stable of lovers. How did *he* fit into the mix?

"You've been there?" Gabe asked. *He* hadn't been invited —yet.

Nick and McNaughton exchanged glances.

"It was a backup bugout site for all of us, not just Justine," McNaughton said. "A necessary refuge." He and Nick gazed at each other once more. "Especially during the last few years."

This was getting complicated because it was clear to Gabe that Nick and McNaughton were in a relationship—and how did that tie into the public involvement that Justine maintained with both of them?

Justine kissed Donald on his lips, a long, lingering caress, and got up. "Eliot, Donald, Gabie looks confused. I think you'd better explain things. I've not taken the time to do it yet."

"Are you certain it's safe?" McNaughton asked.

"Gabriel is not Philip," Justine said. "Neither is Brandon. It's safe. I just—it's not my place to disclose. I've been waiting for the right moment, when you can divulge whatever you're comfortable with saying. I'm checking on our dinner progress. You men talk." She kissed McNaughton's brow, then Nick's, before going inside.

McNaughton sighed. Then he glanced at Donald. "So who goes first?"

Donald shrugged. "I can start. As you've probably figured out by now, Gabe, the divorce was a protective cover for our political activities."

"I had that impression, yes. Tine has said that you, Eliot, and Nick were important elements in her surviving Philip."

Donald nodded. "Eliot—and Nick—were part of that cover."

"I'm bi," Eliot said flatly. "I had a huge crush on Justine while working with her, but figured she was unavailable. I started dating Nick, just before Justine and Donald began their divorce drama." He took Nick's hand. "Justine discovered the relationship, thankfully before Philip did. She laid it on the line—she needed to role play her involvement with another man. I needed to hide my relationship with Nick from Philip. Different goals, but similar concealment needs."

"So all the media was fake?" *Damn.*

"Oh, the divorce was a real thing," Donald said. "As was my involvement with Coral, Francie, and Meg. What wasn't disclosed was that they served as my medical and emotional support throughout—more than they were ever my lovers."

Gabe exhaled. "All of you are superb actors. I followed things from afar, obviously, then got sucked up into my own drama. I hadn't the faintest clue."

"When the stakes are as high as they were, that tends to make one focus on the slightest action that could destroy you," Nick said.

"Yeah," Gabe said. "That part I understand, far too well. Philip never knew?"

"I think he suspected," Eliot said. "But he had his own little harem on the side. He had to keep it concealed because of his role in the Electric Born, and that was often difficult with Mariah

Meyers. If it hadn't been for the hidden indenture contract Philip held on her, I think she would have tried to blackmail him into marrying her. I'm certain that's how she managed to establish herself as first amongst his women."

Gabe snorted. "Mariah does not exactly do discreet." As he well knew, from her role in his and Ruby's divorce. He was still surprised that she had kept her child by Joey, the cyborg Alexander, secret all these years.

Access to her son had been Philip's means of control over Mariah's actions. More than that hidden indenture contract.

"No. She doesn't," Eliot sighed. "To protect us all, Justine threatened to disclose Philip's involvement with his women, at the same time that she was visibly involved with both me and Nick. That revelation would have destroyed everything he was trying to do with the Electric Born, so Justine had the upper hand over him. For once."

"It was a challenging and difficult era," Donald said. He raised his glass. "And thanks to you, Gabe, and my—*our*— beloved falcon Justine, those times are *done*. To a new future."

"To a new future," Gabe echoed, along with the others. He glanced at Brandon, whose expression was studied and blank. He wondered just how much of this his son had already known, due to his time spent working in Los Angeles with the AgInnovator.

Georgy Batineau, the AgI's owner, was one of Mariah's long-term lovers. On her own initiative, or at Philip's direction? Now that Philip was dead, Mariah had sworn off all involvement with men.

Gabe had to wonder how close to the truth that vow really was. He didn't trust Mariah Meyers, not one bit. Even this reformed version.

He had gained that knowledge the hard way, and possessed no desire to repeat the experience.

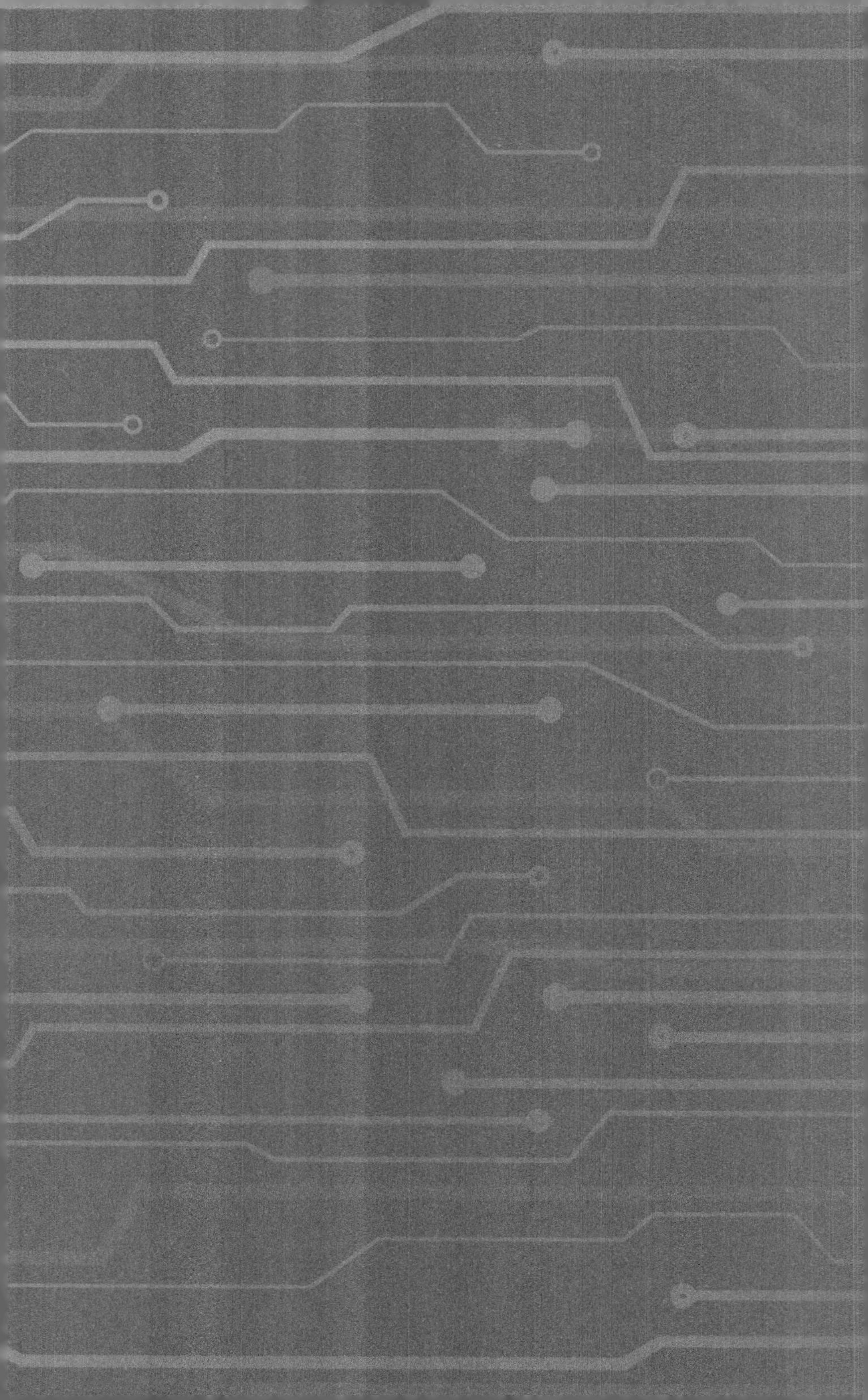

5 / CONSPIRACIES AT THE RODEO

AUGUST, 2060

RUBY

Why did I ever think this was a good idea?

Ruby shook her head. Butterflies in her gut were to be expected, given that she hadn't ridden in a rodeo parade for *years*, much less on Legacy, carrying a flag. But for almost the *entire freaking leadership of the Martiniere Group* to join her in the parade?

Coordination was nothing less than a nightmare.

The various security chiefs—Justine's JSM Corp chief, Shanice L'Étoile; Serg and Piotr for Vygotsky/Martiniere; and Kevin Swait for Swait Secure, the security operation of their business partner Jeff Swait—had been pulling out their hair at the exposure problems. Meanwhile, Thunder County Sheriff Sharon Wilhite had happily handed over security management for their contingent to the Group.

Those too fragile or inexperienced to be on horseback rode in the wagon pulled by the tractor that Charlie Thompson, the Double R ranch manager, drove. Donna-gran, Eliot McNaughton, Mikey (with many protests, but he just wasn't ready to ride even steady Crystal in a parade), Kris with baby

Lily, their business partners Jeff and Kelsey Swait plus the two younger Swait kids, Deontae and JoAnn were in the wagon. The six cyborged brothers rode in the wagon with this group as direct protection.

The mounted contingent included her on Legacy, Gabe on Legacy's dam Casey, Brandon on Blaze, Justine on Pard, Donald on Crystal, along with half her student interns on their own horses and the oldest Swait kids, Wesley and Rae, on Cisco and Buddy.

Breathe, Ruby, breathe, she told herself as she brushed off her old chaps from her year as Thunder County Days Queen. *It's just another rodeo parade.*

And they were one of the first groups, thanks to the Thunder County Days directors, who were falling-over-themselves grateful for the contributions the Martiniere Group had made to upgrading the Thunder County Rodeo and Fair Grounds for this 125th rodeo. Plus the Group's sponsorship of the Old Timer events, and miscellaneous donations that Gabe's old friends in Thunder County had talked him into making from his personal funds.

As a result, Gabe, Brandon, and Ruby rode as the parade's honor guard with the national, state, and rodeo flags, following the Thunder County High School Marching Band that led the parade.

She made her check rounds while Gabe held Legacy and Casey's reins, starting with the tractor and wagon. Big banners draped the wagon, reading:

CONGRATULATIONS THUNDER COUNTY DAYS ON 125 YEARS—FROM THE DOUBLE R RANCH AND THE MARTINIERE GROUP.

The Double R brand and the new Martiniere Group logo, with a larger green and gold trefoil surrounding the red and black one that had been the Group's for years, flanked the words.

Ruby checked the ties on the banners. All secure.

"Everything all right up there?" she called to the wagon riders—McNaughton, Nick, and Donna-gran in the first row; Mikey, Kris, and Lily in the second, and the Swaits in the third. The cyborg brothers spread out through the wagon, Alexander standing in the front, then Carl, Daniel, and Eric sitting in each row, and Frederick and George standing in the back. Their weapons weren't visible but were easily reached.

"All good, Ruby!" Donna-gran grinned big.

Alexander gave Ruby a thumbs up.

"We've got it," Serg said quietly.

The Vygotsky, Martiniere, Swait Secure, and JSM Corp security sidewalkers were dressed in western wear rather than their usual suits. Serg commanded one side; Shanice the other; Kevin following. *They* were visibly armed. Piotr observed from his seat next to Charlie in the tractor cab.

Ruby, Gabe, Brandon, and Justine carried sidearms, ostensibly for appearance's sake. But their pistols were loaded, and the four of them had been practicing daily for the last week, working with their horses to ensure they were desensitized.

At least Pat's not part of the crowd.

Kris's sister Pat Markey was the New Democratic Presidential nominee. She *had* been interested in joining them, along with a contingent of New Dems leaders and fundraisers. It took serious discussion to discourage *that* addition. Bad enough that the four lead principals from the Group were here, much as that thrilled the rodeo directors.

Ruby was just going to be happy when this parade was *done.*

She moved amongst the riders. Not so worried about the local kids—but she paused by Wes and Rae. Their riding skill impressed her during practices over the past week. Both kids participated in Black Junior Rodeo down in Arkansas, and rode in their fair share of parades at home. Still, it didn't hurt to check in since they were riding unfamiliar mounts.

"Doing all right?" she asked.

"Looking forward to it," Rae said, grinning. Thunder County Days had a junior breakaway roping contest, and Rae had been practicing with Buddy ever since the Swaits had come to the Double R for business meetings a week ago. Rae wore one of her championship buckles today.

"We'll make a queen out of you yet," Ruby said.

Rae rolled her eyes. "Nah, I wanna *compete*, not queen."

Well, she could understand that. Unlike Ruby, Rae wasn't going to be dependent on scholarships from queen contests to help pay for *her* college—thanks to the AgSuperhero win, and the Swait share from Barkley-Martiniere-Swait Associates sales. If Ruby had possessed a steady family income like that, things would have been much different—

And she wouldn't have met Gabe.

"Wes?"

Another big grin. Wes was quieter than his older sister, but he sat Cisco with a confident ease born of experience. He also sported one of his junior bull-riding championship buckles.

"Ready to ride bulls," he said, patting Cisco's neck. "He's a good boy. Might even do breakaway roping myself, if I can borrow him, Ruby."

"Sounds good if you want to go for it," Ruby said.

One thing about Thunder County Days, they had a thriving junior rodeo as part of the overall program. Ruby looked forward to watching both older Swait kids perform during the day tomorrow. Possibly even in the evening championships.

She moved on to Donald and Justine. Crystal stood steady like the old packer she was. Donald surprised Ruby when he wanted to ride, but he sat Crystal like a pro, though he looked paler than Ruby was comfortable with seeing before a parade on a hot day. Part of his health issues, whatever they were.

Justine had once ridden high-level showjumpers, but that didn't always translate over to parade riding.

"We're good, Ruby," Justine said. She had borrowed a pair of show chaps from Ruby. They were close enough in size and sometimes shared clothing. But they had to borrow nice chaps for Donald and Brandon. Gabe had his own, of course; had commissioned a pair once he had become the Martiniere, complete with both the Double R brand and the new Martiniere Group logo.

And now to Gabe, Brandon—and Legacy. Bran held the flags and Blaze's reins. Ruby wasn't too worried about Casey and Blaze, but Legacy? The palomino mare had moments like her great-granddam Sunshine, who had been notorious for unpredictable bucking, along with lightning-fast barrel runs.

Still, the golden mare enjoyed showing off. And she was in foal to Star, the new stallion Ruby and Gabe had bought this winter, so that *should* steady Legacy a bit.

Maybe she should have chosen Star instead of Legacy for the parade, but Ruby didn't know how well the dark bay stallion would behave outside of the arena yet, and she was riding with kids. Ruby *knew* Legacy, had raised her from a foal. That made a difference.

"Smile, Rubes," Gabe said. "It's just a parade."

"I know." But there were people out there who wanted Gabe dead. This would provide opportunity. And *that* was the reason for the heavy security.

She took Legacy's reins, eying the golden mare. While Legacy was clearly excited, head high, nostrils flaring, ears flicking back and forth to keep track of all the activity, she stood steady on all four hooves, not dancing around.

Good.

Ruby checked the cinches and breast collar of her Miss Rodeo Oregon award saddle.

Sally, one of the parade organizers, came by. "Going in five, Ruby."

"Thanks."

Ruby glanced at the lineup of marching bands. The Martiniere funding suddenly made Thunder County Days events a lot bigger. Fortunately, the rodeo producers hired experts familiar with larger parades to organize this one. The several high school marching bands lined up one after the other, rather than mixed in with the mounted units and the mechanized floats. Each unit would feed into the lineup in its appointed place.

"All right," she said to Gabe and Brandon. "Let's mount up. Gabe, Bran, then me."

It was easier for her to take up a flag without help. Neither Gabe nor Bran had ridden drill team or handled flags. At least both Casey and Blaze had parade experience.

Her old friend, neighbor, and former rodeo queen advisor Vickie Chandler and Vickie's husband Mike were supposed to be here. So where were they? Vickie's presence would have eased Ruby's mind significantly. However she had ridden in enough parades that Vickie was simply a help, not a necessity.

First, Gabe. Ruby handed him the Stars and Stripes once he was in his saddle, then made certain the pole was secure in its holder. Legacy remained steady with the split reins tossed over Ruby's shoulder. Then Brandon, with the state flag.

Sally reappeared as Ruby prepared to mount Legacy. "Need a hand?"

"Absolutely. Thanks, Sally." Ruby gratefully handed Sally the flag and swung up on Legacy. Sally handed her the Thunder County Days flag, and checked to ensure the pole was seated.

"I'm surprised you don't have help," Sally said.

"I was *supposed* to have help," Ruby said, frowning. "I wonder what happened?"

This wasn't like Vickie and Mike. They were *reliable*, damn it. A host of bad possibilities flitted through Ruby's mind, banished as Sally walked on and the whistle of the first band's drum major blew, signaling the band to start marching in place.

Legacy snorted and bounced.

"Quit," Ruby muttered, squeezing her reins.

Legacy steadied.

The Thunder County High School band stepped out with only a few squawks from the woodwinds. Sally signed to Gabe, and he followed the band. Ruby and Brandon flanked Casey and Gabe.

The Martiniere, carrying the US flag, with the Martiniere-in-waiting carrying the state flag. All symbolic, all meant to project an image.

Legacy pranced and arched her neck, mouthing the roller in her bit as they proceeded down the streets of Lakeside, showing off but not being difficult. There was a bigger crowd than usual. Possibly attracted by the Martiniere presence? Well, that might be an asset to the Thunder County economy. One of Ruby and Gabe's goals was to improve local conditions without losing what made Thunder County what it was.

A delicate balance.

And why they had said yes to the parade and the rodeo.

After all, rodeo was a big part of the story of Ruby and Gabe —a fact that was well-known. Especially after the AgSuperhero competition.

***

It happened toward the end of the parade. Legacy suddenly tensed under Ruby, steps coming shorter and faster, her head shooting up high as her nostrils flared and she snorted. She kept wanting to turn to the outside and face something. When Ruby wouldn't let her, she half-reared, then hopped.

"Quit!" Ruby snapped, squeezing the reins in her left hand. What was setting the golden mare off? She didn't have time to look, but *something* in the crowd bothered Legacy.

A contingent of Martiniere security ran past them.

"Cover Gabe!" Serg bellowed, before they plunged into the spectators.

Ruby sent Legacy forward in a quick trot so that they rode beside Gabe and Casey.

"Should I toss the flag and ride for it?" he asked.

"Not yet. Better that you don't toss *that* flag. Image. I'll cover you."

Gabe nodded. "If I hear shots, it goes, however." His face was tight and hard, defensive. But he still sat up straight and proud, not hunching down protectively.

Only a block more, only a block more—Ruby scanned ahead, scouting a path that wouldn't involve tearing through the band or the parents marching alongside carrying water bottles. Or the crowd.

The band rounded the corner to re-enter the Rodeo and Fair Grounds. Just a few minutes more.

Pop-pop-pop.

"Ride for the trailers, *fast!*" she snapped to Brandon and Gabe once the band was clear. "Don't throw the flags yet!"

Legacy bolted, staying at Casey's side. Ruby didn't look back but she hoped Justine was monitoring Donald and the kids—she probably was.

As they approached the trailers, Ruby spotted a figure slumped on one of the trailer wheel wells, arm in a sling.

"It's me." Vickie Chandler straightened up, her voice quavering, at the same time that her husband Mike hobbled around the corner, flanked by the Thunder County Home Guard.

Ruby slid Legacy to a stop, dropping the flag before she dismounted.

"What the hell, Vickie?" she asked.

"I got jumped in the supermarket parking lot," Vickie groaned. Coming closer, Ruby spotted the black eye and bruising on her face. "Was gonna bring some treats for you all. Didn't have time to bake."

"You all right?"

"Just a sprain," Vickie said. "And the Home Guard got those assholes."

"Any ID on the attackers?" Gabe asked, dismounting after Brandon took his flag.

Mike Chandler's lips tightened. "Deputy Greer says they're modified indentureds. Tattoo is a cross with the old Martiniere logo overlaid."

Ruby and Gabe scowled at each other. *Heaven's Reach.* No mistaking it with *that* logo.

"I'll tell Justine," Ruby said. Damn it, that meant full security for the rest of the rodeo. And she *had* been hoping for a relaxing time, once the parade was done.

***

"SINGULARLY INCOMPETENT," WAS JUSTINE'S VERDICT POST-interrogation of the captured attackers, both Vickie's and the ones the Martiniere/Vygotsky security (coupled with Swait Secure) had chased down at the parade. She, Kevin, and Serg reported to Gabe, Ruby, Brandon, Eliot, and Jeff, all crammed into the living/kitchen area of the big RV that served as head-quarters for Ruby and Gabe during the rodeo. "Firecrackers, no weapons during the parade. Heaven's Reach-connected. Young, half-trained."

"So where are the *real* leaders?" Gabe snapped. "This doesn't fit the Heaven's Reach profile. They don't send out half-trained people."

"It suggests that our screens and scans worked," Kevin said. Swait Secure had handled that aspect of parade manage-ment. "Our staff detected and turned away twenty armed, unli-censed people. Most had a rationale for carrying, local addresses, just didn't agree with the publicity that they needed to leave their weapons at home. All but two returned unarmed."

"It may mean that our pressure on the Heaven's Reach

enclaves is finally starting to work," Justine said. "They may *not* have enough fully-trained agents to send out."

"Or it's a distraction from their real goals," Gabe said. "Meant to lull us into false security."

Justine nodded. "I'm operating on that principle."

"Meanwhile," Serg said, "we've gotten past the most difficult part. Everything from here on can be controlled and managed. It'll be no worse than any other public event."

"I hope so," Ruby said.

Her sister-in-law flashed her a quick smile. "I will make it so, Ruby. I'm looking forward to see you ride Grand Entry. Heard Gabie talk about it enough times that I want to see it in person."

"Speaking of Grand Entry," Gabe said, "it's happening in three hours. Ruby needs to rest. Rubes, are you riding Legacy or Star?"

Ruby planned to alternate Legacy and Star for her run-ins. The dark bay stallion had earned reined cowhorse championships. She could trust him in an arena setting.

"Star," she said. "Parade's enough for the Legacy girl today. She did good."

"Yes, she did." Gabe exhaled. "All right. Keep us posted." He raised his brows at Ruby, and jerked his head toward the back of the RV. "Rubes. Time to rest." His tone allowed no argument.

She sighed and got up, pausing to talk to Brandon. "Mikey's all right?" Mikey, Kris, and Lily had retreated to the second RV. The Swaits had a third one, and Justine, Donald, Eliot, and Nick shared a fourth. Security was headquartered in a fifth. The rental cost was extravagant, but it also provided safety. Plus, between RVs and stock trailers, they had aligned the vehicles in a circle to enclose the portable horse pens for even more protection.

"He's napping with Smudge," Brandon said. "Go rest, Ma."

Ruby rolled her eyes but headed for the bedroom at the back of the RV, Gabe following her.

At least Mikey had his half-grown heeler pup to comfort him.

Just like she and Gabe had each other. And Smudge showed strong protective tendencies toward his young owner.

Most Grand Entries simply involved riding around the arena at top speed. But Thunder County Days included a pattern with the Thunderheads, the rodeo drill team. The patterns hadn't changed since Ruby's tenure as Queen when she was sixteen, but all the same, as she rode Star toward the arena, she was glad this first run was on Star and not Legacy. The dark bay stallion was better at patterns, something she hoped he would pass on to his foals.

Gabe, Alexander, Carl, and Serg walked alongside her, Gabe holding the furled Martiniere Group flag that Ruby would be carrying. The rest of their security sat in the stands with the family members, watching tonight's performance. Ruby wore her old Thunder County Days Queen outfit—or at least as much of it that still fit her. Even though she was still lean, she'd been a lot skinnier at sixteen. Especially her chest.

Vickie met them near the gate. "You got the pattern down?"

"Me and Star both." Ruby patted the stallion's neck. "Big circle, serpentine, crossover, crossover, serpentine, then line up with the rest of the sponsors. National Anthem and prayer. Going out, spiral, serpentine, big circle, exit."

"Watch your timing." Vickie squinted at the stud. "He likes to run."

"He rates pretty well. I'll have more challenges with Legacy. Just like I did with Sunshine."

Vickie rolled her eyes. "You and your palomino mares. All right. You're the first sponsor rider, after the Court and the Thunderheads. Got it?"

Ruby nodded. She liked the way Star felt underneath her. He was alert and focused, attention on the arena, but didn't have that coiled-spring reactiveness that Legacy—and Sunshine before her—possessed. Vickie moved on to talk to the other riders. Gabe unfurled the Martiniere flag and handed it to Ruby, helping seat the pole in its holder. He scratched Star's forehead once he was done.

"You do right by her, fella," he said softly to Star, resting his forehead against the stallion's for a fleeting moment. "I'm trusting you to take care of my lady."

Ruby blinked. *No one* ever seemed to catch a picture of the two forehead-to-forehead, though she had seen it many times. Gabe and Star had a special connection. Star would go to Gabe before her, and always greeted him with a friendly nicker. Gabe rode Star at the ranch. But when it came to performance—it was Ruby in the saddle. She knew the nuances that Gabe lacked.

Alexander, Carl, and Serg remained alert. Ruby didn't think they'd have any issues at the gate, but one never knew.

And then it was time. She moved into line. Star leapt forward when Vickie hollered, *"Ruby, go!"*

"And here we have the 2024 Thunder County Days Queen Ruby Barkley, carrying the banner of our lead sponsor, the Martiniere Group!" she barely heard the announcer say as they charged into the arena. She caught snatches of the rest of his spiel. "—2031 Miss Rodeo Oregon, 2029 Pendleton Round-Up Princess—"

Star snorted as he galloped. But he let Ruby keep him in place behind the rider ahead of them. Big circle to serpentine. Serpentine to the first crossover, loop around for the second, then line up behind the Thunderheads, anchor for the row of other former queens carrying sponsor flags. Ruby exhaled. Star blew and shook his head.

"Good boy," she murmured.

National Anthem. Prayer. Then it was the last pattern elements and another race around the arena.

"Ruby! Need—" She only caught a snatch of that voice, but it was enough to send chills down her spine.

Mariah Meyers. What the fuck was *she* doing here?

No time to think about it. Ruby fixed her eyes on the gate. Star slowed easily as they approached it. Ruby looked around for Gabe—Alexander—*somebody*—once they were out of the arena.

Then Gabe was there, easing the banner out of her hand, Alexander, Carl and Serg with him.

"Mariah's here," she said grimly. "North side of the arena, east end of the covered stands, by the fence. Yelled something at me about need on that last circuit."

"That can't be—" Alexander frowned, then whirled away. "I'll look for her."

Gabe jerked his head at Carl. "Follow him. Have Al bring his mother to the RV. And have someone send Justine over as well." He walked alongside Ruby as she rode away from the arena, Serg on Ruby's other side. "That bitch. That *damned* bitch. Why the hell is she popping up here and now? I thought things were settled with her! She shouldn't be anywhere near Thunder County!"

"Easy, Gabe," she said as Star tensed under her, reacting to Gabe's angry tone.

Gabe patted Star's neck. "Sorry, fella. But damn it, Ruby—" He exhaled.

"I know," she said, halting Star at the Fortress, as she now called the formation of RVs and trailers. Ruby dismounted and let Gabe lead Star inside the enclosure to untack and get the stallion settled. Give Gabe some time with Star to calm down about Mariah's reappearance in their lives, apart from Family Christmas because she was Al's mother and technically Family.

The man needed horse time as much as she did.

By the time the others converged on the RV, Ruby had showered to wash off the arena dust, and pulled on leggings and a t-shirt. No going back to the rodeo tonight, not with *this* happening. She took the bottle of Gabe's favorite whisky out of a cabinet, along with several glasses.

Gabe appeared more relaxed as he and Serg entered the RV. *Good.*

Ruby poured both of them straight shots without being asked, then one for herself, and yet another for Justine. They settled into the L-shaped booth around the kitchen-area table, Ruby in the corner, between Gabe and Serg.

Alexander, Mariah, and Justine arrived together, Mariah entering the RV before the other two. Justine picked up the waiting glass of whisky and leaned against the kitchen counter. She glared at Mariah.

Mariah looked nothing like the last time Ruby had seen her. Her hair was dyed black, face thin and haggard. Instead of her usual immaculate designer clothing, she wore faded jean capris and a t-shirt two sizes too big for her, with tattered sneakers. She shivered as she huddled in the center of the kitchen area, arms wrapped around herself, focused on Justine.

"Should I stay?" Alexander asked, glancing from Justine to Gabe.

"Outside the door, Al," Gabe said, voice harsh.

Justine gestured to one of the swivel chairs as Al left. "Sit *there*, Mariah." Her cold, flat tone sent a chill up Ruby's back. Justine dropped gracefully into the matching swivel chair after Mariah sat, not disturbing the level of her drink. Mariah's gaze followed Justine's movements, almost like a snake-entranced mouse.

"What's this about, Mariah?" Gabe glowered at her. "You yelled something at Ruby about *need.*"

Mariah swallowed hard, not looking away from Justine. "I— what are you planning to do with me?" Her voice grated on Ruby's nerves, atonal and *not right.*

Gabe twitched, forehead wrinkling in worry.

Justine took a swig off of her whisky and set the glass carefully on the side table. Then she uncoiled from her chair like a striking rattlesnake and grabbed Mariah's chin. "Knock it off with the vocal tones, Mariah." Her voice dropped, silky yet menacing. "Daddy-fucking-dearest is no longer alive to protect you, and Gabriel isn't under your spell. What. The. Fuck. Is. Going. On?"

Mariah gulped, staring at Justine as if she were hypnotized. "Programmed again." She half-choked. "Beat it—maybe." Her eyes darted to Gabe and Ruby. "Plot to kill—Ruby and Gabe—capture clone."

Ruby flinched, wanting to check on Mikey.

He's with Brandon. And guarded.

"And just *who* is doing this?" Justine's voice dropped to an even lower, malevolent register.

"B-Brent Colfax." Mariah winced as Justine's fingers tightened on her chin.

"Are you *sure* of that name?" Oh, the compulsions in Justine's voice—Ruby had never heard *that* intensity from her before now.

"Y-yes. With—Heaven's Reach."

Justine released Mariah's chin and straightened up. "Is that all?"

Mariah cringed as Justine towered over her. "There's—there's fresh captives. Taken with me. Young girls—women. Over the state line."

"Washington or Idaho?" Gabe asked, his voice steady even as his free hand fumbled for Ruby's underneath the table and grasped it tightly.

"Idaho," Mariah whispered. "I—I—it was all a mistake! I heard about these girls and I thought I could—but I got caught, *too*—"

Gabe exhaled hard, closing his eyes for a moment, then opening them again. "You were *supposed* to stay in Chicago, Mariah. Where it's safe for you to be. Not go chasing after redemption, damn it!" His voice cracked like a whip, making Mariah huddle into an even smaller shape. "What the fucking *hell* did you think you were doing? I—"

"*Gabriel!*" Justine snapped. "*Stop it.* This isn't useful right now. We have bigger issues." She glanced at Serg. "Secure Mariah. Get Piotr over here to interrogate and deprogram her. Leave Al at the door, take Carl with you."

"Got it." Serg rose. Justine stepped back as he escorted Mariah out of the RV.

Justine tapped her comm. "Shanice. I need Donald here, *immediately.*" She took a big gulp off of her whisky.

"What the hell is going on, Justine?" Gabe's vocal pitch was only slightly softer than it had been.

Justine snapped up an image. "Is this the man you asked me to find and take care of back in January?"

Gabe's nostrils flared as he studied it. "Yes." He took a drink.

"Donald and I have history with him as well," Justine said.

"What the hell?" Ruby asked, her gut tightening. This was *bad*.

Gabe gestured at the image with his glass. "*That man* beat the crap out of me at the behest of my fucking sperm donor, when Philip demanded that I divorce you. *That man* beat the crap out of *our son* at age ten, during the water rights fight. He will pay for that, more than he already has." He took another sip, his voice rising as he continued. "If Mariah's telling us the truth about his connection with Heaven's Reach, and he wants to fucking kidnap Mikey—*that man* is going to fucking pay for that, as well."

"*My* job, not yours, Gabriel," Justine's voice went harder than ever. "We agreed on that back in January. You cannot afford to be connected with this sort of personal vengeance as the Martiniere. Not unless you want to be viewed like our fucking father."

"His connection to Heaven's Reach—"

"I'll *take care of it*," Justine snarled as Donald entered the RV. "Your hands are already sufficiently bloody when it comes to Heaven's Reach, Gabriel!"

"That was *Gabe Ramirez*, not *Gabriel Martiniere*." Gabe glowered at his sister.

Justine exhaled, not flinching away from Gabe's glare. "Damn it, Gabie. You already damned near beat the man to death *once*. This is a matter not just for me as Director of Security, but those girls—that's a Rescue Angel project."

Donald raised his brows as he studied the projection. "So Colfax has reared his ugly head again, hmm?"

His steady voice projected an aura of calm. Justine shivered and her face softened. Gabe's grip eased on Ruby's hand.

Justine nodded. "Mariah Meyers has provided the missing link between him and Heaven's Reach."

"*Finally.*" Donald crossed his arms. "What's the situation, my falcon?"

"Piotr is interrogating Meyers. She claims to have been programmed again, and resisted. There's a plot to kill Ruby and Gabe, kidnap Mikey. Plus a group of young women being held in Idaho. All connected to Colfax and Heaven's Reach."

"The prostitution gig we've been watching?"

"I suspect so. It fits the profile."

"Tine, Don, what the hell is going on?" Gabe asked.

Donald eased himself into the chair that Mariah had vacated. Justine handed him her half-full glass and he sipped from it.

"Brent Colfax was the head of the security team that your father forced on us when we were living at Mist Knoll, before our divorce," he said. "We had problems with him even then."

"He kept tagging after me. I think he suspected that you were in the area and wanted to catch me talking to you," Justine added. "He's also been involved with a host of shady activities tied to Daddy-fucking-dearest. But he's one slippery fucker, and we couldn't make the final connections."

"Justine and I have been tracking Colfax as part of our Rescue Angel activities," Donald continued. "He's tied to recruitment efforts for Heaven's Reach, and trafficking of their victims. We've never been able to make that final connection. Until now, thanks to Meyers." His eyes met Justine's. His brows lifted. Her lips tightened and she arched one brow in return. He nodded. "Rescue Angel will take it over," he said. "I'll coordinate with Piotr and Kevin once we get that information from Meyers."

"What about security levels here?" Gabe asked.

"It's under control, and it's *not your job, Gabriel,*" Justine said. "It's *mine.* Shanice will talk to Sharon Wilhite, and I'll synchronize with Vickie and the Home Guard. Everyone continues with planned activities, and I'll bring more security staff in tonight from JSM Corp." She got up and took the glass from Donald, finishing the drink. "I'll begin the process. Dearest, please calm Gabie down and explain things further."

Ruby slipped her hand out of Gabe's, picked up her drink, and followed Justine out. The tension was just too damned much, and she wanted to check not just on the horses but Smudge and the other dogs.

Justine exhaled after Ruby closed the RV's door. "Ruby, you can't be part of this, either. Same reasons as Gabie," she said, her words brittle and sharp.

Ruby raised her free hand placatingly. "I know, Justine. I'm not arguing for that. I'm just—it's intense in there."

Her sister-in-law's expression softened. "There are times when Gabie is too much like our fucking father—just now, for example." She shivered. "I get it. He spent years working with Rafe Alvarez as a part-time mercenary. His emotions are involved. But Donald and I have dealt with these situations plenty of times in the last fourteen years. Let us handle Colfax." She grimaced. "I've been lying in wait for that fucker for *years.* If this allows us to move in on Heaven's Reach, all the better."

Ruby sighed. "I'm checking on the animals. I think Mikey needs to have Smudge at his side at all times."

"Wouldn't hurt," Justine said. "And now, I have things to do." She walked away.

After checking on the dogs, Ruby went to the horse pens. Star, on the end, stood next to Casey and Legacy in the adjoining pen. Ruby slipped in with the mares and buried her head in

Legacy's neck, straightening up only to take a sip off of her drink. In the distance, she heard the announcer's closing comments.

Star raised his head and chuckled a welcoming nicker to Gabe. He patted Star, then joined Ruby. That dark glower still lingered on Gabe's face, one she recognized from that awful period before their divorce. It tightened her gut, even though she knew that look wasn't directed at her but at memories of the dilemma he'd been wrestling with then, whether he should reveal who he was—until that choice had been taken from him.

By fucking Mariah, no less.

Acting for Philip, but still—her actions.

Therefore, the expression now. Remembrances of a very bad time.

"Aw, Rubes," he said, putting an arm around her shoulder. "I'm sorry. This mess is exactly why I didn't say anything all those years ago. What I hoped to avoid. My family. My fucking family."

"It's not your fault, Gabe." She sighed and leaned into him. "It comes with who you are—who we are. And this time I went into it with full knowledge."

His arm tightened around her even more. "My beloved warrior wife. Have I told you how much I love you, Ruby Barkley?"

"Not within the last half hour."

Gabe laughed and his expression lightened. "I love you more than I can ever say, Rubes." He exhaled, kissing her forehead. "Tine is right, damn it. I can't do this myself. Those days are over. I have to be the Martiniere." His face twisted. *"Boring."*

"Too many people depend on you, Gabe. Including me and Mikey."

"I know," he said softly, leaning his forehead against hers. "But sometimes I strain against the leash. Being here brings back memories of our wild days."

"They were fun, weren't they? But we have to be responsible adults."

Approaching voices startled them. Brandon, carrying Mikey, and Kris, carrying Lily, flanked by Eliot and Nick, and the remaining cyborg brothers, entered the enclosure. Mikey raised his head from Brandon's shoulder.

"Ruby! Gabe! Can I enter the mutton busting tomorrow?"

"*No,*" Ruby said firmly.

"I should say-ay *not,*" Gabe echoed.

"But *why?*" Mikey's voice carried a rare whine, something that only happened when he was overexcited and overtired.

"Hey, didn't I tell you so?" Brandon said soothingly. "Ma never let *me* do the mutton busting as a kid, either."

"Get bigger, and we'll talk about broncs. *Maybe,*" Ruby said.

Gabe laughed at that. Ruby eyed him, as his glower was replaced by a mischievous twinkle.

"*Gabe,*" she said in warning.

"Oh, I agree with you about the mutton busting," he said. "Come on, Mikey. Let's put you and the dogs to bed, okay?"

Ruby followed Gabe out of the pen. He took Mikey from Brandon.

"Night, Ma," Brandon said, as he and Kris headed for their RV.

Ruby let the dogs out of their pen so they could join Mikey, her, and Gabe; deep in thought. She didn't trust *that* twinkle in Gabe's eye. He was up to something, but what?

THE NEXT AFTERNOON AND EVENING FEATURED RODEO EVENTS FOR local contestants, including the championships for the junior rodeo entrants. Old Timers ranch saddle bronc riding for men and women. Wild cow milking. More mutton busting for the little kids. Wild horse racing. Barrel racing. Team roping.

Ruby and Legacy placed in the afternoon barrel racing, which put them in the evening performance for the Old Timers championships. Barrels happened after the men's ranch saddle bronc riding—she was *not* going to compete in the women's ranch bronc riding. She rode enough buckers while starting greenies at home.

She walked Legacy around the warmup pen after a few laps at a gallop, ready to compete again.

To her surprise, Charlie rode Pard into the pen, along with Gabe's old friend Monty. She would have thought Charlie was tired out after a day's haying and not want to compete in team roping, his usual event.

Charlie broke away from Monty. "Thought I'd better give you a heads up. You seen the late entries for the Old Timers men's ranch saddle broncs?"

"No." Her heart sank. Brandon wouldn't, would he? Or Gabe —*damn it, Gabe.*

Now she understood that sudden twinkle in his eyes last night.

Charlie snapped up the entry list. "Take a look."

Second on the list. *Gabe Ramirez, Skydancer's Repeat.*

"Oh, *fuck*," she growled, and spun Legacy toward the gate. "Can I borrow Pard? Need to talk to the pickup riders. I'm gonna pick him up, damn it!"

"Sure."

They rode to the entry gate. Charlie handed her Pard's reins while he talked to the gate crew. Ruby squinted. She couldn't see Gabe in the lineup, but there *was* a chestnut and white Paint in the second chute who resembled old Skydancer.

Charlie came back with one of the pickup riders—Larry, someone she knew, from Thunder County, and an old friend of Gabe's.

"All set, Ruby," Charlie said.

"You want to ride pickup?" Larry asked.

"Yeah. For just one rider. My fool of a husband's in the damn competition," Ruby said. "Second slot. I want to pick him up and start chewing on his ass right then and there."

Larry laughed. "Not a problem, as long as you're on an experienced horse."

Ruby got off of Legacy and handed the reins to Charlie before checking cinches and stirrups, then mounting Pard. "I'm up on Pard."

Larry tipped his hat to her. "Then you're good."

"Will you pass this message to the announcer—Repeat's rider is not Gabe Ramirez. It's Gabriel Martiniere, and he's in a world of trouble right now."

Larry laughed again. "With pleasure, Ruby!"

She suspected that Gabe was due for some teasing from the gate crew, from Larry's smirk.

Good.

The other pickup rider nodded to her as she rode into the arena, not someone she knew. "I'll get the flank cinch, Ruby. Second ride?"

"Yes."

Too damned easy.

Larry rode over to the chutes, yelling up at the announcer. Yeah, sponsors had privileges, especially sponsors who dropped the amount of money the Martiniere Group had on the rodeo, but all the same…something was up.

She kept an eye on that second chute. No sign of Gabe yet.

Oh. Wait. There he was, on the fence, focused on his mount as the first horse and rider combination exploded out of the chute. That rider went flying before the buzzer sounded.

"And now here's Gabe Ram—excuse me, *Gabriel Martiniere,* who's in a world of trouble with his wife right now, on Skydancer's Repeat, out of chute number two. And Ruby is ready to ride pickup."

Gabe looked up and smirked at Ruby as the crowd hooted and hollered. She scowled and pointed an index finger at him. He laughed and yelled at the announcer.

"Hey Ruby, Gabe says you'd darn well better not drop him."

The crowd laughed even louder, and once again Ruby had the feeling that this was a setup.

But no time for that now. The gate swung open and the big horse launched himself into the air. Gabe grabbed his hat—his old black Stetson from years of rodeoing—and fanned Repeat with it while he braced against the horse's thick cotton halter rope, skillfully working his legs and balance to stay in place. Even as Ruby angled to be in place once the buzzer sounded, she had to admit it was a showy ride.

A winning ride? Too early to tell. And would Repeat take off running hard at the buzzer, like Skydancer used to?

The buzzer sounded and Gabe jammed his hat back on his head. Pard, like the experienced former pickup horse he was, sped up alongside Repeat, who fortunately didn't bolt. Ruby braced herself and reached out to Gabe with her right arm.

"I've got you, damn it, you son-of-a-bitch," she yelled.

Gabe laughed. Instead of letting her ease him off of Repeat and onto the ground, he reached further around her waist and pulled himself onto Pard, behind her.

"Gotcha, Ruby," he chuckled into her ear. "And I won the bet with Brandon and Donald. They didn't think you'd be mad enough to ride pickup. Charlie and I did."

"This is a fucking setup?" Oh, she was *pissed* now.

"Exhibition ride, Rubes. Old Repeat is showy but not a hard bucker. Not like his grandsire. Contractor uses him for show rides, not real competition. No score for me."

"But the risk—especially when you won't get on the green broke horses at home—"

Another laugh. "Mikey wanted to see me ride, Rubes, especially since we won't let him try mutton busting. I talked to folks about Repeat to see how crazy he was. Calculated risk, and eight seconds on an experienced old bronc used for exhibitions is different from an unpredictable greenie. Pulled a few strings as a sponsor. Borrowed a saddle from Charlie so you wouldn't see mine gone."

That softened her slightly. Since Mikey had asked—well, that was the sort of request Gabe would do his best to indulge. Mikey rarely asked for much.

"Ladies and gentlemen, that was Gabriel Martiniere on an exhibition ride with Skydancer's Repeat, picked up by his wife Ruby. Let's give them both a hand," the announcer intoned.

"Gimme a kiss."

"I should deck you instead for being a testosterone-fueled idiot."

"But you won't. Gimme a kiss to finish off the show, warrior woman."

Ruby sighed and turned in the saddle as they approached the gate. Gabe's eyes smoldered at her, along with that devil-may-care smirk that had always seduced her. He pulled off his hat and kissed her hard enough that she had to grab for her own so he wouldn't knock it off. The crowd applauded.

Then she rode through the gate.

Brandon held Mikey a short distance away from the gate.

"Gabe! That was great!" Mikey bounced as Brandon laughed.

The huge happy grin on Mikey's face cinched Ruby's reluctant approval.

"As long as you don't do something damn fool like this again," she muttered to Gabe.

"Oh, I'm already paying for the recklessness," Gabe said as he slid off of Pard. "Hurting. But one last go-round—totally worth it." He laughed again.

Another conspiracy at the rodeo. Well, at least this one ended pleasantly.

Who knew how the other one would unfold?

⎯⎯⎯⎯⎯⎯

THE REST OF THE RODEO WAS UNEVENTFUL. RUBY AND LEGACY placed second in barrel racing—at least Legacy didn't emulate her great-granddam and break into bucking.

The Swait kids did well in the junior rodeo, Rae ending up in second place overall, first place in her age division.

And the resolution of the other conspiracy came clear Sunday night back at the Double R, after nearly everyone had gone home. Justine herded Ruby and Gabe, Donald, Brandon, and Eliot into Ruby's office.

"The young women have been retrieved and are safely reunited with their families." She nodded at Donald.

"Courtesy of the Rescue Angel," he said. "The girls were coerced into faked indenture contracts that bullied their parents into letting them—Heaven's Reach—take the girls. All underage."

Ruby swallowed hard. "And the kidnappers' goal?"

"Prostitution," Donald said, his voice the sharpest Ruby had ever heard it. "Until they were beat down sufficiently to cooperate with the Heaven's Reach body modification and experimentation programs."

"What about Colfax and Heaven's Reach?" Gabe asked.

"Dear, dear Brent," Justine said sardonically. "He seems to have been driving too fast on a forest road. Car went off a sharp point on a high ridge, driving way too fast, spun out on gravel, ended up two thousand feet downhill. Identity confirmed."

"That's—anticlimactic," Gabe said.

Justine bared her teeth at him. "Nothing says the fall caused his death, Gabie."

Gabe raised his brows at that.

Donald flicked a file over to Gabe and Ruby. "Rescue Angel, using JSM Corp resources, identified and closed down two illicit Midwestern laboratories that were primary Heaven's Reach facilities. Those present chose to shoot it out rather than surrender."

"Nothing in the news," Brandon said, rubbing his chin thoughtfully.

"That's been taken care of," Justine said.

"One lab had conclusive records showing that it was the location where Mikey was created," Donald continued, waving a hand at the file. "That lab—unfortunately—caught fire. Nothing remains."

Gabe whistled, and reached for the file. "You two don't mess around, do you?"

Justine interlaced her fingers, gazing steadily at Gabe. "I meant it when I said that it would be either you or me succeeding Daddy-fucking-dearest, Gabriel. Donald and I have been doing this for quite a while."

Ruby studied her sister-in-law.

No, she didn't want to cross Justine, especially when Justine was working in combination with Donald. Ever.

Though if it came to Gabe versus Justine—Ruby would bet on Gabe winning. But perhaps she was biased.

GABE

"Do you need me to go to Dr. Sheri with you?" Ruby asked, as they finished cleaning up after breakfast. Mikey was in the barn, riding his Welsh-Shetland pony mare Rose by himself in the arena.

They still avoided talking much about doctors around Mikey. He was much less reactive about the subject than he had been two years ago, but Mikey was still suspicious of Dr. Sheri, reluctantly allowing her to do quarterly checkups to monitor the medications that kept him healthy.

"Nah, I'm good." Gabe feigned lightness.

He didn't blame Mikey for being nervous about doctors. He felt the same way.

Ruby scowled at him. "I know that tone, Gabe. Is this more than a typical checkup?"

He couldn't fool his beloved. Even after twenty-one years apart.

Gabe ran his fingers through his hair, sighing. "I don't know if it's an issue or not. Turning sixty in March. Maybe it's just aging, or the anti-aging serum wearing off earlier than expected. I'm running tired."

No need to tell Ruby about the rest of it yet. The shortness of breath. The occasional chest pains—angina.

"It could just be normal aging."

But he didn't think so. He remembered those symptoms happening before his heart attack eleven years ago.

"Possibly," she conceded.

But there was still that suspicious look in her eye—another factor was the slowing down of his libido, and *both* of them were aware of that. Ruby had seen the full range. Gabe was impotent due to post-G9 viral syndrome when they got together again. Then, after getting the anti-aging serum from Donna-gran, he was as randy as he had been when they were young. Over the past few months, though, his arousal was much less frequent.

"I'll tell you everything when I get back," he promised.

"You'd better," she growled as she slipped her synthetic emerald wedding ring back on. "Or else I'll rub my ring at you."

Gabe laughed, a faint hysteric note slipping in despite his control. Revealing his nerves. Ruby's ring was the master of the Martiniere command rings given to Martiniere wives, tied to the mind control programming. While the two of them had worked out their own compromises when it came to her use of the ring on him, Gabe knew damned good and well Ruby would turn to it if she suspected that he hid important information from her.

His warrior wife kept him honest for the most part, these days.

"Trust me, dear. I know better than to hide things from you anymore." He kissed her before heading out, pausing on the porch to pull on his going-to-town jacket and Stetson.

His bodyguards waited at the truck for him. They let Gabe drive unless he said otherwise. But they were always present, whenever he set foot off of the Double R.

Part of his life as the Martiniere. Would he ever be free of them?

Probably not, even after he handed off the title of Martiniere to Brandon.

Dr. Sheri put Gabe through the full range of tests, including a truly hellish stress test that left Gabe exhausted. This yearly checkup was a mandatory part of his role as the Martiniere. The Martiniere Group paid for Dr. Sheri's whole morning, so Gabe complied, even though he grumbled about it to himself.

But it was necessary. He had endured enough health issues over the years to take checkups seriously, especially for Ruby and Mikey's sake.

Didn't mean he liked what it meant about his life and mortality.

Heart attack, bypass surgery, *two* attacks of severe G9 virus. That didn't begin to take into account his time as a saddle bronc rider, that short stint as a wildland firefighter, injuries from Philip's beatings, working as a mercenary with Rafe Alvarez— and then Philip's cancer and cardiac problems that he was at risk of inheriting.

At last, the testing was done. Gabe sat in Dr. Sheri's office while she frowned at the results.

"All good?" he asked finally.

Dr. Sheri looked up, still scowling. "I'm referring you to your specialist. Waiting for her input about your results, Gabe. Sorry."

"That's all right. I'm glad you're talking to Dr. Caruthers." But his gut curdled. Dr. Sheri hadn't referred his results to Dr. Amy last year, or the year before. Just like Dr. Sheri, Dr. Amy was on a Martiniere retainer, so she would respond promptly.

My suspicions are on point, then. The serum is starting to fail, and it might be triggering cardiac issues. Or worse, cancer.

What did that mean? Would he be subject to post-G9 syndrome once again?

Damn. It.

Dr. Sheri's comm chimed, and she clicked it up. "Good to see you, Amy. What's your verdict?

Dr. Amy's projection looked past Dr. Sheri to Gabe. "Good to see you, too, Sheri. Glad you're here, Gabe."

"Should we arrange for a further consultation?" Dr. Sheri asked.

"Yes. Gabe, I want to see you in Los Angeles, for more testing," Dr. Amy said. "When can you do it?"

"I'll be on site at the Group headquarters in two weeks. We can do it then, unless you think I should do it sooner," Gabe said.

"No, no, two weeks is fine," Dr. Amy said.

At least it wasn't a *get your butt down here now* situation that would make Ruby's birthday and Mikey's Gotcha Day—what they celebrated instead of his unknown birthday—difficult.

"What's going on? Is the anti-aging serum fading in strength?"

"Unfortunately, yes," Dr. Amy said. "I'd like to check Ruby's vitals as well, since she got the serum at the same time as you. But given your medical history—from the documentation that your grandmother Donna gave us, overcoming that many medical problems can lead to an earlier fade in its effectiveness."

Gabe nodded, keeping his face unexpressive. Donna-gran's final dose had lasted a year in her, instead of the projected five years. And the anti-aging serum could make cardiac problems worse as it wore off—that happened to Donna-gran with past doses.

"Are the problems you're seeing cancer or cardiac?"

God, he hoped it wasn't cancer. Watching cancer eat away at Rachel still haunted Gabe. He hoped he wouldn't subject Ruby to that fucking hell. He knew too damned well what *that* felt like —and she had gone through it with her beloved grandmother.

"Cardiac," Dr. Sheri said.

Just as he feared. But at least it wasn't cancer. "What are we doing about it?"

"I'm putting you on different medication," Dr. Amy said. "Sending you the recommendations, Sheri."

"Is a return to post-G9 syndrome a possibility?" That was the hardest question of all, but he needed to know. Prepare for that contingency.

"I want to say no," Dr. Amy said. "But I also want to explicitly rule it out. Our data on that serum is so limited. Right now, I would say G9 post-viral syndrome reoccurrence is *possibly* not a likelihood. However, before I give you a firm no, I want to do more testing. What day works for you?"

"How about Friday the 21st?" The Friday before he spent that week at the Group. It would mean traveling early, and spending more time in LA—but it had to happen. "Let's schedule Ruby as well."

"All right, then, Gabe. I'll see you and Ruby on the 21st. Plan to be here all day."

That meant the full battery of testing.

Shit.

At least they would be able to celebrate Mikey's Gotcha Day and Ruby's birthday before going to LA.

GABE STOPPED IN LAKESIDE TO HAVE LUNCH AT THE LAKESIDE CAFÉ, by Thunder Lake. None of his friends sat at the big round table informally known as the "liars table," where the older, semi-retired, and retired ranchers of Thunder County hung out to visit and swap tales that *might* have a faint connection with the truth.

Gabe selected a table on the deck overlooking the lake, in spite of the overcast and wind, huddling into his coat as he sat with his guards, but wanting that outdoor exposure. He chose to be virtuous, and ordered a salad instead of the greasy fauxburger he really wanted. The Lakeside's fauxburgers were close to the real thing, only with more salt and fat.

Both things that would have to be cut back in his diet—as he remembered from when Rachel had enforced a change in eating after his heart attack. He wasn't ready to give up drinking yet. Food was manageable.

Back at the ranch, Gabe went in search of Ruby. She wasn't in her office, or upstairs in their bedroom. Gabe didn't want to message her. Not for this.

He went to the lab, as the next best place, especially since Mikey wasn't in the house either.

As he suspected, Ruby and Martin supervised Mikey's home school science lab, all three of them working in a clean room. He waited until she looked up, and waved. Ruby said something to Martin and Mikey, then came out, pausing in the vestibule to strip out of her biosuit.

She took one look at him and her face tightened. "Bad news."

He nodded solemnly. "We have appointments with Dr. Amy on the 21st."

"Aw, *fuck*. How bad is it, Gabe?"

"New medication. Cardiac, not cancer, thank God."

"One small favor, though that's bad enough, damn it." She closed her eyes tightly, shivering. Then she opened them again. "And the anti-aging serum?"

"Dr. Amy thinks it's fading in me. She wants to check you." He paused. "And while she *thinks* I won't experience a return of post-G9—she wants to test further before she says for certain."

"Aw, *fuck*," Ruby repeated.

She launched herself at Gabe and wrapped her arms tightly around him. He held her close, burying his head in the intersection between her neck and shoulder, inhaling deep of that mint and lavender scent that always meant Ruby to him. She trembled against him and he thought she was crying.

His warrior wife? In tears? That meant she really *was* worried.

"Hey. Hey." He raised his head. Yes. Ruby *was* crying; small, choked, sobs. "It's gonna be all right. We've got the Martiniere money now. It's not like we're broke and struggling like your grandparents were when they were sick. We can afford the best damn medical care in the world."

She blinked at him and her lower lip quivered as tears streaked down her cheeks. "It's not fucking *fair*, Gabe. We've been working our asses off to fix the Group and get it turned around. We've only had two years back together, and no time to play, not really." Her face twisted. "I *can't* lose you now. It's not fair!"

"That's going to change. I mean it, Rubes. I said when I took on the position as the Martiniere that I wouldn't serve for the rest of my life. This—" he paused before saying his next words. So much left to do. But Mikey turned seven tomorrow, and Ruby was *right*. Two years together again was far too short. "This is the trigger that means I step down, hand the title over to Brandon."

Ruby sniffled. "Are you sure, Gabe?"

"I could spend the rest of my life doing nothing but fighting the evil done by my fucking sperm donor, and it still wouldn't eliminate everything he did." Gabe exhaled. "Bran's ready, especially if I'm around to advise him. He'll be twenty-eight in December. Dad—*Saul*—was younger than Bran when *he* became the Martiniere."

He still had a hard time *not* thinking of the man who had raised him for his first twelve years as his father.

"You'd actually walk away from being the Martiniere? Leave all that power? After everything you did to gain it?" Ruby's voice quavered.

"Yes." Firm. No hesitation. "I had that heart attack and bypass eleven years ago, when I was forty-eight. The doctors told me then that it was due in part to stress and overwork. Didn't know about the genetics from Philip then. I'm sure that stress and overwork is the case now. But I've also had more things happen to me, including taking on a lot more responsibility." He kissed her brow. "You and Mikey are more important to me. Stepping down from the Group and the Family leadership doesn't mean I'll stop working—it just means a lot less work, and more time for the two of you." Another kiss. "And you won't have to work so hard covering for me in our mutual projects."

"How much of a fight is it going to be, however? You've said that leaving the position before death is uncommon."

"The biggest challenge will be selecting the Martiniere-in-waiting. Bran's youth may make that process easier. He's been networking with the other Martiniere heirs his age over the past two years, building his ties. Our son is good at that, Rubes."

She gulped, a faint smile now twitching her lips. "Yes. He is. How soon are you telling people?"

"I'm going to call Bran and Justine now." Family first. "Then Eliot. The Board at the regular meeting in LA." That would take care of the Group leadership. "Do you want to tell Donna-gran as part of the conversation about what your role will be as the Matriarch in the leadership transition, or should I tell her first?"

"I'll talk to her." Ruby's voice steadied in contemplation of the task. "Today or tomorrow?"

"Let me talk to Bran and Tine first, all right?" It was entirely possible his sister might want to be the one to carry the news to their grandmother.

"In case Justine wants to tell Donna?"

He nodded. "And what should we tell Mikey?"

Ruby pressed her lips together, frowning. "Let's play that one by ear. He reads my moods pretty well. I'd like to hold off saying anything to him until the day before we see Dr. Amy, just so he isn't fretting. But if he starts sensing there's something wrong—"

"Yeah." Gabe hugged her again. "So I'd better start making my calls."

She clung to him for a few moments more, then pulled back. "Love you."

"Love you," he said back, then kissed her.

Gabe called Brandon first. He was in the basement office at Moondance.

"Hey Dad." Bran glanced to the side. Checking his calendar? His next words confirmed it. "So what did Dr. Sheri have to say?"

"It's time to hand things over, Bran."

"Bad, then."

"Cardiac problems."

Brandon winced. "How bad is it?"

"Early indicators. Your mother and I have an appointment with Dr. Amy on the 21st. Looks like the anti-aging serum is fading." Gabe took a deep breath. "We won't know if the post-G9 is coming back until then. But—"

"You have Mom and Mikey to consider. And it was stress and overwork that caused the heart attack before." Brandon exhaled. "What timeframe are we looking at for transferring the leadership?"

"We have to find a new Martiniere-in-waiting. You'll have a better idea of who you want as your replacement than I will. That's going to be the major determinant."

Brandon nodded. "I'll start making a list. What then?"

"Let's interview candidates between now and Family Christmas. I still need to talk to Justine and Eliot; we'll need their input as well. Your mother needs to talk about the oath ceremony with Donna-gran, so—" Gabe raised his hands. "It's not happening tomorrow."

"Wouldn't expect that unless you died." Brandon forced a chuckle, grimacing. "So—perhaps March?"

"Sounds most likely. We need the Board to sign off on your choice, and then all the transfer details—"

He was already tired thinking about the work that this transition of power involved.

But he was doing it. If he didn't have Ruby and Mikey to consider, things might be different. Then it wouldn't matter if he worked himself to death for the Family's sake.

Next came Justine.

"Bad news from the doctor, Gabie?"

He sighed. Was he in serious enough condition that *everyone* anticipated this call? Or had Ruby talked to her? He didn't think Ruby would, but—

"I know you were seeing Dr. Sheri today," Justine added. "The timing—"

Of course. Both Brandon and Justine would have that appointment on their calendars. Part of their jobs. He supposed it would be the same with Eliot McNaughton.

"Yes. Cardiac issues, and I see Dr. Amy on the Friday before my regular week in LA. Ruby and me both." Another sigh. "It looks like the anti-aging serum is fading."

"Damn it to hell." Justine scowled. "Fuck. I'm sorry, Gabie. Does this mean you're going to hand the title over to Brandon?"

"Yes. I don't see any options. I'm not going to work myself to death for the sake of the Family and the Group. I can advise Brandon, but I can't take point anymore. I need to think about Ruby and Mikey—"

"Gabie, I *understand*." Her frown deepened. "I completely agree with your decision. Brandon has proven his capabilities. You and Ruby are raising our father's clone. He needs a *good* father figure. Since your health is suffering, you have to prioritize. Not be like Daddy-fucking-dearest and consider yourself indispensable." She sighed. "It's not as if you haven't been vocal about stepping down once you got the Group and the Family on an even keel. This isn't unexpected. Just—" her voice caught, then steadied. "Sooner than I'd like to see it. There's still work left to do."

"It's not happening *tomorrow*, Tine. Bran and I figure March at the earliest. That'll give me time to close out some projects, and resigning gives me the opportunity to focus on particular problems without trying to juggle everything. Plus interviewing potential contenders for the Martiniere-in-waiting. Bran's making a list of prospects."

"That sounds good. Though I'd hoped for five years." She shook her head. "But that's neither here nor there."

"Ruby was going to contact Donna-gran, tell her, plus get coaching about the Matriarch's role in the transfer of power. Or do you want to tell Donna-gran?"

"It's fine for Ruby to tell Donna-gran." Justine smiled weakly. "Ruby *is* the Matriarch, after all. But thanks for thinking of that, Gabie." Another pause. "I'll see if Donald can get away for the weekend, since all three of you will be here. We'll do something fun, for once."

"Feel free to include Eliot and Nick, too." After all, they were *almost* Family.

A bigger smile. "Thanks. You're calling Eliot next?"

"Yes."

"I'll get in touch with Brandon, talk about prospective Martinieres-in-waiting with him. I have a pretty good idea who would be good, especially with some seasoning after heading up Internal Affairs. Just like doing that did for Brandon."

"I think he'd appreciate it."

Justine took a deep breath. "Another thing? Take *care* of yourself, big brother." That choke in her voice, a show of emotion that was so rare in his sister. "I—I don't want to lose you. Too many years apart thanks to Daddy-fucking-dearest. And—you're not the only one who needs to make time for close family. Promise me that you'll take care of yourself. Not just for Ruby and Mikey, but for me. Please?"

"I will," he said, touched by the emotion.

Something he hadn't expected from his sister.

GABE WAS ABSOLUTELY, FUCKING EXHAUSTED BY THE END OF THE testing. Ruby's was less thorough and resulted in a verdict of no accelerated fading of the anti-aging serum, no cardiac problems. She went to Justine's house to be with Mikey.

But it was worth the draining fatigue to see the subtle signs of relief on Amy Caruthers's face when the results came back.

"We can rule out reoccurrence of post-G9 viral syndrome, Gabe," she said. "No traces of G9 left in your system at all. I threw everything at you while stress testing, which should have brought it out. No remnants in your muscles, none in your nervous system, and your antibodies are high enough that you don't need a booster vaccination this year. I'd recommend one next year."

"Well, that's some good news, at least." He steeled himself. "And the cardiac issues? Did the serum accelerate them?"

"Unfortunately, yes."

Then he was doing the right thing. Gabe exhaled. "Please send me this assessment in writing. I need to submit it to the Board."

"Doing that right now, Gabe."

They discussed management of his cardiac issues next. Eventually he'd need another bypass operation, but for now—things were not that advanced. Fortunately.

But it meant quarterly doctor visits. More medication. Those chest pains were definitely angina attacks, so he needed to pay attention to them.

"You're already pretty active on the ranch, and your diet is, frankly, damned good, as I remember from home visits," Dr. Amy said in conclusion. "Not a lot of changes there, Gabe. Meds and monitoring. Reduce your stress load. We'll see how long we can keep surgery at bay, all right?"

And keep you alive went unsaid. But Gabe was thinking that.

HE FELL ASLEEP ON THE WAY TO JUSTINE'S HOUSE.

Ruby met him outside. He took her into his arms, burying his nose once more in that beloved juncture of neck and shoulder.

"No post-G9 likelihood," he said finally. "The cardiac issues are accelerated by the serum, which is fading."

"Oh, Gabe."

"Meds and monitoring right now," he sighed, kissing her.

Gabe ended up falling asleep again on the deck after dinner, rousing only slightly when Mikey climbed into his lap, curling up to sleep. Ruby shook them both awake at bedtime.

He was just *so damned tired.* Had it always been this way, or was he finally admitting to the fatigue?

TO GABE'S SURPRISE AND PLEASURE, JUSTINE RENTED A YACHT FOR A Saturday trip to Anacapa Island to swim, snorkel, and lounge. More pleasant memories from childhood—taking a day off like this was another thing that Angelica and Saul had loved to do.

Fatigue still pulled at Gabe, and he tired easily. But he managed to show off a little bit for Ruby and Mikey. He took a few tentative dives to reassure himself that he could still do it. Then he launched himself into the ocean from higher spots on the yacht.

Gabe's last dive was the highest yet. A thrill raced through him as he smoothly slid into the water, easily angling up to the surface and breast stroking back to the yacht.

Time to quit, before he got too tired.

But he still was able to dive.

No more cliff diving, though, like he had done as a young man. The top deck of the yacht was high enough.

"Wow," Ruby said as Gabe ambled onto the shaded outdoor deck to find a towel. "I didn't realize you could dive like that."

"Not something I'd do in Thunder." Gabe toweled his hair—he wore a t-shirt to cover the scars on his back and chest from Philip's beatings. Ruby was still the only one besides his doctors who got to see them. "But Tine and I grew up doing this regularly. Mom and—Saul—would take us out for the day like this, several times a month. Me, Louisa, Tine, Serg. Saul taught us. I used to dive off of cliffs as well, when I was young and wild."

"Do you think I'll be able to do that?" Mikey asked. "It looks like fun."

"Not right away, and probably not the cliff diving. Listen to Tine. And Nick. I did a lot of low dives before I started doing the high stuff."

Gabe kissed Ruby, then stretched out in the sun to let his t-shirt dry. Donald joined him.

Ruby stayed out of the water and out of the sun for the most part—she had never been a swimmer, and was tart about *spending enough time in the sun at the ranch as it is.*

Gabe and Donald finally tired of the sun and lounged with her in the open but covered deck area. Soon enough, Justine and Mikey joined them. Mikey eventually went below for an extended nap in one of the bedrooms. Justine curled up with Donald, and Ruby with Gabe on the shaded outer deck. Eliot and Nick retreated elsewhere.

"You know," Ruby murmured at one point. "This is the most stereotypic rich person thing I've ever done."

"I'm slacking," Gabe said. "We should be doing more of this. We have this damned fortune; let's use it to make our lives more pleasant once in a while." He kissed her hair. "I promise you, my love. More goofing off and less work in our future."

"I'll hold you to that," she said, giving him *that look* that was purely his warrior wife.

Gabe didn't answer but nuzzled her again, suddenly all too aware of *time running out.*

GABE TOOK A DEEP BREATH BEFORE BEGINNING THE MONDAY morning Board meeting. He felt almost as tense as he had been before testifying against Philip's abuses all those years ago. Insomnia had ravaged his Sunday night. His fatigue was worse than ever—he'd gotten maybe two, three hours of sleep.

"You'll notice that I just opened access to the first agenda item," he said, after the opening routine.

"What the hell, Gabe?" David was the first to react. "You're resigning as the Martiniere—*now?*"

"How are we going to keep the Family factions from tearing the Group apart?" Charles glowered across the table at Christopher. "We're pretty damned weak, and *some of us* still want to take the Group public."

"I think going public is the best idea," Christopher countered. "Especially with Gabriel stepping down."

"Wait a minute. Did you even read the full statement?" Justine asked. "This isn't a casual impulse. Gabriel has health issues."

But the arguments swirled past her objections, the Family leaders bickering.

"STOP IT!" Gabe slammed both fists down hard on the table, but that didn't seem to make an impression. He started to rise— and pain clobbered his chest, radiating to the fingertips of his left arm. He fell back in his chair, panting, grabbing at his left shoulder. Oh God. Was it already too late?

"QUIT!" Brandon bellowed from his seat at Gabe's right. "Eliot, get the medics in here, NOW. Justine, call Mom down from her office." He bent over Gabe. "Dad. Meds."

"Left. Jacket. Pocket," Gabe gasped, barely aware of the sudden silence around him. The pain dominated everything else.

The little pill that Brandon slipped under his tongue didn't ease the agony one bit.

"Hang on, Dad. Hang on," Brandon said over and over, his voice steady. A focus.

Then his son stepped back as medics swarmed around Gabe, easing him onto a stretcher. Blood pressure cuff. Hand-held scanner. Shot that *finally* dulled the pain.

Ruby's hand in his.

Breathing coming easier. But God, he was tired.

"How bad?" he whispered, after another shot.

"Angina," Ruby murmured in his ear, a faint fearful note in her voice, so unusual for his warrior wife. "A very bad attack. They're giving you blood thinners just in case, but the scanner doesn't detect any blockage or clot. Running blood tests now."

He nodded, and tightened his grip on her hand.

The stretcher started moving.

"Hospital?" he asked.

"No. Your office." That worried tone still echoed through Ruby's words. "No further issues. You just need to rest."

He focused on her hand in his as they left the conference room. Once they were in his office, the medics helped him lie down on his couch. He heard Ruby talking to Dr. Amy via comm, over by his desk, but was too wiped out to pay attention.

Ruby returned. "Dr. Amy confirms scanner diagnosis from the tests the medics sent her. Angina, probably caused by stress, coupled with what appears to be an anxiety attack. The medics are leaving the monitors on just in case. It's on a direct feed to her office. She's adding an anti-anxiety medication to your daily regime that you are to take right away. While she doesn't recommend you go back to work today, she says to tell you that if you *do* decide to do so, you are to *take a nap first.*"

That pissed tone in Ruby's voice was actually a relief—back to her usual self. He must be improving if she sounded angry instead of scared.

"We're to give that med to him in a shot," one of the medics said. "Fast-acting."

"Good," Ruby said.

"Will you stay with me?" he asked as the medic injected him.

"Of course, Gabe." Her voice softened. "Sleep now, all right?" She moved away.

"Let me do that," one of the medics said as Gabe heard the faint sound of dragging—sounded like one of the heavy but comfortable office chairs.

"Thank you," Ruby said. Then she picked up his hand. "Sleep, Gabe. I'm here."

He obeyed—not that he could do anything else.

GABE STIRRED. "HOW LONG HAVE I BEEN ASLEEP?" HE ASKED.

"About an hour." Ruby stroked his cheek. He nuzzled into her palm, smiling up at her worried face. "Shall we go back to Justine's?"

He sighed. "No. I'd better find out what's happened with the Board while I've been down. Or did Brandon adjourn the meeting?"

"They reconvened with him as the chair and it's still going. Are you sure about this, Gabe?"

"It's either that or hand things completely over to Bran right now—and I'm not ready to do that. I don't have to *do* anything, but I'd better make an appearance."

He exhaled. The tension that had been winding him up since Sunday afternoon was still there but distanced, not clutching at him like it had been. The effect of the anti-anxiety med? Possibly. Damn it, though, he hated the notion of anti-anxiety medication —too close to the psychotropics that Philip had used on him. If it could get him through this week without further attacks, however—

Gabe sat up slowly. He didn't need Ruby's help to stand, though she went with him to the bathroom, leaning against the counter with her head in her hands as he used the toilet, washed his hands, then straightened his clothing and hair. At least he didn't need to resort to his backup shirt or suit. Then he kissed Ruby.

"Time to return to the fray," he said.

Ruby scowled. "I'm coming with you. Wait—" she said as he started to speak. "I'm the Matriarch. And your wife. If the Board doesn't like it, they can take a flying leap."

Gabe chuckled at that. *Definitely* his warrior wife, ready to do battle. He took her arm and they went down to the conference room.

Brandon raised a hand to stop discussion as they entered. "Are you here for the rest of the meeting?"

"Just to observe," Gabe said. "Keep on going, Martiniere-in-waiting."

Brandon nodded sharply. Eliot pulled another chair over next to Gabe's for Ruby. The Board members silently rose, then clapped as Gabe and Ruby sat down.

Ruby held his hand throughout the rest of the meeting. Gabe added a comment or two, but otherwise deferred to his son.

They returned to his office as the meeting wound down. Gabe did not want to get sucked into long discussions and justifications afterward. He was *tired*, damn it. And Ruby needed comforting after this scare.

He did, too. They sat on the couch, holding each other.

A knock on the door. "It's me." Justine opened the door a crack.

"Come in," Gabe said.

Justine dropped in the chair by the sofa.

"Well, that was *one* way to prove your point about needing to step down," she said wryly. "Daddy-damned-dearest never did get carried out of a Board meeting on a stretcher, though there were a few times when he should have been."

Gabe rolled his eyes. "Sounds like Philip, all right."

"I suppose you could call him a product of that era of corporate leadership," Justine sighed. "And Brandon rose to the occasion. If there were any questions from the Board about his ability to be the Martiniere—most of them got answered today."

"Good," Gabe said.

"One thing they did decide before you returned—you *will* have a Family title after Brandon becomes the Martiniere."

"Good grief. Can't the Family let go of me?"

"You're kidding, right, Gabie? It's nothing big." Justine's lips quirked in a half-smile. "The Martiniere Emeritus. Some privileges, a little bit of power, mostly within the Family, not the Group. Advisory within the Group."

He could live with that. "So who pushed that notion?"

Justine managed to look a little abashed. "Um. Me. I can foresee times when it would be good for you to have a voice with some weight behind it. Brandon is perfectly happy to let you preside over Family ceremonial events." She paused. "The Family is very aware of all you have done to improve our circumstances after the mess that Daddy-fucking-dearest made of things. Some events—like the Gala, and Christmas dinner—won't be the same without you heading them."

"Mostly social, then."

"Pretty much. Your vision is important, even after you step down, Gabie. You're a unifier, not a divider. We still need you in that role."

Damn Family. But Gabe was well aware that the Family would not let him go again—not until he died, and if the Family could find a means to cling to him after his death—then they would.

All part of being a Martiniere, damn it.

December, 2061

. . .

Brandon's choice of the Martiniere-in-waiting happened faster than Gabe thought it would. He picked one of the British Martinieres, Seth, a cousin of Christopher, the current head of the British families. Seth was Bran's age, and had been too young to be sucked into Chris's abortive attempt to overthrow Philip. His experience was in finance, not research or programming.

"A good thing, really," Justine told Gabe. "Neither Seth nor his father Robert have been tied into any factions. That continues on the unification pathway you and Brandon have established. Plus Seth's financial background is a good backup for Brandon—one lack Bran has is in the financial management side." She scowled. "What I don't like is that Seth enjoys high risk sports more than he should. At least for my liking. But perhaps I'm just getting old."

"Eh, well, let's hope Bran holds the title for a good long time," Gabe said. He eyed his sister. "Have you given any thought to *your* replacement yet?"

Justine snorted. "Gabie, I'm seven years younger than you, and the worst thing that ever happened to me was that damn hysterectomy when I was twenty. I don't have Daddy-fucking-dearest's cardiac issues, and cancer?" She shrugged. "If that happens, well—I don't have anyone affected by it."

"Wrong. You have me and Brandon. Ruby. Mikey. Donald. Eliot. Nick. I'm not the only one who needs to think about what happens next," Gabe said. "Just saying. You don't have children, and neither does Serg. There aren't any young Vygotskys. Someone reliable needs to be groomed to take over security."

Justine nodded curtly. "Taking it under advisement. Don't worry, Gabie. I've been talking to Kevin Swait. That—may provide an option that keeps things independent. Which the Director of Security really needs to be."

Gabe raised his brows at that, but it made sense. The Swaits had been heavily involved in the work of freeing indentured workers, and they'd been working with Justine even before the AgSuperhero and the formal connection with him and Ruby.

The Group could do worse than bringing a few of the Swaits into leadership positions. And—perhaps—Jeff Swait's youngest daughter, JoAnn, seemed to be striking up a friendship with Mikey. Both kids were fascinated by tech and video games.

A possible match which would make the Swaits part of the Family, not outsiders?

Too early to tell—and who knew what would become of either of those kids at this point? Mikey was just seven and JoAnn six. A lot of years were ahead of them.

MARCH, 2062

THE ASCENSION CEREMONY FOR BRANDON HAPPENED AT Moondance. Donna-gran was too sick to attend, but to Gabe's eye, Ruby did admirably well administering the oath of office to both Bran and Seth. As the Matriarch and the Martiniere Emeritus, they were the first to swear loyalty to both men.

Still, Gabe was glad enough when it was over, and he, Ruby, and Mikey could go back to the Double R.

Gabe went to bed early.

He startled awake at full daylight. No warmth on Ruby's side of the bed, so she had risen quite a while ago without waking him—usually she got him up if he slept through the alarm.

What the hell?

Gabe called up the time.

Eight o'clock. Damn, he was going to be late starting the day's meetings—

Wait a minute.

Gabe blinked. His son had become the Martiniere yesterday.

He didn't have those morning meetings.

Ruby hadn't begun the handoff of responsibilities from Barkley-Martiniere and Barkley-Martiniere-Swait.

But Mikey should be headed for the barn by now for his morning ride, before he started his home school classes.

Damn it, why had Ruby let him sleep in? He still had things to do.

Gabe tossed on clothing and hurried downstairs. Ruby was washing dishes, and his heart sank. He needed to scrounge his own meal. Worse, he had missed breakfast with Ruby and Mikey, one of the high points of his day. Damn it. Why hadn't Ruby gotten him up? Yeah, he had been tired after everything yesterday, *but—*

"Sleep well?" Ruby turned from the sink and grinned at him.

"I missed breakfast with you and Mikey," Gabe grumbled. "Slacking. And we've gotta shift responsibilities, now that I'm no longer the Martiniere—"

"C'mere, you." Ruby opened her arms. They hugged, and then she pulled back, looking up at him. "Listen. You were wiped out after yesterday. I could tell." She gave him a little shake. "It's your first day of official retirement. You don't have to burn up the world doing something new, *Gabriel Martiniere*. For today—" she poked him in the nose. "You need to go to the Lakeside for breakfast. Spend some time drinking fake decaf with the liars. Learn to slow down a little bit."

"You want me to become a *loafer*?" He couldn't quite keep the outrage out of his voice.

"Two or three mornings at the Lakeside won't make you a loafer. It's good for our image for you to start showing up there, give some input into community opinion—and you know as damned well as I do that the Lakeside table is where a lot of informal decisions are made. We've been talking about getting more grassroots influence within the community, making things better for the future. This is one way to do it. You have the time to be there now."

"True," he admitted.

"And maybe—just maybe—I'll have a husband who'll live for a few years longer if he learns to relax. Got it?"

Gabe laughed and hugged her. He definitely heard the worry in her voice.

He stopped in the arena to watch Mikey ride Rose before leaving. Ruby had been working with Mikey on reining maneuvers.

"Want to watch me ride a pattern?" Mikey asked.

Gabe cocked his hat as he leaned on the gate. "Sure."

Mikey and Rose managed a credible reining pattern and Gabe applauded. Ruby came up beside him.

"Hey, I thought you were going to town," she said.

"I am. I just stopped in to see Mikey."

"All right." She kissed him. "Now, *go*. Your bodyguards have been waiting. They're a little worried."

Gabe laughed again. "Eager to get rid of me?"

"No more lollygagging. You need to eat and take your meds."

"All right, all right." He headed for the truck, checking his pocket to ensure he remembered his pill dispenser.

When he got to the Lakeside, his friends Monty and Larry were among the ranchers sitting around the liars' table.

"Well, there, Gabe," Monty said. "How does it feel to not be the big boss of the Martinieres anymore?"

Gabe took a deep breath as he sat down and checked the menu the server handed him. He noted it was a healthy senior menu. Heh. Probably the standard for every other person at this table. He ordered the cardiac special—fake egg and cheese omelette, faux bacon, one slice of toast—and faux decaf.

Then he answered Monty.

"You know, I think it might just start to feel pretty damn good."

Oh, he still had things to do. The Electric Born weren't completely eliminated as a threat. Ruby had carried the full weight of managing Barkley-Martiniere and their part of Barkley-Martiniere-Swait for two years, and that needed to be remedied. And he wanted to be more involved in bringing up

Mikey. Plus research, the inevitable problems that would come his way as the Martiniere Emeritus, and whatever local projects he took up.

But for this morning—Gabe sipped his coffee, relaxed in his chair, and joined in the flow of talk.

Time to learn a different role for his life.

How hard could that be?

RUBY

RUBY SCOWLED AT THE CLEAR BLUE SKY AS SHE SAT ON ONE OF THE growboxes placed on the trailer behind the crawler. It needed to be overcast and either splatting her with icy wet snow or a steady rain—she didn't care which form of precipitation happened in March, as long as it was liquid soaking into the ground.

Not enough of either rain or snow this past winter. That meant the potential for a smoky hot summer, crappy hay harvests, and prospective crop failures. Crop failures weren't a problem for the Double R these days, but—she and Gabe might end up bailing out struggling Thunder County locals. Ruby hated to think what the situation might be for the less fortunate if Martiniere money *wasn't* available to help them. She could remember what *those* days looked like in the County. The prospect of tough times ahead still made her uneasy. Remembering the toll it took on families.

And it's always the best of the families that go down.

She shifted her weight. A definite concern, but a deflection from more immediate worries.

Still no sign of Gabe and Mikey—now Mike. What was taking them so long to ride up to the Homestead field? Ruby was reluctant to start the test of the new growbox self-transport mechanism without their help. Just in case *that piece* failed.

They already had complexities with the bots in the boxes. The payload included the new two-year duration RubyBots carrying self-reproducing microbial treatments intended to strengthen drought resistance in grain crops, along with perimeter-patrolling Guardian killbots meant to repel sabotage biobots. She wasn't as worried about the Rubys as she was the Guardian bots. The RubyBots were proven tech. Guardian was a mutual development project with Swait Secure, and it was a cranky, cranky bot, either overreacting or underreacting.

This was also Mike's first time running a scanner to monitor and record biobot release performance. He was excited about learning this technique—so why were he and Gabe running late?

As always, the possibility of crisis came to mind.

Was the delay due to problems with Gabe's health? Mike's? Both were moving slow this morning. But Mike's meds were supposed to be stable, and Gabe—well, who knew for sure about Gabe, thanks to all the variables in his health. Or it could be a call from Brandon, Eliot, or Justine—even though it had been a year since Gabe's retirement from being the Martiniere, things still came up that required his input as the Martiniere Emeritus.

Or it could be something involving the Swaits, or, or, or—

Stop fretting, Ruby.

Gabe had stabilized over the past year. Mike's meds were projected to be stable until he hit puberty, hopefully still a few years off. He was only eight, after all.

The delay was probably business-related, and *that* was always unpredictable.

Focus on the land. Focus on the here and now. Breathe. Inhale. Exhale. Even if it wasn't raining, at least it was a beautiful morning out here on her land.

The steady four-beat rhythm of galloping hooves shifted

Ruby's mood. That meant Gabe and Mike were racing up the final stretch from the Draw field just below Homestead. The two of them engaging in impromptu horse races was fairly common these days, as Mike's riding skill grew. Or crawler races. Arthritis kept both of them from foot races, or she suspected those would be happening as well.

Ruby slid off the growbox and walked to where the road dipped into the draw, hands on her hips, waiting. The horses and riders came into view, the horses almost the same color except for Star's light brown nose and the rusty tinge to his winter coat. The difference between a truly black horse like Pard and a dark bay like Star was more evident in summer, when Star turned dappled light brown under black guard hairs.

Gabe restrained Star from outpacing Pard, while Mike bent low over Pard's neck, doing his best to encourage the old gelding to run harder.

Three and a half years since Mike first sat on a horse, and now they could hardly pry him off a horse's back. Unless he was sick—which was far too often. Still. Or unless he was engaged in a tech or programming challenge.

All the same, the sight of Gabe with Mike made Ruby wistful. Brandon *said* he didn't envy that Mike was growing up with a full-time father. But sometimes she wondered. Would Bran have been more interested in programming and systems design if he had matured around Gabe's daily presence, instead of weekend visitations? Would he have developed the same deep love for horses that Mike had, instead of an amused tolerance? At least Bran shared Gabe and Mike's fondness for dogs; had a couple of Border Collies at Moondance.

Don't chase might-have-beens, Ruby!

Their son was a successful Martiniere, deftly guiding the Martiniere Group while leaving much of the Family leadership to Gabe. Had been a successful videocast producer in his own right, and still made 'casts as part of his management of the

Group. Just because he wasn't like her and Gabe when it came to science and tech research didn't mean his work wasn't valuable.

But all the same—she enjoyed Mike's obsessions that were in common with hers and Gabe's; regretted they didn't share them with Brandon.

Ruby put brooding thoughts aside as the horses approached.

Gabe sat up to ease Star back as Mike and Pard shot ahead, galloping past Ruby.

"Whoa," he said softly to the dark bay stallion.

Star didn't stop as hard as he would in the arena with skid boots on—too hard on his fetlocks and the experienced stallion knew it—but he halted without Gabe needing to touch the reins. Mike had a few more problems with Pard, finally turning him to trot back to Ruby, Gabe, and Star.

"Sorry it took us so long to get here," Gabe said. "Mike and I stopped at the lab to check his scanner, and it kept glitching."

"Better you found out down at the lab than when trying to use it here." Ruby frowned. "Weird. I thought those scanners were solid tech. I've not had problems with them before."

Gabe shook his head as he dismounted. He pulled off the stallion's bridle, untying the lead for the rope halter Star wore underneath the bridle from the saddle horn, then hanging the bridle and reins on the horn. There was a fenced-off grass patch on the other side of the road from the cultivated field so that they could turn horses into it while working at Homestead, if they chose to ride up. All of the ranch horses had been trained to graze while trailing a lead rope—easier for catching.

"It surprised me and Martin as well. We ran a virus scan on all the devices at the labs. Worm-type virus, something new showing up only in certain scanners. Martin's rewriting protocols and talking to Kevin about the Swait labs. Still no idea where the worm came from."

"Sabotage?"

"Very possible. Martin's not issuing a verdict yet." Gabe

shrugged as he held the gate open for Mike and Pard. "You got the scanner, Mike?"

Mike nodded, patting his backpack. "Don't trust the saddlebags."

"Good idea."

Ruby exhaled as Mike dropped Pard's lead rope. "All right. Let's get going before it's too warm for optimal release. Mike, let's see your first display."

Mike eased the backpack to the ground, next to the crawler. He knelt and rummaged inside the pack until he retrieved the scanner, then opened the first screen.

"So what variables are you looking for?" she asked. A test.

"Distribution of the RubyBot and the Guardian." Mike showed her the variance settings. "If they go beyond that, we have problems, right?"

"Correct. Let's put you here—" Ruby guided Mike to the optimal monitoring spot. "Don't get excited about variances until all the bots are in the field. You'll see some wide ranges. They need about five minutes to spread properly."

Mike nodded, biting his lower lip as he concentrated on the display.

Ruby returned to the trailer.

"Shall we see if the tracks work?" Gabe pursed his lips, studying the growboxes.

The Swaits had first devised self-transport growboxes. But they used propane-fueled jets to move theirs—not as much an issue in Arkansas as it was in the arid West. Enough of the RubyBot customers were in dry and borderline areas that finding a different transport method was a priority. Ruby and Gabe focused on solar-charged batteries, to avoid fire danger and reduce complications. However, making reliable growbox self-transport function properly proved to be more difficult than expected.

As always.

They lowered the trailer ramp. Gabe stood on one side, Ruby the other.

Ruby exhaled. "Let's get it done. You want to flip the switch?"

Gabe shrugged. "You came up with the latest fix. Go for it."

"Blame me if it doesn't work," she snorted.

Ruby picked up the remote controller that rested next to the growboxes, scrolled down the list, and pressed the ACTIVATE button for GB ONE. A soft whine came from the growbox as the tracks lowered—but not a grinding or screeching sound that indicated problems. Good.

Ruby carefully watched—did the growbox stay level as the tracks engaged? That had been the latest problem, uneven angles which interfered with the auto-emptying function of the growbox.

Level. Good. Another step accomplished. Ruby pressed FORWARD. From here on, she could use the directional arrows to guide the growbox—if it worked. The damned remote wasn't always functional.

She and Gabe hovered close to the growbox, ready in case the box threatened to tip over as it descended the ramp. Another past problem.

Ruby realized she had been holding her breath when the growbox reached the bottom without tipping. She exhaled, and tapped the button to turn it toward the field. One track caught on a long, tough strand of grass which spun the growbox around in circles until it wobbled, threatening to fall over. Ruby pressed STOP as Gabe kept it steady. She knelt to pull the grass free.

"Another thing to work on," Gabe muttered.

Ruby nodded. She stuck the controller in her back pocket and they carried the growbox to the edge of the field. Then she and Gabe returned to the trailer to unload the remaining three growboxes, using the remote to get them off of the trailer. They carried each one to its proper place for the bot release.

"Whew." Gabe blew and stretched after they handled the last

growbox. "At least we didn't need to unload each box. Just getting them on and off the trailer like this is a big advance, and my back is grateful for *that*." He grinned at Ruby. "We're getting somewhere, Rubes."

"Not fast enough," she sighed.

"It'll come. Have faith."

"We'll see. If anything goes wrong, it sure seems to be in this field."

"Which makes Homestead the perfect trial field," Gabe said.

"Yeah. Mike! You ready to monitor?"

"Yes." Mike's jaw tightened and he stared at his display.

Should I tell him to relax? Nah. Won't make a difference with first-timer jitters, especially with Mike.

Ruby toggled all the growboxes, and hit the RELEASE command. Gabe stood ready as the containments opened, watching to ensure that the doors didn't stick. Swarms of biobots half the size of ladybugs emerged from each box. The majority glowed bright red—the shade the RubyBot had taken from the very beginning and which had been the source for its name. The Guardian bots were teal and brown. The latest version came with a camouflage capability, but Ruby wasn't certain how effective it would be here. Most likely, perfecting that aspect of the Guardian would take localized research and programming.

"All releases good," Gabe called.

He joined Ruby and put an arm around her shoulders. She leaned into him as they watched the bots skim across the field, spreading within the programming parameters to their charted locations. Homestead's difficulty didn't come from the mapping component—all of the Double R fields were mapped in excruciating detail, part of Ruby's work over the twenty-some years she had spent crafting the RubyBot. Homestead was thoroughly mapped in more detail than other fields *because* it was a difficult field. Its challenges came from the winds, microclimates, and temperature extremes that the field was subject to. Not to speak of connectivity issues, which was an ongoing problem with Homestead.

But damn, when everything came together—Homestead was one of the Double R's most productive fields. That was one reason why Ruby struggled to keep it in cultivation rather than turning it into grazing. It was also an excellent proving ground for testing bots—another reason to keep it as something other than pasture. Homestead regularly defied bot cultivation. However, every tweak of the RubyBot to meet Homestead's challenges meant that the bot worked in a greater range of conditions elsewhere.

Ruby pursed her lips, worrying as she noticed that the distribution of teal-colored bots didn't appear to be uniform around the edges of the field.

"Hey Ruby. There's a problem with the Guardians," Mike said.

She and Gabe joined him.

"Input distribution control, and reboot parameter definition," she said. While she itched to take the scanner from Mike, enter those commands herself—it was time he learned how to do this.

Under supervision, of course.

"Got it."

"Hit disperse again." She squinted at the display. Mike *was* inputting commands correctly, but it sure wasn't being reflected in the data. She looked up.

"It's getting worse," Gabe said. "Concentrating on that right corner. You don't suppose we have an issue over there?"

"Scanned the field before you two got here," Ruby said. "Nothing showed up that would interfere with a bot release."

Gabe pulled his scanner out of his pocket and punched in commands. "Damn it, mine's not working."

"They're all going to that right corner!" Mike's voice rose, quavering slightly. "Ruby, they won't obey me!"

"It's just the Guardians, right?" she asked.

"Yeah."

"Rubes, can I borrow your scanner?" Gabe scowled at his. "I should have checked mine as well as Mike's. I'm going to that corner to see if I can spot a reason for those Guardians to act like that."

Ruby looked at Mike's scanner again. The RubyBots were settling in—so it was just a Guardian issue. "Let's all go to that corner. Maybe it's an issue of transmission range."

"That could be." But Gabe didn't sound convinced.

She really wasn't, either.

Mike scampered ahead of them. He halted at the corner and scowled at his scanner.

"It's still not working," he grumbled as Ruby and Gabe joined him.

Ruby handed Gabe her scanner. He entered several commands. No response.

"There's no logical reason for the Guardians to act like this," he said.

Ruby sighed. "All right. I wonder if they'll obey a command to re-enter the growboxes, or if we need to hand-collect samples before hitting auto-destruct?"

"I think we'd better hand-collect and auto-destruct," Gabe said. "I know," he said as Ruby winced. "It's a pain with these Guardians. But I'd just as soon avoid the risk of them disrupting the Rubies. Whatever this is targets the Guardians."

Ruby couldn't argue with that logic. "All right. I'll get the Guardian sample nets and boxes from the crawler."

"I'll help." Mike scrambled to join her.

"Thanks."

This wasn't how she intended to spend the morning. But it was another task that Mike could learn—the precautions for handling rogue Guardian bots when gathering them for sampling purposes.

Hopefully, the bots would obey the kill command and they wouldn't have to spend the whole day clearing the damn bots from the field. Rogue Guardians were *nasty*. They often turned on humans.

But at least Ruby remembered to bring protective gear for all three of them. Maybe that would make the process easier.

She hoped.

A COUPLE OF HOURS LATER, AFTER WRESTLING WITH RECALCITRANT Guardians, Ruby, Gabe, and Mike stood outside of a clean room, watching Beck and Martin, the lab managers, run assessments on the Guardian samples. Ruby's gut tightened as Beck and Martin talked, Beck shaking her head. At last, Beck headed for the vestibule, stripping out of her biosuit before exiting.

"It's two things. Martin's checking further, but it looks like we have a problem with that stem line. I have to trace it further." The stem cell lines powering the biobots were Beck's specialty.

"Originating here or at Swait's?" Ruby tensed. The stem lines for this generation of Guardians had come from Swait Farms.

"It's partially a Swait issue," Beck sighed. "There's also been a problem with programming—and that originates here. So fifty-fifty."

"We'd better call Jeff and let him know about this issue," Gabe said.

"Yeah. Let's schedule a meeting and take them some samples. Beck, what's the programming issue?" Ruby thought through their schedule. Tomorrow would work, if Justine had a jet free to go to Arkansas.

"You'll need to talk to Martin about that one," Beck said. "He thinks it's related to the problem with Mike's scanner. Some sort of worm that doesn't appear consistently."

Gabe frowned. "Could his scanner have been the source of the programming problem with the Guardians?"

Beck shrugged. "More Martin's venue than mine, but I think that might be a what-came-first issue. Or both could have been infected from the same source simultaneously. Want me to send Martin out?"

"No, we'll wait until you two are done," Ruby said. "Gabe, Mike, I think we've learned what we can right now. Let's aim to have a solid preliminary report to send to Jeff by this evening, and meet with him tomorrow. Sound good?"

Gabe and Beck nodded.

"Mike?" she asked. "Does that sound good to you?"

Mike's eyes widened. "You're asking me?"

"You're part of this project, and you'll be composing your own report to Jeff this afternoon," Ruby said. "So yes, you have a say in the meeting plans."

"Does this mean I go with you to Swait Farms?"

Ruby wasn't sure if that was apprehension or excitement in his voice. "Yes."

Mike grinned. "Yeah. Can you help me write the report?" Now trepidation showed up in his voice.

Ruby side-hugged him. "Mikey, just write down everything you did and that you observed. We'll edit it from there."

Mike *was* a decent writer, for an eight-year-old.

Then again, while Mike's progenitor had been a psychopathic ass, no one could deny that Philip Martiniere had been brilliant when it came to research. It wasn't surprising that Mike displayed a comparable degree of precocious intellectual ability.

Now if they could just keep Philip's clone from turning into the psychopath that Philip had been....

***

No matter what time of year, there always seemed to be a drastic climate contrast between the Double R in Northeastern Oregon and Swait Farms in Arkansas. Not that Ruby was paying much attention to the surroundings. Swait Secure used SUVs with blackout windows to whisk them quickly from the jet to the main offices adjoining the Swait labs.

"Sorry about the rush from the airstrip," Jeff apologized when Ruby, Gabe, and Mike entered his office, after they handed over the Guardian samples to Jeff's lab manager Sally, one of his cousins. "Things are getting rough again. Safety issues, especially for people arriving on airplanes. Drones that are evading our measures. They don't show up during takeoff or landing, just when people are exposed out there."

"Again?" Gabe raised his brows. "Need Justine to provide backup?"

"Both she and Temira Cho are coming in this afternoon," Jeff said. "It's possible that your problems are affected by larger issues."

"So, sabotage might explain what happened with the Guardians?" Ruby asked.

Jeff nodded. "Yep. And there's more going on. Gabe, you eliminated the Martiniere Group indentured program. But we're seeing new problematic indentured contracts from other sources, and that's where our issues may lie. Pushback against President Markey's executive orders phasing out indentured workers. That may be tied to the Guardian hack."

"Which makes it personal," Gabe sighed. "Does Brandon know?"

There are times when it is a real pain in the ass to be related to the President of the United States.

Pat Markey, the current President, was Brandon's sister-in-law. The Martiniere Group as well as Gabe and Ruby personally had contributed heavily to her campaign. With Pat up for re-election next year, a lot of political jockeying was taking place.

"Yep," Jeff said. "That's why Justine is meeting with Temira Cho, here, this afternoon. Safest location."

Ruby raised her brows. Justine *had* mentioned she would be at Swait Farms today, but not why or with whom. Temira Cho had been the other competitor for the AgSuperhero award besides Ruby, Gabe, and Jeff. She had been cut, but managed to win funding at the next level down, the AgSuperstar, and was still doing well with the AgInnovator.

The AgInnovator. The ag funding game show that brought her and Gabe back together. Fixing problems with the AgI was another reform Gabe started during his short stint as the Martiniere—doable thanks to Philip's partial investment in AgI. Brandon took it further, buying out Georgy Batineau, AgI's owner. The AgI was now a competitive grant program with no social media voting, harkening back to a vision that Saul Martiniere had tried and failed to create during his years as the Martiniere. Brandon and Kris's past experience with the show enabled them to identify the dead weight and budget padding, and Kris now managed the grant program.

"I'll be glad to see Temira," she said.

"Maybe you will," Jeff said, a gloomy note in his voice. "Things are pretty intense. That's why Justine is getting involved."

At least this shouldn't be Heaven's Reach.

Those people seemed to keep slipping away from a final resolution.

Ruby would scream if this situation was tied to Heaven's Reach. That would be enough for her to agree to Gabe leading an attack on wherever the hell it was that they were based. She'd happily join Gabe in doing that, and damn any consequences. At this point, it was an issue of keeping Brandon's daughter Lily as well as Mike safe in the long run.

Aw, fuck. It is a Heaven's Reach issue.

Gabe's former informant within Heaven's Reach, Doug Gates, arrived with Justine and Temira. Ruby cringed inside when she saw him—no mistaking who he was. At least Doug looked better than he had when she first encountered his case in the Indentured Recovery Project.

Ruby bit her lip as Justine, Temira, and Doug entered Jeff's office. Justine raised her brows, and eased by Ruby.

"It's not Heaven's Reach," she whispered. "Doug's my indentured issues expert. Gabie recommended him. Doug knows a lot about that world thanks to his Heaven's Reach connections."

"Good," Ruby murmured back. She turned to Temira—hollow-cheeked and thinner than she had been the last time they met. *Hope this doesn't mean she has health problems.* "How's the family doing?"

"I've had to send them into hiding," Temira said grimly. "But it's not perfect, and they keep having to move. They keep getting harassed—I talked to Jeff and he suggested I meet with Justine."

"What the hell?" Temira wasn't involved in anything political —was she?

"It's because of my opposition to indentured labor pools," Temira said. "Getting death threats. Kids and Alan being followed when they go off the farm. Sabotage. Drone attacks. Killbots. And more. It's linked to the Real Truthers and animal rights—specifically, We Love Animals and Nature."

Ruby winced. Philip had been the major undercover financier of WLAN, using the organization to harass agtech competitors. It wasn't until after his death that Gabe and Justine got their hands on *those* financial records within the Group databases. And Philip was not the only big WLAN contributor—just the largest and most powerful. Tracking those non-Family ties was much more difficult.

Damn it, are we ever going to get away from Philip's toxic legacy?

"Of course," Ruby sighed. "It *would* be WLAN. Are you losing animals to the sabotage?"

"Five of my best sows in one incident," Temira said grimly. She brushed away tears. "I wanted to—the deaths were inhumane. Horrific." She gulped. "That was when I turned to Jeff, looking for help."

Temira's farm focused on closed cycle boutique pork production, selling ethically raised farm-to-table meat. She raised her own feed as well as growing vegetables for a small farm-to-fork cooperative that catered to high-end restaurants. Her operation regularly earned the highest compliance certifications from agricultural animal welfare oversight organizations.

"I'm sorry to hear that, Temira. If there's any way that we can help—" Gabe said.

"If we can plug that jamming hole in the Guardians so that they will work consistently, that will make a huge difference," Justine said. "Effective Guardians coupled with a protective force means that Temira's family could come back to the farm safely." She scowled. "With WLAN playing such a big role in the harassment, it's clearly tied to former allies of Daddy-damn-dearest."

"Heaven's Reach?" Ruby asked tensely. Yes, Justine had *said* they weren't involved, but all the same....

"No," Doug Gates said firmly. "Not them, nor the Electric Born." He snapped up a screen. "Take a look. I've been following the money flow. Terence Braun. Head of Zingter Enterprises, WLAN supporter and proponent of indentured labor pools. He's taken over Philip's role both financially and strategically, not just in the Real Truthers but in WLAN. Major drone developer. We need to get our hands on some of his drones and compare specs to confirm his participation in these attacks—that opens up legal and civil remedies. Access to his company's drones is highly restricted to begin with. And any potential purchaser tied to the Martiniere Group is interdicted. That's been the challenge. Sure, we can do extralegal stuff within the shelter of the Group, but—we really need the ability to pursue legal remedies."

Gabe raised his brows. "Tine. Terence Braun. Is that—?"

"Walter's grandson," Justine snapped. "Another reason for the Group to be a target." She exhaled. "Philip tried to force me to marry Terence Braun's grandfather, Walter, when I was seventeen. Braun was blackmailing Philip, and I was supposed to be the payoff to keep Braun silent. I married Donald to escape that fate, with Gabriel's help. So yes, there's some bad blood between our families."

"But why me?" Temira asked.

"You're a visible Martiniere ally," Gabe said. "And you're prominently anti-indentured labor. So if we can get our hands on some drones, lure them out—that might open up those legal and civil channels Doug's talking about. Not that I have major confidence in their long-term effectiveness. It's been years since civil and legal sanctions have worked. But I'm biased. For damned good reasons."

"Understandable," Gates said. "And those systems are going to take a lifetime to change."

Ruby bit her lip. They didn't have a lifetime to change things, not anymore.

Another fucking thing that Philip Martiniere stole from us.

In the long run, fixing things—if possible—was going to be a job for Mike. Lily. The Swait kids.

"We'll be able to catch those drones," Kevin Swait said. "I'm confident of that. This worm in Mike's scanner—it's not the source of the problem in the Guardians, but it also doesn't help the situation." He scowled. "I've been trying to trace it, and it just—disappears." He threw up his hands. "As if it's not there. I can't replicate it consistently, and it slips through every lure or trap I set up for it. It will interfere with biobots that share the Guardian programming formats, but not all—and it's specific to the Guardians. Not the RubyBot, not the Swaitbot."

"Then we'll get him a new scanner," Ruby said. "And I'll talk to him about cybersecurity. Mike's good, but he's still a kid. Stuff happens."

RUBY WAS ONE OF THE LURES FOR THEIR FIRST DRONE CAPTURE attempt, against Gabe's protests. She and Jeff wandered around the airstrip, apparently discussing the fields next to it, while carrying Kevin's fob-based devices that would electronically knock down and capture the drones. Jeff had one version; Ruby the other. Gabe and Justine were monitoring surveillance screens at the Swait Farms security offices, along with Kevin Swait.

"If we can get the Guardians to work on this field, I'd plant Swaitrice and run the Swaitbots on it," Jeff said as they stood at the end of the runway, gesturing toward the hayfield. "The field profile works beautifully for that combination—"

Ruby's fob buzzed. "They're coming," she murmured.

"No sign on mine yet," Jeff muttered. "Kev, you got that?" he said into his comm.

"Monitoring," Gabe snapped. "No signs on any screens."

"I've got something," Justine said. "Coming from the southeast."

Ruby whirled to face that direction. She raised her fob. It twitched and vibrated hard enough to make it difficult to hold with one hand. She waited. Waited. Waited. Finally, the approaching drones appeared—difficult to see because they were so small. It was only because of pattern recognition skills gained from the years spent working with the RubyBot and its relatives that she spotted them.

Her grip tightened even more on the juddering fob.

Not yet. Not yet.

"Trigger now," it finally droned.

Ruby pressed the button. The approaching drone swarm shuddered to a halt.

Then small explosions popped off, little sparks that flared bright and fell to the ground. When it stopped, Ruby and Jeff hurried to where the remnants had fallen.

Nothing but ash and cinders. They carefully used long-handled scoops and tongs to gather up what pieces they could.

"Damn it, programmed self-destruction," Jeff growled.

"Well, at least it gets rid of the darn things," Ruby said.

"Not good enough for protective purposes, though," Jeff said. "And we still don't know how they run interference with the Guardians. Or what infected the scanners at the Double R. No drones working there."

"True," Ruby conceded.

Two separate problems.

No solutions, at least that day.

Gabe and Justine called Brandon privately, from Jeff's office, to discuss the Cho family issues. Ruby visited with Temira. At last, Gabe came out.

"Tine and Bran are making the final arrangements," he said. "We have two safe locations for Alan and your kids, Temira. Moondance, and Justine's house in Los Angeles. Both heavily sensored and guarded. The Martiniere Group is picking up the bill for defending your farm. Justine's sending people and more sensors. Eventually, that should reduce your losses and allow your family to go home." He ran his fingers through his hair. "Not a perfect solution, I'm afraid. I wish we could do more, but it looks like we'll need to provide defense for you long-term."

"Gabe, you didn't have to—" Temira began.

His face hardened. "It's part of my father's damn legacy because it's tied to the Real Truthers and Terence Braun, all right? You're a Martiniere ally, and it's not fair to you and Alan to be put in this position. Both Moondance and Justine's house are spacious and set up for long-term guests. It's not an imposition."

"Thank you," Temira said. "I appreciate this, Gabe."

"It's one means of fixing things." Gabe eyed Ruby. "Meanwhile, it's getting late. We didn't come prepared to stay the night."

"Neither did I," Temira said.

"Justine will take care of that," Gabe said. "Rubes, let's gather up Mike and head for home." He sighed. "Keep in touch, Temira. I feel responsible for what happened to you, and if there's anything more the Martiniere Group can do—Brandon and I are both committed to assist you."

"Getting those legal and civil remedies to work effectively will be one big help," Temira said.

"Well, let's hope we can get Pat Markey re-elected," Gabe said, running his hand through his hair again. "We'll be talking, Temira. Stay safe."

"I will."

It took a few minutes to extract Mike, buried in a build-a-bot game with JoAnn Swait.

"You two can play it online," Ruby said finally. "Mike, we have to go."

"You'll give me access?" Mike asked. Ruby maintained a tight restraint on Mike's online accesses outside of school and research. But when it came to JoAnn—and this particular game—

"*After* you do schoolwork, chores, and exercise," Ruby said. "Understand?"

Mike nodded eagerly.

It wasn't until bedtime that Ruby and Gabe had the time to talk privately.

"I don't think the Guardians are going to be fully effective for a few more years," Ruby said as they lay in bed facing each other. "I started working through the potential holes on the way back from Swait's, based on the newest data from Kevin."

"It sure seems that way, doesn't it?" Gabe said. "Let's hope it doesn't take the twenty-some years to develop, like the RubyBot did."

"And more, because we're still tweaking it." Ruby paused. "But—things could change. Did you take a look at the bot that Mike and JoAnn were working on as part of their game?"

"Not very close, I'm afraid."

"I went through sequences, because I wanted to know the full reach of the game before I gave Mike unlimited access. Potential cybersecurity issues. It's—interesting."

"How so?" Gabe propped himself up on one arm, smiling down at her.

"Those two are demonstrating design skills in collaboration that go way beyond what I was capable of doing at that age. Beyond what a lot of adult designers can do. Close to what you and I can do now."

"Well, Mike is Philip's clone, after all, and if there is one thing about my sperm donor that I can't deny—Philip was brilliant, in his own way. Dangerously so."

"But was Philip much of a bot designer?"

Gabe frowned, chewing his lip thoughtfully. "No. Not really. Programmer, yes. Understanding psychological algorithms, yes."

"So perhaps Mike is developing different skills from his progenitor, based on being raised in an environment where bot development is a higher priority?"

"Could be," Gabe said. He stroked Ruby's cheek with his free hand. "That's an encouraging thought. He *is* growing up around research that has a very different emphasis from what Philip did."

"And—" Ruby paused. "JoAnn brings out a lot of positives in him."

Gabe chuckled. "Matchmaking, Ruby? It's way too early."

She laughed back at him. "Even if the two of them don't become romantically involved, I think their ability to cooperate bodes well for Barkley-Martiniere-Swait. They work well together. It's not just something I've noticed. Jeff commented on it to me."

"Building a future." Gabe stroked her cheek again. "After today—God, Ruby. I thought we could turn things around within a few short years. But it sure seems more complicated than that."

"Mike, Lily, and the Swait kids are our future."

"True." Gabe turned more solemn. "I just wish that I didn't have this weird foreboding whenever I'm around Lily." He grimaced. "Martiniere juju. Superstition, tied to the Medicis. All the same—I hope that Bran and Kris are able to have more kids."

Ruby shivered. She knew what Gabe meant. Their granddaughter was a lovely little girl, but her personality—even at almost three, Lily exhibited mood swings that troubled Ruby.

Her family—Barkleys and Ryders alike—had a load of mental health problems, including early-onset schizophrenia. So did the Martinieres. And then there was the hormonal tampering that had been Kris's legacy from being sold into indenture by her parents in her early teens. Hopefully, Lily was free from those legacies.

Hopefully.

Ruby shivered again.

"You okay?" Gabe asked.

"Just one of those thoughts," Ruby said.

"Maybe I need to distract you." Gabe kissed her.

She laughed and kissed him back, hard.

8 / CHASING AFTER SHADOWS
APRIL, 2064

GABE

Damn it.

Even after a year's worth of work, no matter how much he poked at that Guardian bot's file designs, Gabe still couldn't isolate that damn worm that came and went within it. The bot would work just fine for a while, and then everything fell to pieces. At first, he and Ruby had thought it was tied to Mike, somehow, but the latest manifestations originated from files that Mike hadn't handled.

His comm chimed. *"Donald Atwood."*

Gabe answered, relieved to have a distraction from wrestling with that Guardian design. "Don. What's up?"

His ex-brother-in-law frowned, an unusual expression for Donald's normally unreactive face. "Gabe, have you noticed any memory oddities when working with those Guardian files you sent me?"

"Hasn't affected our systems in that manner," Gabe said. "At least not according to our tracking records."

Donald shook his head. "No. Not electronic memory. Human memory."

"Wha—no. Not at all. Why?" A chill that had nothing to do with the alternating rain and sun outside prickled Gabe's forearms. "Who's affected?"

"Justine. No impact on me—just her. We've been recording it."

Aw, fuck.

"How extensive?" Gabe asked, uneasiness clenching his gut, thinking through the possibilities, fighting back fear.

Not my sister!

Was this really caused by whatever was going on with the Guardian files, or was this something organic in Justine? After all, she had undergone enough beatings from their father to possibly cause brain damage that might surface only now, as she aged.

Or was it the mental illness that was one of the Martiniere *subjects we don't talk about*?

"The memory failures are strictly limited to knowledge of that occasional bug in the Guardian bot," Donald said.

Gabe slumped in his chair and pinched the bridge of his nose. That was a minor relief, at least.

"That fucking Guardian," he said. "The problems are coming from our end, not Swait's. Ruby and I have been over and over the programming, as have the Swaits. Guardians that have no contact with Martiniere files? Kevin's been running those just fine the last six months, except for some quirks in the stem cell lines that aren't tied to the programming issues. He almost has the stem cell pieces fixed." He dropped his hand. "Does it have any effect on you?"

"No—and that's the disturbing part. Justine doesn't remember that the bug is a reoccurring situation, at least until I remind her after each incident." Donald scowled harder. "It has her spooked, Gabe. Me as well."

"I'll talk to Ruby and Mike, ask if they see it in me." Though he doubted that. He'd been pounding his head against that damned worm's existence for well over a year now. How on earth could he forget about it?

"Thanks, Gabe." Donald's frown softened.

"Wait. Actually, Don, call Martin. He'll have observed it in all three of us if that's the case, and he's definitely not a Martiniere. I'll talk to him, too."

"That sounds like a plan. I'll get back to you once I know more, Gabe," Donald said.

"Thanks, Don."

Gabe sat still for a few minutes, tapping his chin with his index fingers as he thought it through. Should he go down to the labs and check with Martin right away, or give Donald time to talk to him?

Wait.

Besides, he had other things to work on besides the Guardian problem.

Justine wanted him to make fundraising calls to high-end donors for Pat Markey's presidential re-election campaign. That might be a more productive effort than fretting about those damned Guardian bots. They needed four more years of Pat in office to yank political structures back into place and finally eliminate indenture.

Pat's re-election wouldn't eliminate all those years of the Real Truthers undermining the Honest Republicans and the Classic Democrats.

But eight years of a New Democratic administration might further some progress toward eliminating indenture beyond the structures of the Martiniere Group.

He hoped.

GABE WENT DOWN TO THE LABS THAT AFTERNOON. RUBY AND MIKE were busy with the broodmares, so he would have uninterrupted time to speak with Martin without worrying about either of them overhearing their conversation.

"It's an interesting situation," Martin said in response to Gabe's question.

"*Have* you seen traces of memory loss in any of us, whether it's connected to the Guardians or not?"

After all, both he and Mike had potential ties if this was a Martiniere issue.

"Yes," Martin said, without hesitation. "You, Brandon, Mike, and Ruby. It's not consistent, and not to the degree that Donald described happening to Justine, when I talked to him."

Brandon too, damn it. And why is Ruby affected when Donald apparently isn't?

"How is it showing up? Because I certainly remember that there's an intermittent problem with the Guardians."

"It's incident-related. Ruby and Brandon have recorded worm encounters that they logged—and then come to me a few days later, asking if someone's hacked the reports, because they don't remember making those recordings."

"Here only?"

Martin shook his head. "Both Moondance and the Double R."

That meant a focus centered on the Martiniere and his family, then, not the labs.

But still—why Ruby and not Donald?

"And me and Mike?"

"Mike partially recalls that there have been times when he's coded something he doesn't recognize. You forget that you've issued alerts about glitches."

"So it's not consistent even between those of us who are exposed," Gabe sighed.

"Exactly. And it's small things."

"I honestly don't remember those instances of forgetting, Martin."

"I thought as much," Martin said.

"Should I issue a general alert to the Group and the Family?"

Martin shook his head. "Not yet, Gabe. Let me ask around and see how extensive this situation is."

"All right."

It wasn't a perfect answer, but at least it was—something.

Both Ruby and Mike frowned when Gabe brought up the subject while they prepared dinner.

"All of us, then." Ruby deftly dumped chicken chunks into the frying pan and stirred them. "How is it targeting us?"

"Mind control programming of some sort?" Gabe laid out the plates on the kitchen table while Mike gathered silverware.

"Then why am I affected and not Donald? Neither of us have experienced significant Martiniere mind control programming." Her scowl deepened as she stirred the chicken. "Gabe, how on earth would that work?"

"Philip slipped nanos into you somehow during that second appearance at the AgSuperstar, before our divorce," Gabe reminded her. "Enough of an influence to trigger me."

And Ruby has gone right to the heart of my concerns. Why her and not Donald?

"Philip would have had much more access to Donald over the years that Donald and Justine were married than he ever had to me," Ruby countered. "And his contacts with Donald would have been in the same time period as the AgSuperstar."

"And what about Brandon?" Mike piped up.

"Mmm, that could have happened while Brandon worked for AgI," Gabe said. "But that's a good point, Mike." He leaned against the kitchen counter. "The common ground is a Martiniere connection. Why Donald mentioned not noticing any loss affecting him surprises me. He and Justine are—ahem—" he caught himself, remembering that Mike was still only ten years old. "Involved once again. I would think that would provide exposures."

"Safeguards Donald has that we don't?" Mike suggested.

"Entirely possible," Ruby said. "And it's also likely that it affects Donald in a different manner. It appears that our reactions to whatever the hell this is varies. Let's check with Kris as well. *Then* let's start discussing the situation within the Family." She dumped the bowl of chopped vegetables in with the chicken. "Gabe, grab some spices, all right? Your choice."

He grinned and complied. Mike liked bland and Ruby spicy food. Gabe's preferences satisfied both of them.

July, *2064*

WEATHER CONDITIONS DISTRACTED THEM FROM TRACKING DOWN what was going on with that damn worm. Temperatures skyrocketed in late May and early June, melting snowpack faster than usual and speeding up the first hay cutting. Irrigation became crucial, as the temperatures overwhelmed even the RubyBot-treated grain fields.

Gabe spent most of his time wrestling with bot programming, trying to integrate Ruby's design ideas for more durable bots into their prototypes. At last he was able to do the field work he had been longing to get back into, with Ruby—and now that it was here, he could barely keep up. Taking time to track down that transient worm in the Guardian bots just wasn't a priority, especially since the Swaits seemed to make them work —as long as no Martiniere touched the programming.

Frustrating, especially since the Guardians were *supposed* to be a Barkley-Martiniere-Swait cooperative venture.

Labor was also short that summer. Gabe ran a swather until he got light-headed and Ruby spotted him leaning against the rig, shaking his head, trying to stay upright, not trusting himself at the controls. Even with an air-conditioned cab it was *hot*.

Mike puked on the hottest day yet, while raking hay.

Ruby kicked Gabe and Mike out of the hayfields after those incidents. "The two of you don't need to be in this heat."

But it was *Ruby* who ended up collapsing from heat exhaustion.

Not once, but twice.

The second time, Gabe took her to the ER, over Ruby's feeble protests.

"You're more vulnerable after the first collapse," Dr. Sheri scolded Ruby. "You have the money to hire help. Do it, damn it."

The fact that Ruby didn't immediately snarl back at Dr. Sheri worried Gabe more than anything else.

Oh well. As a Martiniere he had money to pay higher wages to bring in a larger crew and rotate them through on shorter shifts so no one else got sick.

It solved *that* problem, and Gabe ended up helping out several Thunder County ranchers in a similar position.

But managing harvest and production logistics for the Double R, Moondance, and half-a-dozen other operations meant there wasn't a hell of a lot of time to dedicate to the issues of whatever the hell that programming worm was.

"GABE! I NEED YOU IN THE LABS NOW!" RUBY SCREECHED INTO THE comm.

The urgency in her voice, coupled with Mike screaming in the background, forced Gabe out of his chair, running from his office, through the house, and out the back door.

"What's wrong?" he panted as he ran.

"Mike's having a meltdown! Bad!"

"Be right there!" Gabe switched off his comm and sprinted faster even though it was hotter than hell, the midday sun turning Northeastern Oregon into something like the Southwest had been twenty years ago.

He careened into the labs, looking around.

Where the hell are they?

Julie, one of the staff, nodded toward the programming room where Mike spent a lot of his school hours. "In there, Gabe." Her voice quavered, face pale under brown.

What the hell had happened? Julie wasn't easily rattled.

Gabe inhaled sharply, seeking to calm himself before bursting in. Then he opened the door to the programming room.

Ruby and Mike were on the floor, Mike moaning and coiled in a fetal curl, half in Ruby's lap as she rocked him, murmuring soothing tones. Smudge pressed hard against Mike's legs.

"What happened?" Gabe dropped to his knees next to them, rubbing Mike's back. Physical contact had helped bring Mike out of meltdowns when he was younger—hopefully that still worked.

Ruby shook her head. "I have no idea. I was working in Clean Room Four when Julie paged me. I came in to find Mike on the floor, screaming." Worry crinkled the skin around her eyes as she looked up at Gabe. "He kept repeating *clone* and *I am Philip*. Then he passed out." She jerked her head toward a projection. "I haven't dared look at it yet."

"I'll call Dr. Sheri." Oh God. Didn't Mike already understand that he was Philip's clone? Oh shit. How could he have *not* understood that?

It seemed to take forever for Dr. Sheri to arrive instead of the ten minutes it would normally require for someone to drive from her Lakeside office to the Double R.

Mike started moaning as Gabe talked to Dr. Sheri.

"No. Clone. I am Philip."

"Mike. *Stop.*" Ruby managed to project some of her strongest vocal tones. Mike stopped groaning, but kept sniffling as she rocked him.

"Clone?" Dr. Sheri frowned. "I thought Mike already knew he was a clone."

"So did I—"

Mike screamed louder than ever, trying to curl up tighter, quivering hard, as if he'd undergone the harshest possible use of mind control tones.

Oh God.

The word *clone* seemed to be the trigger.

Somehow, between Gabe and Ruby, they managed to keep Mike still enough for Dr. Sheri to inject him with a sedative.

Gabe gathered Mike into his arms after the sedative took effect, suddenly noticing how light his adopted son was for a boy his age. Had Brandon been this lightweight at ten?

He couldn't remember.

Gabe didn't try to mess with that file—not a good time for it. But he eyed the projection to figure out just what file this was, before carrying Mike to a crawler waiting outside.

Subject PJM-M-13-Michael.

And from the quick glance, he saw enough to realize that it contained Mike's cloning records.

What the fucking hell—where did that come from?

Those records were supposed to be in a secure archive, damn it.

AS SOON AS MIKE WAS SETTLED UNDER RUBY'S SUPERVISION, GABE rushed back to the labs. That malignant file's projection still shimmered, waiting. Tempting. He could *almost* read the details from three feet away. The urge to move closer and study it in detail called him in closer, almost hypnotic in its lure.

Read me. Read me.

Why had Mike reacted so dramatically to it? Especially the word "clone"?

His job to find out. Just what in hell would make his boy react so dramatically to a simple file? Mike was pretty damn stable these days, so why had he melted down so intensely? Even if the file did contain details of his creation—it shouldn't be *that* bad, should it? And just how the hell had it gotten out of that locked archive?

Only one way to find out.

He should wait for Ruby. For Martin. Justine. Someone to back him up. That thought faded away as quickly as he considered it.

Gabe took a deep breath, then tentatively reached out to scroll through the file.

An electric shock lashed through him as he touched the projection, knocking him halfway across the room before he landed on his rear.

Rage like he hadn't felt for *years* roared through him.

Kill. Hurt. Rip. Shred. Motherfuckers, I'll make you all pay—

Wrong. Alien.

Not my thoughts.

Gabe clenched his fists, panting, fighting back the anger.

Mind control trigger.

He closed his eyes and shook his head to clear it.

He had suspected that likelihood already, given the intensity of Mike's reaction. But he didn't like the implications.

Something had to be done about that file. But what? If a simple contact was so reactive—and *how the hell was that happening?*

Gabe thought it through. What could best insulate him from actual physical contact with the file? His chest ached on the left side—damn it, had that fucking thing triggered another angina attack?

Deep breathing, and the ache eased. It might have just been muscles reacting to that nasty zap.

Biosuit.

He pushed himself up from the floor, his body throbbing from that damn electrical jolt, and went to the lab's stash of cleared biosuits, specifically the style designed to work with the RubyBots while introducing the initial programming into the biobots. Maybe he didn't need to wear much more than the gloves—no.

Full suit. Safer.

Gabe pulled it on, made certain the anti-static precautions were active. As an afterthought, he grabbed one of the styluses that Ruby had devised to implant codes into the assorted biobot lines. More precautions.

This time, he approached the projection cautiously. Studied what he could see without contact.

A picture of Mike, clearly taken just before his rescue.

Part of a table of contents.

Part of a narrative about the cloning process.

DNA sequence codes.

The file order seemed to be jumbled. A reflection of what had been done to it when it zapped him, or a deliberate disorder, unless you had the right keywords?

Gabe tentatively touched the projection with the stylus. Bright light flared around the stylus and his hand, something pushing him back, thankfully without that nasty jolt.

The projection flared red and yellow. Data swirled, and the file slammed shut, retreating to a file directory mixed in with Mike's studies, last in a sequence of *Subject PJM* files—*all* of those fucking clone files. Gabe tried to tap it open again.

BIOMETRIC ACCESS DENIED popped up, followed by a third jolt nearly as hard as the first. Gabe dropped to the floor, gasping for breath, clutching at his chest.

Damn it—too far.

Then his eyes widened as Philip's form took shape in front of him. A younger Philip, identical in expression and attire to what he had looked like the day he demanded that Gabe divorce Ruby.

Complete with that mocking, self-satisfied sneer.

"You will be mine eventually, Gabriel," Philip cackled. *"All of you will be mine! I am going to win!"*

"No," Gabe groaned, somehow finding the strength to rise. What the hell was this—a hallucination? "You're dead, damn you, and not a single one of those I hold dear will ever be yours!"

More laughter.

The image faded.

Gabe stood, shaking, gasping for breath.

What the hell had just happened?

He didn't remember a damn fucking thing, except that he was wearing a biosuit, held a half-melted stylus in his right hand, and that damn file was closed.

Why was he wearing a biosuit and holding a half-melted stylus?

Why did he feel like he had been beaten within an inch of his life?

Most importantly, what had caused this sensation of dread that made his heart pound so damn hard?

***

ONCE MIKE WAS SAFELY OUT OF THE WAY THE NEXT MORNING, GABE held a council in his office with Brandon, Justine, and Ruby. The only ones who knew about those damned biometrically-locked *Subject PJM* files.

The only ones who could easily shove them into Mike's records.

And not a one of them knew how it had happened.

"I think there was a trigger of some sort in that file," Ruby said after the meeting, while washing breakfast dishes.

"A mind control trigger?" Gabe asked.

Ruby nodded. "I thought I knew Mike pretty well by now. We've served as his parents for half of his life. This extreme a reaction to learning he was Philip's clone was not what I anticipated."

"Me too. I thought he knew more than he apparently did."

Ruby pursed her lips as she put her emerald wedding ring

back on. "Tracing the links to that file with Justine last night—Gabe, it has ties to some sort of worm. Maybe the same one that keeps popping up with the Guardians." She bit her lip. "And the possibility that it's a worm is something I keep forgetting."

Gabe scowled. There was something else that had happened yesterday in the labs—but what?

"You did lock down your *whatthehell* files, right?" she asked.

He tensed. If Mike reacted that poorly to learning that he was Philip's clone, then what would happen once he discovered the degree to which Philip had abused Gabe?

"As tight as they can be locked," he said.

"That's what we thought about these files." Ruby frowned.

"I know."

"Mike needs more protection—and I have an idea, based on Smudge's reaction to his meltdown," Ruby said. "I think I can do some epigenetic manipulations in Smudge's descendants to increase their potential as therapy dogs. Maybe even horses."

And then she described recent research into augmentation of cyberawareness in horses and dogs, currently being developed for show training.

Smudge's gene markers showed potential for further development.

So did Ruby's mare Legacy, and Legacy's daughter Heritage.

Gabe considered the potential of this line of research.

Well worth it.

At the minimum, it would add to Mike's protection.

Too bad Lily was so afraid of dogs, even the Border Collies who had been around her from babyhood.

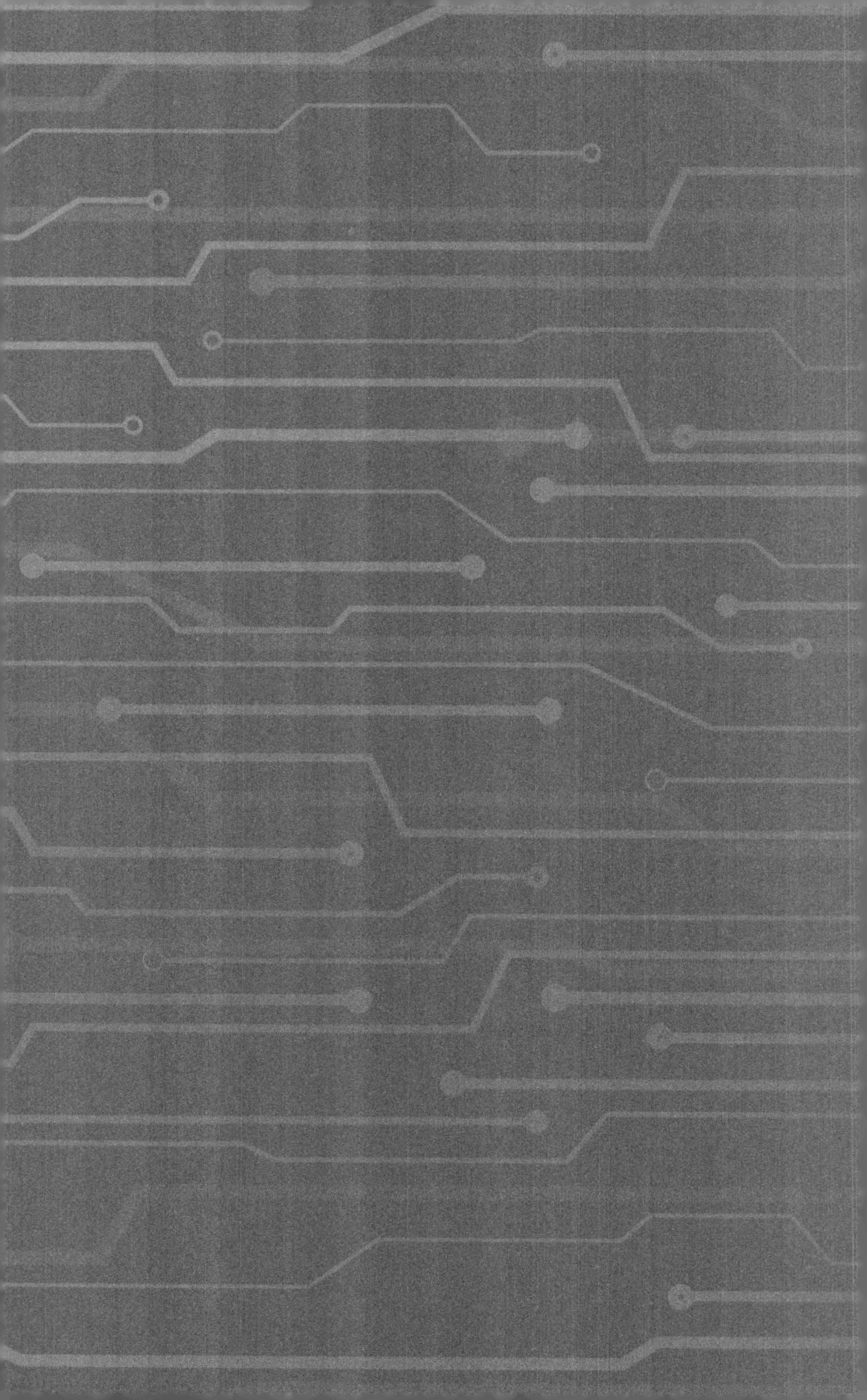

RUBY

"WANT TO DO SOMETHING SPECIAL FOR OUR FIFTH ANNIVERSARY?" Gabe leaned on the doorframe of Ruby's farmhouse office.

Ruby looked away from the ranch end-of-quarter financial reports.

Reviewing ranch financials had been a grim duty when single and trying to keep the family ranch afloat, while trying to launch the RubyBot. It was no less onerous now. But the prospect of losing the ranch was no longer a dread concern lurking in her thoughts. Remarrying Gabe—and discovering that he was an exiled heir of a wealthy and powerful family, not a broke and brilliant ranch hand evading student loan indentured servitude—made a big difference.

"Five years is longer than we lasted the first time we married," she answered. "I think that's cause for celebration."

Gabe chuckled as he came into the office, hobbling a little. Ruby suppressed a concerned frown. Was he limping worse today?

Just a limp. You have much worse things to worry about when it comes to Gabe's health.

Like his cardiac problems.

"If you want to add the two marriages together, it's eight years, but all the same—" He came around the corner of her desk and leaned against it, arms crossed. "We should treat this as a landmark anniversary. I promised you we would play and have fun when we remarried, and again when I retired. I've been slacking at doing it."

"What do you have in mind?" she asked.

Uh-oh.

When Gabe pronounced that *I've been slacking* at something, that meant his contemplated remedy involved some form of overcompensation for his perceived slighting of—whatever bothered him.

Gabe tilted his head from side to side. "Oh, I don't know. Lots of possibilities, but I wondered what *you* might want."

She shrugged. "I've enjoyed what we've done on our anniversary so far."

"Hey. We can go anywhere in the world. Do anything, within reason. What would *you* really want to do that would be special?"

Ruby considered how they had celebrated their anniversary previously. Special dinners, special outings. Most of the time with Mike. Often with Brandon and Kris, Justine and Donald, and other Family members. Never just the two of them, except for the dinners. And that was, what? Two, three hours at most?

"Something with *just us* sounds pretty good," she said. "Mike can stay with Brandon and Kris, and this is enough advance notice to warn them."

"Just us, hmm?" Gabe rubbed his chin thoughtfully.

"Yeah. I love the Family, but—" she sighed, letting her voice trail off.

Five years as part of the Martiniere Family—always with a capital F. It wasn't the novelty of extreme wealth as much as it was the novelty of the Martiniere *togetherness* that constantly niggled at her. Family in the past had just been her grandparents.

Not so with the Martinieres.

Family Christmas with *all* the high-level Martiniere heirs, ranging into distant cousins, was fun, but exhausting. Gatherings with the Canadian, British, or French Martiniere Family branches which also involved lots of cousins. Business meetings of the Martiniere Group, which turned into social occasions and Family events.

Gabe's position as the Martiniere Emeritus meant that Ruby and Gabe were the leaders of non-business Family affairs. Sometimes their Family-related responsibilities were just plain tiring.

"Yeah," Gabe said after a few moments. "I hear you, Ruby." He took her hand. "I've been having the same thoughts. Thirty years away from the Family has an impact, and now—" he sighed, an echo of hers. "I've been wanting to get away for a while. Completely disconnect."

"That sounds really good to me."

"So—urban? Mountains? Ocean?"

"Someplace quiet." Ruby glanced outside. "It's been a long, dry summer so far, and we're only getting started. It would be nice to go someplace cool. Where we can be by ourselves for a few days. Read books and *relax*. Maybe do some hiking but nothing more than that. Just quiet. Just us. No need to hurry anywhere."

"Coastal, then. Atlantic or Pacific?"

"Pacific. Not California—I love the excursions to Anacapa Island with Justine, but that's always a Family thing. Not on a boat, either. Or swimming. That's not what I want to do."

"Got it." Gabe snapped his fingers to bring up his computer display. "We're thinking alike, once again. I've found several possibilities. Rank them, and I'll make reservations."

Ruby flipped through the choices and made her selections. "Do you think we'll actually get any of these places? It *is* only a month out."

"We'll see. I suspect that farmhouse on the river estuary will still be available. The coastal ones, especially *that* one—" he flipped back to her first choice, a house isolated on a rocky point above the ocean. "Might prove to be challenging." He grinned. "But I'll sure do my best."

"That's all we can do," Ruby said.

He kissed her and left.

Ruby turned back to her spreadsheet with renewed energy, though the occasional thought of a few days on the coast in August kept popping back up.

Much as she loved the Double R and the mountains and prairies surrounding it, really hot, dry summers got on her nerves. The last five years had featured dry springs followed by hot, smoky summers. Fire was a constant worry.

Normally, she shunned even the idea of the coast in August because of crowds. But if Gabe could find them a quiet, private place to stay, it sounded like a nice break—and they had the money to buy isolation these days.

Too bad it was a month or so before they could do that. She was ready for cool weather *now*.

August, 2064

Ruby exhaled. They'd made it. Not to the cliff house—as she suspected, it was booked. But they would take Mike to Moondance tonight. Travel to the Coast tomorrow, flying into Astoria and taking a helicopter to the place they had reserved.

Tomorrow.

Even staying at the old farmhouse on the estuary sounded nice. Private.

The farmhouse would be warmer than the coast proper, but still cooler than the Double R. No wildfire smoke. It featured hammocks, easy hikes down to the estuary, and was off of the main road.

She was taking hard copy books to read—nothing electronic, nothing that would lure her into checking her email and messages more than twice a day.

"Good news," Gabe said as he entered their bedroom and pulled his roller bag out of the closet.

"Oh?"

He smirked at her. "The cliff house. I threw enough money at the manager that we got it."

"That's fantastic!" No swimsuits, then—wait. There was a hot tub at the cliff house. Depended on how private that was. But definitely more cool-weather wear than the farmhouse.

Gabe's smirk widened. "Absolutely." His expression then turned more serious. "I'm worried about you, Rubes. This year's haying took a lot out of you, and we still have another cutting plus grain harvest ahead. Not being able to give you any significant help with any of that work bugs the hell out of me. Mike's too young to be of much assistance, and with *his* health—"

She shrugged. "I need to step back, not overdo, and hire more hands and interns. That's what Gramps did, and he lived into his nineties."

"Your grandfather also had the two of us working the ranch at the end of his life, instead of seasonal help," Gabe reminded her. He took her into his arms. "We put in the long hours that he couldn't. And let's face it—our generation has a shorter lifespan than our parents and grandparents. We're sixty-two and fifty-six, and neither of us have lived an easy life, until the last five years." He took a deep breath. "So that's why I busted my rear getting us the cliff house. You deserve it, and we have the money now. Damn it, I *want* to enjoy life with you, and I've been slacking. Getting distracted by work."

Uh-oh. That again.

Gabe piling guilt on himself.

"Hey," she said softly. "It goes two ways. I haven't been after you to take it easy, and maybe I should have before your heart started acting up."

"It might not have made any difference," he said, stroking her cheek. "Not with my family history. Not with the side effects of the anti-aging serum. I worry that your fatigue and heat exhaustion after the first two cuttings of hay this summer is an indicator that the damn serum has worn off in you, too. That you'll start having cardiac problems. We have to be careful."

"You're really being morbid today, aren't you?"

Gabe buried his head in his favorite place, the junction of her neck and shoulder, inhaling deeply before raising his head. "Let's just say that I'm feeling my mortality, and I shouldn't be. Not with a fifth anniversary coming up." He pulled her even closer. "And if it hadn't been for my stupidity years ago, this would be our thirty-first anniversary, not our fifth."

"That would have been in June, not August. Gabe. That doesn't matter anymore. What *does* matter is that we're together again, and we're going to have fun and no responsibilities for a few days. All right?"

"All right," he conceded.

She still didn't trust that look in his eyes. Gabe was up to something.

But what?

FOG DELAYS ON THE COAST MEANT THEY DIDN'T REACH THE CLIFF house until almost dark.

"Typical," their pilot said as they waited in Portland for clearance. "Hot in Portland, heavy fog on the coast. It'll lift soon, though. That's the pattern."

Instead of taking a helicopter from the airport, their security drove them to the cliff house. It was located on a spur road off of the main highway, and they passed a few houses clustered along the road before passing through a set of iron gates to drive up to the main house. To Ruby's surprise, the property manager waited for them underneath the overhang sheltering the front door.

Maybe it was a result of all that money Gabe had thrown around to get this place. Ruby was *still* learning that money earned a lot of personal service. Gabe tended to avoid being ostentatious, unless they were in Europe or around the Family, so when money did make a difference, it still surprised her.

"Here you go, Mr. Martiniere." The property manager handed Gabe a key ring with multiple keys and fobs. "Your paperwork is on the kitchen counter."

"Everything?" Gabe asked. "Furnishings as specified?"

"Everything, including furnishings. It's a pleasure doing business with you."

"And with you." Gabe exhaled. They bowed to each other as security carried Ruby and Gabe's luggage and their food inside, before retreating to their quarters. Then the manager left.

"It's a bit old-fashioned," Gabe said, slipping a key and a fob off of the key ring. "Key for the doors, fob for the gate. Here's your copies."

"Multiple keys for just a few days?" She raised her brows at him as she took them. "Especially since we're not going out very much?"

"C'mon," he said. "Let's check it out."

Gabe slid his arm around Ruby's waist and guided her inside, steering her into a kitchen that opened onto a living and dining area. "Three bedrooms, two baths, hot tub on the deck that can be enclosed in bad weather. Separate quarters for security by the gate, helicopter pad nearby—that is, when we're not socked in with fog or storms. Smaller than Moondance, but we don't need something that big here."

"Gabe." She sharpened her tone, but he avoided looking at her.

What the hell is he up to now?

This was *definitely* Gabe being evasive.

"Electric fireplaces for heat. Solar, wind, and wave generator power with lots of battery backup. Everything's up-to-date." His voice went tentative. "I hope you like it."

"For a few days why should it matter—" And then she saw the paperwork on the kitchen breakfast bar to her left—granite counters, nicer than the setup at Moondance.

A sales contract.

She thumbed through the papers. Ownership deed, for Ruby Barkley and Gabriel Martiniere. Paid in full, and she gulped at the price. They were billionaires now, but *still*—

"*Gabriel Martiniere.* You didn't say *one word* to me about this!"

He looked abashed. "Happy anniversary, Ruby."

"You didn't have to—"

"I *wanted* to." He took a deep breath. "Ruby, you're right. We need a place like this which is *ours*. Sure, Mike can visit, same for Brandon and Kris, Justine and Donald—but you are absolutely right. We need a refuge for *just us*. Not the Family. A hideaway for Ruby and Gabe."

"You could have given me *some* idea of what was happening."

"Hon, until yesterday morning, I wasn't certain we *had* this place. Negotiations. Closing complications. I threw a lot of money around to make it happen, and every damn penny of it was worth it. Even more to ensure we had adequate furnishings that weren't junk and would be set up in time to make us comfortable for the next few days. We can add more later." He smiled, that slow grin coupled with that smoldering *come-hither* look in his brown eyes. "I wanted this to be a surprise. A gift."

"Oh Gabe." How could she argue with this sentiment? It wasn't a question of finances—and, really, this was the first time he'd given her—them—something *this big*.

"I wanted to make up to you for all those years of hell," he said. "And this—just struck me as one way to do it. Especially since—you getting sick during the haying scared me. It brought me down to earth. We *don't* have all that much longer left, and—

I want to spend it with you, my love. With the chance to escape to our private getaway. Here."

"You've been working on this for a lot longer than a month." She knew damned well that real estate didn't usually work that fast, even with large amounts of money to lubricate the transaction.

"Four months, to be exact. I've been half-looking for the right place for some time now. I've had the same wish to get away from the businesses, from the Group, from the Family. This seemed to fit. Totally different from the ranch; reasonable distance from the Double R; decent medical access. Our vacation place. I had to move fast, and it was a very, very competitive process. I probably spent too much, but that was the kind of stupid money that was being thrown around for this property. Yes, we can afford it, especially since we don't do the billionaire stuff very often. And I wanted it for you."

Now his expression shifted to that puppy-dog pleading look. *Did I do all right?*

"Oh, Gabe," she sighed again. But she couldn't keep a grin from forming. "So were you going to buy the farmhouse?"

"Hell, no. It was this place or nothing. The farmhouse was just a booking." He eased her away from the kitchen island. "Let's take a tour of our new domain." He guided her to the right. "Bathroom. Guest bedrooms on each side of the bathroom." They glanced into each room—unlike Moondance, these bedrooms didn't open onto a deck. But they did have fireplaces, and the bathroom was a full, luxurious bath.

Gabe guided her across the living area. "Primary suite." He dropped his arm, standing in the doorway.

Ruby walked in. Twice the size of the other bedrooms. No deck here, either, but an even bigger electric fireplace directly across from the bed. A long sofa under the great picture window looking out over the Pacific, with reading lamps set at each end. Empty bookshelves begging to be filled with *real* books. *Huge* king-sized bed that looked very, very comfortable and held at least six pillows—with nightstands and reading lights. Walk-in closet, and—she went into the bathroom. Big tub separate from the shower. Two sinks. Well-lit mirrors.

"You like it?" Gabe asked.

"It looks very, very comfortable." She grinned and nodded at the sofa. "Big enough for both of us to use. But no office space?"

"This is a *vacation* home, Ruby. A place to relax. C'mon." He waved her over, and clicked on the fireplace. "Let's look off of the deck."

Compared to the bedroom, the living and dining area didn't seem quite as cozy as they walked back through it, even though Gabe clicked on that fireplace as well. Part of the deck was taken up by an enclosed hot tub, with a shower right there. Ruby shivered as they stepped out on the deck. The contrast between here and the ranch—oh, it felt good, but it was also *cold.*

"I don't want to do the hot tub tonight," she said. "Maybe in the morning. That setup looks *freezing.*"

"It's why I turned on the fires in the bedroom and living room, to warm up my always-cold sweetheart. Charcuterie tonight so all we need to do is relax and cuddle." He held out his arm. "Come on. I'll keep you warm while we're out here."

Ruby tucked herself under Gabe's arm. Watching the hypnotic pattern of ocean waves relaxed her, and the distant *boom* of waves against the shore—she peered over the edge carefully; there was a tiny strip of sand before the cliff walls—added to a growing calmness.

Gabe nuzzled the top of her head. Ruby grinned and looked up at him.

"You've been wanting a coastal place for a while, haven't you, Gabe? I've been watching you when we're staying with Justine at her Los Angeles house. You get that same blissful expression on your face when we're out on her deck, and it seems like you relax there more than anywhere else."

"Childhood memories," he said. "My first twelve years. Mother and Saul loved the beach, and took us out on the ocean regularly." He sighed. "Those same memories are why I didn't look in Southern California. Or Northern, for that matter. And memories of Rachel—why I didn't want to do Puget Sound. I wanted to find something like *this*, that would be just *us*. Still the ocean, but not what I grew up with. Not what Rachel and I did, either." His arm tightened around her. "After all these years, the inland is my home. But it's nice to have someplace like this to escape to. A setup where we don't have bodyguards and security in our face, but can still enjoy the ocean."

"I've never had much experience of the coast," Ruby said wistfully. "Maybe a few times growing up, a quick trip in August between haying and harvest, crowded on the beach with everyone else escaping to cooler weather. So this is marvelous."

"I'm glad you like it," he said. "I hope to make many happy memories here."

Ruby shivered.

"Cold?"

"A little," she said. "But—something else. A feeling. Wondering about how much time is left."

"I understand," he said softly. "Let's go inside. I think food and a glass of wine will help. Not exactly regular meals today with the travel."

Once inside, Gabe wrapped Ruby in a blanket and set her on the couch close to the fireplace. He poked around in the refrigerator and produced a tray of cold cuts, cheese, crackers, and vegetables—something they ate regularly these days when they didn't want to cook. She waited until he had brought over plates, opened the bottle of wine and poured it, then dove in.

After they had finished eating, they snuggled.

"Better?" Gabe asked.

"Yes," she said.

She ended up falling asleep on his shoulder, waking only when he carried her into their bedroom. A quick round of evening medications, brushing her teeth, and Ruby crawled into bed. Gabe wrapped himself around her and she eased back into sleep.

COOLING CAUSED BY GABE'S ABSENCE STARTLED RUBY AWAKE. SHE shot up with a gasp, looked around, disoriented, then spotted him on the couch with a fleece blanket thrown over him, glasses on, reading a physical book. Still dark outside.

"You all right?"

"Just woke," she said. "Realized you weren't there."

"My back and knees ache, and I couldn't get back to sleep. I didn't want to disturb you by reading in bed." He paused. "Do you want to cuddle? I can come back to bed to read."

"Or I could join you. If you're aching, no need to go back to the bed."

That big, warm smile in response. "I'd like that."

Ruby joined Gabe. He turned on his side, and carefully made sure that the blanket covered them both. She nestled in tight, sliding down slightly so he didn't have to contort himself to hold his book. In spite of being shirtless, with just pajama pants on, Gabe was *warm*, while she was cold even in pajamas, always had been.

Gabe adjusted his arms, rested his chin on the top of her head, and she drowsed off again.

At some point she woke once more. Gabe's book was on the floor, glasses on top, the reading lamp turned off, Ruby still tucked under his chin as he curled around her with both arms holding her tight, one leg over hers. Holding her secure so she wouldn't roll off of the couch.

The faint boom of waves against the cliff roared louder than before—high tide, perhaps? The gray light of dawn barely showed the outline of the bed—still early. Probably about the time Ruby normally rose at the Double R, but she didn't feel like stirring.

Five years together this second time around. Five-and-a-half, really, if one counted the period before their remarriage, when they were working toward being a couple again, relearning each other after an acrimonious divorce and twenty-one years apart.

Did she regret those twenty-one years?

Mostly.

But the circumstances that had forced Gabe into exile had also been a huge factor in breaking them apart. From everything Ruby had learned over the past five years, Gabe had been right to fear for her and Brandon's safety, which had been his primary motive for hiding his identity. They *would* have been targets for Philip Martiniere's wrath. Even after their divorce, Gabe had done what he could to protect her and Brandon—and there had still been incidents.

Gabe continued to apologize for his secrecy. For not telling her all those years ago that he was on the run because he had testified against Philip's approval of human rights violations against indentured workers and not, as he had claimed then, due to student loan debt bound by indenture. No matter how many times she told him that she understood why he had kept it a secret, he felt the need to say he was sorry.

Ruby suspected he would feel guilty about his secrecy until the day he died.

Meanwhile—this moment, this breath of time, was sweet. Resting in the arms of the man she loved, had always loved, even in the depths of her anger during their divorce. A man she could spend several days with in a retreat such as this house, cuddling, reading books, hiking—and just being together.

If only it hadn't taken twenty-one years to repair the broken ties.

Gabe stirred, and nuzzled the top of her head. Ruby giggled. He chuckled, and turned her to face him. He kissed her forehead, then her eyelids, easing down to her lips, a soft kiss which grew more passionate.

"I think we might want to move to the bed," he murmured.

"I agree," she said.

Their lovemaking was slow, measured, and utterly exquisite. Afterward, they lay in each other's arms, drowsing.

"Amazing what a night's rest and a break can do," Gabe said finally. "Oh God, Rubes, this should have happened earlier."

"We've been on the run just trying to keep up with everything over the past five years," she sighed. "Mike. The Group. The other businesses. The ranch. The Family."

"We're taking time from now on. We have this house. Let's use it."

"Yes. Let's." She kissed him, then rolled away. "I'm starving. Time for breakfast!"

***

THEY HAD THREE MORE UTTERLY BLISSFUL DAYS SPENT READING, napping, and exploring the property.

"Need to have a handrail put in," Gabe muttered the first time they carefully edged their way down the narrow path to the small beach. "Among other things. This little trail needs a lot of work to make it safe. I'll call about it when we get back to the house. Schedule the work for after we leave."

But they reached the bottom and sat on the small sand strip for a while, leaning against each other.

And when they headed back to the Double R, stopping by Moondance to discuss business with Brandon besides picking up Mike, Ruby felt energized and able to handle the rest of the summer.

Especially since she now had escapes to the cliff house to anticipate.

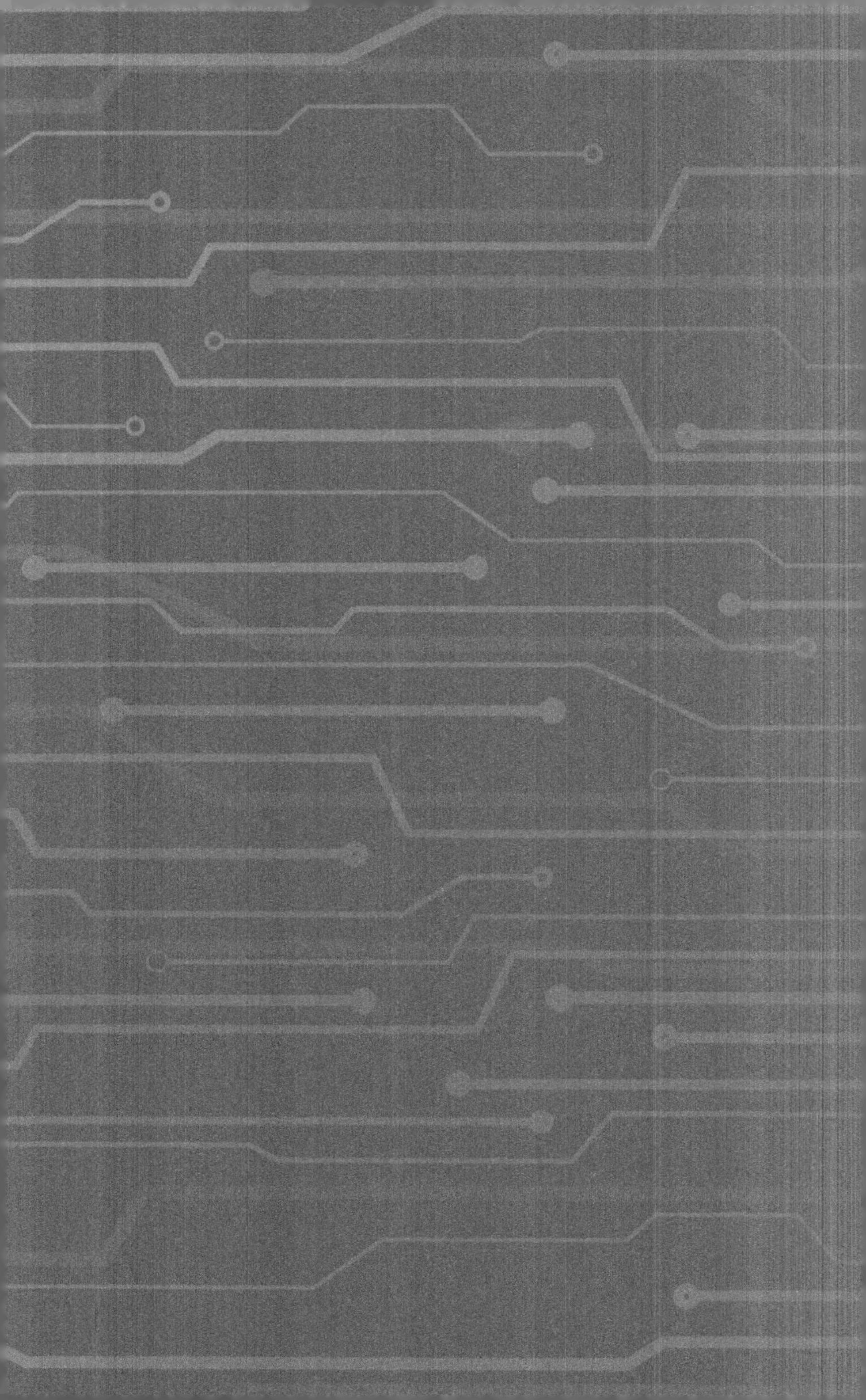

10 / MARIAH

GABE

"Dad, I need help." Brandon's expression in the projection was a mix of sadness, perplexity, and concern.

"What's happening?"

Nothing related to the Martiniere Group should be problematic. Quarterly reports were done. Financials looked good. As far as Gabe knew, there weren't any new contentious flares between Family branches. He had adjudicated a few and by now, the Family was well aware that the Martiniere Emeritus didn't tolerate petty power squabbles that did nothing but tear down the Family.

Personal, then. A problem with Lily or Kris? Or the upcoming election?

Kris *was* lending a hand with her sister Pat's presidential re-election race, but that should be under control.

Kris's continued poor health was troubling, but there wasn't much Gabe could do about that.

Lily—their granddaughter was a handful, and made him nervous at times. Something about her reminded Gabe of Philip.

But she was only four-and-a-half years old—too young to get into any major trouble.

Right?

"It's Mariah. She's in the hospital. Apparent suicide attempt, not expected to survive. Al is not taking it well."

Aw, shit.

Gabe tightened his lips. Mention of Mariah brought up too damned many memories, all bad.

"I didn't realize that Al was that close to his mother." Gabe tried to keep his voice neutral.

"Apparently he has been." Brandon rubbed his chin. "He reports contacts with her to me; that's been a criterion we set up shortly after I became the Martiniere. His idea. But this happened without warning." He winced. "Al was able to intercept a statement she made. It's not pretty."

"Of course." Like everything tied into Mariah. "How far did it spread?"

"Kris has it locked down, and Justine is investigating whether it truly came from Mariah."

"I hope you set parameters for your aunt Justine."

His sister had certain triggers that brought out a side of her all too much like their father. Gabe never understood exactly why Justine disliked Mariah so intensely. It went beyond Mariah's role in his divorce—something about the way Mariah had behaved toward Justine during her tenure as Philip's primary mistress?

Very possible.

Whatever it was, his sister hated Mariah with the same intensity that his wife did—and, a rarity for Justine, was not as good at concealing her feelings as Ruby. Then again, Mariah's demonstrated deep feelings for her son Alexander, oldest of the cyborg brothers, had gone a long way toward mellowing Ruby on the subject of Mariah. They might not be the best of friends, but Ruby and Mariah could be in the same room these days without arguments exploding.

Not true for Mariah and Justine.

"I know how Justine feels about Mariah," Brandon said. "Al needs onsite support as she passes, Dad. I can't give that to him as the Martiniere. Image. Can you—without getting Mom involved?"

"I can help. But—your mother will be involved," Gabe said firmly. "For my sake."

"Mom's presence may attract more attention than we want, given your past history with Mariah," Brandon cautioned.

"I need your mother there," Gabe insisted. "And considering our past—I wouldn't think of leaving her out of this situation. So where is Mariah, and where is Al?"

"I'll send you the hospital details as I have them," Brandon said. "Justine is moving Mariah to a private location—she ended up in an indigent facility. In Los Angeles. As for Al—he's ready to leave as soon as Justine gives us the details."

Gabe nodded. "All right. I'll get Mike and your mother ready, and talk to Justine so she knows we're coming in. Have Al wait for us to come to Moondance—I'd be more comfortable if Mike could stay with you, so we don't have to take him to LA."

"Not a problem," Brandon said. "I'll let Al know. Thanks, Dad."

"You're welcome." Gabe disconnected and rubbed his eyes, pinching the bridge of his nose as he exhaled.

God, Mariah, even in your dying you cause trouble.

Gabe leaned his head against his chair back, organizing his priorities.

Tell Ruby first.

Then Mike.

Get the travel packing started, and whatever actions need to be done to cover ranch operations for an indefinite period.

Call Justine, have her route the jet for Al to the Double R first to pick us up, then get her take on the situation.

He was damned sure there was some sort of situation, not just because it was Mariah but because she was in LA, not

Chicago. Mariah was *supposed* to be in Chicago. Her financial support from the Martiniere Family Trust was contingent on her *staying there*, away from the Family except at Christmas.

Mariah had probably gotten sucked into yet another misguided attempt at atonement for the things she had done as Philip's mistress. While Gabe hadn't investigated, he was certain that he wasn't her only victim.

He didn't really want to know about the others. Bad enough that Mariah had nearly landed in prison for her blockchain tracker scam—and he wondered how much of that situation Philip had engineered, so that he could keep Mariah on a hidden indenture contract.

———

RUBY'S LIPS TIGHTENED AFTER GABE TOLD HER.

"Do you know what her current condition is? Obviously bad, but is she coherent? At risk of dying before we get there? I'd like to know what we're facing."

Gabe shook his head. "I haven't called Justine yet. I wanted to ask you to come with me first. Then get Mike ready. I'm just —" he sighed. "Even in dying she causes trouble. I want you by my side because I—I need you. And Al needs you."

Ruby nodded. "I hadn't thought he was that close to her, but it's not been my concern."

"His mother, his business," Gabe agreed. "Al has been reporting contacts regularly to Bran. He says they're close."

"Give me half an hour to ensure that Terri has everything lined up for the third cutting of hay and for the grain harvest. Everything should be in good shape, but I want to be certain we're covered." Her mouth quirked. "We'll go to Justine's house?"

"Most likely. I don't know for how long yet. Bran's all right with Mike staying at Moondance."

"Good. He shouldn't be anywhere near Mariah." Ruby

scowled. "Too many traces of your father about her. She might be able to trigger some programming in him. After that incident with him and the mysteriously appearing clone file—I'd sooner err on the side of caution."

"Absolutely." Gabe came around her desk and leaned against it, taking her hands. "And Rubes—thank you for not making a scene about this situation. You would be justified if you did."

A quick smile crossed her lips, then faded. "There is one thing, Gabe."

"What's that?" He steeled himself, tightening his hands on hers, expecting a demand of some sort—not the usual thing from Ruby, but she was entitled.

"Bran's certain it was a suicide attempt, and not murder?"

The question took him by surprise, and yet—

"I plan to ask Justine for more information."

"Good." Ruby's lips tightened again. "Because of all the people who have suicidal tendencies? Mariah Meyers is one of the last people *I* would expect to exhibit them. Unless she tried something spectacular and it failed."

And there it was. Ruby articulating something that had been niggling at Gabe, as she so often did when he couldn't clarify a problem.

My beloved warrior wife.

"You're right," he said. "Why is she in LA? Why an indigent facility? She should have enough money to be comfortable in Chicago."

"Exactly," Ruby said. "There's more to this story than a suicide attempt, Gabe. I wonder how authentic that statement of hers is."

"THE STATEMENT DOESN'T RING TRUE TO ME," JUSTINE SAID WHEN Gabe called her to reroute the plane. "Current evidence suggests it's fake."

"How bad is Mariah?" Gabe asked.

Justine grimaced. "Fucking ugly. Poison. Maybe twenty-four hours before complete liver and kidney failure, and she's in bad health to begin with."

"Ruby and I are coming with Al."

"That's good. He'll need your support. She's still somewhat coherent part of the time, and knows that Al is on his way. She's asking for him."

"Do *you* think this was suicide?"

Justine paused, tapping her lips with her index fingers. "I don't know how much of what I'm seeing is caused by the poisons in her system and how much of it is mental deterioration. She took a mixture of acetaminophen, drain cleaner, and bleach."

"Aw, fuck." And deft avoidance of his question by his sister —which might be the answer he sought.

"I have questions. She rambles. God, Gabie. Yells at Daddy-damned-dearest's ghost. Rants about Georgy Batineau—and others."

"Including me?"

"No. Nothing about you, nothing about Ruby. However. There are ligature marks on her wrists."

"What the hell?"

"The owners of the complex where she was staying said she has—a certain reputation. Bondage. They thought she was a prostitute."

"Brandon said she was in an indigent facility."

"No evidence of an income," Justine said. "She was living in that complex for six months. It doesn't fit, Gabie. She should have had enough money to live in a better place, even in LA."

"And she has been drawing her money regularly from the Family Trust?"

"It appears she went back to Chicago monthly for the mandated inspections."

"This doesn't make sense."

"Neither does her alleged statement." Justine exhaled. "It's ugly. But—given her state of mind—I don't know for certain, Gabie."

Early-onset dementia?

Entirely possible. Or mind control gone awry—an ever-growing concern within the Family as their awareness grew about how those processes could go wrong over time. How much had Philip's programming twisted Mariah?

"We'll be there soon," Gabe said.

"Good."

UGLY WAS AN UNDERSTATEMENT. GABE WRAPPED ONE ARM TIGHTLY around Ruby's waist as Al bent over to talk to his mother. They stood with Justine, as far away as they could get and still be in the same room.

Al's time. Al's moment with his dying mother.

But God, the shape Mariah was in. She had always taken care of herself, maintained a high-end beauty regime. Now she was emaciated, skin sagging on her face and arms, and she appeared to be years older than Ruby, even though they were the same age. Her hair looked like it had been roughly hacked short with no regard to styling. *Not* the Mariah he had known.

An argument for mental deterioration? Dementia? Certainly. Now whether that was influenced by mind control programming or natural—he couldn't say.

But there was no mistaking the adoration in Mariah's expression as she gazed at her son. Alexander had been a means for Philip to keep control of her, until he sent partially-cyborged Al back to his mother, programmed to kill Mariah when triggered.

Gabe's lips tightened, remembering Mariah's words when pleading with Ruby to break Al's programming.

Destroying your marriage earned me a full week with Alexander. And that was when he finally called me Mama.

He shuddered. Yet another one of Philip's evil actions.

And once both she and Al were free of Philip, Mariah ended her old seductive habits.

At least that was what he had thought. Justine's report—raised questions.

Ruby's arm tightened around his waist. "You okay?" she whispered.

He nuzzled the top of her head. "Memories."

"Yeah." She bit her lip. "Me too."

Al straightened up. "Gabe?"

"Yeah."

"She wants to see you."

Another shudder. Ruby dropped her arm from around his waist. He took her hand, gently urging her to come along as he walked that ever-so-long-seeming distance toward Mariah's bed.

Up close, she looked even worse. Lips eaten away.

What the hell was in that mix?

He forced himself to meet her gaze.

"Gabe." He had to listen close. "Sorry. So sorry. Listen. Zing —" Her body convulsed as alarms went off. But her eyes remained fixed on him, even as medical staff pushed them away, then herded them out of the room.

"I heard you, Mariah," he said, raising his voice above the cacophony. "I heard you."

"Heard what?" Ruby asked, once they were in the hallway.

"Zing."

"Zingter?"

"I suspect so." He squeezed Ruby's hand, seeking comfort there, even as she frowned at him, a troubled expression crinkling her eyes.

That convulsion sure as hell looked like a block created by poorly-executed mind control programming. Justine had hinted just last month that an investigation of hers suggested Zingter Enterprises had accessed some of Philip Martiniere's secrets. But no definite information—yet. A project she was still working on.

Had Zingter accessed Philip's mind control programming records? Gabe wouldn't discount it.

We're looking at murder for certain, not suicide. Mariah, damn it, what the hell did you get yourself into?

And am I glad you blundered into this, before it blew up on us unexpectedly?

I'm not sure.

Mariah never regained consciousness. Al was the only one allowed back in with her once she was stable, and he sat with his mother for two hours before she died. Gabe held Ruby's hand as they sat in the waiting room, while Justine paced.

"We need to order an autopsy after she's dead," he said to Justine during one of the few moments she sat.

"You sure about that, Gabriel?"

"I'll fucking pay for it." He used the firm, hard tone that didn't allow for argument.

Justine nodded curtly, then started pacing again. "I'll make certain it happens, then, Gabriel."

"It's the right thing," Ruby said quietly. "I heard what she said, Gabe."

"If it's Braun—Tine, are *you* going to be able to manage this?"

"I *have* to be able to handle it, Gabriel." She shook her head. "We need to discuss this elsewhere."

"Understood." He tensed.

Did full-on, corporate war between the Group and Zingter Enterprises lie ahead?

Not something he would hand over to Brandon to control, unless forced.

But God, was he capable of managing what this corporate war might lead to, given his own health?

It's not Heaven's Reach, at least.

However, Terence Braun was twenty years younger than Gabe.

THEY BURIED MARIAH IN THE LOS ANGELES FAMILY PLOT, NEAR Philip and Joey's graves. Gabe and Ruby flanked Alexander at the simple graveside service. Afterwards, Gabe lay flowers at the graves of his mother, his sister, and Saul while Justine and Al left.

It still hurts.

He lingered by the graves. Ruby slid her arm around him, and he leaned on her.

"When it's time, do you want to be buried by them?" she asked.

"No," Gabe said. "I want to be buried wherever you are. You're my family now."

"The cemetery at the Double R, then."

He nodded. "I miss them. My life changed so much when they died. And yet—"

"We wouldn't have met if this hadn't happened."

"We *would* have," Gabe said. "Only I would have met you as Gabriel Martiniere, potential Martiniere-in-waiting, looking for talented bot developers to bolster my qualifications to succeed Saul as the Martiniere. Not as Gabe Ramirez, broke saddle bronc rider."

"You really think so?" Ruby looked up at him.

"One of your competition bots from high school caught Cousin Arthur's attention when I was interning in his agricultural technology division during my time at the University of Paris. If it hadn't been for Philip's insistence that I start work in the Los Angeles labs, and—my testimony in *US vs Martiniere Group*—I would have approached you during your junior year at Oregon State. Talked to you about considering a future with the Group. If Saul had survived, Philip's notions about women in positions of power wouldn't have dominated the Group, and the Martiniere Grant that died with Saul would have been available to you. Hell, I would have been the person interviewing you for it. I have no doubts that you would have become quite the force in the labs, even without our relationship. But I like to think we would have gotten together."

They stood silently, thinking about that possibility.

"That would have been a very different life," Ruby said finally. "But *that* Gabriel Martiniere would have married a high-society woman."

"Not likely," Gabe said. "I was pretty resistant to high society mamas throwing their daughters at me. I would have still won your heart. Even as Gabriel Martiniere, I had an eye for a brilliant, beautiful horsewoman who could hold her own with me in the labs. More so than yet another pretty face."

She chuckled. "Ah, Gabe. Lots of ifs, could-haves, would-haves, and should-haves."

"And that's one reason why I won't be buried here. Los Angeles is the Martiniere Group's past. Tied to Philip and his aspirations. The Double R and Moondance point to the future."

Ruby shook her head. "I'm amazed at that prospect."

He sighed. "And now it's time to think about that future."

THEY HELD THE WAR COUNCIL AT MOONDANCE THE DAY AFTER Mariah's funeral—Justine, Brandon, Gabe, Ruby, Serg, and Kevin Swait. It started in Brandon's office.

"The autopsy report supports our suspicion that Mariah's death was murder, not suicide," Justine said grimly. "I have staff working with the authorities, and made it known to them that the Martiniere Group is *very interested* in seeing Mariah's killers being brought to justice. Not that finding those people will finger the persons behind the scenes."

"What do we know about her activities in Los Angeles?" Brandon asked.

"She was seeing a lot of the Zingter principals in LA," Kevin Swait said.

"Define *seeing*," Gabe said.

"Apparently having sex with them," Justine said.

"The other piece is that we've made connections between her activities and Zingter indentureds disappearing over the border into Mexico," Serg said.

"So she was to trying to atone for her past. Once again." Gabe shook his head.

Justine raised her brows. "It's possible that she stumbled across this rather than deliberately sought it, Gabriel."

"Terence Braun could easily have targeted Mariah," Gabe said.

"Yes, Gabriel," Justine said. "Donald is doing *that* investigation through Rescue Angel. No results—yet."

Gabe leaned back in his chair, steepleing his fingers. "Bran. I can't dictate as the Martiniere Emeritus, but I can advise. Any actions that we take need to be kept separate from the Group."

He glanced at Ruby. She nodded. They had discussed this probability last night.

"Your mother and I are willing to take the lead on whatever results from Donald and Justine's investigations," he continued. "As the Martiniere Emeritus and the Matriarch."

"Family, and not the Group?" Brandon asked.

Gabe nodded. "This may not be a Group issue, but it *does* affect the Family. Mariah was one of ours, through Alexander. Therefore, she's Family. It will also be—cleaner for Pat's re-election campaign if you're not connected."

Brandon turned toward Justine. "Your opinion?"

"Speaking as the Director of Security, this is a preferred approach," she said. "And since my authority extends to the Family as well as the Group, I see no conflict in continuing this investigation under Gabriel's supervision."

"And as a representative of Swait Farms, because this impacts Barkley-Martiniere-Swait Associates, I see no conflict in assisting with this investigation," Kevin said. "Especially since indentured management may be involved."

"Good," Brandon said. "You'll keep me briefed about any problems, Dad?"

"Yes," Gabe said, taking Ruby's hand. "Serg, Justine, Kevin. Let's move out of Bran's office to make our plans."

Step one.

Donald met with Gabe, Ruby, Kevin, Serg, and Justine at the Double R that evening.

"Mariah had a definite pattern of contact with both Zingter principals and Zingter indentureds," Donald said. "It appears that one of the Zingter principals was working with her to move indentureds across the border to Mexico. And that Zingter principal is tied to Mariah's just-captured killers."

Gabe winced. "Mariah and this Zingter principal weren't going through the established indentured contract challenge protocols set up by the Markey Administration?"

"Some contracts slide through the challenges," Kevin said. "Usually the sleaziest ones that end up being hard to break."

"The contract challenge piece matters, but what's more important is the Zingter principal who was Mariah's primary contact for moving indentureds, and who has also been connected to Mariah's killers," Donald said. "Terence's daughter Natalie. She has approached the Rescue Angel before, wanting to be involved."

"Natalie—Weimer?" Kevin asked. "Is that who you're talking about?"

"Natalie Braun-Weimer, yes," Donald said. "She used the Braun name in approaching us."

"Weimer in her contacts with Swait Secure," Kevin said. "Blatant, with no subtlety. There's no way I'd incorporate her into anything confidential. Our assessment was that she was a crude attempt to infiltrate our organization."

"The same here, yes," Donald said. "I sent out warnings to all my people to avoid anything but the most superficial connections."

"So why would she use Braun in approaching Rescue Angel, but Weimer with Swait Secure?" Justine rested her chin on her clasped hands. "Braun would be a major red flag for both me and Donald—the connection is well-known."

"She didn't strike me as the brightest person in the world." Kevin grimaced. "It's a cliché to talk about the *clueless rich white girl*, but that's exactly how this woman came across to me. And she was racist as fuck."

"How old is she?" Ruby asked.

Justine flicked her a file. "Here's the details."

Gabe rolled his chair over to scan the file along with Ruby.

"She's young," he said, thinking out loud. "Barely in her twenties. That could explain some of the lack of subtlety. Especially if Terence and his father Frank followed Walter's pattern in dealing with women of their family. Keep them pregnant, keep them confined, don't educate them."

That brought him a hard scowl from Justine. "I understand *that*, Gabriel. It would fit how Zingter handles their indentured contracts, and Terence's role in taking over our father's political positions. *But*—" she stabbed at the air with an index finger. "Unless Mariah was in cognitive decline, she'd also see the red flags in Natalie Braun-Weimer's behavior. I can't believe that she would be that naïve on purpose."

"Mariah may have seen the red flags, and thought that she might be able to expose something involving Zingter." Ruby frowned. "Gabe, did you notice this piece?" She highlighted a section of the file. "Who Natalie's husband is? His connections? There's something hinky here."

Gabe brought it up. "Berendt Weimer is a minor

programmer in the Zingter labs. They married when they were seventeen and they're both twenty—you're right, they're both too young to have the degree of responsibility their bios claim. Not even Mike would be working at this level in the labs when he reaches that age and he's a fucking genius—" He pulled up Weimer's picture and data. Inhaled sharply. "Oh *fucking hell.* Weimer's father Reinhard works in regenerative organ cloning. For Zingter."

He skimmed the files. Where was a picture of Walter Braun at Berendt's age?

There. He exhaled with relief. Significant difference between the two. All the same, he flipped through other pictures of Terence Braun, and Reinhard Weimer.

Not a clone.

But still—he took another hard look at Natalie Braun-Weimer, just in case. Something about her looked familiar.

And then it struck him. He pulled up a picture of Natalie's mother Mathilde. No. Terence's mother Katrin. Not quite.

"Gabe, what is it?" Ruby asked.

He ignored her, frantically searching for a picture of his sister at the same age.

It hit like he'd been kicked in the gut when he found the picture and flicked it up for all to see. *"Tine. Donald."*

"What—" Justine gasped at the two pictures. "How the *hell*?"

"There were twelve clones before Mike," Gabe said harshly. "He's almost ten years old. Braun-Weimer's ten years older than Mike. How many clones a year did Philip create?"

Donald joined them. "Clone, or cosmetic surgery?"

"Why would they do cosmetic surgery?" Justine asked. "Walter Braun died before we divorced, dear. Terence would have been a baby then, and he wouldn't have an interest in replicating *me.* Would he?" She tapped her chin, voice going cold and hard when she spoke again. "And just how the hell would they get their hands on my genome? To my knowledge, I've never had it charted."

Donald expanded the pictures. "It's not a clone, dear falcon. Small differences. Look at the nose."

"She didn't go through abuse." Justine absently touched her nose where Philip had broken it when she was fifteen.

"Shade of eye color. *That* won't be affected by surgery or beatings." Donald snapped up pictures of Mike and Philip at age ten. "Look at Mike and Philip. Much more congruence." He frowned. "But I should have seen a resemblance between her and you, dear one."

"Not a clone but genetic manipulation," Ruby said. "We need a sample to confirm it, but if they were able to get their hands on some of Philip's genetic material, then that could account for the resemblance. Or your genetic material, Justine."

"It would have needed to be before 2044 if they were using mine." Justine tapped her chin again. "Could they—no. I became Director of Security in March of 2044. Plenty of access for a sample, but not enough time to create Braun-Weimer."

"There *is* the incident of 2037," Donald said. "When Hallock broke your thumb while you were downloading the data about the Electric Born and Heaven's Reach. Let me call up your treatment records, see if it would be at all possible for Greg Hallock to have taken a sample during *that* blowup."

"How would he have carried it?" Serg spoke up for the first time. "I made certain that Hallock was clear before I took him to my father for a memory wipe."

"Eliminate that possibility? I still want to keep it on the table, but—" Justine's voice trailed off as she studied the larger pictures of her and Natalie Braun-Weimer. "I think you're right, Ruby. Genetic engineering. But why try to duplicate me?"

Gabe exchanged a glance with Ruby, thinking about that file describing Mike's cloning that had popped up out of nowhere in July.

He lifted a brow and raised his chin. Mike was upstairs at the moment.

Ruby's brow raise matched his. She glanced up, and nodded.

Then she pursed her lips thoughtfully. She rolled her lips into a tight line and nodded again, sharper than before.

"It could be an attempt to hack your biometric accesses, Justine," she said. "I don't know if the difference in eye color could throw things off but—if it's close enough otherwise—" Her voice trailed off.

Now it was Justine and Donald's turn to exchange glances and expressions.

"I'll take care of it," Donald said. "I can refine your accesses to avoid potential security breaches, my dear."

"Nothing says that the genetic manipulation was successful," Ruby said. "It may be an ongoing project."

"So why was she working with Mariah? Is this a trap?" Gabe decided to shift the discussion.

"That's a good question," Donald said. "Clearly we're not going to know the answer to that until we talk to Natalie Braun-Weimer ourselves."

"I'm working on that even as we speak," Justine said.

***

STEP TWO.

"Where do you want to interrogate Braun-Weimer?" Justine asked the next morning, as Gabe came into the Double R's kitchen. She was settled into her favorite workspace at the ranch, the green Formica and chrome kitchen table.

"You've run her down already?" Gabe poured himself a cup of coffee.

"In the custody of JSM Corp operatives, supervised by Shanice," Justine said. "Just need to tell them where she goes."

Gabe sat across from her. "Ruby will be down in a minute. Let's ask her what she thinks. I'm inclined to bring her here, but only after she's been scanned for tracking devices. Still. Ruby's property. Ruby's call."

There *was* the cliff house on the coast. But it wasn't as isolated as the Double R, and it wasn't set up to receive direct transport of someone in custody. And taking Braun-Weimer to Moondance would defeat the purpose of keeping this action separate from Brandon.

"What's my call?" Ruby entered the kitchen, heading for the coffeepot.

"We have Braun-Weimer," Gabe said. "Do we question her here—or somewhere else? Where is she now, Justine?" That might give them a third option.

"Chicago."

Then no, nothing there. Bran and Kris had a condo in Chicago, but again—that brought them into this mess.

Ruby leaned against the counter, sipping from her coffee. "Can't do Donald's Nameless Island because that's taking her out of the country. Don't think we should do it in Los Angeles or any of the other big cities where we have facilities, for security reasons and avoiding snoopy authorities. Don't want to do it at the cliff house." She sighed. "So. Here. Not really a choice."

"I'm sorry," he said. "I promised you we wouldn't do much Martiniere business at the Double R."

She shrugged. "Family business, Gabe. It makes sense." Her voice hardened. "Besides, we have secure lab facilities on site. We can answer the question of cloning versus genetic engineering very easily, and if she thinks she wants to take off? Easily discovered and captured."

"All right," Justine said. "Sending the message now." She tapped on her virtual keyboard, then dismissed it, grabbing her coffee mug. "She'll be here in two hours."

Step Three.

The minute Gabe set eyes on Natalie Braun-Weimer, he knew she wasn't Justine's clone. Braun-Weimer was shorter and heavier-boned.

But that face—even though Braun-Weimer carried more weight than his sister, it was a close facsimile.

"About fucking time," Braun-Weimer snarled as she faced Gabe and Ruby with Shanice L'Étoile, Justine's security chief, standing close by. "You keep yourself pretty well isolated, *Gabriel Martiniere*." Her face shifted slightly, more than just the normal play of muscles. Gabe tensed, uneasiness pulsing through him. L'Étoile edged even closer to her.

"I have my reasons." He kept his voice unreactive and flat.

"It shouldn't have taken Mariah Meyers's death to bring you out," she said.

"So what do you know about that?" Ruby asked.

Instinct made Gabe grab Ruby and spin her away just before Braun-Weimer spat.

"Kiss Protocol!" he bellowed. Oh God, had she infected Justine's people? Damn it, *that meant Heaven's Reach was involved!*

No, thank God, they were all gloved. But not masked—*shit.* Wait.

L'Étoile yanked a membrane over Braun-Weimer's face. "Second layer, everyone!" she yelled. "We engaged Kiss Protocol from the beginning, sir. Orders."

"I suspected this likelihood, Gabriel," Justine said. "And protection against all contaminants—including the Kiss from Heaven's Reach—is standard protocol for my security. It's a transparent membrane."

"Take her to the labs and start running checks," Gabe said grimly. "We're not going to get anything useful out of her for at least another six hours." Depending on when she'd been injected with the Kiss, of course—so two hours plus however long Justine's people had Braun-Weimer in their custody—was this the twelve hour or the twenty-four-hour version?

And damn it, why weren't Ruby and I given those protective membranes?

As L'Étoile and her staff herded Braun-Weimer toward the

labs, Gabe let himself start trembling. If he hadn't been aware of that subtle facial movement—oh dear God, *Ruby*—

"Gabe. Gabe. I'm all right." Ruby's voice quavered. She had also read about the effects of the Kiss potion developed by Heaven's Reach—he'd handed her the file about Kiss effects and protective measures himself after they remarried, *just in case.* Now Gabe was glad he'd done that. She knew the risk.

He enfolded Ruby in his arms, holding her tight.

Heaven's Reach allied with Zingter. Definitely a worst nightmare scenario.

Oh God, if Ruby—

No. He didn't want to go there. Even in his imagination.

Six hours later, Gabe still seethed in his office. The one thing that kept him from raging around the house in sheer terror was that he had called Dr. Sheri a couple of hours ago about a supplemental anti-anxiety dosage and taken it. The med kept his fury distanced, something he could observe objectively instead of letting it ride him.

Philip in me, damn it. My fucking sperm donor's legacy.

But still. Zingter was allied with Heaven's Reach. That meant a connection with the Electric Born as well. So what role did Braun-Weimer play in all of this, and how did it relate to Mariah?

Answers. He wanted answers, damn it. L'Étoile had messaged Justine that they could talk to Braun-Weimer now. Ruby and Justine were down there with Kevin and Serg.

Not you as well, Ruby had said firmly. *If we find a reason for her to talk to you, then yes. You may be her target.*

And he couldn't argue with that.

His comm chimed. *"Terence Braun."*

The motherfucker himself. He must have finally discovered that his daughter was in Gabe's custody. Gabe took a deep breath, wishing now that his anger wasn't distanced. This conversation called for a full Philip-esque tantrum.

On the other hand, you've experienced enough of them that you could easily replicate one of your sperm donor's meltdowns.

Gabe snapped his comm open. "So what do you want, Braun?"

Braun glowered at him. "You have my daughter."

"She's a person of interest in the death of a *Family* member." Gabe steepled his fingers as he glared at Braun, stressing *Family* hard enough to impress upon Braun that he'd fucked around with the Martinieres and crossed a line. "Furthermore, it appears that she's been gene-modified using Martiniere proprietary cell lines."

That kept the authorities off of their backs—Beck O'Toole had been able to identify gene mods in Braun-Weimer that *did* originate from Justine's cells. That finding made this Martiniere business, and not something that law enforcement agencies wanted to touch with a ten-foot-pole.

Legacy of the aftermath of *US vs Martiniere Group,* and multiple Supreme Court rulings that gave Philip free rein to do as he damned well pleased when it came to genetic engineering —at least in the United States. Gabe had been working to change that legal situation—but right now, he was glad those structures were still in place.

"You have evidence?"

Gabe bared his teeth at Braun. "Right here." He flicked over the file that Beck had sent him shortly after she performed a genetic quickscan as well as identified the strain of Kiss potion in Braun-Weimer. "You've got some nerve to use my sister's cells."

Braun skimmed through the file. "Not something I was aware of." He shrugged.

"Are you calling me a liar?" Gabe's voice went quiet and cold.

None of this fit, damn it, unless Mariah had been set up to lure him into—*something.*

"It's been done since she married Weimer. Who knows what her father-in-law's been up to?"

"My understanding is that Reinhard Weimer works for *you*. In *your* labs. Are you telling me you don't have control over a middle-level *cloning expert*?"

Braun exhaled through bared teeth. "I want her back."

"I want to know what the hell she was doing with Mariah Meyers. Along with Reinhard Weimer, Berendt Weimer, and five other Zingter principals linked to Meyers's activities in Los Angeles."

"Then why don't you—"

Gabe's office door slammed open. Ruby marched in, followed by Justine.

"*You!*" Ruby yelled at Braun, pointing at his projection. "You motherfucker! To do that to your *own daughter!* I thought Philip Martiniere was bad, but damn you—"

Gabe quickly surveyed his wife and his sister. They were *pissed*, the sort of deeply-rooted fury that would make *him* back down.

Something more than the use of Justine's cells had happened. Something more than administering the Kiss.

"My father was an evil son-of-a-bitch," Justine snapped. "But he never went so far as destroying the brains of his children."

"What the—?" A chill ran down Gabe's back. Physical—or mind control programming?

Fuck. How much of the Martiniere mind control programming does Braun know?

Damn it, this *was* verging upon Martiniere Group involvement.

"Can't you control *your women*, Martiniere?" Braun taunted.

Ruby rubbed her ring and pointed her left index finger at Braun's projection, straightening up and somehow making her lanky figure seem larger and looming.

Fuck. I'd forgotten that Donna-gran taught Ruby how to project command codes over comms using her ring.

"I am *my own woman*, Terence Braun," she said, her voice cold, hard, and just *loaded* with Martiniere command tones. "Unlike your unfortunate child who has been effectively lobotomized through mind control programming. Not to speak of the fucking genetic engineering that made her vulnerable to it!"

Braun flinched back. "You—you can't be serious."

Another rub of her ring. "Was it you who approved it? Had to be, as deep as the programming goes."

"You—you don't know that," Braun blubbered.

"*Like hell.*" Ruby dropped her hands and clenched her fists. "*I am the Matriarch of the fucking Martinieres, damn it. Donna Martiniere taught me the deep secrets of the Martiniere mind control programming before her death. Serg Vygotsky was trained by his father Piotr. My sister-in-law also knows these techniques. We all agree. Natalie Braun-Weimer has been subjected to deep mind control programming, poorly executed in combination with gene mods to the degree that she has been functionally lobotomized. So tell me. Who approved it?*"

Braun's eyes bulged. "My—my father with my help when she was twelve." His words came out slow, forced. "But—but this wasn't supposed to be the result!"

"A Martiniere Family connection is dead. Your daughter is intimately connected with that person's killers. Triggers tied to their apprehension and then our interrogation of her instigated a cascade of flawed mind control programming that left *your daughter* at the cognitive level of a four-year-old," Justine snapped.

At least Braun paled at Justine's words. *At least.* Gabe's stomach churned.

"That can't—no, that wasn't supposed to happen," Braun blubbered. "I swear it wasn't supposed to happen. Isn't there something you can do?"

"Thanks to the coupling of mind control programming with the gene mods, no," Ruby snarled. She rubbed her ring again. "Now. Tell me where it was done."

"I-I-I—"

"Tell me *where it was done.*" Ruby stepped closer to the projection.

Justine crossed the room and handed Gabe a pair of ear filters. She leaned over and whispered, "Put these in, *now.*" She did the same with another pair.

Gabe shakily complied.

He couldn't hear what Ruby was saying, but by the time she finished, Braun was a gibbering, drooling, mess.

However, Ruby had coordinates that she flicked to Justine.

Gabe noticed that Justine waited to remove the ear filters until Braun's projection winked out.

"*There,*" Ruby growled. "That son-of-a-bitch is *fried.* How soon can we go after the motherfuckers who did this, Justine?"

"Getting it together now."

"I'm going to be part of it," Gabe said.

"As am I," Ruby said. "*God.* That poor girl." She stormed out.

Gabe eyed his sister. "I didn't realize Ruby's tones were that powerful."

"Donna-gran gave Ruby the full training that she wouldn't allow me to have. And, apparently, Ruby's aptitude for tone usage is higher even than Donna-gran's."

"Can we save the kid? How bad is it?"

Justine exhaled. "It looks like they may have done the same thing to both Braun and his daughter, judging from his reaction. Ruby only used a quarter of—*that*—strength on Natalie and she —God, Gabie, it was horrible. The impact not only on the kid but on me." She shook her head. "I've called in a specialist to see if we can help Natalie. But there's not a lot of hope. Serg—he had to puke afterward. Awful. Just fucking horrendous. I *hope* Ruby did the same damn thing to Braun, only more so."

"I'd better go find her." He *knew* what executing this action must have done to his darling.

"Yeah," Justine said.

Gabe hurried out of his office. Mike was upstairs so no, she wouldn't retreat to their bedroom.

Barn. Horses.

Legacy was in a pen by the barn, with this year's foal, Heritage, preparing for weaning. Ruby would turn to Legacy for comfort.

He strode to Legacy's pen.

Ruby sobbed into the golden mare's withers. Legacy's chestnut filly nuzzled Ruby's back as Legacy wrapped her head and neck around Ruby. Gabe gently rested a hand on Ruby's shoulder.

"Rubes. I'm here."

She turned from Legacy to throw herself against his chest, wailing. Gabe held Ruby as both Legacy and Herrie stayed close, mare and filly continuing to brush their noses against Ruby's back.

Ruby raised her head, gulping. "Damn it, Gabe. I *did not* want to hurt her like that! God damn it! Damn those sick fucks that programmed her—" She gulped again. "And I *enjoyed* destroying him! What have I become?"

"A Martiniere," he said bleakly. "Completely so. But better you did this than us having to hunt him down and kill him. Because that would be what needed to happen. *Fuck.*" Gabe paused. "Are you sure you want to participate in destroying the labs where this was done? It is damned likely to become another bloody mess. Like the original Heaven's Reach action."

"I want them gone, Gabe. I want them eliminated off the face of this earth." Ruby wiped away her tears. "And if my vocal tones can help us at all—" she swallowed hard. "But when it's done? I want to spend several days in the cliff house. Just us. Alone. Because God—coming to terms with it—with *myself*—I can't think about it now. But I will need to do that afterward."

"I understand," he said. "Completely."

Even his warrior wife had her limits. Thank God for that.

Taking care of Braun's illicit labs connected to Heaven's Reach wasn't *quite* as bad as cleaning Heaven's Reach out of North Fork. Gabe personally ensured that Justine's cell copies and every record on that damned site were eradicated. He sent copies of the files to Donald for analysis. Those files were safe with Donald, safer even than with Justine.

Gabe let Justine and Brandon deal with the political fallout from Zingter and the incapacitation of Terence Braun and Natalie Braun-Weimer. He and Ruby led the destruction of the labs.

Delegation of responsibility.

Both Reinhard Weimer and Berendt Weimer died along with others at the source lab when drones destroyed it. Shrapnel from one explosion clobbered Gabe's right thigh—not bad enough to break through his protective armor, but enough to leave him sore and hobbling.

A price to be paid.

Ruby was at his side the whole time, at least.

And when the damned bloody mess was finished, Gabe and *this* wife, his *warrior wife*, went to the cliff house.

They spent the first day sitting together on the deck overlooking the Pacific. Neither able to pick up a book, watch vids, or anything else to distract from the memories of destroying the labs.

Neither able to keep even the slightest bit of food down without vomiting.

Just listen to the ocean and the cries of seagulls, arms around each other.

And drink bourbon straight from the bottle, puking it up before drinking more. But alcohol brought the shadows into sharper focus, instead of blurring them.

It still felt good to do.

Ruby cried multiple times. Sometimes she swore and raged, beating on Gabe's chest.

He didn't resist.

Their sleep that night was troubled, one or the other waking up screaming from nightmares.

When they *could* sleep.

A price to be paid.

———

THE SECOND DAY WAS BETTER.

Both of them were able to eat small amounts without puking, and they didn't touch the remaining unopened bottles of bourbon in the liquor cabinet.

Gabe coaxed Ruby into the hot tub.

This hadn't been what he had in mind when he bought this house as a retreat, but God, now he was grateful they had it.

———

BY THE THIRD DAY, THEY MADE LOVE.

The steady thunder of the ocean waves against the small sandy beach at the bottom of the cliff soothed both of them. They didn't venture down the narrow cliff trail this visit. Just hearing the faint roar of the ocean mixed with seagull cries was enough.

———

"ARE YOU READY TO GO BACK?" GABE ASKED RUBY ON THE FOURTH day, as they sat on the deck, Ruby in his lap. A soft autumn drizzle mixed with fog muffled the sound of gulls and ocean waves.

"I don't know. I didn't think I was capable of doing things like this," Ruby said. "Breaking people like I did Terence Braun.

Killing—" Her voice cracked. "But it had to be done. I just—if we didn't, what would they do to Mike? To Lily?"

"I know," he murmured.

"Better we did it ourselves rather than handing it off to others," she said. "Oh God, Gabe, the nightmares. Now I understand why you had so many of them when we got back together."

"I wish I could have spared you this," he said. "The price of being a Martiniere."

"But it would have meant life without you," she said. "I—don't think I could have tolerated that." She choked. "Twenty-one years apart was bad enough. So yes. Even if I had known about—this—I don't regret it. Not one bit."

He nuzzled the top of her head, unable to speak as he held her tight.

THEY RETURNED TO THE DOUBLE R ON THE FIFTH DAY, MORE OR LESS patched together and ready to face whatever came next.

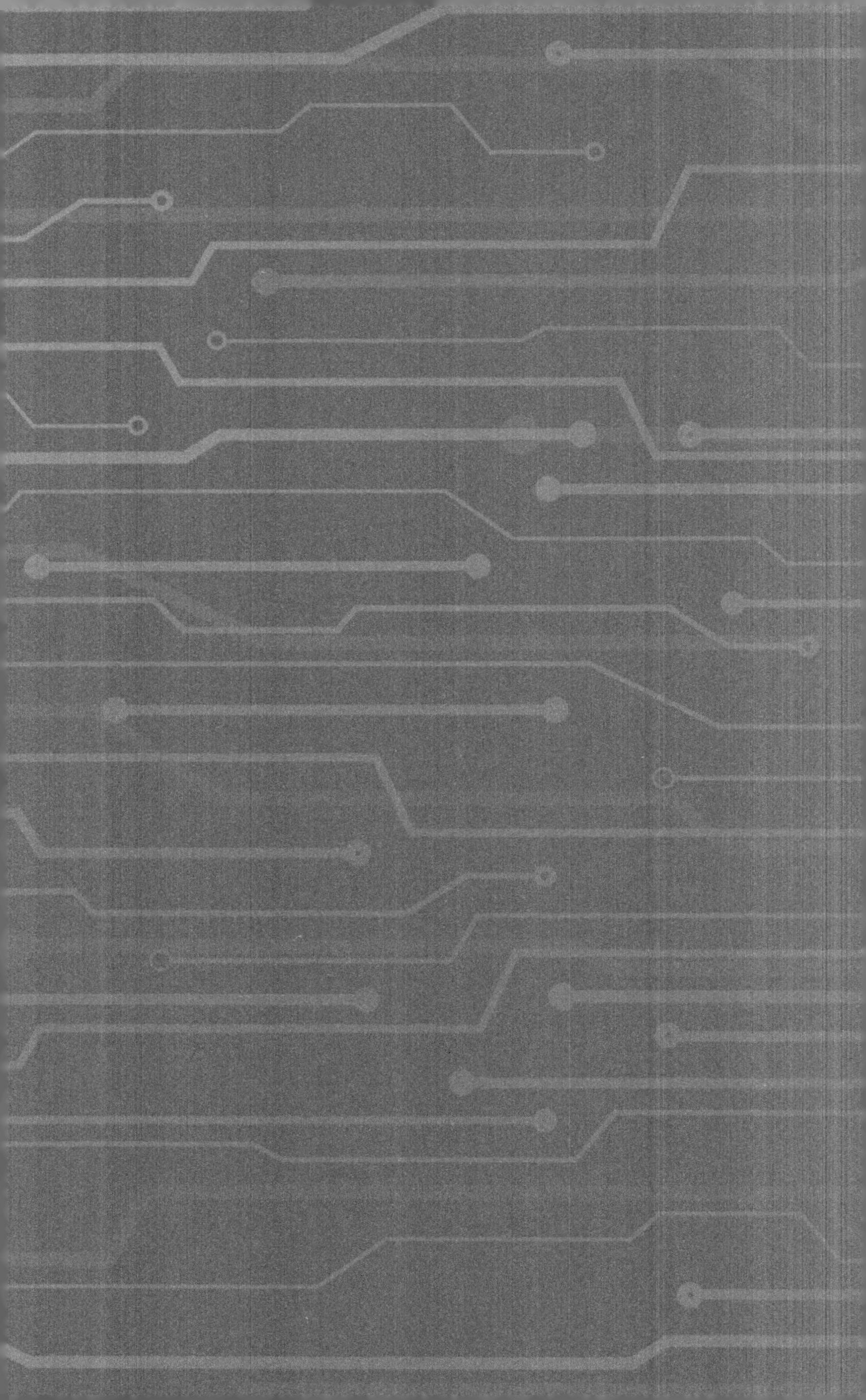

RUBY

AS IF EVERYTHING ELSE WASN'T ENOUGH....

Ruby scurried through the hospital hallways, heading for the obstetric surgery unit in Portland's University Hospital. Gabe was back home with Mike. After yet another *weird* unexplained file appearance, this time Gabe's old *whatthehell* file that chronicled everything that Philip had done to him—she and Gabe had decided it wasn't a good idea to leave Mike with non-Family supervision. Mike hadn't melted down about the *whatthehell* file, but considering that damned worm they only remembered part of the time, and everything else—best Mike had a close Family member around. Just in case.

Which made things tough when Kris miscarried—*again*. It was clear from Brandon's tone when he called to tell them about Kris that he desperately needed support. Help with Lily. And Mike didn't need to be a part of this, especially since *doctors* and *hospitals* were involved—same for Gabe, who was as skittish as Mike about medical situations.

That meant she was the one available to help Brandon.

Parenting never really ends.

Ruby screeched to a halt when she saw the appropriate signage, then went through the sliding doors of the obstetrics wing. Brandon sat in the waiting room, trying to read to a squirming Lily.

Lily saw her first. "Grandma!" She twisted away from Brandon and ran to Ruby, wrapping her arms around Ruby's waist—Lily was going to be tall, like Ruby and Gabe, not like Bran and Kris, both of whom were shorter.

Ruby held her seven-year-old granddaughter tight with one arm as Lily sniffled into her belly. Brandon put his tablet aside with a relieved sigh and stood. Ruby raised her other arm to him, and he joined them in the hug.

"Mama was bleeding *bad*," Lily murmured. "And they won't let me see her!"

"She's not out of surgery yet." Brandon's voice caught. "That's why you can't see her, Lily-hon."

Surgery. Hysterectomy? Oh God, that means just Lily for the next generation, means the Martiniere leadership may pass out of this branch of the Family. Unless Mike....

No. She and Gabe agreed about that. Mike was *not* in line to become the Martiniere, at least as long as they had a say in the situation. It wasn't fair to him. Not with his heritage and his shadows.

She raised her brows at Brandon and mouthed the word *hysterectomy*.

Brandon shook his head. "D and C. So far." He exhaled. "Hydatidiform mole, not so bad as to require—that." His mouth tightened. "It's taking longer than they said it would. And they wouldn't touch it in Pendleton or Walla Walla. I'm worried."

Ruby winced.

Hydatidiform mole.

Years ago, early in her marriage to Donald, Justine had a pregnancy become a hydatidiform mole, growing into uterine tissue, bad enough to require a hysterectomy. Justine rarely talked about it unless she had been drinking heavily, and even then, she didn't say much. Her hysterectomy had put Justine in the position where, even though she was a woman, Philip considered her capable of working in a responsible role in the Martiniere Group.

As always with Ruby's dead, woman-hating father-in-law, that responsibility came with a price. Bran and Kris had been around for at least one drinking session where Justine ranted about the degree to which Philip taunted her about *no longer being a real woman* after her hysterectomy. Repeatedly and continuously, up until his death.

So *hydatidiform mole* was a touchy subject amongst close family. That it had struck again was worrisome—Ruby hadn't told anyone, not even Gabe, that her miscarriage during their divorce had also been a hydatidiform mole, not severe enough for a hysterectomy.

Until their remarriage, she hadn't thought much about it.

This made three separate occurrences in their close family. No logical connection, and yet it was a shadow that stalked the Family. At least their branch of it.

Fucking Philip Martiniere. If I didn't know better, I'd say it was a curse he put on us.

"Oh, Bran." Ruby wanted desperately to talk to her son, to reassure him that Lily would be enough. She and Gabe didn't need a passel of grandchildren. But it wasn't something to discuss in front of her young granddaughter.

He exhaled. "If Kris didn't want to keep trying, I'd—" His voice trailed off. "And I *won't* sneak a vasectomy past her. Not fair considering—everything—her past—"

"I wouldn't push her into accepting it," Ruby said. Too much had been done to Kris when she had been an indentured worker with no control over her own body.

But it *had* been one thing after another for Kris since Lily's premature birth after a difficult pregnancy. Multiple miscarriages. And Lily had issues that concerned Gabe and Justine, not to speak of Gabe's uncle Gerard and the other Martinieres who remembered Philip as a child. Philip's great-granddaughter exhibited behaviors too close to his at the same age, and *everyone* worried about that.

Behaviors that Mike, as *his* clone, should have manifested—but didn't.

The quick, uncertain temper. Irrational explosions that didn't seem right for a child her age. References to *voices* that didn't fit the fancies of a young child. An obsession with Mike which led to behaviors that, again, didn't fit a child Lily's age.

Maybe Lily will grow out of it, or maybe we'll find the right medication to keep her from going down Philip's pathway.

Right now, the behavior of the lovely child crying into Ruby's belly was completely normal for a little girl whose beloved mama was undergoing surgery. So perhaps there was hope.

Brandon leaned his head into Ruby's shoulder. Not quite like Gabe did, but very similar. Ruby held steady, comforting her son and her granddaughter, stroking their backs. Doing her best to be the *one who was reliably there* for her family, just as her grandmother had been there for Ruby and her grandfather.

"Justine should be here soon," Brandon choked into her shoulder. "Should I tell her what's going on?"

"Yes. She can give you better advice than I'll be able to do."

Besides her own case, Justine had run into other instances of hydatidiform mole while working with the Rescue Angel operation. Ruby had heard *those* stories as well, when Justine was drinking hard and haunted by shadows of her past. Those sessions usually just included the two of them, no women of reproductive age or men around to hear the horror stories of pregnancy gone wrong and botched abortion attempts.

So many ways for a pregnancy to turn problematic. *Too* damn many ways.

Justine hurried into the waiting area. Ruby heaved a relieved sigh. Brandon pulled away from her and spoke quietly to Justine —who blanched. Then they joined Ruby and Lily. Justine rubbed Lily's back and Lily raised her head.

"Auntie Justine."

"Lily-hon." Justine took Lily's chin in one hand and brushed away the tears running down Lily's cheeks with her other. "Your mama will be all right. I've seen these situations before. They look awful and scary. But they really aren't, especially because of our money. We can buy the help your mama needs, not like other people can." She swallowed hard "It's when people don't have money that it's a problem. Understand?"

"Uh-huh."

"Donald's Portland condo is available for us to use," Justine continued, releasing Lily's chin. "He'll be here as soon as he can, to help with logistics if necessary."

"Thanks, Justine," Brandon said.

"Meanwhile, maybe Ruby or I ought to take Lily to the condo, hmm? No need for all of us to hang out here, and I'm sure Lily would prefer to be somewhere else."

Lily stuck out her lower lip. "Don't wanna go until Mama's okay."

"Honey, there's nothing here for you to do," Brandon said, a tired note in his voice. "Maybe you can swim at the condo's pool. Or someone can take you to a dance class?"

Ruby recognized her cue. "I'll set that up."

"But I don't have my special slippers," Lily grumbled.

"We can get some on the way to the condo," Ruby promised. "Slippers, leotard, tights—everything."

"Will they have slippers in my skin color? The slippers won't be broken in. And Mama can't sew my elastics."

"A Portland dance supply store will have slippers in your size and skin color. You go through plenty of slippers, so you might as well break these in," Ruby reminded Lily. "As for the elastics, I'm perfectly capable of taking care of those—though it's about time you learned to do that for yourself, don't you think?"

"You'll show me?" Lily's mood switched abruptly.

"Yes," Ruby said. "I may not be a dancer, but I can cut and sew elastic. You'll have to figure out where we place them. You can do that, right?"

"Right."

"Ruby, I'm messaging you the condo codes," Justine said.

"Thanks. All right, Lily, let's go," Ruby said. "We can pick up dance supplies on the way to the condo, and I'll track down a class or two for you, all right?"

"Yay!" Lily bounced on her toes.

Thank you, Brandon mouthed, before Ruby put an arm around her granddaughter's shoulders and guided her out of the waiting room.

Ruby's heart ached for her son and daughter-in-law as she and Lily went to the waiting car.

Couldn't Brandon and Kris have this one little thing go right? If they couldn't have another child, couldn't Lily turn out to have escaped Philip's far-too-long shadow in their lives?

This was one legacy that she and Gabe *couldn't* repair.

THE BALLET SCHOOL WAS *MORE* THAN HAPPY TO SCHEDULE LILY into classes. Two years ago, Lily's ballet teachers in Pendleton and Walla Walla had recommended that she try out for the Nutcracker in Portland, and Lily had earned a role as one of the second act angels, repeated last year. This year, she aspired to dance as either one of the party attendees, or Marie (or was it Clara? Ruby could never keep the different roles straight, as one version the company performed called the main female child lead Marie, and the other one called her Clara).

But Martiniere donations and sponsorships didn't hurt Lily's chances for a prime Nutcracker role, either. And they made it easy to slide Lily into classes whenever she was in Portland.

They had just enough time to pick up appropriate brown

slippers, tights, and leotard as well as Lily's preferred purple leg warmers from a dance supply store, then sew the elastics in before Lily's first class. Ruby was grateful that a sewing kit was one of the things she always, *always*, slipped into her bag when traveling—a habit carried over from rodeo queen days. She was finishing up securing Lily's hair—another thing to be thankful for was the time spent with Kris learning how to do Lily's hair *right*—when Justine arrived at the condo.

"Is Mama okay?" were the first words out of Lily's mouth. She jerked toward Justine. "Where's Daddy?"

"Hold still," Ruby murmured. "This old white lady still isn't as good at Black hair as your mama." She secured the last strands of Lily's beautiful dark hair into the single bun that Lily preferred for her classes, as opposed to the three buns that Kris usually put into Lily's hair.

Justine dropped onto the couch. "Your mama is all right, Lily. Your father stayed at the hospital so she's not alone. He'll be back in time for dinner." A pause, then she continued. "Your mama will be discharged tomorrow afternoon."

Ruby silently sagged with relief and stood up. "We're just heading out for Lily's dance class. We'll stop at the grocery on the way back and pick up dinner."

"Are you going to watch my class along with Grandma, Auntie Justine? Please?"

Justine exchanged a glance with Ruby. "Sure. Why not? The three of us can choose dinner on the way back."

And we'll get the chance to talk about Kris privately, while Lily's in class.

Justine slipped Ruby a flask after they settled in the viewing area. "Since security's driving, I thought you might want a nip. God knows I need one after *this*."

"Thank you." Ruby sipped, then handed it back. "What's the situation?"

Her sister-in-law grimaced. "Well, it could have been worse. One area of invasive tissue that the doctor thought *might* force a hysterectomy, but with some careful work they avoided doing that."

"I don't know if to be relieved, or further worried."

"Same here." Justine rolled her eyes. "My personal, *informed*, opinion? Kris endangers her health by trying for another child. They were lucky to have Lily survive to viability, thanks to what was done to Kris under indenture. But Kris wants more children, has always wanted several."

"Adoption. Surrogacy."

"They won't go there, even though there's always kids who would benefit from being adopted. Or surrogates if they're bound and determined to have their own kids." Justine shook her head. "But I'm not going to argue with Brandon and Kris. I've dealt with enough of these situations in the Rescue Angel. I recognize the pattern. Some people—I just didn't think I'd encounter that mentality in my own damn family! Maybe I'll try one more time. I *am* really worried about Kris's health."

"Bran and Kris's dynamics aren't the usual," Ruby sighed. "Kris—everything she went through in indenture. Bran, as a result of me and Gabe divorcing when he was so little. And all the crap that went along with that. He keeps telling me he's not jealous about Mike having a full-time father. But sometimes I wonder. He was *so* determined to get us back together eight years ago, after Rachel's death, and *so* happy when we did."

"You never thought about anyone else? I mean—it didn't stop Gabie from remarrying."

Ruby tapped her chin with a forefinger, remembering. Her absolute, utter *fury* at Gabe's involvement with Mariah Meyers, and her lesser anger when she learned he was marrying Rachel Alvarez. Even now—knowing that her emotions had been shaped by Philip Martiniere's mind control programming, and that Gabe had undergone more severe manipulation which removed his ability to choose his actions—the anger still stirred when she thought about everything that happened during their divorce.

Only now her rage focused on Philip, not Gabe.

"No," she said finally. "Not even to give Bran a stepfather." She shook her head. "Gabe was the first man I completely trusted." A bitter laugh. "The *only* man I've ever trusted. That's why it took me a while to agree to remarry him—rebuilding that trust. And after the divorce, there just were damn few people around Thunder County who weren't either a relative or someone looking to grab my land. Or the RubyBots."

Justine took another swig off the flask and handed it to Ruby. "I had an exit strategy that involved several men when Donald and I divorced."

"Why *did* you divorce?" Ruby held the flask, not quite ready to take another sip. Justine's divorce from Donald was yet another subject where she tended to evade direct questioning.

"Politics," Justine said curtly. "You going to take a drink, Ruby?"

Ruby sipped and handed the flask back. "But you didn't marry any of those men."

Her sister-in-law took a longer drink this time. "No. And much as Donald and I care for each other, we're not remarrying." Another drink. "Have you talked to Gabriel about me, Eliot, and Nick?"

"No."

"Ask him. He knows what the situation was, and I—" She shook her head again. "Too much. After today. After Kris."

The class moved away from the barre. Lily led the four dancers through chaîné turns, then piqué turns. Ruby admired the elegant, precise lines of her granddaughter's movements. Lily was so graceful and coordinated. Darker-skinned than her great-grandmother Angelica, who had been working her way up the dance ranks when she broke her ankle, then had been courted by the Martiniere brothers, Saul and Philip. That rich dark-brown shade of Lily's skin, coupled with the seductive big brown eyes that came straight from Gabe, and her black curly hair, added to her beauty.

Ruby smiled, remembering her first sight of Lily as a newborn. The awe of realizing that she was a grandmother, and that this beautiful, tiny, near-perfectly formed little girl was her granddaughter.

Those big eyes, and all those curls. Prettier even than Brandon as a baby.

And their son had been *so* cute as an infant and toddler, growing into the same darkly handsome presence as Gabe. Even Gabe at newly sixty-five still took Ruby's breath away. He aged well, and that *come-hither* look of his when aroused, coupled with that slow, intimate smile—well, the combination always made her stomach flutter and warmth flood through her.

Her granddaughter was gorgeous, hearkening more to her Martiniere ancestry than Kris's or Ruby's. Too bad Lily didn't care for horses, otherwise she might have made a lovely rodeo queen.

Perhaps Lily would follow in Angelica's footsteps as a dancer. It would be a better future for her than to force Lily into Martiniere Group leadership.

Lily and Mike *both* might be better off if the title of Martiniere went to a different branch of the Family.

"She's beautiful," Justine said. "If only—"

"Yeah." Ruby reached for the flask. "If only."

If only the shadow of Philip Martiniere didn't hang so heavily over his great-granddaughter.

SHE WAITED TO CALL GABE UNTIL LATER IN THE EVENING, ONCE LILY was in bed and Brandon had retreated to his room. Ruby excused herself from the living room where Donald and Justine watched a movie, and went to her room. She carried a drink—last one of the day.

"Wondered when you were going to call." Gabe leaned back in his office chair, a matching straight shot of whisky in his hand. He must have poured it to be ready for her call so they could drink and talk—one thing they always tried to do in the evenings when they were apart. "Everything's all right with Kris?"

"Well, everything except that Justine thinks Kris shouldn't keep trying to have her own babies." Ruby sipped from her drink. "In her *informed* opinion. Hydatidiform mole. Not so bad that it required hysterectomy, but bad enough."

Gabe winced. "Oh, that has to be tough for Tine."

"It is." Ruby pondered her drink, wondering if this was a good time to ask about Justine, Eliot and Nick.

Not now, she decided. *In person.*

"How are Brandon and Lily holding up, and when is Kris being discharged?" Gabe sipped from his drink.

"Bran is—as well as could be expected. Some tension between him and Justine, because she's pushing for them to stop trying for a second child."

"And they don't agree."

Another sip. "No. Justine told me she wasn't going to push—but she tried one last time at dinner. Bran shut her down hard."

"She's right. But that's not going to make a difference, is it?"

"Pretty much. We made a stubborn kid, and while that has its blessings, it's also been a challenge over the years."

Gabe smiled wryly and saluted Ruby with his glass. "Our son gets it from both of us."

"Boy does he ever. And Lily is Lily. She had a class at the Ballet School today, two tomorrow, so she's happy and occupied. Kris gets discharged tomorrow afternoon. They're staying one more night, then going home."

"That's a relief. When are you returning?"

"Tomorrow afternoon, once Kris is here at Donald's condo.

Justine and Donald are staying, just in case. But I figured I should be around until then, at least."

"A good idea."

"How's Mike?"

"No new appearances of the damned worm, if that's what you're wondering."

"That's good." She took another sip. "You and Mike could always come down here day after tomorrow, and we could go to the cliff house. Either all three of us, or I could ask Justine if she wants some time playing auntie with Mike. I need a break." Mike and Justine liked going to the museums in Portland, both art and science, and it had been a few months since they had done that.

But having *that many* people here in the condo—probably best to wait until Bran and Kris went back to Moondance. Especially if Lily went into one of her moods.

Gabe contemplated his drink. "The thought is tempting, even if it means waiting another day to see you. I don't think we should throw Mike and Lily into such close quarters, especially after—*this*. The stress could complicate things. I'd just as soon avoid causing one of her meltdowns. Or his."

"Lily has been pretty stable, thanks to her dance classes, but —I agree." Moondance was one thing. Mike and Lily had separate suites, were in different wings of the house. Mike could isolate himself from Lily any time he wanted if she slipped into a mode where she wanted to stalk him.

Not so in Donald's condo.

"Let me know if Justine's up for minding Mike for a couple of days." Gabe blew Ruby a kiss. "Love you, darling, and miss you."

"Miss you too." She blew him a kiss in return.

Talking to Gabe about Justine's history could wait.

"Time with Mikey? You bet," Justine said, grinning, when Ruby brought it up after breakfast. Brandon was working, Lily doing schoolwork in the office with him, before going to her first dance class.

"Maybe we can go to a baseball game," Donald suggested, a matching smile on his face.

"They start this early in the year?" Ruby didn't have a clue about non-equestrian sports. She had never possessed the time to care, her grandparents hadn't been into sports, and Gabe was like her—interested in equestrian sport, especially rodeo, but nothing else.

"Exhibition games. I'll see what I can do about tickets." Donald finished loading the dishwasher and started it.

"We might stay down there for several days," Ruby cautioned.

"After this last session on Nameless, I'm more than ready to do some urban things," Donald said.

"You won't need to rush back?" Justine furrowed her brows at him.

"Finally have this caretaker trained," Donald said. "Might even be able to stay for a couple of days once Mike, Ruby, and Gabe go back to the Double R."

Justine smiled. Their gaze locked for a few moments and Ruby felt like she might be intruding. She slipped out of the kitchen to prepare for taking Lily to class.

The question nagged at her all the same.

So why was Donald tied down to Nameless Island, to the degree that a caretaker's training made a difference? Did it have something to do with why Justine wouldn't remarry him—and why *wouldn't* she remarry Donald, given that they were still clearly in love with each other?

Gabe and Mike arrived around noon the next day, shortly after Brandon and his family left. Mike looked around the living room cautiously.

"Lily's gone," Ruby said.

Mike exhaled in obvious relief.

"Feel like going to a baseball game this afternoon, Mike?" Donald asked. "Gabe, you can join us if you'd like."

"Thanks, Don, but I'd like to get down to the coast fairly quickly. There's a storm due this evening."

"Ah. Understand."

But the intense scrutiny that Gabe fixed on Ruby suggested to her that there was more involved with his urgency to get to the cliff house than beating a storm.

That look sent tingles up and down her body, and the way he stalked toward Ruby made her shiver in anticipation. Gabe's *come-hither*, seductive gaze was amped up to full burn. He took her into his arms and kissed her hard.

No, this urgency to get to the cliff house wasn't about racing a storm.

Springtime, perhaps? Or just missing her presence?

No matter which this was, Ruby was going to take full advantage of the situation. Lovemaking when Gabe was in this mood was marvelous. These occasions had significantly declined as they aged and Mike entered his teen years.

She was most *definitely* ready for a few days alone with her husband.

Gabe held Ruby's hand all the way to the cliff house, periodically rubbing his thumb across her palm. Then he would raise her hand to his lips, kissing it. Their eyes met each time and that little tingle ran through her, in expectation of what would happen once they were alone in the cliff house. Oh, this was *so much* like the first date that led to them becoming lovers.

Maybe not in location but *that gaze.* The way her heart pounded.

The question was, who would act on it first?

———

BOTH OF THEM, AS IT TURNED OUT. ONCE SECURITY HAD CLEARED out of the house, and they finished arranging kitchen supplies, Gabe glided toward Ruby. She grabbed him around the waist and pulled him close, backing up until she leaned against the kitchen island. Gabe purred as their lips met and parted, tongues teasing each other before he began kissing her chin, running tongue and lips down her neck, fingers fumbling with her shirt snaps.

"Bedroom," Ruby finally gasped. "Too old to screw in the kitchen."

"Agreed," Gabe growled. "Bed. Now."

She clung to his hips as he backed her into the bedroom, his hands supporting her upper body firmly against him. Some fumbling as they kicked off shoes and pulled off clothing, but before long they were on the bed.

Oh. She was on fire, *so* on fire, and so was he, enough to think that they were in their twenties again.

———

THEY CRAWLED UNDER THE COVERS ONCE THEY WERE SATED, holding each other. Gabe stroked Ruby's face with his index finger. She closed her eyes, thrilling to the contact.

Gabe chuckled. "Sixty-five and fifty-nine, and we can still get it on like we were kids. Occasionally."

Ruby opened her eyes. "No complaints from this party. I think it must be going around, from the vibes that Justine and Donald were putting out."

"Mmm, didn't hurt that Mike and I were working with

broodmares. Both Crystal and Legacy came into heat, pretty intense." Another chuckle from Gabe. "Star wasn't complaining. They're *definitely* bred. But I also missed you pretty bad."

"It *has* been a while since we've had time for just us."

"Too long."

"I won't argue with that." Ruby reached up to cup Gabe's cheek.

He turned his head to kiss her palm, then sighed. "Poor Bran. Poor Kris. I did speak to Bran last night, as the Martiniere Emeritus, to advise him that they shouldn't feel pressure to have another kid just for the Family's sake."

"I've told him that as well. So has Justine. Probably with similar results. I don't think their desire for more kids is about the Family."

"That's my impression, too. How's Tine been taking this situation with the hydatidiform mole?"

"She drank pretty heavily the first night, once we were settled in the condo. We were sipping from her flask while watching Lily's class." Ruby paused. "That led to a conversation about our divorces. She said she had several men lined up as backup, but wouldn't say anything more except to talk to you."

"Yeah." Gabe propped himself up on his elbow. "Justine and Donald's divorce, given that it happened just before ours—honestly, I hoped it would be a distraction for Philip. That the timing of the AgInnovator would give us a break."

"It didn't."

"I knew Don and Justine's divorce was coming. They had agreed to it before their marriage."

"What the *fuck*, Gabriel?"

He sighed and stroked her shoulder, beginning to trace the Martiniere trefoil on it, an action which usually marked their discussion as involving Family politics.

"Their prenuptial agreement included a mutual pact to divorce after seven years, unless they rescinded that aspect of it."

"Wow. She said it was political."

"Very much so. Tine married Don to get away from Philip, to avoid being drugged into compliance so she would marry Walter Braun."

"I knew about that part."

Gabe's lips tightened. "I don't know all the details of the divorce proceedings. But her hysterectomy made it inevitable, because Philip dragged her into the Martiniere Group, and she and Don decided that what she could do in that position was more important than their marriage."

"Philip forced *their* divorce, too?" Another instance when she wished that she could resurrect her late father-in-law and *make the asshole pay.*

"Yes. Tine's involvement with Eliot and Nick was a coverup; nothing more than friendship and alliance, meant to distract Philip from scrutinizing her further clandestine work with Don. They chose Rescue Angel's survival over their marriage."

"Fuck." What else could she say? "She's pretty adamant about not remarrying, which really surprises me."

Gabe shook his head. "I have no understanding of my sister's rationale. To all appearances, she and Don are as close a couple as they were before I left the Family."

"She won't give a reason. And Don's tied down to Nameless. He said something about finally training a caretaker, the first night we were all in the condo, so he could have a few extra days."

Gabe shrugged. "Eh, who knows? Those two have always kept their long-term plans to themselves. I'm just happy they're our allies and not our opposition." He pushed a strand of hair back that had fallen into her face. "But here's something else to think about. Remember when we talked about how things might have been different if my family hadn't died, after Mariah's funeral?"

"Yeah."

"I had some *very* vivid dreams about what that might have

been like over the past few nights." He smirked. "Somewhat erotic, in fact."

"Aha." She chuckled. "I *knew* there was more to your mood than separation or horses breeding."

Gabe's laugh echoed hers. "Yeah, you were just as hot—if not hotter—in those dreams as you were as a twenty-one-year-old barrel racer. But it was an interesting set of dreams. Sequential. Detailed—or at least what I remember of them."

Now *that* was interesting. "What kind of details?"

"Four years age difference between us instead of six. While I still spent time in Philip's house, it was only two years, and I hauled Justine out when I left. She spent her teen years growing up with my sister Louisa, and oh were they *ever* a pair." He kissed her forehead. "You and I married within a month of meeting each other, because I became the Martiniere and Philip had threatened to kill me. I didn't know if I would live to see our first anniversary. Our mutual science and technical interests were a huge factor in how fast we became a couple, because there just wasn't anyone else that clicked like we did."

"Close enough to our real lives. So *did* you survive to our first anniversary?"

"I never did dream the rest of the story, at least not anything I remember. The last pieces included the two of us fighting Philip at the Double R. We both nearly died, but you killed both Philip and his girlfriend in a shootout."

"Damn, that's a dream I really wish I could have shared, just for the part about killing Philip."

More forehead kisses. "And then we were in Paris, still recovering from our injuries from fighting Philip. That was the last part I remember."

"Sounds like you did survive. That's good."

"Yeah." His fingers kept tracing the trefoil. "No indenture in that world, but accelerated climate change. And—no Brandon. No Mike. A quick flash of Justine and Donald with a daughter, but that was it. No indication if we stayed married."

"I don't know if I like the sounds of that world." She considered the possibilities.

Gabe was silent long enough that she would have thought that he had fallen asleep, except that he kept tracing the trefoil on her shoulder.

"We were both a lot more emotionally and physically damaged by what happened to us in that world than we are in this life," he said finally.

"That says a *lot*. You and I are pretty screwed up, overall. At least we're broken in similar ways."

"No kidding. I like this world better. Even if we spent twenty-one years apart. I have the distinct sense that we died before we reached our fifties, in that universe."

Ruby yawned. She turned and snuggled in close to Gabe. "Then I definitely like this world better."

He nuzzled her ear and threw one arm over her. "Living to a ripe old age is the best revenge, as far as I'm concerned. I just— regret the years we lost."

"Nothing to do about that, except to make our remaining years the best that they can be."

"Agreed."

POUNDING RAIN ON THE WINDOW WHILE IT WAS STILL DARK STIRRED Ruby from a restless, foreboding dream that featured Philip laughing and promising future vengeance. No further details came to her, except an ominous fear that the rain, and the storm, foretold problems ahead.

Stop it. You're just being fanciful.

But no amount of self-reprimand could banish her sense that shadows were gathering to do them harm.

She pressed closer to Gabe. His arms tightened around her, but he didn't waken.

Please. Keep everyone I love safe, she thought, imploring—the

Universe, she supposed. She had never been a church-goer.

Normally that invocation settled her concerns. Not this time. Instead, further worries about Brandon and Kris, Lily, Mike, and —Gabe, oh Gabe, her beloved—roiled through Ruby's thoughts, each one darker than before.

Ruby lay wide awake in Gabe's arms, troubled by that lingering sensation of dread and doom, until darkness started to fade into gray dawn, and she had a reason to get up and make coffee.

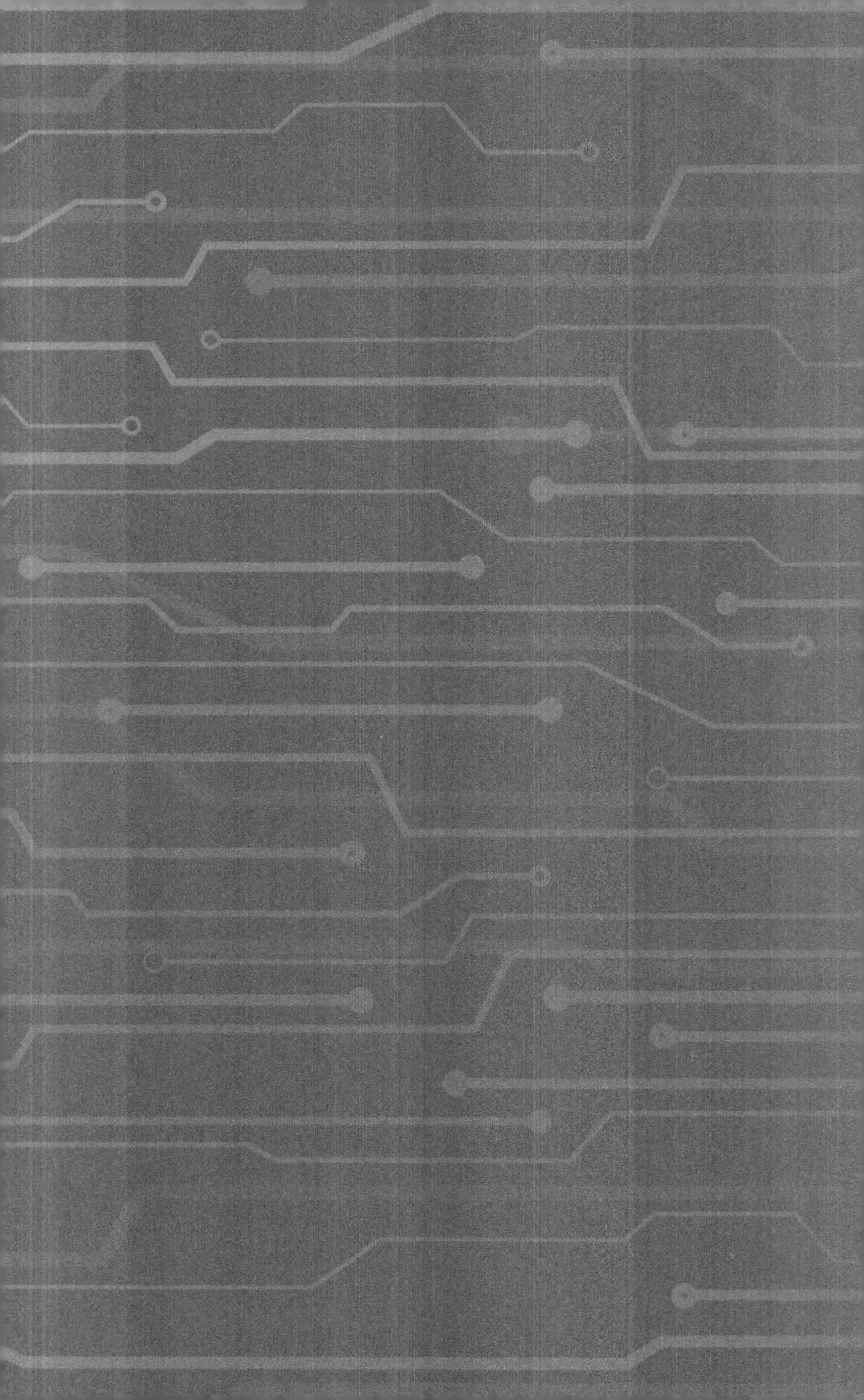

MARCH, 2068

GABE

"ARE YOU *SURE* YOU SHOULD BE RIDING BOOMER TODAY? ESPECIALLY on the low route?" Gabe asked Ruby as he leaned against the back porch doorframe, watching her garb up for the day's ride. She planned to join the Chandlers next door to move cattle, riding across fields to meet up with them. Their security now reluctantly allowed them to go out on the place by themselves, since things had finally settled down with Zingter.

Normally, Gabe wouldn't be bothered by Ruby's ranching plans. And Boomer, though only four years old and lightly started, was a steady-minded colt. They were considering him as a junior stallion prospect. Fresh blood to cross on Star's daughters.

But the weather varied between sunshine and storms, with a brisk northwestern wind. Both he and Mike were moving slow and sore today. Plus Gabe just had—oh, he couldn't explain it, but it was one of his *feelings*. Nothing he could quantify. Last week Star had been jumpy and snorty on the low route to the Chandler place. The big stallion rarely acted like that, but, as a possible, non-dire explanation, every horse had their moments.

Even a stud as steady as Star was. And it *was* spring, coming into breeding season.

All the same, Star's behavior suggesting that there was a problem in that area still made Gabe uneasy, especially with Ruby riding a green colt through it.

Ruby finished lacing her boots. "Eh, Gabe, I'm carrying my saddle rifle, if security's what you're worried about."

"Kinda," he admitted. "Sure you don't want to trailer over to the Chandler place instead of riding over? Or find something else to do? I'm sure the Chandlers will understand if you don't join in."

Ruby frowned. "Boomer needs the warmup he'll get from the ride over. This drive will give him some seasoning. It's the best cattle drive this spring for a young horse like him. Close to the ranch and over by midday."

"Not happy about you taking that low route. Star was pretty skittery when we rode out to check the fields last week."

Ruby shrugged. "It's shorter and better for Boomer."

"Wish I was going with you." Maybe that was it. He ached, and that somehow kicked off his worry about Ruby.

"You still could." Ruby pulled on her heavy jacket.

Gabe shook his head. "Hurts to raise my bum leg. You'd have to pry me off of Star."

"I'm sorry you're having a rough day." She kissed him. "I'll message you when I get there, and again when I'm on my way back."

"All right." He could concede that much.

"See you this afternoon." She headed out the door.

On my way back, Ruby messaged at twelve-thirty. *Boomer's a good boy. Cowy and smart. See you soon.*

Be careful, Gabe answered. He calculated the time. She should be back at the barn by one-thirty. He scowled at the dark clouds hovering over the prairieland to the north, promising a hard squall coming soon.

Sure you don't want me to run over there with the trailer and pick you up? he sent. *Weather looks rough.*

We're good.

Gabe wanted to argue further with Ruby. But odds were that she was already on her way, far enough along that she was in the dead spot where she couldn't make or receive calls. A short enough distance, maybe about ten minutes out of reach, but damn it, that area worried him.

***

One-forty-five. No Ruby at the barn.

Should he ride out?

No. Fifteen minutes late was within reason. Even though a hard, driving rain had set in.

Gabe paced the alleyway, peering out the barn door every circuit.

Nothing but a downpour.

***

Two o'clock. Still no Ruby.

No message saying she was delayed.

The rain had eased off.

Gabe tried her comm, just in case.

Nothing. Fear tightened his gut. He tried again.

Still nothing.

Damn it, she *had* to be within comm range by now.

He limped up to the house.

"Mike!" he hollered from the kitchen. "I need help!"

He *should* call on security for help rather than Mike. But if Ruby was just dawdling on her way back from the Chandler place, or had stopped to check on fence or something while still in the dead zone, she'd be pissed at him for overreacting and getting security involved. If he and Mike rode to meet her, however, they could plead cabin fever and wanting to get out as an excuse, now that the sun was shining.

If everything was all right, that was.

"What's up?" Mike hobbled into the kitchen, his heeler Smudge right behind him.

"Ruby's half an hour late getting back from the Chandlers," Gabe said. "No response to her comm. And she's riding Boomer. I can manage to get up on Star. Can you handle a crawler?"

Mike's face tightened and he nodded. "No problem, Gabe. Meet you at the barn."

Gabe headed back to the barn. Luckily, Star was stalled, in quarantine after traveling to the breeding station for sperm collection, and not in the field with his mares or in a pen. That made it easier for Gabe to groom and tack the big stud. A quick swipe with the brush over back and belly, then Gabe heaved the saddle onto Star's back. Before Gabe bridled Star, he leaned his head against the dark bay stallion's forehead.

"She's late, big fella," he said softly. "I'm worried. Help me find her."

Then he straightened up. The stud nuzzled Gabe before he pulled the bridle on over the halter. He tied the lead rope to his saddle horn.

The faint rumble of a crawler announced Mike's arrival. "Still nothing?" he asked, walking into the barn.

"Nothing. Let me try again."

No response.

"I'll try," Mike said. "Just in case your comm's out of commission."

Should have thought of that myself.

Mike snapped up Ruby's contact. They stood there, waiting until Ruby's recorded message responded.

"All right, then," Gabe said grimly. "Let's go."

He didn't want to take the time to haul the mounting block

out of the indoor arena, and there were issues with mounting in the arena, then going outside. Fortunately, Star was comfortable standing next to the crawler. Gabe clambered up on it, Mike steadying him. From there it was an easy step up and over onto Star's back. Even better than the mounting block.

Mike started the crawler, and Gabe guided Star behind it until they came to the first gate—this one could be opened from horseback. Mike sped through and ran ahead while Gabe shut the gate. Star easily caught up with the crawler. Nothing new; they'd followed the crawler many times before. Gabe rose in his stirrups to look ahead, hoping to see Ruby and the blood bay colt ambling toward them.

Nothing. And that overwhelming, paralyzing sensation of *something's wrong* throbbed through Gabe, worse than ever, tightening his chest.

Second gate. No Boomer pacing with an empty saddle—which would be likely if he managed to dump Ruby. The colt would head for home.

Mike whistled to Smudge after they drove through the gate. The heeler hopped out, ranging by the crawler, venturing on short forays away from the crawler track as he sniffed out scent trails, then returning.

But no reaction out of the ordinary, no alert that suggested he smelled Boomer and Ruby.

Gabe rode Star alongside Mike. No more gates for a while, and if Boomer wasn't running loose here—

"I'm gonna gallop ahead, to the next gate," he yelled to Mike.

Mike nodded, his jaw set grimly.

"Help me find her," Gabe murmured to Star. "Both of them." He clucked and rested his calf against Star's side to cue him, leaning forward and extending his left hand to ask for more speed.

Star picked up his easy gallop. In other situations, Gabe would be enjoying a run along the level crawler trail that paralleled the Double R hayfields. Star was *fun* to gallop. But he kept looking, and watching Star's ears. The stallion *should* spot Boomer and Ruby before he did. He was well aware of the younger stud's presence on the ranch.

They rounded a corner, just at the start of where Star had gotten nervous last week, and Star's head shot up. He skidded to a stop, looking off toward the creek, then neighed imperiously.

Gabe squinted. Was that the blood bay colt standing near the bushes?

Yes, his head down.

What the hell—

He shifted his weight and urged Star toward Boomer. Star bellowed another neigh as they approached the colt. Boomer raised his head but not very high. Something restrained him—

Fuck, fuck, fuck, Ruby's off, this has to be bad—

Gabe halted Star. He couldn't see Ruby. Boomer shifted his feet nervously, eyes fearful and open wide enough to show white sclera, nostrils flaring red with anxious roller snorts. Star rumbled deep in his chest and Boomer—*oh God, he's caught up in wire.* Remnants of an old fence along the creek, had to be. But how did he end up in it?

Gabe dismounted and untied Star's lead rope from the saddle horn. He looked around for a tree stout enough to tie the stallion, and away from any wire, ignoring the stiffness and pain in his legs and hips as he secured Star and wrapped his reins around the saddle horn.

Smudge loped up to Gabe as he hobbled over to Boomer.

"Back to Mike!" Gabe ordered. Last thing they needed was for Smudge to startle the colt into hurting himself further—and maybe step on Ruby. Even though there was no sign of her.

He approached Boomer carefully, choking back his fear so that he didn't project it onto the colt. At the same time, he looked for something, *anything* that indicated where Ruby was.

"Steady, boy, steady," Gabe murmured as he eased toward Boomer.

Oh God.

Wire tangled around Boomer's legs, and he was bleeding. Bridle gone—maybe Ruby had pulled it off in her fall. Soaked halfway up his body—so the colt had plunged through the creek. Halter on, lead rope still tied to the saddle horn but snagged on some branches. Deep cut on his haunches, claw marks—*aw fuck.*

Mountain lion or bear attack.

Damn good colt. Boomer could have ripped himself up a lot worse, and he had apparently dragged the wire, but he stood still as Gabe freed him—no wire cutters handy, *damn it.* And Boomer had dumped Ruby at some point during the attack —*where?* And what had happened?

Gabe considered possibilities as he worked. The track crossed a bridge about a quarter mile further along and doubled back along the hayfield on the other side of this creek, running underneath rimrocks before it climbed up and turned toward Chandler's.

Late, hard winter; mountain lion or bear hungry and desperate enough to risk attacking a horse and rider. Ambush. Boomer spooked, Ruby—*where?*

Did the predator get her?

She hadn't pulled her saddle rifle out of its scabbard. Taken by surprise. Unusual for Ruby. But on a green colt, not raised here—

Mike stopped the crawler near Star, approaching Gabe and Boomer cautiously.

"You armed?" Gabe asked.

"Yeah," Mike said.

"Keep an eye on the horses and Smudge." Gabe led Boomer away from the wire, pulling Ruby's saddle rifle out of its scabbard. "Mountain lion, I think. Maybe bear. Call security. Get a medic team out here. I'm looking for Ruby."

Mike took Boomer, murmuring to the colt to soothe him. Gabe climbed over the wires, reading Boomer's tracks, heart pounding scarily as he reached the flooding creek and there was no sign of Ruby. Willows obscured a full view downstream.

God, Ruby, where are you? Did you get dumped in the creek? Are you drowned?

"Ruby?" he called. He wanted to bellow but damn it, that would scare Boomer. They didn't need to have Mike hurt as well.

Nothing.

"Ruby!" Louder.

A soft groan in response. Gabe thrashed through the willows toward where he heard it. Motion as he broke free from the brush. Ruby lay on her side, in the water up to her waist, wire tangled around her as well. She clung to a slender willow branch.

Oh God.

Gabe scrambled to her, putting the rifle down.

"Rubes, it's me, I'm here," he gasped.

She raised her head slightly, blinking at him. "Gabe?"

"Don't move." Oh God, he had to get her safely out of the water before she lost her grip. Did he have to untangle the wire first? Or could he just pull her out and then unwrap her?

"My leg," she whispered. "Hurts. Bad. Cold."

"Don't move." At least she could feel her leg, but were there spinal injuries? Hard to tell.

"Tried to pull out of creek. Tired. So tired."

"I'm gonna get you out, but we've gotta be careful. Give me a moment."

Risky, damn it, but Ruby was turning hypothermic, blue around her lips and nostrils. Hypothermia and shock. He had to get her out of that creek.

What about that damned wire?

As he investigated, it became clear he would have to loosen it to get her out of the creek in the first place. The strands wrapped tight around Ruby and trailed into the creek. Gabe plunged into the cold flow, up to his waist, muttering curses that he hadn't thought to stick a wire cutter into his belt. The wire strands connected to a post on the bottom of the creek. He yanked at it, fighting the chill and the damned stubborn wire and *he had to get Ruby out of this damned mess.*

The post came loose and Gabe staggered back, falling on the bank. He heaved the post next to Ruby. The process ripped two strands loose, easing the bind on her. He yanked the third free. Now he *might* be able to get her untangled—how the hell had both she and Boomer gotten into the wire? It looked like the wire had been cut once, so at least he wasn't fighting with an entire line of fencing, but why hadn't it been removed?

No time for that.

Get Ruby out of the creek. Now.

Gabe muttered a prayer to the God he no longer believed in. She could move her head and neck, so...he stripped off his heavy duster coat and used it to rig a sling under her arms, then slowly pulled her free of the creek, doing his level best to keep her spine straight.

Ruby screamed as he tugged her onto the bank; wordless, heart-rending shrieks that tore at Gabe's guts, cries of the sort that he hadn't heard from her since Brandon's difficult birth. She gasped for breath once he had her out of the creek.

Gabe undid his coat from under her arms, doing his best to wrap it around her torso. He stared at her broken leg and the blood now slowly staining her jeans. Dare he do more? She was bleeding so much—he started unbuttoning his shirt to make a tourniquet, ignoring the warning pains in his chest.

Voices. Help.

"She's down here!" he called. "Broken leg. Maybe spinal injuries. Hypothermia. Get MedicFlight in here now!"

Security thrashed through the willows, then scrambled around him, lugging a backboard. They rolled her onto the backboard carefully, tossing Gabe's coat back to him as they wrapped her in an emergency blanket. Gabe grabbed Ruby's saddle rifle on his way back up the bank. He knelt next to the backboard, holding her hand as they waited for the helicopter.

She was *so damn cold.*

The ranch manager, Charlie Thompson, rested a hand on his back. "Horses are taken care of, Gabe. Vet's on the way."

"Good. Call Fish and Wildlife to send someone out here to track down that fucking mountain lion. Bear. Whatever it was that attacked Boomer."

God, his chest hurt. But probably just angina. Help for Ruby was more important right now.

"I saw those claw marks. We have it under control."

He nodded, his focus on Ruby, ignoring the pain rising in his chest. God. If he hadn't been so anxious about her—

The *whomp-whomp-whomp* of the MedicFlight helicopter was the sweetest sound he'd heard in ages. Gabe argued when they wouldn't let him ride with Ruby.

He prevailed, but only because the pain in his chest got so bad that he doubled over and started gasping for breath.

LAKESIDE MEMORIAL SEPARATED THEM, EVEN THOUGH HIS CHEST pain eased enough that he could argue again. It took Dr. Sheri's stern glare to calm him down.

"Ruby's in surgery, Gabe," she snapped.

"Then I want to be with her once she's out," he insisted.

Dr. Sheri shook her head. "We'll see. I don't like the look of your vitals."

"Put us in the same room, damn it."

"Gabe—"

"You want Ruby crawling out of bed to find me once she hears *I'm* down?"

That comment got results, mainly because his beloved was still remembered at Lakeside Memorial for dragging herself to Brandon's side when they were both so sick with that damn killer flu all those years ago. His bed was wheeled into a double occupancy room.

No Ruby yet.

The door opened. Mike burst in. "Dad—Gabe—oh not you too!"

Brandon followed as Mike flung himself on the bed.

"Hey, hey," Gabe said, trying to soothe Mike as he buried his head in Gabe's chest.

Mike *never* called him Dad. *Never.* It spoke of the young clone's fear.

Brandon exhaled. "I swear, the two of you...." He shook his head. "Mom's still in surgery, Dad. She lost a lot of blood."

Gabe's throat tightened.

God. No. Not Ruby!

"And when I heard you had been admitted as well...." Bran shook his head again. After a moment, he continued. "Mike was frantic when he called me. Didn't know anything, couldn't reach you, and he was the only one who could keep Boomer calm while the vet worked on him."

Gabe nodded. "Mike. Mikey." He ruffled Mike's hair.

"Yes?" Mike sniffled as he raised his head.

"Everything's going to be all right. You did good. How's Boomer?"

Mike gulped. He sat up slowly and slid off of the bed. "Deep wire cuts on all four legs. He banged his forelegs around pretty bad, like he stumbled over a rock pile or something. Bruising and a bone chip on one knee. M—might be permanent tendon damage. Too early to tell."

Damn it. Fucking wire.

He would make damn sure that every bit of that fence wire was *gone*, along with whatever had spooked Boomer and caused this much damage to Ruby and the colt.

"And how are you doing?" Gabe's voice went softer and he held onto one of Mike's hands. Mike was twelve, the same age Gabe had been when he lost his entire family. True, Mike had Bran and Kris, Justine and Donald—which was more than Gabe had when the plane went down with Saul, his mother, and his sister. All the same, he *knew* what Mike was going through right now.

Had to be strong for the kid.

"Scared." Mike's voice trembled as he whispered. "Medic said you were having a heart attack. Ruby's hurt so bad—so much blood—"

Gabe tightened his hand on Mike's. "They're keeping me for observation, Mikey. I felt good enough to pitch a fit so that Ruby will be in here with me when they're done with her. I'm not gonna die right now and neither is Ruby, all right?"

Mike nodded.

"I don't want you to worry. We'll get through this."

"Mike," Bran said. "You'd better wait in the hallway like you promised Dr. Sheri." He glanced at Gabe. "Dr. Sheri gave him five minutes with you. Sneaking, because he's too young to be in here. He had a meltdown in the waiting room until she allowed it."

"C'mere." Gabe pulled Mike close and kissed his head. "You listen to Brandon and the other adults you know are safe. It's up to you to keep track of the ranch for us. We'll all be back home together before you know it. No more meltdowns, all right?"

Mike sniffled. "All right." He hugged Gabe, then slowly left the room.

"You *did* have a mild heart attack, Dad," Brandon said once the door closed behind Mike. "I've talked to Dr. Sheri. Luckily it happened right there with the MedicFlight crew, so they gave you a shot."

Gabe exhaled. "I thought as much. Went blank for a bit. Any word on your mother?"

"Multiple breaks of that leg. The thigh fracture isn't the worst one." Brandon winced. "And blood loss. She'll be down for a while." He paused. "I shouldn't leave Mike alone for too long. He's fretting now that he doesn't have anything to keep his mind occupied—building up to that meltdown. No self-mutilation—

yet. Justine's on her way; she'll stay with Mike at the ranch. Donald may be coming as well."

"So plenty of support. Good. And Mike will be around the horses and dogs at home. Best for him."

"Mike really did good, Dad. Held it together until he called me from the field, then collected himself to help with Boomer."

"*Good*," Gabe repeated. "Especially given his anxiety issues."

A quick smile flitted across Brandon's face. "He's a Martiniere, Dad. He'll rise to the occasion."

"Yeah." Gabe closed his eyes for a moment, suddenly weary. "Any idea what set Boomer off?"

"Not yet." Brandon patted his hand. "I'll let you rest."

"You'd better keep Mike company. I'm not going anywhere. And I'll have your mother with me soon enough."

Besides, he wanted to nap.

Gabe woke when they rolled Ruby into their room. Her leg was elevated and rigged up with some complicated device he was too tired to figure out, her face pale against the sheets, even her freckles washed out and faded, eyelids fluttering. And her head was bandaged, too—he hadn't noticed a head injury.

Brandon trailed after the nurses and moved to the side of Ruby's bed as the attendants set her up. She glanced around.

"Gabe?" A frantic note came into Ruby's voice. "*Gabe!*"

Oh God, she sounded so frail and frightened. *Not* her normal self. Not like his warrior wife.

"I'm here, hon." He wrestled his bed rail down and rolled off toward her, staggering and almost falling in the short distance between their beds.

"*Damn it, Dad!*" Brandon snapped, hurrying to Gabe's side and supporting him. Gabe slumped on Ruby's bed. Brandon huffed an exasperated sigh. "You'd better move their beds close enough together so they can at least touch fingertips, preferably hold hands," he said to the attendants. "Otherwise, you're gonna have issues."

Gabe ignored the commotion, focusing on Ruby.

"I'm here, Rubes," he said. "Right here."

She blinked blearily at him. "Why are *you* wearing a hospital gown?"

No way to avoid it; he'd better tell her now.

"I *may* have had a small heart attack while rescuing you," he admitted. "They took care of it, but Dr. Sheri wants me to stay overnight."

"*Gabriel Marcus Martiniere.*" Ruby squinted, her focus sharpening. Oh, it was so good to hear that scolding tone in her voice, feeble as it was. "What am I going to do with you?"

He grinned at her. "Hard to get rid of me, Rubes. I'm tough as nails and meaner than a rattlesnake. How about you?"

She closed her eyes. "Everything's fuzzy and I ache. I can't remember what happened. One minute Boomer was getting antsy, the next—hurting and cold. Wet. Grabbing at the willows so I wouldn't get sucked into the creek. Then your face, hovering over me."

"Oh Rubes." He stroked her face gently, avoiding the bandages.

Something bumped against him.

"Come on, Dad, let's get you back into bed," Brandon said. "We're putting the bed close enough so you can hold Mom's hand. All right?"

"All right." He *was* tired.

Gabe allowed Brandon and the aides to help him back in the bed, then finish pushing their beds together. Once he was able, he turned on his side and took Ruby's hand. She couldn't move her body, but shifted her head so she could see him.

Alive. She was *alive,* and while it might take some time, she was going to get better.

Gabe watched Ruby as she closed her eyes.

"Wish I could turn on my side," she mumbled.

"It'll be all right, hon. I'm here."

Could he stretch far enough to stroke her cheek? He tried. Not quite. But he could lift her hand to his lips and kiss it.

She smiled and slid a couple of inches toward him, still not enough for him to touch her face. The smile lingered as her breathing steadied into sleep.

Watching Ruby sleep made him drowsy, but Gabe wasn't quite ready to join her, reluctant to drowse off because —because—

So close, so close.

He had almost lost his Ruby today. That sudden jolt of fear was enough to make him wakeful again.

All the same, soon enough, he felt sleepy. He drowsed off, still holding her hand tight.

Dr. Sheri discharged Gabe the next day, with additional medication and a stern order *to get more rest and I don't want to see you back visiting Ruby until tomorrow.*

As Gabe waited for his ride home—at least Brandon had dropped off some clothes that weren't bloody and still wet from the creek—he lingered with Ruby, carefully leaning on her bed so that he could kiss her forehead, kiss her cheek, her lips, fret over his hurting darling.

"Damn it, use the self-admin button for the painkiller," he said once. "That's why they give it to you. Don't make yourself suffer."

"Don't want to get hooked," she muttered. "Not like my parents. Daughter of addicts. More susceptible."

"That's not true and Dr. Sheri told you that just this morning," he insisted. "It's legit, Ruby."

She finally yielded. Gabe sat on his bed, holding her hand.

It was taking a while for someone to pick him up. On the one hand, he appreciated having more time with Ruby.

On the other—he wondered what was going wrong *now*.

Justine finally appeared. Ruby blinked awake as his sister entered the room.

"Hi Justine," she said feebly.

"Hey Ruby," Justine said, her voice softening as she eyed the traction apparatus fastened to Ruby. "God, that looks horrible."

"It *feels* horrible," Ruby tried to laugh and coughed instead.

Justine patted Ruby's hand. "Well, I'm taking this man back home."

"Wish I was coming along."

"You will, soon enough," Gabe bent to kiss her. "And I'll be back tomorrow. Unless you'll bring me in tonight?" he asked Justine, hoping.

His sister shook her head. "Dr. Sheri's already cornered me. I have my orders. Ruby, I'll be back to see you in a bit. Get away from the testosterone circus at the ranch."

"Testosterone circus?" Gabe asked.

Now what?

"Fish and Wildlife showed up this morning," Justine said. "Hunting down the mountain lion that started this whole mess. Apparently, it's a chipped animal, with a history. So all the *boys* —" she stressed that word. "—on the ranch had to march out on a hunting expedition. *Including* Donald. Ruby, I'll be back. Come on, Gabriel."

Gabe sighed. He kissed Ruby one last time. "I'll miss you. Don't do anything I wouldn't. Love you."

"Love you." She was already drowsing off again. He lingered, worried because she hadn't snarked back about *don't do anything I wouldn't*—which was *so* not normal for Ruby—until Justine pulled at his sleeve and just about dragged him out of the room.

"Who all is off on this hunting expedition?" he asked Justine once they were settled in the farm truck. Maybe he might be able to sneak along if they got back to the ranch in time.

Justine rolled her eyes. "Brandon. Mike. Charlie. Donald.

Serg. The lady from Fish and Wildlife—Mari, is her name, I think she's a former high school classmate of Brandon's."

"Must be Mari Petersen. She was one of Bran's girlfriends but they never really hit it off. Ruby would know more."

"Sounds right. They took off with crawlers before I left, so no, *Gabriel*, you *aren't* joining them. I made sure they were gone before I came to get you."

"Tine, damn it—" Sometimes his little sister could be *so damn bossy*.

"How many cardiac incidents does this make since you retired from being the Martiniere?"

"Only the third. First heart attack. The rest have been angina."

Justine nodded, her lips tightening. "Your sixty-sixth birthday is next week. I want you to live to see that one and many more, damn it. With Ruby down, you need someone nagging you."

"Tine—"

She interrupted him again. "Mike needs you. Ruby needs you. The rest of us need you, and you *have* to take care of yourself."

"Being up to my waist in an ice-cold creek so that I can free my injured wife from a wire tangle and pull her out of that same damn creek is *not* an everyday event," he said. "Tine, we're talking major stress."

"True." His sister sighed, then gave him a half-smile. "And since Donald won't let me nag him about *his* health, you get it all."

"Harrumph." He *still* didn't understand his sister's relationship with her ex-husband. Maybe this was one reason why they didn't remarry—both were fiercely independent.

And yet the same could be said about him and Ruby. What was the difference?

As they pulled into the farmyard, Gabe spotted several crawlers parked by one of the equipment sheds.

"Looks like they're back already," he said.

"Mari had a tracker on the cat's chip. She didn't think it would take very long." Justine drove up to the shed. "I suppose you'll want to hang out with the boys."

"Absolutely." Gabe slid out of the truck, wincing as his bad leg twinged at him. He hobbled over to join the others while Justine parked the truck.

The mountain lion carcass hung from the skinning hook. Mike, garbed in a mask and protective gear, carefully skinned it under Brandon's supervision while Donald, Serg, and Mari watched. Charlie must have gone back to work.

"So this is the culprit?" he asked Mari.

"Yeah. Third strike. She killed a colt over at Reed's and several calves at Chandler's. GPS record placed her near where you found Ruby and Boomer, at the same probable time that they were attacked," Mari said. "Vet gave me samples from that claw mark on Boomer's butt; matches her DNA. Couldn't get permission from the higher-ups to do anything about her until it was confirmed that she had attacked a horse and rider. Believe me, I expedited the process." She shook her head. "Brandon was ready to call down the full force of the Martiniere on my bosses, but I talked him out of it. Better political move. But he *did* get their attention."

"Pregnant? Cubs?"

"Neither. Just old, and we suspect illness, either that or got into the habit of looking for easy prey. I'm taking the carcass to check, make sure she doesn't have rabies or something like that."

"Surprised you're letting Mike do the skinning."

"Mike was the one who shot her, and both he and Brandon made a good argument for turning the skin into a rug or blanket for Ruby, if it's clear from any nasties." She shrugged.

"Thanks for responding so quickly, Mari."

She pursed her lips. "Bran asked, and I owe Ruby." A hesitation. "Plus, my bosses pay attention when *the Martiniere* makes a request."

"Way of the world," Gabe said, sighing.

A few years ago, he would have cringed at the thought that Martiniere privilege bought them better service. But damn it, that animal had been the cause of Ruby's injuries. Besides, from the sounds of it, she was becoming a problem.

"In any case, she's done her part for the species," Mari added. "Raised several litters of cubs, and her descendants are out where they're supposed to be. She's only become a problem in the last six months, which makes me think she had a health issue. Not a young cat. Not fat and well-fed. Her teeth are worn, so that could be it."

"Yeah."

Before Gabe could say more, another crawler roared up. Charlie and his assistant Terri climbed out.

"Looks like Ruby and Boomer stumbled into a stack of posts and wires, scattered it all to hell and back, dragged a big chunk into the creek," Charlie said. "Terri and I scoped it out. She's assigning several interns to haul it away."

"How long has that mess been there?" Surprising that Ruby hadn't cleared it out by now. Then again, she had other things to focus upon, and if this was a project her grandfather Ron had started and not finished—well, there were other priorities on the Double R.

Charlie shrugged. "Overgrown enough that I suspect it could be thirty, forty years."

Most likely something Ron Ryder couldn't complete due to his health, then.

"How's the colt?" he asked Charlie. He didn't want to interrupt Mike's focus to ask him.

"Hurting but on all fours," Charlie said. "I'm surprised he didn't break a leg, after seeing the mess."

Gabe scowled. "I'd better look at him. Ruby will want to know."

They went to the barn. Boomer was in one of the smaller stalls, an extra partition added to keep him from moving around too much. His legs were bandaged, his dark red coat was speckled with white where medicated cream had been applied, and he stood with head lowered. He raised it, ears flicking forward, as Charlie and Gabe looked through the bars of the top half of the stall.

Boomer's nostrils fluttered and he nickered softly, extending his nose and making eye contact with Gabe, ears pointed directly at him. He licked his lips.

"I'll get him a couple of treats," Gabe said. "At least he feels good enough to beg for them." He grabbed a handful from the feed room, then slipped into the stall. Boomer moved stiffly toward him. Charlie stood in the doorway as Gabe assessed the blood bay colt.

As Mike had said, *too early to tell*. Cuts over his body, not just the claw marks but where the wire had dug into him. Gabe scratched Boomer's neck and fed him cookies, crooning softly to the colt. At last he sighed, patted Boomer, and left the stall.

Justine met them coming out of the barn. "You need to *rest*," she insisted.

"Soon enough, Tine, soon enough." He headed back to the others, just as Mike finished the skinning job. Mari and Brandon bagged the mountain lion, then carried it to the Fish and Wildlife truck.

Mike packed away the hide. He looked up and startled. "Gabe."

"Sounds like you did good, son," Gabe said. "I'm proud of you. What's your plan for the hide?"

Mike flushed. "I need to hear back from Ms. Petersen before I do anything with it," he said. He carefully started stripping off his protective gear and dropping it into a bucket that Serg produced. "Just in case. But—I don't know, I was thinking a lap robe or something for Ruby, but it's not really shaped right."

"I know some folks on the Reservation that might come up with something," Gabe said. "It'll make a nice gift for her."

He waited until Serg sprayed Mike down with decontam spray before ruffling his hair.

"Why don't we go to the house? You can clean up and tell me about the hunt," Gabe said.

Mike smiled shyly. "Sure."

Before they walked off, Gabe turned to Justine. "Tell Ruby that Boomer felt good enough to beg a couple of treats from me, all right?"

"All right, Gabie," Justine said.

Then Gabe walked to the house with Mike. Brandon fell in on his other side.

Warm pride flowed through Gabe.

Here I am, with my sons.

Mike was unexpected, unlooked for, a happy accident.

And while Mike was Philip's clone, he was Gabe's *son*, as surely as if Gabe had sired him. Just like Gabe had been Saul's son, even though Philip had sired him.

Repetition of a pattern, except—

Mike was a fortunate accident.

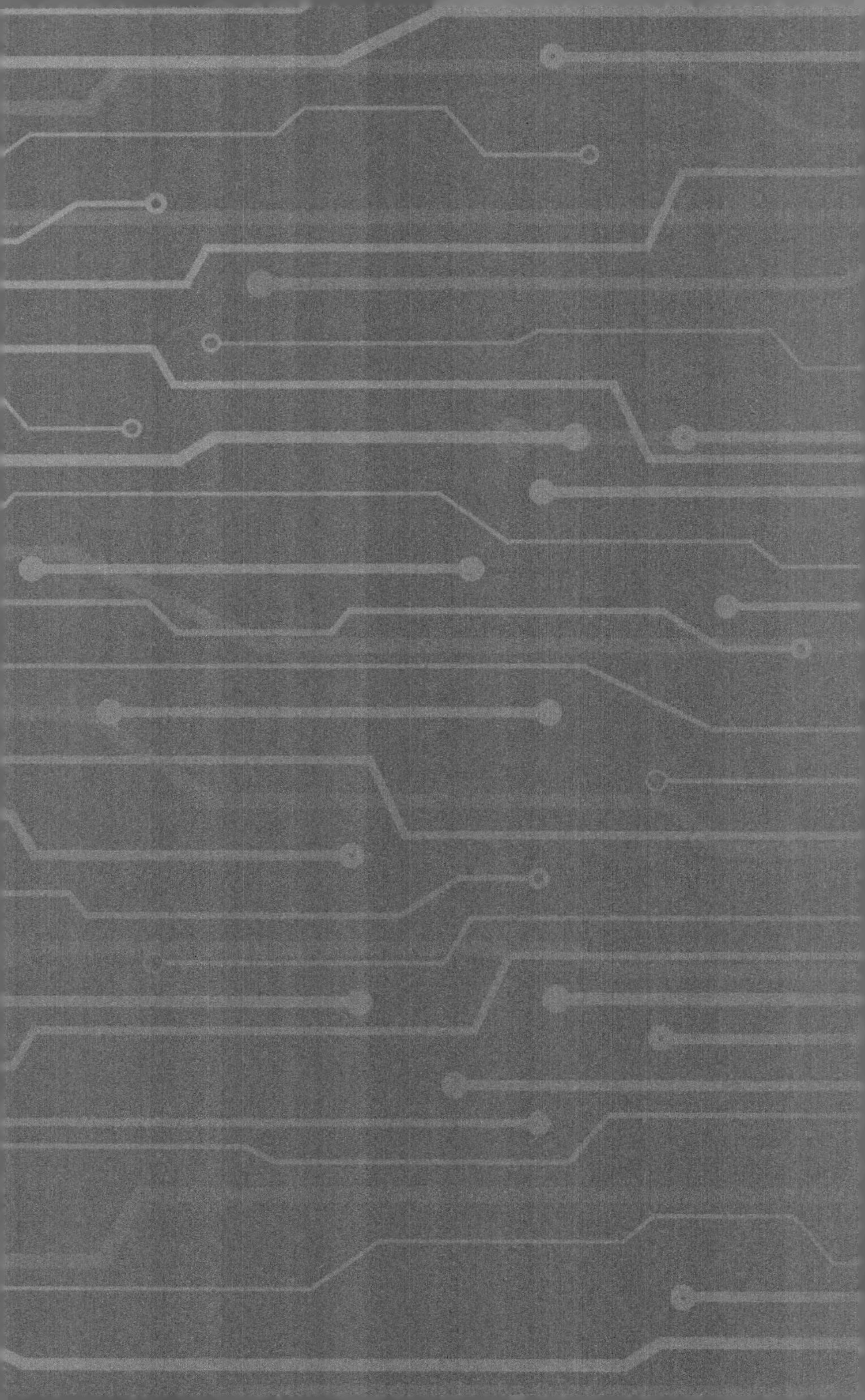

RUBY

"I'M NOT SURE WHAT GABIE'S GOING TO THINK ABOUT THIS. JUST A little bit nervous." Justine carefully set a stained, brownish-white, cardboard banker's box on the Formica and chrome table in the Double R's kitchen.

"Why?" Ruby eyed the unmarked box. Part of her wanted to pop the lid off and poke around in it, intrigued by what might be inside. The other part wanted to yield to sloth after this morning's intensive physical therapy. She would have to take her leg off the chair in order to reach the box, probably even stand up. That would hurt and be a lot of work—the kind of effort that seemed to get more difficult the older she became. Right now, she felt every one of her almost-sixty years.

"The archivists are *still* turning up surprises from Daddy-damned-dearest's hidden records stashes at the Group head-quarters. Most of them are electronic, but then they run across something like—*this.*"

"What is it, Tine?" Gabe glided into the kitchen. "Why are you concerned about what I think?"

Justine frowned at her brother. "Snooping again, Gabie?"

Ruby hid a grin. She was used to Gabe's light step. But it was an occasional point of contention between him and Justine.

"No, was just coming to get more coffee and heard you talking." Gabe waved his cup. "I have a couple of moments. So what's in the box?"

"It's—some of your mother's things. Clearly personal." Justine took a deep breath. "Mostly memories about you."

No wonder Justine's concerned.

Gabe's expression went blank. He reached for the lid. Hesitated, hands trembling slightly. Then he lifted it in a smooth swift motion, resting the lid upside down next to the box. He squinted inside the box, blinking, lips tight.

Then he extracted a ballet shoe with ribbons wrapped around it, smiling faintly.

"One of Mama's pointe shoes." Gabe turned it over. "Ah. She wrote on it. *Last shoe from my final Swan Lake.* The one I hoped it was. Mama had sold all her shoes to collectors except this one, which was displayed on a shelf at home—and they can't be found. At least that was what I had been told. I had hoped to come across this one someday, to give to Lily." He set it down and picked up an album. "My baby book." He picked up the pointe shoe, put the book in the lid, then placed the shoe on top of the book. "Family pictures."

Gabe didn't pull the pictures out, but continued to thumb through the contents until he retrieved a notebook.

"A diary," he said. A quizzical expression tightened his face as he studied the plain black notebook held closed by a faded elastic band. The band snapped as he slid it off and opened the notebook. "Dated from June 2001 to March 2002, and it's been read and reread. Someone made notes in a different handwriting —" his voice faltered. Gabe dropped the book into the box. "*Where* was this located, Justine?" His voice was tight and hard.

"A triple-locked closet in Philip's office archives at the LA Group headquarters, Gabriel." Justine's tone was flat. "The archivists had to bring security in when they finally got it open, because there was a lot of sensitive material. Not Group files and records. Personal."

"His blackmail files?" Gabe's nostrils flared and his brows furrowed.

"Quite likely. This is the only Family-related item."

"Figures. So why was it found only now?"

"Hidden door, Gabriel, one of several that were only locatable after checking blueprints—not anything official. I supervised the opening, then checked each box myself. No one else has seen the contents."

"Thank you, Justine." Gabe delicately set first the baby book, then the pointe shoe back in the box. "I'll take this to my office." He scooped up the box and left the kitchen, leaving his coffee cup behind.

Justine raised her brows. "Well. Both better and worse than I expected."

"Yeah," Ruby sighed. She eased her leg off the chair, then pushed herself up. "I'll take Gabe's coffee to him."

And check on his state of mind.

At least she had graduated to a full-leg boot that didn't require crutches to get around, so that she could carry his cup as well as hers. Whatever Gabe had seen in that diary had definitely bothered him.

***

Gabe looked up from gazing at the baby book as Ruby hobbled into his office. "What?" he snapped. "Oh. Sorry. I just got so much into—this—that I forgot my coffee. Thanks, Ruby." He waved to the loveseat against the wall. "Sit down. I'll show you my baby book. I thought it was lost." He placed the book on the coffee table in front of the loveseat.

He helped Ruby find a comfortable position before he retrieved the box and put it on the floor next to the loveseat.

Then he sat, leaning forward to sip his coffee before picking up his baby book.

"You thought this album was lost?" she asked.

"It disappeared, along with these other things, after the plane crash. A lot of things that were personal to Mama, Papa, and Louisa did. I never knew if those items went into Family archives or thrown out. They were *supposed* to be in Family archives, but when I checked after becoming the Martiniere, there was no record of anything belonging to the three of them. I expect this means that there are personal things of Saul's and Louisa's floating around in yet another hidden space. Or so I hope." His nostrils flared and he shook his head.

Ruby hugged Gabe.

Damn you, Philip Martiniere.

Even after death, the son-of-a-bitch was still capable of hurting Gabe.

"So. I used to look at this baby book a lot when I was little. Mine and Louisa's both. I wonder where hers is?" He opened the book. The first picture was oh-so-familiar, including that suspicious-yet-regal glower at the photographer.

Gabe chuckled. "I had that glare down even as a baby."

"You were a cute baby even with that expression. Looks a lot like Brandon—and yeah, I see you in Lily as well." Ruby studied the first picture. Newborn Gabe possessed long dark lashes and wavy black hair—lots of hair. Definitely resembled her son and her granddaughter at birth. Ruby had *thought* that Brandon looked more like Gabe when he was born—but now, seeing the infant picture—there was no question. Brandon was clearly a Martiniere. For that matter, so was Lily.

I would marry a prepotent man! the horse breeder in her thought. *Stamps his get.*

Oh, she saw her mannerisms in Bran and Lily—just about the only part of herself that Ruby could identify in her son and granddaughter.

But Mike picked up on them as well—no biological connection *there*.

The next picture was of Gabe with his parents. Angelica Ramirez Martiniere, dressed in a loose-fitting, flowing lavender top with matching lavender fleece pants, sat tall in a white wingback chair, baby Gabe in her arms. Saul Martiniere leaned on the chair, smiling down at mother and son. Angelica gazed at Gabe.

"That was the official Family birth announcement portrait." A bitter tone came into Gabe's voice. "*Of course*, nobody mentioned who my biofather was."

"Were Saul and Philip identical or fraternal twins?" Ruby studied Saul. He did look a lot like Philip—but there was a difference that she couldn't name. Posture? Or a regal bearing similar to Gabe's?

"Identical." Gabe flipped the page. "Official baptismal portrait." His voice sharpened. "And look. Philip was my godfather, along with Renate as my godmother. Philip left the Catholic Church shortly after Joey was born, to create his damned cult."

Ruby pulled the book closer and fingered through it. There were lots of pictures. A lock of black curly hair, so much like the one she had kept of Brandon as a baby. Many shots of Saul with Gabe. Saul beaming proudly down at Gabe as he toddled next to Saul on a beach. Playing in the sand. Gabe and Saul in a swimming pool. Gabe sleeping on Saul's bare chest, Saul gazing fondly at him—Ruby had a similar one of Gabe and Brandon.

Smiles in all the pictures, except formal family portraits with Philip.

Telling.

"You were a very loved child," Ruby said.

"For twelve years." Gabe leaned forward to retrieve his coffee.

Ruby continued. The last picture was of toddler Gabe, seated in a child-sized rocking chair, grinning at a baby carefully tucked into his arms. "Is this your sister?"

"Yes." Gabe's voice softened. "I used to call her Weeza because I couldn't quite say Louisa when she was a baby. It stuck for the rest of her life, especially since she insisted *I's Weeza!* when she was first able to speak." He stared off and smiled. "She adored me. Always tagged along behind. And I—damn it, I—" he choked, shaking his head and resting his forehead in his hands. "I didn't think it would hit me like it—damn it, Ruby. Yeah, I was on the brink of my teen years, but damn it—" He gulped.

"You were a boy. You thought you had forever," she said softly, guessing that it was one of *those* childhood squabbles. Except—the timing of this one.

Gabe rubbed his face and exhaled sharply. "Yeah. I called Weeza a *snot-faced brat* and got into a fight with her the last time I saw her alive. At least I apologized. The last damned thing I said to my sister was my apology for being mean and calling her names. She forgave me, like she always did. God. Oh God." He buried his head in his hands again, groaning.

Ruby kept her hand on his thigh, squeezing it slightly. Gabe raised his head and dropped one hand on hers as he leaned back.

"I wanted to unearth that baby book after their deaths." He swallowed hard. "The only pictures I had of my family were what I could locate online. Philip claimed he couldn't find any family mementos, that someone had broken into the house and stolen a bunch of things before he could get them boxed up."

"Fuck, Gabe. I'm so sorry."

No wonder he had reacted like that when he saw what was in the box.

He laughed bitterly. "It's been—what? Fifty-four years? You would think I'd be over it by now."

"Do we ever get over something like that?" Ruby closed her eyes tightly.

2014. Gabe's family killed in a plane crash, and—well—she had nightmares about her father beating her mother to death that year. Of the terror sharpening her focus as she raised the pistol, just like Gramps had taught her, when her father turned on Ruby with that bloody tire iron—

2014. A nasty, bloody year for both of them.

"I guess not," Gabe said softly. "After all, you still wake up screaming from nightmares about *your* childhood trauma. Ah, Rubes. You and me. Two broken people." He sighed. "I'm almost afraid to look at the rest of what's in that box. Maybe I should just put it aside, deal with it later."

Ruby side-eyed her husband. "Yeah, yeah, *right*. I know you, Gabriel. You'll say *put it away, deal with it later*. Then, the minute I leave, you'll go to your desk. You'll come back to the loveseat and either grab the box or sit here. You'll rummage through it and brood, maybe splash some whisky in your coffee, and drink. Let's talk about what's in that box, *now*. Something bothered you, more than just memories getting stirred up. What was in that diary that spooked you so much?"

Gabe shook his head, features relaxing, smiling faintly. "You called it, Rubes." He pinched the bridge of his nose. "There were notes in Philip's handwriting in that diary, from the very first fucking page. He went through this box. He *knew* about it, *God damn him!*"

Fuck.

"It just keeps getting worse and worse, doesn't it?"

Gabe nodded. "I want to read what Mama wrote when she was pregnant with me. But the handwriting—gahh! I won't be able to read it without thinking of *him*. I wonder how much he scribbled over it. What kind of hateful shit he wrote."

"Would it help if I were to transcribe it? Not what Philip wrote, but what she did? Or did you want to read it in her hand-writing?"

Gabe exhaled. "If you could do that—don't feel like you have to." His voice caught. "But just to *know*. She hated Philip. I knew that. She loved me—I think. Even though I was *his* son."

"Gabe. I understand. I'll do it."

"You are far too good to me, my love. Thank you."

"It's the least I can do. Do you want me to—summarize any rough parts?"

"I—shouldn't. But Rubes—use your judgment. Please."

"I will."

OF COURSE, THIS HELLISH PREGNANCY WOULD BE CONFIRMED ON ONE of the most dismally hot days of the year. IVF has succeeded. The embryo has implanted. I am carrying Philip's son. So far, apparently, Renate has yet to implant one of Saul's embryos. It makes me want to scream.

Ruby didn't know what was worse, the bleak first entry in Angelica's diary, or the obscene rape fantasies that Philip had scrawled in and around it. She forced herself to transcribe the despairing entry, arguing with herself about whether she should tell Gabe about this, much less give him the transcript.

Perhaps it would make more sense to thumb through the damn diary first, flag what areas she *could* easily give to Gabe—if there were any.

And yet a part of her rebelled against that easy path. Gabe would know if she sugarcoated the damn thing too much—and unlike him, she was crappy at lying, especially about emotions.

Still bitter about him hiding the truth about himself, before mind control lockdown rendered him silent on the subject no matter what he wanted to do, Ruby-girl?

Oh, he had improved—but for things like—oh, the secrecy around his buying the cliff house, Gabe was still good at duplicity. Even though the cliff house was intended to be a present, the fact that he could pull off deceiving her about the purchase still hinted that if he tried, and Ruby didn't get suspicious enough to rub her ring at him—he could still lie to her.

On the other hand, thumbing ahead might give her something pleasant to anticipate.

Renate is pregnant — finally! After three months' worth of attempts. And our son is moving inside of me. Saul approaches this pregnancy with the determination that he will make *this boy* ours. *Not Philip's. His enthusiasm is catching. I remind myself that Saul and Philip are identical twins, and that this boy could end up looking more like Saul than his biofather.*

But then I think about Philip's mental instability, and I become afraid. Again.

Philip's annotations were inconsistent throughout the book. The entry about feeling Gabe move was one left untouched. Perhaps the comment about Philip's mental state?

Ruby shuddered as Gabe came into her office. "How's the transcription going?"

"Rough," she admitted. "Not just what your mother wrote. Philip's—Gabe, he was delusional as well as psychopathic. I'm reading things that remind me too much of Lily. It scares me."

Gabe dropped into a chair, frowning. "You don't have to do this if you don't want to."

"I promised to transcribe this for you, and I am. You don't need to read Philip's crap."

Besides, the more I see of Philip's thought processes, the more likely it is that I can help figure out how to circumvent them in Lily.

"What about Mama?" His face tightened.

"She's—well, she was understandably depressed early on. But never hating you." That was stretching things a little, because there *had* been resentment of her unborn child in those first entries. Ruby hoped her voice didn't betray her. "I'm looking ahead. Some portions are unreadable, thanks to Philip's scribblings. I just read a section where Renate is confirmed pregnant, and Saul is determined to make you *his* son."

That brought a faint smile to Gabe's lips. "That sounds so much like Papa—Saul."

"No question in my mind that he loved you deeply. Those expressions of his throughout your baby pictures."

"Saul was a very positive thinker." Gabe chuckled softly. "At least he always was with me. Even when I was being defiant, I could be brought to heel by knowing that I had seriously disappointed Papa. Yes, he was lenient with me when I started getting really wild—and yet he decided that it was time for me to go to military school."

"I don't know, I've not heard any stories that make me think you were any wilder than kids I knew."

"It's different within the Family." Gabe laced his fingers. "I regularly beat the crap out of Joseph at Family gatherings. Was on my way to becoming a bit of a bully, like Philip."

"You? A bully? I'd believe it of Joseph, but not you, Gabe. Not the way you're respected now."

Gabe snorted. "Remember some of the issues you ran into when approaching the Family on my behalf, gathering support to dump Philip as the Martiniere? Some of those objections were rooted in things that happened when I was nine, ten years old. I'm sure my parents got pressure to bring me into line because, as the Martiniere's son, I could have become a potential threat. A year of military school started to change that—" he gulped. "And then I learned what *real* bullying felt like, after my family died. It was a relief to escape to Northview Military Academy once I was in Philip's custody."

"I suppose Bran's wrestling competition served the same purpose for him. Though he went through real bullying as well." Ruby tightened her lips.

She hadn't recognized the signs of abuse, when Brandon had been bullied at school. The water rights fight that set up the bullying had drawn all of her attention—had to, in order for her and Brandon to survive on the ranch. Though she ended up sending Bran to Gabe for a year, because Bran was skipping school—and was at risk for kidnapping. Or worse.

"It was a good outlet. And it turned him into a sneaky fast

fighter—which paid off when we were battling Philip. It wasn't really an outlet I had—being the Martiniere's son meant I had to be protected. Northview—was a dose of reality that I needed. And later, a refuge."

"I guess," Ruby said. "I suppose it's a good thing that I didn't have to deal with raising the Martiniere's son."

"Eh, it would have been different. No divorce, for one thing. And your upbringing was totally different from Mama's. The Ramirez family was wealthy, Cuban and Mexican money, in finance. I was acting enough like Mama's brothers and cousins that she didn't see the issues with my behavior. I think you would have kept Bran more centered, and there would have been siblings. Cousins." Gabe exhaled, grinning wryly. "I remember thinking how I needed to bring the hammer down on Bran that day you sent him to me, after that last epic school skip. I kept remembering what a snot *I* was at his age. He was *so* pissed about the lockdown bracelet."

"That's why I sent him to you. Not just desperation and fear —I just couldn't handle what I was afraid I was seeing." Ruby's voice went even lower as she remembered *those* dark days. Her fear that Brandon was turning into something like Tony Barkley, *her* psychopathic father. A deep-down dread that was enough to overpower her anger over the divorce and ask Gabe for help.

"That turned out well enough," Gabe said.

"It did."

Silence fell. Then Gabe got up. "I'll stop bugging you about the transcription. With that stuff going on in your head, thanks to Philip's scribbling—I'll be patient."

Ruby smirked as he left.

Patient? Gabriel Marcus Martiniere? Hah!

She would be willing to bet that promise *might* last twenty-four hours. Maybe.

Ruby returned to puzzling out the diary. After all, Gabe might surprise her and *not* pester her about the transcription progress for several days.

Maybe by then she would have something positive to give him.

Angelica's moods swung from anticipation to apprehension. Mentions of Saul seemed to bring out the most rage in Philip's reactions, sometimes to the degree that Ruby couldn't read what Angelica had originally written because Philip had overwritten her words several times.

All the same, she gained a deeper appreciation for Angelica and Saul. Definitely a love match—Gabe had alluded to that on the rare occasions when he talked about his family. Saul seemed to share his wife's concern about what this child would be, and went out of his way to cheer Angelica.

Gifts of flowers. Jewelry.

Ruby recognized that aspect of Gabe—something he must have learned from those years spent with Saul. Even when they were first married and broke, Gabe would bring her *some* small gift, almost daily. A flower he had picked or a pretty rock that caught his eye out on the ranch. A small food treat she had been craving during pregnancy. A book—often used, because they had no money, but by one of her favorite authors. She suspected that he had regularly cruised by the local Little Free Libraries and garage sales to find things he thought she would like.

Now? Flowers. Jewelry. The cliff house. Books—ebooks and real books alike. The lab of her dreams. And more.

Gabe kept his word and didn't pester Ruby.

The diary transcription became easier as Angelica's pregnancy progressed. Apprehension faded, possibly because of Saul's attention and concern. Philip's comments slowed—perhaps because he couldn't stand Angelica's praise for Saul.

Saul talks to the baby every night. He tells the boy about his day, about how he's looking forward to seeing him. About how he can be so much more than his biological father. For what it's worth, the baby responds to his voice.

All the same, Family Christmas in Paris is rough. No one knows about the IVF. They think it's an interesting coincidence that Renate and I are both pregnant with boys, due dates so close to each other. What sort of nightmare have we created for these children's future?

Philip continues to be an ass to both me and Renate. Saul is speculating about taking his child away from Philip and Renate shortly after birth, and raising the boys together. The only problem is that means I might have to give up this child if Philip insists. Philip's son—but mine as well. They will take this boy from me over my dead body. If only there could be an accident—I could happily cooperate with Renate in raising the boys.

Not with Philip. Never with Philip.

A FEW DAYS LATER RUBY WAS DONE WITH THE TRANSCRIPTION. Angelica fell madly in love with her son after his birth, marveling at his beauty and his big brown eyes.

Gabriel Marcus Martiniere. Definitely well-loved, by both parents.

Ruby printed out the transcript, proof-read it, then hobbled to Gabe's office.

"Here it is." She dropped it on his desk and sat in a chair.

Gabe's nostrils flared as he eyed the stack of paper. "So—how scary is it?"

"She was ambivalent at first, as would be expected. Then apprehensive and anticipatory. Saul did a lot to ease her fears."

Gabe still eyed the paper nervously, as if it were a snake that might choose to strike at him. "I'm kind of afraid to touch it."

Ruby pushed herself up and limped behind the desk to lean against him. "Gabe. You may have been forced on her, due to that damn arrangement—but you were loved." She ran her fingers through his hair, then kissed his forehead.

"I guess I just have those moments of wondering, you know? How much did you have to edit out?"

"This is the whole thing—except for what I couldn't read due to Philip's scribbling."

Gabe exhaled and pulled her onto his lap. "Thank you for doing this."

"It's the least I could do. You don't need that toxin in your head."

"But you have it in yours."

"Not really."

She kissed Gabe, to keep him from forcing further confessions from her.

Truth was, she had learned a *lot* about how Philip Martiniere had thought.

The depth of Philip's hatred toward his biological son was terrifying. Because the notes and reactions also laid out potential paths for Gabe's destruction—all written in the years immediately after Angelica's death. The years while Gabe was in Philip's custody.

How and why Philip kept from killing Gabe when Gabe was a teen, I'll never know. But I'm glad Gabe survived.

GABE

GABE WAS CONDUCTING MARTINIERE BUSINESS IN SEATTLE, covering for Brandon, when Kris went into labor. The meetings kept him in Seattle until early evening, trying to get everything handled so that both he and Bran could focus on family.

The sun had set over Pendleton when his jet landed at the airport, a welcome spring drizzle making the tarmac glisten under the airport lights.

"Everything okay with Kris?" he asked the security head who escorted him to the waiting SUV.

"As far as we know."

Not much of an answer, but at least it meant the worst hadn't happened.

Once settled into the middle seat row while security drove, Gabe leaned back, nervous. Ruby hadn't messaged him yet. That could mean labor complications—or that she had her hands full managing both Lily and Mike. He wasn't even sure if Ruby was at the hospital. Bran might have asked her to take the kids to Moondance, get them out of the way. Lots of possibilities.

It made sense to stop at the hospital first, find out what was happening.

Gabe tapped his fingers on the seat. Pendleton traffic wasn't anything like Seattle, but it still seemed to take too long before they reached the hospital. Security in the SUV handed him off to another set of security stationed at the hospital entrance, headed by a young woman who followed Gabe as he strode through the reception area, and reached the auto-receptionist.

Gabe brushed his index finger across the screen to activate the speaker. "Brandon and Kris Martiniere, labor and delivery. Gabriel Martiniere. I'm on the list."

That announcement brought a live human scurrying through the sliding glass doors to meet him. Nurse, chunky, male, carrying himself with the authoritative aura that indicated years of experience. The young security person excused herself to sit in the waiting area.

"You'll need to wear PPE. Just a coverall, no need for masking if you test clear." The nurse eyed Gabe's bespoke suit. Unusually formal for Pendleton, but it couldn't be helped. The Seattle to Pendleton flight was too short for him to change safely, especially given turbulence, and Gabe had rushed directly from his last meeting to the jet Justine had waiting for him. She wasn't here because Donald was sick—again.

"I'm good with that. I would have changed, have my own supply, but—" Gabe shrugged. "Any idea how the labor has progressed?"

"Mother is still in surgery. Delivery by c-section." The nurse swabbed Gabe's nose. When it came back negative for common viruses and infections, he handed Gabe a suit to pull on over his clothing, relaxing slightly at the ease with which Gabe donned it.

Oh, still in surgery doesn't sound good.

But Brandon and Kris finally had their second child. At least *this* pregnancy had succeeded, in spite of everything.

I just hope—damn it, I hope they don't think they have to make more babies. This hell has to end. For Kris's sake.

Gabe followed the nurse down the hallway to a private room.

Ruby sat in a hospital recliner, crooning at the bundle in her arms, the tip of her long, silver-streaked red braid escaping the loose surgery bonnet on her head. Mike and Lily looked on, both wearing full PPE, like Ruby. Gabe hesitated, suddenly struck by the likeness between Mike and Lily—despite the difference in skin color, the features of great-grandfather's clone and biological great-granddaughter were *so similar*. Perhaps more so due to their closeness in age.

Then Ruby looked up, grinning.

Lily whirled. "Grandpa! Come see my baby brother!"

Happy Lily. A relief, because almost-ten-year-old Lily had been so cranky and jealous at the prospect of a baby brother.

Lily ran to Gabe and hugged him. He picked Lily up and spun her around—their normal greeting when Lily wasn't plagued by the voices that turned her into a raging fury. Spinning was something that Saul had done with Louisa—and with Mama. His dancer granddaughter grinned, giggling as she pointed her toes while he spun her. Just like Mama did when Saul had spun her around.

And that giggle. *So much* like Mama's. Louisa's. Oh God, Gabe wished Saul and Angelica had survived to see their descendants. Even if his grandkids were Philip's biologically, not Saul's.

"*Gabriel*. Don't mess up your back!" But Ruby's chiding tone, also typical for this greeting between grandfather and granddaughter, faded quickly as she kept smiling at him. "Come see your grandson."

He set Lily down and knelt in front of Ruby, holding out his arms.

She eased the small bundle into them. "Meet Mr. Ronald Marcus Martiniere."

A solemn-faced infant gazed up at him. Subtle differences between Ronald and Lily, Ronald and Brandon. Skin a shade darker than Lily's. The Martiniere forehead, brows, nose, and chin. Kris's lips. Full head of curly dark hair. Chubby and healthy despite coming four weeks early.

Another gorgeous, lovely, Martiniere baby descended from him.

My grandson.

He had a granddaughter *and* a grandson now.

Descendants.

Funny, he didn't feel that old.

"So they settled on Ronald Marcus?" He didn't look away from Ronald's steady gaze, the infant studying his face.

"Ronald for Gramps, and Marcus for you."

"*Good.*" The first choices—Saul Gabriel, or Ronald Gabriel, had been names Gabe vetoed, hard. Like he did with any Family member who wanted to name their children after him and asked first. Right or wrong, he felt the names *Gabriel* or *Gabrielle/Gabriella* ill-wished anyone related to him.

And, of course, no one wanted to name a child after Philip.

But *Marcus* was safe. Gabe couldn't explain why, but he'd given that middle name to Mike at his adoption, and recommended *Marcus/Marcia* to those who wanted to honor him.

"Grandpa, can I hold him?" Lily squirmed next to Gabe, breaking him out of his thoughts.

"Just a moment." Gabe snapped his fingers to activate the small recorder cam that lurked behind his ear when he was working. As it flew out, he cradled Ronald and grinned up at the bot, getting several shots.

A similar picture to the ones he'd taken with Brandon, then Lily, as newborns.

"Whatcha doing, Grandpa?"

"I took pictures like this of your dad, then you, to send out as birth announcements to the Family. Now it's Ronnie's turn." Gabe flicked through the picture projections until he found the one he wanted, added text, then sent it out.

Ronald Marcus Martiniere, born April 7th, 2070. My grandson.

A portentous date in so many ways.

"Now can I hold him?" Lily bounced impatiently.

"Sit in the chair first." Ruby got up.

Gabe noticed the wistful expression on Mike's face. "First you, then Mike. Sister, then uncle." He was not not *not* going to say *great-grandfather*.

Once Lily was settled, he eased Ronnie into her lap. Ruby hovered watchfully, waiting for her to tire—which happened soon enough.

"Okay." Lily squirmed. Ruby eased Ronnie out of Lily's arms as Lily bounced up, and Mike took her place. Teenage gawkiness hadn't really set in with Mike yet—surprising, because Gabe remembered himself as being lanky and awkward at fourteen. Then again, he got his height from Angelica, not Philip—Philip was slightly shorter than Saul, at least from what Gabe remembered. The Martiniere twins had been short men. That was probably the difference.

Mike beamed down at Ronnie, his face softening. Ruby stood and put one arm around Gabe's waist, as Lily settled in another chair, watching a video on the new comm Brandon had given her.

Ruby leaned over to whisper into Gabe's ear. "They had to do a hysterectomy. Bran is with Kris—they let him stay."

Gabe nodded. "Lily's been cooperative so far?" he murmured to her.

"For Lily."

Ruby seemed to be able to handle Lily's volatile behaviors best of all the Family. She negotiated children like she did horses or difficult interactions between Family members in her role as the Matriarch—deftly, calmly, and without drama.

She should have been able to have more children than just Brandon.

And that thought brought up memories tied to this date. The fact that the two of them only had Brandon was squarely Gabe's fault, no matter what damned Philip had done.

April 7th, 2036. Thirty-four years ago. The date I left Ruby and gave into Philip's demands that I divorce her.

Gabe swallowed hard and squeezed Ruby tighter. She glanced at him, raising her brows questioningly.

He tightened his lips and shook his head. They could discuss this later—if Ruby remembered to bring it up.

But he hoped she didn't.

Once Kris was cleared from surgery and back in her room, later that evening, Gabe and Ruby took Mike and Lily to Moondance so that Bran, Kris, and baby Ronnie could have time together.

While Mike settled into his suite quietly, Lily insisted on doing a ballet workout in her studio before going to bed—she had missed one of her classes because of Ronnie's birth. Ruby supervised because Lily was in a manic mood, and might well dance all night if someone wasn't there to insist that she stop and take her medications, then go to bed.

Gabe checked on Mike—completely absorbed in an online video game with Jeff Swait's daughter JoAnn in Arkansas—and extracted a promise that he would sign off in fifteen minutes and go to sleep. Mike could be just as obsessed as Lily about his interests, but tended to be more secretive about it. Gaming with JoAnn was rapidly becoming one of those obsessions.

Secrecy was a definite Philip characteristic shared with his clone, accented by Mike's early years, before Gabe and Ruby adopted him. Mike hid his emotions until he couldn't manage them anymore. Having his horses and dogs around, especially the young dog Striker, bred with Ruby's epigenetic tweaks toward cyberawareness, seemed to modulate Mike's tendency toward internalizing his emotions until he melted down.

But counseling still was a requirement. And, occasionally, anti-anxiety medication.

Gabe snorted at that thought as he poured himself a shot of whisky in the kitchen, then went to the great room where he was within earshot should Ruby require his help. *He* still needed anti-anxiety meds, and sometimes they weren't enough. How much of that need was due to Philip's abuses of him, and how much was because he was Philip's son? Justine never talked about taking meds in order to cope. But she drank heavily.

Just like he did, sometimes.

For the same reason? Probably. Her life with Philip had also been a living hell, until she married Donald.

Gabe exhaled. Even though this recliner was new, a replacement for the one burned up in the fire eleven years ago, and the great room as decorated by Brandon and Kris looked nothing like it did when Gabe lived here, there were enough similarities to the original Moondance to bring back memories—and not the good ones.

Sitting here after Rachel's death, drink in hand, mourning the loss of his wives, one to divorce, the other to death.

Brooding about how he could have prevented the divorce from Ruby.

Lonely.

Loneliness was the emotion Gabe most attributed to Moondance. The place where he put himself back together after the divorce that had, as Philip hoped, destroyed *who he was* much more than a painful death would have. Even when he and Rachel lived here during their marriage, there had been an aura of loneliness around Moondance. The cancer that ate away at Rachel, before the G9 killed her. That awful year after Rachel's death, before he and Ruby reunited.

In many ways, the fire that had burned down the old Moondance house had been a welcome event. Oh, Gabe regretted what he lost of Rachel—her beautiful art quilt projects among other things—but he had none about the death of the *lonely* place.

This new Moondance was where he remarried Ruby. Where Philip died, and Gabe became the new Martiniere. Where Brandon became the Martiniere. Where Lily and soon—hopefully—Ronnie would fill the place with the sounds of children playing.

However, tonight, this house felt like the old one. Loneliness lingering in the shadows. Sitting by himself in the recliner, drink in hand, thinking about the past. The *bad* past, not the more recent, pleasant parts of it.

Ronnie was born on the date that everything went to shit for me and Ruby. I hope he changes things around, for all of us.

Gabe closed his eyes and shook his head. He shouldn't be thinking about this. Such thoughts brought up vague recollections of the shadows that sometimes whispered to him. The dreams that suggested *things could have been different, if only something had changed.*

But that refusal to think about those dreams pushed Gabe toward yet another, diverse set of shadows.

Philip's voice echoed in his memories.

You will be mine eventually, Gabriel. All of you will be mine!

What on earth did that really mean, and why did those sentences come back to him irregularly? Clear as could be when he heard those words in his head, true to every inflection in Philip's voice, with just a hint of mind-control tones.

So why did they occasionally pop up in his thoughts without warning? Why did they fade away when he tried to tell someone?

Just like that damn programming worm in the Guardians that *still* evaded detection.

Memory skittered away as the *clack-clack* of Ruby's boot heels on the polished wood floor alerted him to her presence. *Loneliness* ebbed as she stood beside the recliner.

"So here you are, brooding again." She crossed her arms and frowned at him.

He half-laughed and slid over, patting the big seat. "Join me."

She slid into the space—Ruby managed to stay lithe and slim, even at sixty-two—and eased the glass from his fingers, sipping from it. "Sitting alone in a mostly darkened room, glowering out the window, drink in hand, especially at Moondance—oh, I know your habits, Gabriel. What the hell is bugging you?"

Damn right you know me, Ruby.

"Just thinking about the date and the resonances around it."

"The date? Oh. Yeah." Her lips tightened. "Coincidence. Just like Branny was born on the same date in December that Justine had her hysterectomy. Ronnie will grow up to be his own person. Like Bran did."

"I wasn't thinking so much of Ronnie and his future. Just—" he sighed. "I fucked up so bad years ago, Rubes. You're so good with the kids. Maybe if I had stayed, our daughter would have survived."

Ruby shut her eyes for a moment, wincing. Then she drained the glass, reaching over him to set it down carefully on the side table. "Gabe, it was a hydatidiform mole. Just like Justine's and Kris's, only more like Kris's. No hysterectomy for me."

"God damn it, I should have still been there to support you." The revelation stunned him. *Three* instances of hydatidiform mole in their close family? It wasn't a genetic phenomenon, at least as far as he knew.

That—doesn't seem right.

"I *tried* to tell you. You kept blocking my texts until I used Remy's phone."

"I was being an idiot. A total fucking fool." He shuddered. "I should have fought Philip then."

"You were under mind control, remember? Unable to tell me a damn thing about what was going on whether it was voice, handwriting, or typed."

He groaned. "And yet I could have thought of a way to tell you. I overlooked an obvious possibility."

"Like what?"

"Remy Trask had that file that would have qualified you to draw on the Martiniere Family Trust in the event of my death. She was one of the assistant US attorneys working on *US vs Martiniere Group.* Even though I didn't know *that* at the time, I knew she was practicing law in Los Angeles during the trial—and would have been aware of my testimony. I had seven days after Philip gave me that ultimatum. There would have been time for me to act."

"To do what?" Ruby frowned at him.

"To tell her to disregard my original instructions not to open that envelope unless I was confirmed dead. I should have told her to share that information. The two of you would have figured it out. Maybe even contacted Justine or Donna-gran, figured out a way to beat my programming."

Ruby pursed her lips. "Given the condition you were in after Philip and his goons beat the crap out of you, I doubt you had much brain space to think about something like that. And—" she arched a brow at him. "Remember, you theorized he introduced more psychotropics and nanos into your system while battering you when he made that demand. That's another factor why you didn't think of that option. He intended to block your ability to act, period."

"All the same, I was fucking stupid. I should have thought of Remy. We might have brought Philip down one hell of a lot sooner."

"It still wouldn't have saved that pregnancy, Gabe."

He gulped. "I slipped away from Mariah and lit a candle in church after you told me you miscarried. Broke down crying on the prie-dieu in front of the candles. It was the only damn thing I could do in that whole mess." He exhaled. "Something weird happened after that. An older woman, in blue, the shade associated with apparitions of Mary. She touched my shoulder and made the sign of the cross on my forehead. Couldn't see her features clearly because my eyes were blurry with tears, but she kinda looked like my aunt Elena Ramirez—who had been killed years before."

Actually, more like Mama.

But he wasn't going to say that. Even though he still half-thought his mother had returned to comfort him.

Ruby cupped his cheek. "I didn't think you believed."

He turned his head to kiss her palm. "I still don't, or at least nothing more than is expedient to keep the Catholic traditionalists in the Family happy. But it soothed me. Not sure why. It was probably one of the older parishioners who had seen my face in a vid."

"Aw, Gabe. So why are you beating yourself up over this now?"

"Because you're so good with the kids. Not just Mike and Lily, but Bran. A good mother." He took a deep breath. "I always thought that sooner or later you would remarry and have more kids with someone else. Had resigned myself to it at one point."

"No, Gabe." She shook her head. "There wasn't anyone promising in Thunder County. You're—" her voice broke and she swallowed hard. "You're the only man I've ever trusted in a relationship. I had a really rough time in college because so many guys were chasing the rodeo queen. But you were polite. Respectful. Interested in my mind, not just my body. Honestly a horseman. Oh, Monty Montgomery sniffed around me a little bit a couple of years after the divorce, but I told him I wasn't interested, that screwing him would be too much like getting back in bed with you."

"That damn Monty." But Gabe smiled, even as he shook his head. "You know the man carried a torch for you for years, right?"

"He was also fifteen years older than me, and—" she sighed. "I just didn't have the heart for anyone else, Gabe. It hit me hard when you and Rachel got together. So why didn't *you* have kids with her? I could say the same back to you—you're great with the kids, and Rachel was a good stepmother to Brandon."

Ouch. But he'd asked for it, by finally asking Ruby this question.

"I had a vasectomy nearly a year before I started dating Rachel. I just—after the divorce, and everything else—I was already worried about what Philip would do to Branny. Once I started making enough money to hire escorts when I went to National Finals, I decided I didn't want to risk any more hostages to fortune. More weaknesses for Philip to hold over me as a lever, to force me to dance to his tune."

"Vasectomies can be reversed."

"Rachel couldn't have kids. Hysterectomy, as part of her first bout with cancer."

"I see. That sucks. And no nieces or nephews? Bran didn't mention any Alvarez kids. Just your friend Craig's grandkids, and after a couple of years not even them." Ruby leaned her head into his shoulder.

"Rachel's brother Rick liked to play the field, never settled down before he died from the G9 virus, and her other brother Rafe—he and Serg were lovers. So neither of them had kids. Serg and Rafe would never have been able to adopt—besides the increasing restrictions on gay adoption thanks to Philip, the hostages to fortune thing was an issue as well, with both of them so deep into security work. And we didn't adopt—well, I'm not sure why we didn't. The possibility never came up, I suppose because Rachel was worried about the cancer returning."

"Well, we have Mike and the grandkids, at least."

"And the Swait kids. And the interns at the Double R."

Ruby laughed. "I think that's why I kept sponsoring and helping a couple of girls with their horses every year. Couldn't always do money, but even just loaning trained horses as queen rides helped girls who couldn't compete otherwise."

"At least you did *something*."

"Ah, Gabe. Stop beating yourself up. What's past is past, and we have a future ahead of us."

"True," Gabe conceded.

He just wondered how many years were left for them together. He was sixty-eight, and Ruby would be sixty-three in October. Neither of them had lived easy lives. His heart. Her family history of cancer.

Gabe wrapped his arms tightly around his Ruby.

Cherish the moment.

God, he remembered doing just this, *here,* holding Rachel close as cancer ate away at her, day by day.

He hoped he wouldn't need to do that with Ruby.

DECEMBER, 2070

THE WIND HOWLED AND WHIPPED ICE PELLETS AGAINST THE NORTH-facing bedroom windows when he woke. Gabe exhaled. His throat ached. The air moving through his nostrils burned warmer than usual. He didn't want to move, arms and legs feeling like sandbags were piled on them.

Hell of a day to get sick. First real winter storm.

Maybe he could push himself enough to help Ruby feed this morning, since most of their staff were down sick. But Gabe couldn't help groaning as he sat up, leaning on his hands after he swung his feet to the floor, trying to summon the strength to stand.

That brought Ruby to his side, frowning as she rested the back of her hand on his forehead. "You're running a fever."

"Not much of one. I can help you feed."

"No. Mike can help." She crossed her arms, glaring at him in that bossy manner he knew all too well. "I don't need you having a heart attack in the field."

Gabe would have argued, but the way he wobbled slightly when he stood made Ruby's case. He let her guide him down-stairs, into the living room. She kindled a fire in the wood stove, and settled him in his favorite rocker with a side table nearby. Then brought him coffee.

Something about the way Mike moved when he refilled Gabe's coffee made him take a second look at the boy. Mike had grown *up* but not *out* over the past summer. His face seemed thinner and paler than it should be. The one thing that looked right about him was a faint scattering of acne across his nose. He hunched over this morning like he was in pain—probably was, Mike had arthritis like him and Ruby.

Yet Mike put in a full day's work on the ranch and in the labs. Every day. And schooled horses.

After all, Philip had been a slight man—and nowhere near as active as Mike.

Probably nothing.

Gabe leaned his head against the back of his chair and dozed off, barely rousing when Ruby left his breakfast on the side table and kissed his forehead.

———

The sudden shrill of his comm startled Gabe out of a sound sleep.

"Ruby Barkley."

What the hell? Why was she calling him? Something had to be wrong in the field. Gabe answered, his heart pounding hard with fear.

"GABE!" she screamed. "Mike's collapsed in the horse field and I can't get him up! He's out cold! MedicFlight is sending a ground ambulance but—oh God!" Ruby gulped. "Trying to get him into the cab now. He isn't responding!"

"Hang on, sweetheart, I'll be right there."

Oh fuck.

Gabe called Brandon as he staggered to the back porch, quickly told him what was happening.

"I'll get there as soon as possible. You don't sound good, Dad," Bran said as Gabe coughed, a deep wracking hack that brought up phlegm and doubled him over.

"I'm down sick. So is just about everyone else on the ranch— security, lab, ranch hands, and probably Mike now." He wrestled with his heavy insulated coveralls. Thank God for Ruby's habits of bringing out their heavy clothing in mid-November, even when the fall had been mild like it had been until today's storm. He didn't have exert the energy to search for his coveralls, jacket and boots.

"Why didn't you tell me?"

"Happened just this morning." Gabe sealed the coverall, wrapped a scarf around his neck, pulled on a heavy wool cap, finishing with his jacket.

"You be careful, you and Mom both!"

"Got it." He wrenched on his insulated boots and headed out the door.

The tractor was moving by the time he got to the horse field, hightailing toward the gate, even as Gabe heard the faint but welcome wail of the ambulance siren. He opened the gate wide as Ruby steered through, secured it, then hurried as best as he could after the tractor.

Ruby stopped it in the middle of the barnyard. Gabe clambered up the tractor's side. She held Mike in her lap, sobbing, her arms wrapped around him. Mike's eyes were closed, his face pale, a blue tinge around his lips and nose, but at least he was still breathing, nostrils fluttering slightly. His heeler, Striker, nudged frantically at Mike's limp hands, whining. Gabe thought about opening the door but no, Ruby had a heater running in the enclosed cab. Better he didn't let the storm in.

"I'll guide the ambulance over!" he called.

Ruby raised her head, nodding. God, she looked deathly pale. His worry heightened as she started coughing.

Both of them down sick, damn it.

He let himself down carefully. No need to rush and make things worse by slipping on slick surfaces. Gabe staggered toward the driveway, straining to see those red and blue flashing lights.

He guided the paramedics to the tractor, after warning them about the potential that Ruby and Mike were sick as well as him, waiting for them to mask up before they got out. Watched, worried, as they eased Mike out of Ruby's arms and onto a stretcher. Grabbed Striker and dragged him to the kennel when he would have followed the stretcher, the dog protesting all the way. Made sure the kennel heater was working and that Striker had food and water.

Ruby shivered next to the ambulance when he returned to her, arms wrapped around herself. "I'm sick now too," she gasped. "Gabe—oh Gabe—they think he's had a heart attack. I'm running a fever. I can't go to the hospital with him."

"Bran's on his way." A chill unrelated to his illness ran down his spine. *Heart attack. At fifteen. Too fucking young. This has to be a clone effect. And so close to Kris dying from a heart attack in September* — "I'll send Bran to the hospital—let them know."

Gabe took care of the niceties, calling Brandon to let him know he needed to act in their stead as temporary guardian to approve treatment. Issuing the necessary approvals. Together, he and Ruby put the tractor in the hay shed. Then they leaned against each other as they staggered back to the house.

Ruby was in worse shape than he was. Gabe managed to haul himself upstairs to their bedroom and retrieve sweats for both of them as she shivered over coffee in the rocker he had abandoned. He pulled her into the first-floor shower with him so they could warm up, then helped her dress. After stoking the fire in the wood stove, he curled up with her on the living room couch.

"How can he have a heart attack so young?" Ruby moaned. "Oh God, Gabe, it was scary. Mike just staggered away from the bale, grabbing his chest, then fell in the snow and didn't get up. Striker kept the horses away from him, Striker and Spree both."

Spree. Mike's prized weanling filly, soon to be a yearling. Bred so he could compete in reined cowhorse competition with a horse of his own breeding and training. Mike had been working toward this goal for *years*.

And both Striker and Spree had benefited from Ruby's epigenetic manipulations.

Gabe didn't answer Ruby. *Couldn't* answer, because he knew the possibility too damned well.

Fucking Philip Martiniere. This is either a clone effect, or a weakness he made in Mike.

Instead, he held Ruby tight, worrying about his beloved and the clone who was their son.

And then there was Brandon, newly widowed, with a daughter spiraling into madness and an infant son. What sort of viruses was he exposing himself to—and his children—by coming to Thunder County where God-only-knew-what was spreading?

Am I losing my second family?

In a slower manner than the plane crash that took away his first family?

God, Gabe couldn't stand *that* possibility. He had spent his life trying to keep his second family from suffering the fate of his first one.

It wasn't fair. *It just wasn't fair.*

BRANDON BROUGHT DR. SHERI TO THE RANCH TO CHECK ON GABE and Ruby. Gabe was happy to see that both Bran and Dr. Sheri wore heavy-duty filtration masks.

"Flu," Dr. Sheri sighed, after running diagnostic tests and examining the projection readouts. "A variant that wasn't in your vaccination this fall. Lots of it in the County right now. Luckily, this one responds to antiviral treatment. The two of you need to quarantine for three days, but at least you'll feel better."

"Probably the same thing for the others," Gabe muttered as she injected him.

"I'll check your security and ranch workers once I'm done here. Brandon told me everyone was down sick."

"Pretty much. What's the story with Mike?" Ruby asked.

Dr. Sheri sighed again. "Heart attack, and something else.

White blood cell counts are way down." A third sigh. "We're testing for the cancers that Philip Martiniere had. Fortunately, Mike doesn't have this bug."

Cancer. Fuck.

Ruby sobbed into Gabe's chest after Brandon and Dr. Sheri left the house to check on the other ranch residents.

He cried with her.

Sixty-eight years old, and Gabe would happily trade his life for Mike's. He had lived his life.

Mike hadn't, and damn it, the young clone deserved a chance to thrive, separate from the shadow of his fucking progenitor.

2071

CANCER TURNED OUT TO BE THE LEAST OF MIKE'S PROBLEMS. HE also had significant heart and lung failure, tied to being the clone of a seventy-eight-year-old man. His system wouldn't handle a standard transplant, and clone regeneration in someone who was already a clone suffering from clone effects? Not likely.

Cyborg heart and lungs were possible—but expensive and time-consuming to create.

Plus the psychological issues. Mike cut himself off from everyone dear to him once it became clear that his health problems went beyond cancer to heart and lungs, plus significant osteoporosis that manifested in his arms and legs. All clone effects. All reflective of Philip's health problems at the time Mike was created. All those health issues—that kept him off of horses.

Mike huddled in his darkened room with only Striker for companionship, refusing to talk to anyone beyond bare necessity. Lily shied away from Mike—and that, given her past obsession with him, frightened Gabe even more.

"Our fucking father had those moments in his last years,"

Justine said during one of their late-night drinking sessions in the Double R's kitchen in late July. "Nights where he would summon me to keep him company while he stared out the window. Sometimes he drank, but most of the time—dead silence. Especially during Family Christmas."

Gabe winced. "Shit. I do that."

Justine bit her lip and nodded. "Yeah. Same here. Like father, like son and daughter."

"He's still Mike. Not *him*. But if it wasn't for Striker—" At least Mike still kept his dog close. Gabe dreaded to think what dire *thing* would emerge from Mike's bedroom, wearing his beloved son's face, if Mike didn't have Striker to keep him connected to the world.

"Ruby says Mike told her to sell Spree today." Justine tossed her whisky down her throat and poured herself more. She held up the bottle. "Another?"

Gabe eyed it, and shook his head. Alcohol couldn't chase *this* horror away.

Ruby had cried herself to sleep in his arms.

He's giving up, Gabe. We can't let him do it.

But what could they do? Bran couldn't reach Mike either. Nor Justine. No one.

"I've tried to talk to Mike. I've asked his counselor what we can do." He got up, paced the kitchen. "We can't do much more in the way of medication, given everything else going on." Gabe stared out the kitchen window, toward the barnyard. A couple of whitetail deer drifted through, sniffing after wisps of hay scattered from today's stacking. "And Lily isn't any better. She's hearing voices regularly. God. We're losing Mike. We're losing Lily. I don't know what to do, Tine. I know what made Mike tell Ruby to sell Spree. He couldn't brush half of one side of her today without having to sit down. That filly is so well-behaved with him, even at her age—"

Justine's eyes widened—she had been a horsewoman once herself, understood what it meant and how unusual it was for a yearling filly like Spree to be that mannerly. "Shit. But there are ways—"

"He won't talk to JoAnn, and they were best friends, heading for a romantic relationship—Jeff and I spied them holding hands last summer, typical early teen shy nerd romancy stuff. Mike won't talk to any of the kids he hangs out with locally. None of his online connections." Gabe returned to the table, sitting down hard. "Fuck."

"Maybe a visit with Donald." Justine's voice sounded unconvincing.

"Mike won't willingly leave the ranch unless we're taking him to see a doctor. Can Don travel?"

"I'll talk to Donald." Justine pressed her lips together. "See what he might be able to manage."

"Thanks, Tine."

<hr>

WHILE TALKING WITH DONALD BRIEFLY HELPED, THINGS GOT REALLY bad around the one-year anniversary of Mike's heart attack in December. Mike finally exploded at Gabe, or at least as best as he could shout with limited lung function. Gabe let Mike yell himself out, mainly repetitions of *I don't matter to anyone, who cares if I live or die, maybe I'm better off dead, I'm just a crippled clone boy and the image of an evil man.*

God. The darkness Mike had been carrying within him. Where had all that negativity come from? Not from anything that Gabe or Ruby or anyone else had ever done or said, at least that Gabe knew.

That damned worm? Whatever it was that kept yanking files out to rub Mike's origin in his face?

Whatever it was, it was evil. It was wrong.

Mike was *cherished* by the Family. An example of what Philip *could* have been.

Gabe sat by Mike's bed and took his hand.

"You matter to me. To Ruby. To Bran. To Ronnie."

That last one got to Mike—Gabe could tell. Baby Ronnie was the only one who didn't let Mike's moods put him off, but insisted on cuddling with *Unca Mike.* The only time Mike smiled was around Ronnie.

They talked it out, and Mike's moods were never quite as dour after that.

A good thing, because shortly after that talk, Mike went into the hospital in Portland. He would either leave with a cyborg heart and lungs or—he'd be dead.

TECHNICALLY, THEY WERE SUPPOSED TO BE STAYING WITH JUSTINE AT Donald's Portland condo.

Realistically, Gabe and Ruby stayed with Mike, with short separate trips to the condo to change and shower.

Mike faded as each day ticked by. Panic attacks struck at any hour, at times so bad that the only means they had to soothe him was Ruby—as the lighter and more agile of them—in bed with Mike, holding him in her arms, while Gabe leaned over the bed and lent his support, hugging the two of them as best as he could. Gabe crooned old lullabies he faintly remembered from babyhood, a mix of Spanish, English, and French. Ruby told stories from Ryder family history.

After Mike settled, Ruby and Gabe took turns staying awake to watch while the other one found sleep the best that they could in the big hospital recliners.

His chest started to hurt in a familiar manner.

But Gabe could not, *would not,* leave Ruby and Mike alone in this vigil as long as he could stay upright.

No matter what the cost.

Maybe his sacrifice would save Mike.

Gabe ended up in surgery the day before Mike. A massive heart attack, requiring a quadruple bypass.

Martiniere money bought him a bed in the room next to Mike, so Ruby wasn't running between hospitals.

Money's good for something, for once.

December, 2072

Gabe's recovery was faster than Mike's, in part because the severity of Mike's osteoporosis limited what he could do for physical therapy. For the first time in two years, they were able to go to Vienna and Paris in December, for the Spanish Riding School's Winter Gala and Family Christmas. Gabe took advantage of the opportunity to book a private stable tour of the Lipizzan stallions—best for Mike, since he was now in a wheelchair.

Mike finished the tour with damp cheeks. The stallion in the last stall hung his head over the stall door, stretching his nose out to Mike. He carefully raised his hand to let the stallion sniff it, then scratched up the horse's long nose to the spot just above his eyes, a favorite with most horses. After Mike dropped his hand, shaking with fatigue, the stallion eyed Mike. Then, carefully and oh-so-gently, the stallion nuzzled Mike's forehead and cheeks, blowing softly.

Silent tears trickled out of Mike's eyes, even as he grinned.

"He *will* ride again," Ruby murmured into Gabe's ear. "If I have anything to say about it."

Gabe nodded, blinking back his own tears.

Something had to work out for their boy. *Something.*

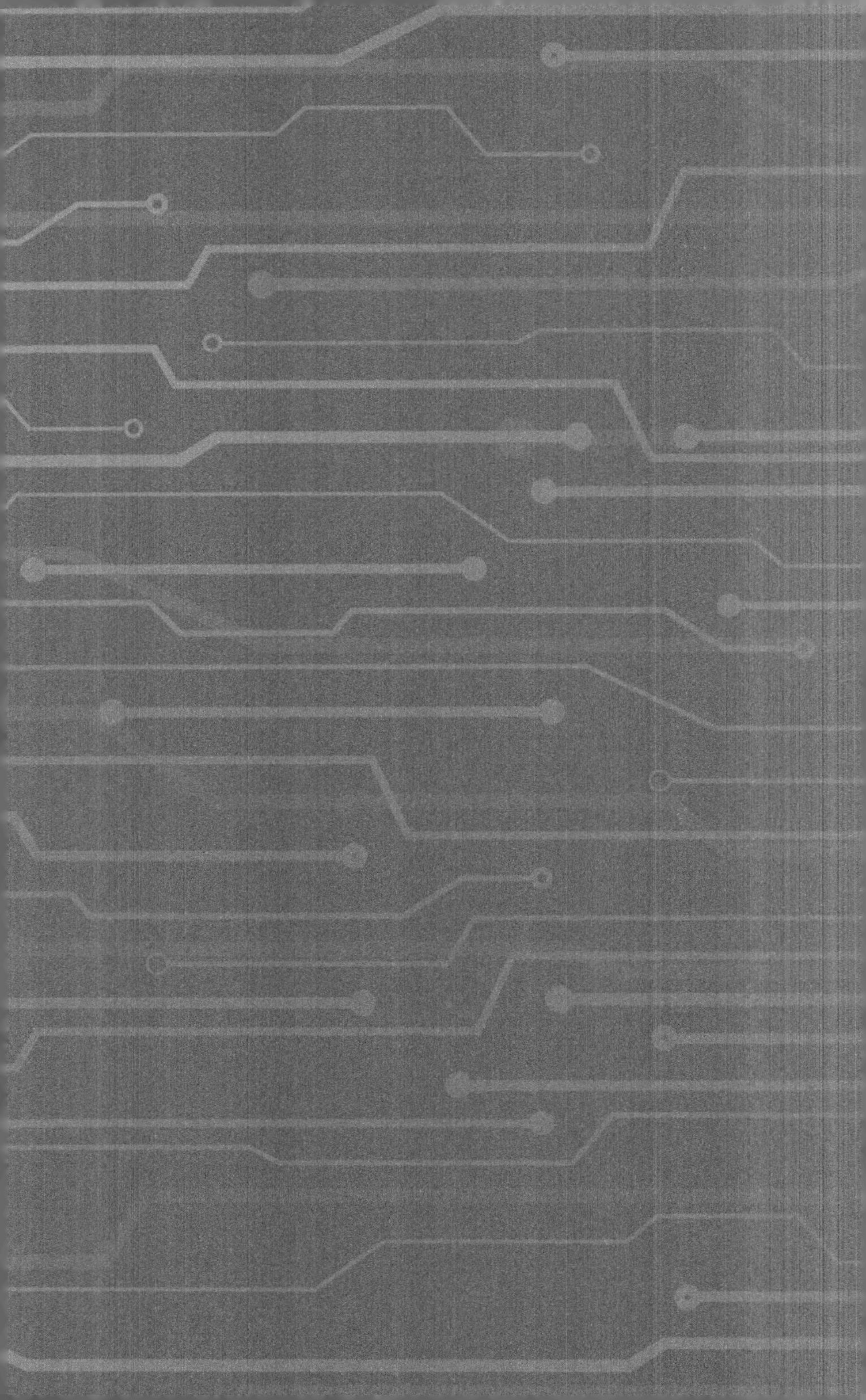

15 / WINDING DOWN THE YEARS

RUBY

RUBY OPENED HER EYES, WAKING SLOWLY FROM A SOUND SLEEP. THE distant screech of seagulls, coupled with the faint roar of pounding surf, reminded her that they were at the cliff house, though the cloying damp and cold also served as a notice that they were on the coast, not at home at the Double R.

Gabe curled around her, bare flesh to bare flesh, arm thrown over her waist, pressing close. Ruby smiled, remembering last night's lovemaking. Her husband might be turning seventy-one years old today, and his arousal less frequent, but he still was as passionate as he had been when they first became lovers.

Almost forty-three years ago. Thirteen years since we got back together.

A sweet thirteen years, in her opinion.

And she had plans for Gabe's birthday morning. They had spent a week between Portland and the cliff house, Mike staying in Portland with Justine and Donald as he underwent preliminary tests and prep for his arm cyborging in April. So far, it looked good for the process being able to replace the bones only, with minimal intrusion and side effects. They would know for certain tonight, when they joined Mike for Gabe's birthday dinner, along with Justine and Donald.

But the morning at the cliff house was theirs.

Ruby eased carefully out from under Gabe's arm. He snuffled and turned over, exhaling heavily. She paused, waiting to see if he was waking up. When he settled deeper into the bedding, she rose and pulled on a robe to stave off the worst of the chill, and slid her feet into a pair of slippers. A quick visit to the bathroom, then into the kitchen to take her morning medications. Ruby started coffee, and turned to her first project, mixing her quick-rise biscuits.

Biscuits set to rise, Ruby poured herself some coffee, then made quiche using the last of their dried morels and a home-made crust she had left in the freezer after their last trip to the cliff house. Maybe they would be able to get into the woods in a few weeks to harvest more mushrooms this year, and maybe not. Gabe had problems walking very far without either a cane or a walker anymore, and it seemed like every year the mushrooms retreated further and further into the forest, to areas where it was difficult for him to walk.

Might need to think about cultivating some morels. Or just buying some.

Though Ruby hated to give up the morel hunt, traipsing through the woods as the season changed from winter to spring. Finding calypso/ladyslipper orchids. Watching meadows transform from soggy, mushed-down-by-snowbanks dried grasses to the fresh green of spring. That special ox-eye daisy patch she loved, near the shooting range. And stumbling across morels, suddenly spotting a single shy, convoluted, gray-brown-black mushroom, then realizing they were all around her.

But eras changed, and perhaps it was time to let go of mushrooming, as they had done firewood cutting.

On the other hand, Gabe could ride in a crawler while she hunted mushrooms. Maybe it wasn't time to completely give it up yet.

In any case, she had stashed these remaining morels for just this occasion. Gabe loved them, especially in her quiches, and what better for his birthday than a quiche filled with morels? Even if they were rehydrated dried ones.

Shuffling sounds alerted her and she turned her head to grin at Gabe as she slid the quiche into the oven. He no longer glided silently around the house, but hobbled, unable to silently sneak up on her—or Justine—or any other Family member. But that broad, joyous smile that spread across his face when her eyes met his, and that matching *come-hither* twinkle in his eyes—no, that hadn't changed. Like her, he wore a light robe, unbelted, more for keeping the chill off back and shoulders than modesty.

"So what have we here?" He wrapped his arms around her.

"Your birthday breakfast quiche." She turned within Gabe's arms. "Quiche, and biscuits are rising. I need to put them in after a bit."

"Mmm." He pulled her close for a kiss, soft at first, then more intense. At last he raised his head, smiling at Ruby.

She smiled back and stroked his cheek and temple with her right hand. Age lines on his face, of course, and his once-solid-black hair was now mostly gray and silver, with streaks of black.

"Seventy-one today," she murmured.

Gabe scowled. "Don't want to think about the number of birthdays. Getting to be too many of them. Just want to kiss my pretty wife."

Ruby snorted. "Flatterer. I have stretch marks. Saggy tits. Gray and silver in my hair. Wrinkles."

His hands slid down her back and wrapped around her butt. "And firm horsewoman's ass, muscled-up legs that go on forever, and no droopy skin sag under your arms. You're still the gorgeous, brilliant, beautiful redheaded rodeo queen who stole my heart and soul. My queen. The queen of my heart." His dark brown eyes gazed solemnly into hers.

"My love." As always, he was *so warm*, bare skin against bare skin. "My wild bronc rider turned corporate leader. The man who believed in my biobot vision. The only man who has ever possessed my heart."

"And see where it took us." Gabe exhaled. "Ah, Rubes, the best birthday presents were when you took me back into your life, then remarried me. Best. Ever. For life." He kissed her forehead as his hands moved back to her waist, his lips brushing little feathery kisses down her cheek. "Thirteen years together again, and far too short. I'm so damn grateful you managed to forgive my stupidity."

"Are you ever going to stop saying you're sorry?"

"Never. Getting stampeded into divorce because I was so afraid to tell you my real identity was the stupidest choice of my life. I will always regret it."

Ruby shuddered, a sudden unreasonable sensation of *dread* and *desolation* sending chills through her, joined with a vision of a future without Gabe, somehow worse than divorce had been. She buried her head in Gabe's chest.

Seventy-one. How many more years do we have left?

His hand stroked her hair. "Rubes. What's wrong?"

"Just—I don't know, that sensation of someone walking over my grave. Or yours. Something like that."

"Death will happen someday." His voice was quiet. "We've had some close calls over the years. Together and apart. But we're both getting up there in age. It's not like we have forever left to us."

"It's not enough."

"No. It's not." Gentle lips on hers again. "But it's what we have. And on my birthday, as far as I'm concerned, being able to spend another year in the presence of my brilliant, beautiful wife is the best present ever."

"Good, because besides your breakfast, that's what you're getting this year."

"I'd take you to bed after breakfast, except last night—" He smirked.

"That was a good time, wasn't it?"

"Yes. And I look forward to an equally good time celebrating *your* birthday in October."

"I'll hold you to that," she said.

But that same premonitionary chill tightened her gut. Ruby clung to Gabe.

It wasn't so much the prospect of facing the world alone that sent the fear racing through her. After all, she had done just fine by herself after their divorce.

It was the potential absence of *Gabe*—now and forever—that struck dread into her heart.

May that day be long in coming.

---

*A*PRIL, **2073**

MIKE HID HIS FEAR ABOUT THE UPCOMING CYBORGING REASONABLY well. They spent the night at Moondance to celebrate Lily's birthday before reporting for surgical prep in Portland the next morning. Ruby overheard the conversation between Mike and Brandon as she walked by the kitchen, heading toward Lily's room to help Gabe get her settled. She paused out of sight, to listen.

"I'm afraid it's gonna hurt." Mike's voice quavered a little. "I —it's silly to say anything about this to Gabe and Ruby. I mean, Ruby's broken leg with Boomer, and Gabe and the G9, and his surgeries, and—"

"Bro, you'll be *fine*," Brandon said. "You've been through a lot yourself. Chemo. Heart and lung cyborging. More."

A cough. "Yeah. But this is creepier. Replacing my bones with some weird composite? What if the anesthesia doesn't work this time? It was weird during the cyborging before. Now—"

"It'll be all right. Trust in that."

"No!" Lily yelled, her voice echoing down the hallway from her studio, distracting Ruby from Mike and Bran's conversation.

"Lily-hon, we need you to cooperate." Gabe's voice held an unusual edge. Normally Lily didn't set him off.

Ruby sighed, and continued toward the family wing to deal with the drama. After settling the difference, Ruby returned to the kitchen. As she walked in, Mike fell silent, looking half-guilty. Brandon raised his brows at her, and Ruby realized he didn't want her to say anything.

Bran probably saw me.

He *was* sneakier than Mike, almost as sneaky as Gabe.

After dinner, Mike went to the nursery to put Ronnie to bed, and Lily to her studio. Ruby and Gabe settled with Brandon in the great room. She shared the big recliner with Gabe while Brandon sat in a rocking chair.

Ruby glanced around the space—mostly empty these days, except for the recliners, couch, and rocking chairs by the slider door leading to the big deck. Voices echoed when there were only a few people in here, and that gave her the heebie-jeebies.

Far too many memories here, both good and bad. Marrying Gabe. Kris and Brandon's wedding. The final confrontation with Philip. Kris's death. Those occasional nights when she found Gabe brooding over a drink—something about Moondance sparked a certain moodiness in him that she rarely saw at the Double R or the cliff house. He seemed to prefer this room when moroseness slipped over him.

Well, it *was* a replica of the previous house, and Gabe had spent a good chunk of his life here.

Brandon sighed. "Lily's getting worse. Dad, Mom, I don't know what to do. Maybe we can keep her from being committed to a psychiatric facility, but it seems less and less likely. She keeps talking about hearing voices. I've found her dancing with an imaginary companion."

"She's not as fascinated with Mike as she has been in the past few years." Gabe stroked his chin. "Perhaps she's gotten over the obsession with Philip."

"She's more fixated on Philip than ever. Who do you think her imaginary dance partner is? Today was a good day." Brandon laced his fingers and leaned forward, staring down at his hands. "Part of the problem is that her new meds have impacted her coordination. She can't dance anymore—well, at least not in performance. Dr. Soren thinks things will get better —maybe."

"Maybe she can dance again, after she adjusts to the meds?" Ruby swallowed hard. Dance had kept Lily centered, just like horses and now Striker had provided support for Mike. If Lily lost dance—unlike Mike, she had no other outlet. No pets. No other creative endeavors.

"No. Even before we changed meds, her behavior had become more erratic. She needs a minder with her at rehearsals, and I've yet to find someone who Lily will accept." Brandon shook his head and raised his hand before Ruby could speak. "Not you, Ma. I'm grateful for all the time you've put in with Lily, but—honestly, I'm worried about your safety with her anymore. She's dangerous in some moods."

"That bad?" Gabe scowled.

"Yes." Brandon ran a hand through his black hair that was just starting to get streaked with gray, like Gabe's was now. "It requires the right person. Trust me, I've been looking. I'd *like* to keep Lily dancing. But between medication issues and the very real risk she can pose to others due to her dissociative episodes, she's not sufficiently stable to perform. And I don't dare send her to classes without a minder present to intervene if she has a problem."

"Perhaps a small local company?" Surely there had to be an answer. Something to provide a focus for her granddaughter.

Brandon sat up, sighing. "And that's where I run into further problems with Lily. Even if I could find someone to serve as a minder, she considers dancing with a smaller company to be a significant hardship. She refuses to think about the possibility." He raised his hands. "She's right. She's a better dancer than the others in the local amateur companies, either in Pendleton or Walla Walla. But there's issues beyond her meds. She's just—too erratic. Won't hold up to the stress. Dr. Soren has been quite firm with her about it, and she's *verbally* in agreement with this decision. But coming to terms with that reality is a different story."

Mike came into the great room, brows furrowed in worry.

Ruby sat back and listened as he told Brandon about Lily dancing with an imaginary partner. Gabe's hand tightened on hers as Bran explained Lily's circumstances to Mike.

Another heavy exhale from Bran as Mike left for his suite.

"You know that Mike's scared stiff about this surgery."

Was that relief in her son's voice as the topic turned to Mike and not the twists and turns of Lily's situation?

Probably.

"He hasn't wanted to talk about it," Gabe said.

"He's spent a lot of time alone with Striker, so I'm not surprised," Ruby added. "Was that what you two were talking about in the kitchen?"

"Yes."

Good. At least Mike's talking to someone.

"It *is* a scary surgery." Ruby tapped her fingers on her leg. "And while we're trying to preserve his muscles and skin, there's always the possibility that may not work. That he may need to go full cyborg with his arms—and his legs."

"He's very aware of that." Brandon ran his hand through his hair again. "But there's more to it. Anesthesia worries him."

"This is a different situation from his heart and lung cyborging, but I can sure see how it would affect him. After all, he damned near died before the cyborging happened." Ruby frowned.

Could Mike's surgery be the source of her foreboding?

Entirely possible.

As it turned out, Mike wasn't the problem that caused her dread. The surgeries—it took several to complete the cyborg arm replacement—were uneventful. Recovery and physical therapy needed to be slow, in order to integrate muscles, tendons, and nerves with his new bones.

"Excellent prognosis," was the verdict of Mike's surgeon a week after the final surgery. Dr. Pramula was a cyborging specialist from Los Angeles who had started a clinic in Portland, funded by the Martiniere Foundation. "Much better than Mike's heart and lung surgery. It reflects his improving health."

"What about my legs?" Mike mumbled.

"Not yet. We need to see what the long-term impact is on your heart and lungs first."

A small victory, but *that* was worth rejoicing.

Ruby and Gabe went out for a celebratory dinner, walking from the condo to a Thai place they had been getting takeout from during Mike's previous hospitalization.

On the way back, Gabe turned to look at a vehicle. His foot missed the curb, and he fell into the street.

Ruby screamed and dived for him. Security pushed her back.

Gabe's face went paper-pale as they helped him to his feet. "Fuck, fuck, *fuck*. Aw, *fuck* that hurts. The bad right knee."

Ruby hovered until they got him out of the street and settled on a nearby bench. She sat next to Gabe and held his hand while security checked him.

"We'd better transport to the ER," was the final assessment.

So back to University Hospital they went.

Torn meniscus and anterior cruciate ligament, was the verdict. Which meant a surgery date for Gabe as well.

Ruby sighed at the thought of a summer of physical therapy ahead, with *two* grumpy Martiniere men to handle.

"It's more work for you, Rubes," Gabe fretted once they were safely back at the condo, leg elevated, knee in a brace. "And I'll miss morel hunting, even in a crawler. Tie you down to the house all summer. No getting outside."

It matched her own thoughts. But she had some notions about how to handle Gabe and Mike.

"We've been talking about setting up an outdoor office during the summer anyway," she said. "I'll park you and Mike on the lawn, then go ride and train. It's not like we don't have staff around to help you two, and we weren't going to do much this summer anyway because of the length of time Mike needs to recover."

"True," Gabe conceded.

<hr>

AND YET…WHILE SURGERY AND RECOVERY FOR MIKE WERE uneventful events, Gabe had problems. Spiking blood pressure during the operation revealed more heart issues. It took him longer to recover than anticipated.

"Cumulative effects of two bouts of G9," Dr. Amy Caruthers, Gabe's personal specialist, told Ruby. "And side effects from that experimental anti-aging serum."

"That didn't really work well after five years," Ruby muttered.

May raced by as both Gabe and Mike grumped around the house. The weather switched quickly from cold and damp to hot and dry. Normally, Ruby would fret about the hot, dry weather —it still concerned her, but the change meant fewer aches and pains for both men. And she could set up the outside office under the Jeffreys pines on the front lawn—at least until it got too warm.

A canopy for lawn chairs, as a sun break. A hammock strung between the two closest of the trees, with posts set for support getting in and out. A lawn swing. Tables. Chairs. Hammock and swing angled so that both had a clear view of the Thunder

Mountains. Staking out Star or one of the broodmares on the lawn.

Gabe claimed the hammock while Mike settled into the swing. Getting outside to work—Gabe, managing their assorted projects, Mike, wrapping up the high school studies he missed during his illnesses and recovery—seemed to improve their outlooks.

Still, Ruby worried. She couldn't put a finger on exactly what niggled at her. Gabe seemed slower. His memory wasn't as accurate. He got frustrated by obstacles much more easily. In spite of the difficulty he had with climbing the stairs to their bedroom, he refused Ruby's suggestion that they move into the downstairs bedroom that had been Gramps' during his last illness.

"I'm not that damn fragile," Gabe muttered whenever Ruby brought it up. "I want to stay in *our* bedroom, not the invalid's room."

And whatever project it was that obsessed Gabe the most seemed to be more and more problematic. He wouldn't talk about it, and Mike wore earbuds to help focus on his academics. So he would have no idea about what was bothering Gabe.

She *was* tempted to rub her ring at Gabe several times. Then again, Ruby only remembered her concern about this secret project whenever she was away from Gabe's presence.

What is happening to us?

JUNE, 2073

STAR COLICKED AND DIED IN MID-JUNE, WITHOUT WARNING. RUBY found the big dark bay stallion in the field, with his mares and foals gathered around him in silent tribute.

"I'm burying him myself," Gabe insisted.

"Gabriel." Her voice sharpened, and she *almost* inserted a command tone. "Your knee, and the shape you're in—"

"I'm not a fucking invalid, damn it!"

Ruby flinched. *He* wasn't hesitating about using a tone, and even though she wasn't programmed, the resonances hit her hard. "Damn it, Gabe! You're also not in the best condition." She used a slight tone on him.

He glowered at her, lips tight, eyes hard. "I owe it to the old man. Damn it, I wanted to get one last ride on him but I'm *so fucking weak*—" His voice quavered and he blinked. "Damn it. Another thing my health has taken away from me!"

"We'll *both* do it," she said.

God, this was awful. Especially since Gabe's eyes glimmered with unshed tears. Star had been *his* horse, more so than any other on the ranch.

They buried Star in the field where he died.

"No need to trim mane and tail hair," Gabe said. "That's just sentiment." But his voice caught and he blinked hard. "He was romping with his foals just day before yesterday."

Ruby managed to sneak in and clip enough hair to braid into a bracelet for Gabe. Despite his tough façade, he had loved the big stallion, and the two of them—

Gabe and Star. The big dark bay stallion had been Gabe's preferred saddle horse. Lords of the Double R, she supposed. The Man of the Place and his stallion.

Neither Gramps nor her long-dead uncles had been horsemen. She had to go back to the late nineteenth century to find an equivalent to Gabe and Star in the ranch's history. Her great-great-grandfather David Ryder had been a horseman, with his own stud, Blue. *David Ryder and Blue* had been famous amongst Thunder County ranchers, for Blue's ability to work cattle and outrun just about any horse put up against him. Legacy was a Blue descendant, as were a lot of Thunder County-bred horses.

Gabe Martiniere and Star had earned a similar regard.

Ruby sighed.

End of an era.

She hoped that was the only thing ending.

Gabe seemed somewhat diminished after they buried Star. For the first time he appeared to be frail, hands trembling as he used utensils over dinner, slightly hunched over and slumping instead of sitting tall. He went to bed early that night.

Ruby had a hard time getting to sleep because she kept startling awake, to check on Gabe.

Is this an omen?

She hoped not.

At last, when sleep refused to come, she got up and went down to her office, where she had placed Star's hair to dry after washing it.

Keychain and bracelet, she decided, and began to rummage through her storage closet for her jewelry kit. The familiarity of the braiding preparation process calmed her thoughts—it was something she had done since her teen years, both for herself and for friends, to create a remembrance of special horses. Gabe's bracelet would include green and gold beads, a commemoration of his preferred Martiniere colors.

Several days later, she presented Gabe with the keychain and bracelet.

"You didn't have to do it," he protested, as Mike hid a smile.

"I wanted to do it," she said as she fastened the bracelet around his wrist.

Gabe didn't say anything more. He touched the bracelet, eying it with a wry smile. Then he kissed Ruby.

"Thank you."

She noticed that the bracelet stayed on Gabe's wrist, except when he showered. And afterward, it went right back on.

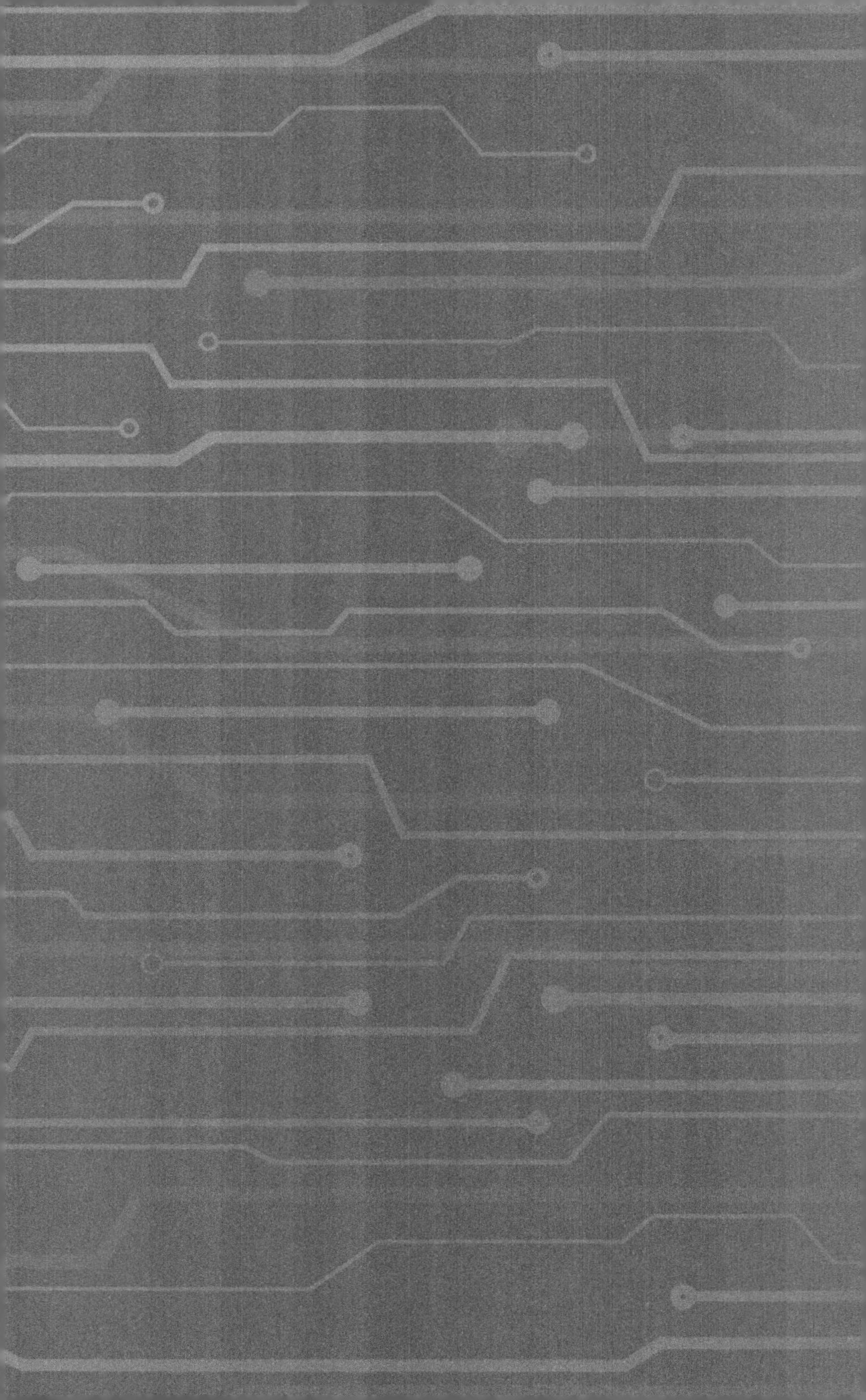

GABE

RUBY'S ETERNAL WATCHFULNESS WAS GETTING OLD. OH, GABE understood *why* she was herding him and Mike as tight as one of his Border Collies from past years would have done to a herd of cattle. She had come pretty damn close to losing both of them at various times during the last couple of years. He had been the same way with her after that godawful accident with Boomer.

Sure, he was seventy-one. Hadn't been in the best of condition lately. Losing Star was—losing Star. The big stud wasn't *that* old, after all—he had been seven when they bought him, twenty at his death, in good health with vision intact and teeth in good shape. Still rideable. Never colicked before. Never foundered. Never—

It just didn't seem right that Star was *gone.* Just last week, Ruby had staked him in the front yard to graze near their outdoor working space, where both Gabe and Mike could hobble over to commune with the big dark bay stallion when they took breaks from their work.

No longer. And while Ruby would stake out Legacy or Herrie and their latest foals by Star on the lawn to keep Gabe and Mike company, all Gabe could think about was that he was seeing Star's last foals. Except that wasn't true—both Legacy and Heritage were in foal to Star, as were the other five mares in the broodmare band.

All the same, he kept thinking of the palomino and red dun fillies as Star's last babies. A premonition, or something else?

Yeah, he'd been pretty shaky the day they buried Star. Fatigued both physically and mentally. Had nearly collapsed before going to bed early.

That *still* didn't mean that he needed to be cosseted and kept in bubble wrap. Deep inside, he was still the same Gabe Martiniere who had been the cliff diver. Gabe Ramirez, the wildland firefighter, ranch hand, farm worker, frozen peas factory line worker. Gabe Ramirez, the bronc rider. Gabriel Martiniere, who had finally stood up to his psychopathic sperm donor Philip, defied him and *won*. Who had finally managed to make indentured servitude a thing of the past again.

Perhaps that was the issue.

Had he *really* won?

The lassitude and occasional forgetfulness was *supposed* to be aging. But Gabe had suspicions.

"You can expect to have some loss of memory, Gabriel," Dr. Sheri said when he brought the subject up at his latest examination. "Loss of memory, loss of muscle mass, slow physical recovery—all that is to be anticipated. Considering the impact on your body from the G9 virus, mind control and the drugs associated with it, the anti-aging serum—all of those insults catch up to you. Eventually."

Except that whatever was ailing him didn't quite feel like aging. It reminded Gabe of the early days post-divorce, when he went through whole days in a blur.

The blurring of activity wasn't as bad as it had been with Mariah feeding him drugs all those years ago. All the same, he had days when he was barely aware of his surroundings, doing —what?

Things he barely remembered. Programming work that he *should* be able to recall. Especially since some elements of it were problematic and needed to be reworked. It had been *years* since he made such simple programming mistakes—well over fifty years since he had been writing more complex programs during his high school years at Northview Military Academy.

Losing his mind to dementia? Or was this something worse?

Then, just before and during the divorce, Gabe had been under a tight mind control programming lock created by Philip. That shouldn't be the case now. Philip had been dead for thirteen years. Those links had been erased and purged from Gabe years ago, after the first attack of the G9 virus. The only people still alive capable of creating that sort of mind control programming were Ruby and Justine. Neither woman had gone through the level of training required to do it. Justine might be able to figure out how to do that programming—but why would she do it?

Could Philip's links have been restored somehow?

Damn it, he was only seventy-one. Philip had lived into his eighties, had been dispensing his venomous thoughts and concocting his devious plans right up until his suicide, in spite of his cardiac and cancer issues. Say what one would about Gabe and Justine's damn toxic father, Philip Martiniere had been sharp and rational—for *some* degree of rational—up to the very end of his life.

This felt like something interfering with *both* Gabe's mind and his body.

Could it have to do with the worm that he occasionally remembered?

Could Philip have implanted some sort of long-term compulsion meant to cripple Gabe in his elder years?

If only someone would *listen* to his worries, instead of assuming his growing weakness was simply old age.

But Gabe wasn't so sure he could trust Ruby or Justine with these concerns. Brandon had enough to worry about with Lily.

Perhaps Donald?

EVENTUALLY, GABE MANAGED TO SNEAK AWAY FROM RUBY'S supervision, with the help of Terri Granger, the ranch manager now that Charlie Thompson had retired after his husband Martin's death. Gabe stayed behind when Ruby and Mike went to Portland for a maintenance check on Mike's cyborg parts, and an assessment of Mike's progression toward needing his legs to go through the cyborging process.

Charlie would have insisted that Gabe not go out on the ranch alone. Mike would snitch to Ruby if Gabe tried to sneak out while he was around. But Terri—well, he could easily sweet-talk her into letting him take a crawler out alone for a day-long expedition on the ranch. The old *persuasive Gabriel* magic, with just that tiny touch of mind control *pushing* in his vocal tones.

He took along a locator—Ruby had that much influence over Terri. Fixed a lunch, included a small flask. Not a lot of whisky, just enough to sip as he drove and thought. The locator and an ancient tablet were the only electronics that Gabe carried with him. And he switched off notifications, leaving only the emergency app running.

This trip was an experiment. If what he was feeling was something that Philip had planted in him, something long-term and dangerous, perhaps getting to the parts of the ranch that still had connectivity issues might reveal something.

Or it might not.

Worth testing his hypothesis.

NORMALLY, IF HE WERE JUST RUNNING THE CRAWLER AROUND THE ranch, he could make the circuit in four hours. Gabe planned for longer—and advised Terri of that, to avoid triggering any concern. Promised to hit the alert button on the locator if he started feeling bad.

He took plenty of water, and a blanket. At some point a nap might be a good idea. Both walker and cane, just in case. A pad and pen, so he could take notes. That tablet—not his daily work electronics, but an old one he used to have for field work that didn't connect with the ranch networks anymore.

Just in case he came up with a programming idea.

At the very least, he would be *getting outside.* Not the tame outside that being limited to the front lawn included. The *real* outside. On the ranch he had grown to love, more than he ever could Moondance. He and Ruby had wrestled with the Double R for all those years, *together.*

If his mind and body really were failing, then today would be a good farewell.

Gabe started his expedition by cruising to the upper fields. Bridge field. Draw field—and that bridge where little Mikey had shown his horsemanship mettle during his first non-arena ride by sticking on through Crystal's giant leap, because the old Paint mare disliked crossing bridges.

Gabe grinned at that memory, then sighed.

Would Mike ever be able to ride again?

Not with Mike's legs in their current condition—and they weren't failing badly enough to start the cyborg process. Unless Ruby and Mike learned otherwise today. And even then, Dr. Pramula, the specialist in charge of Mike's cyborging, urged caution. Part of that caution was technology-driven—the longer Mike waited for the initial cyborg work, the better the long-term results were likely to be.

Gabe continued on, driving the crawler up the steep incline to Homestead field.

Ah, Homestead. The field with cranky center pivot sprinklers that never wanted to work right, back when he was a young man doing his best to keep the ranch producing income. Every summer before divorcing Ruby, Gabe had spent hours fighting the Homestead pivot line. Irregular connectivity and water pressure, and no funds to do anything about it—then.

Part of his first summer as *Gabriel Martiniere* on the Double R had involved *fixing* that pivot line for good.

He stopped the crawler here and hobbled to the edge of this year's wheat, still green and forming kernels, leaning on his cane as he looked past the field to the Thunder Mountains. So many memories. Worth a sip of whisky.

Homestead. The field where Ruby had continually fought interference with the RubyBot signals, especially during the pivotal year of 2059, during the AgInnovator. Where Mike's instruments screwed up and they started to learn about that mysterious worm, when trying to perfect the Guardians—still a lost cause. Only the Swaits could handle the Guardians. If any Martiniere touched them, they went awry.

Why?

Homestead was relatively tame now, but even with improved connectivity and water pressure, it still could be a challenge to run bots on it, or deal with electronic pivot controls. Something about the underlying geology of the field—not something Gabe knew that well. But it was a good test field simply because of those issues.

And his thoughts still held that *fuzziness*. Not a good sign.

Gabe clambered back into the crawler. He steered around the edge of the field and into the draw that separated the Double R from the Reed place next door.

If things didn't change here—

This was where the testing of his hypothesis would really begin. Ladyslipper Draw and Ladyslipper Spring, named after the rare calypso orchids that still sprouted in a damp year. No connectivity here.

And it was a pleasant place to eat lunch, take a break, another sip of whisky, and a nap, especially on this nice warm day. Gabe parked the crawler near the plastic pipe outlet that funneled water from the fenced-off area into an old iron water trough. He hobbled around, spreading the blanket on a partially sunny hillside spot under big Ponderosa pines, then carried his lunch, flask, and water over to it.

Was it wishful thinking that he seemed to be able to move better?

Before settling on the blanket, he knelt beside the outlet and carefully scooped himself a handful of the spring water. Terri tested the ranch springs regularly, and Ladyslipper had always produced sweet-flavored water.

It didn't fail him now. Still as cold and sweet as ever. Gabe drank another handful, catching more in both hands to rub over his face and rinse off dust.

He didn't need to use his cane to get back up and limp over to the blanket. And he didn't hurt as much.

Not imagining that.

After eating and sipping the whisky, he lay back on the blanket to drowse, using his old black Stetson to shade his eyes.

He already felt better. His mind seemed to be clearer. Now if he just took a nice little nap, where there were so many memories.

Ladyslipper Spring. The most private location on the Double R. Where Brandon had most likely been conceived on a hot spring day. Where Gabe and Ruby began their serious reunion discussions, after learning about the degree to which Philip and the AgInnovator had compromised Brandon's freedom. Where kidnappers —sent by Philip—had left Gabe to die, thirteen years ago.

Despite that last memory, he still loved Ladyslipper.

And perhaps, after a nap....

Gabe startled awake, trembling and sweaty despite the fact he was in full shade. He sat up and shook his head.

"Now *that* was a weird dream."

As he spoke, two whitetail does at the water trough spooked, flipping their tails high, waving them side-to-side to signal a warning. Gabe chuckled at the does, hoping to dispel the uneasiness washing over him.

But that dream—

It had seemed *too damn real.*

Unlike most dreams, it unfolded like a complete memory, as if he had really lived it. And he remembered the whole thing.

It opened with him en route to that fateful meeting with Philip on April 1, 2036, which led to their divorce. Ruby's calls, that he rejected. Then *that text*, from Remy Trask's phone.

Answer your damn phone, Gabriel Marcus Martiniere. You're in serious danger.

Obeying the next time it rang, shaken by her use of his real name, that she shouldn't have known.

Remy says turn back, Gabe. Philip will kill you. She was one of the assistant US attorneys working on US vs. Martiniere Group. Please. I know everything. Justine is on her way here to help you—Remy called her. Come back.

Braking the truck, turning around in the highway.

Black SUVs suddenly in his rear-view mirror, in both lanes of the highway, gaining on him even though he had the accelerator pushed to the floor.

Desperately talking to Ruby as he did his best to outrun those black SUVs driven by Philip's security. Encountering a blockade of them.

Gunshots. Trying to return fire as Ruby wept, not having a hand free to disconnect and spare her the battle as he did his damnedest to stay alive.

SUVs ramming him as he tried to evade them by four-wheeling across a wheat field. Shot in his shoulder. Flipping the truck. Unable to break loose from his seat belt and get on his feet.

Philip's laughter as he marched up to Gabe.

I have you now, you worthless sprog. And I'll destroy you, just like I will your wife and child.

Screaming *I love you Ruby Barkley* as Philip placed his pistol against the back of Gabe's head, hoping she heard. A loud roar, a moment of overwhelming pain, and then—

Darkness.

Gabe rubbed his face. He could still *feel* the impact of that bullet in his skull. With trembling fingers, he explored the back of his neck, poking and prodding.

Nothing. Not even a sensitive spot, as if he had accidentally rested his head on a rock or stick or pine knot while sleeping.

Just your imagination, Gabriel.

But what in hell had triggered *that* vivid a dream? Or was it like the other occasional dreams that gave him glimpses of himself in a different life? *Those* dreams had been about meeting Ruby as himself, based on the notion that the plane crash which killed his family hadn't happened.

This one—

Well, that *had* been the outcome he feared that fateful day, on April 1st, 2036. But the other pieces? Ruby getting mad and calling Remy because she thought he was leaving her? Pulling up his hidden messages on the computer to read Philip's demands? *Ruby knowing who he was because Remy told her?*

No, that hadn't even been close to the reality.

Gabe pushed himself up, shaking, and went to the spring. This time he used water from the trough to splash over his upper body, taking off his sweat-drenched shirt to dip it into the water. Something he had done for years to cool off after working hard in the heat of the day. An old pleasure. He shivered as he pulled the shirt back on.

Then he returned to the blanket to write down his dream. As Gabe made notes, other memories started flooding back.

This wasn't the first time he had this dream. And others, connected to it. Hovering in their bedroom, watching but unable to do anything to comfort Ruby while she sobbed, overwhelmed by the revelation of his true identity and her widowhood. Her alliance with Justine and Remy. The birth of their daughter, Gabrielle Marguerite, redheaded like her mother, seven months after his death—*not* a hydatidiform mole like the reality. Ruby and Gabrielle's vengeance on Philip, aided by Justine and Brandon. Gabrielle becoming the Martiniere in her twenties...and nothing more beyond that.

Other universes, where Ruby's pregnancy with Brandon triggered him telling her who he really was.

And the one he most clearly remembered, those dreams where he met Ruby as Gabriel Martiniere, and Gabe Ramirez never happened. Where there were no indentureds.

Huh. Maybe I should take up writing science fiction. Apparently, I have the imagination for it.

Gabe snorted at that thought.

But then there were other memories. Repeated visions of Philip.

You will be mine. All of you will be mine.

Flashes of the past few weeks, tied to those moments when the mental fog cleared and he stared at whatever the hell it was he had just programmed that didn't make sense.

"You know, Gabriel," he said out loud. "Those instances are also tied to your brief awareness of that damned worm."

He should write every incident down—except his hands ached at the prospect. He thought for a moment. Then he set his tablet to *record*.

The worm seemed to ignore video files. So if he kept them short, maybe, just maybe, he might be able to keep it from trashing *them*.

RECORDING THE FILES, THEN WRITING A SIMPLE UPLOAD PROGRAM that would duplicate the video files and stick multiple copies in many separate folders, took longer than Gabe wanted. But for some reason he had more energy than usual. He wrote a stronger security program for the videos.

When he was done with that, he wrote one final program—

an automatic sync to trigger the upload once he returned to connectivity, then disconnect.

One way or another, he was going to *beat* Philip.

———

HE DIDN'T NEED TO USE HIS CANE TO LOAD EVERYTHING BACK UP IN the crawler—another data point. Gabe checked the time and grimaced. No way he could make a circuit of the lower fields now. On the other hand, those were fields that he *might* be able to have Ruby drive him to for a look-see. He had learned what he needed to know after this trip to Ladyslipper Spring.

And if he could get her to drive him up here, then perhaps—

There was enough time to continue up to Lone Pine, where Ruby had moved the broodmares after Star's death. Then back to the house.

Fatigue crashed over him as he drove out of Ladyslipper Draw.

Remember the dream, he told himself repeatedly, as he continued to Lone Pine. *Remember Philip's appearances. Get Ruby to bring you back here, to Ladyslipper.*

By the time he reached the gate to Lone Pine, the aches and pains had reasserted themselves. Gabe stuck some horse cookies in his pocket, grabbed his walker instead of the cane because he hurt too bad to trust his cane, and hobbled over. Herrie and Legacy were still at the main ranch. But the other five mares— three more with Star's foals at their side, all bred—Star's last foals would be born next spring.

So why did he keep feeling like the babies he saw now were Star's last ones?

Gabe leaned on his walker, watching the mares and foals. Eventually, they wandered over to the gate. He didn't dare go into the field with his walker, but he could scratch the horses that came near. They snuffled at him, and he fed each mare a cookie in turn. The foals got scratches—Ruby believed in *treats only in the bucket* for young horses, until they were well into ground training and had proven their understanding of proper manners around humans.

Once the treats were gone, the mares drifted off, one-by-one pausing to lick the salt block, the lower-status mares waiting their turn. Then their heads rose, turning to look down the track leading to Lone Pine.

Gabe wheeled the walker around. Ruby rode Boomer, now gelded and part of the saddle string, scowling as she halted Boomer next to the crawler and dropped his reins to ground tie him after she dismounted.

"Terri says you've been gone all day." She put her hands on her hips, her frown deepening. "You turned off everything but the emergency locator, and you popped off her screens for a while. She was frantic, but I saw that you were down in Ladyslipper and told her it was all right. Just what the hell are you up to, Gabriel?"

"Just a little cruise. Ate lunch and took a nap at Ladyslipper. Getting out."

"By yourself? *Gabriel.*" She gulped, and he heard a little bit of the tone that had been *that other Ruby crying.* "If something had happened out here, especially at Ladyslipper, by yourself—oh God, Gabe. I could take you and Mike out and about if you wanted. Please. Don't do this alone anymore."

"You're so busy with both of us. I didn't want to trouble you. I just wanted to get out."

Should he tell her his suspicions?

Yes. Too many secrets.

"I'm sorry, Gabe." Her expression softened and she came to him, holding him tight. "But you scared me."

"I intended to be back at the house by now. Just spent too much time at Ladyslipper."

"Doing what?"

"Oh, a nap, and—thinking." He took a deep breath. "I've learned—"

"No! You will not tell her anything!"

That pistol jammed against the back of his head. Gabe tightened up, body jerking into a convulsion. Fear crossed Ruby's face.

Then Philip laughed, and pulled the trigger.

"Not gonna be that easy, ignorant sprog!"

Darkness. Obliteration.

HE WOKE IN A HOSPITAL BED. RUBY, PALE-FACED, CLUNG TO HIS hand.

"Oh thank God," she breathed as he opened his eyes.

"Wha' happened?" His words didn't want to come out clear. Gabe coughed and swallowed. More difficult than it should be. His tongue felt thick and awkward.

"You had a seizure—or something. I was terrified that you had a stroke, but the doctors don't think so now. They don't know what happened. Dr. Sheri thinks you overdid. Gabriel Marcus Martiniere, damn it, you scared the crap out of me!"

Philip smirked behind Ruby, waving a chiding index finger at him.

"Told you that I would make you pay, ignorant sprog."

Gabe blinked and shook his head. Philip's image faded away. *What the hell is going on?*

NOW IT BECAME A GAME OF CAT AND MOUSE. GABE WAS BACK HOME after twenty-four hours, but the incident had taken its toll. The left leg that had withered as a result of post-G9 syndrome fourteen years ago reverted to that post-G9 status overnight.

Another issue to puzzle the doctors.

Gabe found one of the video files he had made at Ladyslipper. But when he tried to show it to Ruby—Philip and the pistol struck again.

Another hospital stay.

Trying to tell Mike wasn't quite so bad, not enough to land him in the hospital, but bad enough. Gabe decided it wasn't worth trying to tell Justine or Donald.

As long as he didn't tell anyone, he could work with the video files. The security program was strong enough to keep Philip out of those files, so—

He still didn't have an explanation for those manifestations of Philip.

Or why that pistol had such a devastating effect on him. It wasn't *real*, damn it.

Except that every time Philip shot Gabe, it ripped away more of his ability to move and think.

A*UGUST*, 2073

G*ABE* *REMEMBERED* *THE* *DREAMS* *OF* *THOSE* *OTHER* *WORLDS* *MORE* clearly now. The one where he had the most ability to move freely in his dreams was that horrible, devastating universe where he died at Philip's hands. Gabe spent time around that world's Ruby. Maybe if he could *talk* to her, then she could communicate to *his* Ruby.

No such luck.

But he kept dipping in and out of the timeline, trying to find an opening. The one good thing was that he learned how to control his movements in that world.

It wasn't until Gabe stumbled across the adult Gabrielle Marguerite that he had his first breakthrough. She was sitting in her office at the Double R—once *his* office—a year before she deposed her grandfather Philip. As he popped in, she looked up from the screen she was studying, and smiled.

She saw him.

No one *ever* saw him in these dreams. No matter what he did.

"Hello, father," she said softly. "I've been expecting this visit." She snapped the screen to a larger resolution, and he recognized what she was watching.

One of his recent videos.

"How?" Gabe dropped into one of the chairs. Not that he needed it, but he felt better when he wasn't just floating around.

"These videos started popping up in my feeds about six months ago. I—" she bit her lip and looked down. "I've been fascinated by them, if somewhat frustrated. No one else can view them. Not Mom, not Brandon, not Justine. They glitch." She gulped. "I've heard so many stories about you—well, this world's version of you. I ran an aging program on the pictures I have of you to confirm your identity. To see the father I've never known, in his elder years, talking about something that I've started to suspect—"

"Do *you* know what's happening?"

Her lips pressed together, *so much like Ruby's* when contemplating a problem. "When I broke into Philip's files a year ago, I came across a reference to *digital thought clones*. He's been experimenting with them. I started to do the same thing, trying to devise an algorithm. Using what video files I have of you— including these." Gabrielle gestured toward the video. "I thought that maybe, just maybe, I could talk to some version of you, get some advice. Instead, it looks like I lured in the real thing—just from a different universe."

"In my world, I'm dreaming. I'm still alive. I'm not a clone, digital or otherwise. What the hell are digital thought clones?"

"Digital thought clones are created through an algorithm using existing media files to construct a digital personality that thinks like the original person." Gabrielle frowned—and *that* frown matched the glower he sometimes saw in the mirror, nothing of Ruby. "The more data, the more useful the digital clone is."

"So what's Philip trying to do? He created physical clones in my world."

My world.

Amazing how quickly he assumed this was real and not just dream logic.

Gabrielle grimaced—this time a Ruby feature. "He's chasing immortality."

"That's what he tried with the physical clones. He made thirteen of them, used them for blood donations. One survived to the age of five, and Ruby and I found him. We raised him. He's almost eighteen now—Mike. The thirteenth clone."

"Aw, *shit.*" Gabrielle leaned back. "He's not been able to make physical clones in this world. Only digital." She exhaled. "I think Philip has discovered the algorithm to go digital. It's entirely possible that he exists physically and digitally in this world."

Chill crept down Gabe's spine. "He's been dead for almost thirteen years in my world. But I've been seeing manifestations of him. There's a worm in the Martiniere programs that forces us —me, Ruby, Mike, Brandon, Justine—to forget about it."

Gabrielle blanched. "And you have a living physical clone in your world?"

"Yes. Mike."

"And there are manifestations of Philip."

"Yes. I can't tell anyone what I see, except in those videos, and I'm being careful talking about them. I don't want anyone thinking I'm experiencing delusions. Especially since—" Gabe swallowed hard. "If I try to tell someone, Philip shoots me. Just like he did to me in this universe."

"And the effect?" Oh, that was *so* a Ruby expression on her face now, that tight-lipped thoughtful mode.

"Every time it happens, I lose a little bit more of what I can do physically. It's as if I've had a stroke, only the doctors can't find any evidence of a stroke."

Gabrielle shook her head. "He's experimenting on you, damn it. Trying to find a way to possess a live body."

"And his goal?" Though Gabe already thought he knew.

Mike.

"He wants to possess the clone in your world. He mastered physical clones in your world, and digital clones in mine. If he can transfer that knowledge across worlds—"

"I wouldn't call it mastery of physical clones. Mike has significant physical issues. Heart attack and cancer at fifteen. Severe osteoporosis. He needed to have heart, lungs, and arm bones cyborged. Odds are quite high that Mike will not live as long as his progenitor. And Mike's not material for a secondary clone—the degeneration of the source DNA is even worse."

Gabrielle rubbed her face. "Well, that's something to be thankful for—I guess. Unless Philip's had better luck in another world."

Gabe shrugged. "I don't know. I won't know. This world and my own—well, there's another where the plane crash that killed my family didn't happen—are the only ones I have much experience with."

"We have to stop him."

"I don't know how much more time I have, dear." Time to face up to the reality. "I'm fading. Seventy-one and struggling. Come close to dying several times ever since digital Philip's taken to shooting me."

Gabrielle pursed her lips. "Would you be willing to try to become a digital thought clone? Maybe the reason my algorithm dragged you in was because you're still living in your world."

"But why me and not another version of me?"

"No idea." She threw her hands up—now that was a Justine mannerism—and sighed. "I don't know how to best communicate the algorithm in a means that you can use."

"My videos crossed the worlds. Maybe if you made one, for me—" He tapped his lips with his index fingers. "Ah. I wrote protective algorithms for the videos. Let me dictate them to you. That—might be a factor."

"I'm willing to try. And in return—any advice that *you* can give about fighting Philip would be helpful. After all, you managed to beat him in your world."

"Dear girl, whatever it will take."

Her tooth-baring grin in response was so like his that it was scary.

She's my daughter, all right.

GABRIELLE TWEAKED GABE'S PROTECTIVE PROGRAMS, WHICH MADE IT easier for them to exchange videos through a process he still didn't understand. They just—*appeared*—in his email. And for whatever reason, if he responded directly to her emails, they went through. If he tried to write a new email to the same address, delivery failed.

He created the necessary algorithm over two weeks, detailing the process in short videos that he placed along various online nodes. Gabe's awareness of digital life shifted as he built the digital clone version of himself. Sometimes, he almost felt like he was inside the digital world, and could nearly—but not quite— reach to Gabrielle in that manner. She didn't seem to have the same blockage that he did.

As August temperatures soared, Gabe and Mike retreated to their inside offices, so he had more privacy. But he had to be careful. If Ruby came into his office and asked what he was doing—Philip might strike. His growing knowledge of how digital information flowed helped him identify several holes in his protections that Philip could breach and he couldn't block.

A problem. He couldn't tolerate many more times being shot by Philip. Sooner or later, those incidents would weaken him enough that he would die.

There were times when he wondered what he was really

doing. Was Gabrielle just an old man's fancy, as he slid into delusions?

Hard to say.

But if these were delusions—well, except for Philip shooting him, they were pleasant ones.

GABY—Do you think it's safe to tell Ruby, Brandon, Justine, and Mike about digital thought clones? They need to know. —Papa.

Better we wait until it's finished. You only have a few more tweaks. The clone version of you is more realistic now. —Gaby.

He kept recording videos, structured now toward Ruby, Justine, Brandon, or Mike, dealing with branched likelihoods. He didn't mention anything about multiverses, or different worlds —that might be too farfetched for any of them to believe. Getting them to accept digital thought clones would be difficult enough.

Gaby identified the foundation of Philip's digital clone as being in Gabe's universe. Where—she wasn't certain.

But it was tied to that damned worm that had caused them so much grief.

The worm that had something to do with Lily's escalating decline.

Gabe raged—quietly—when he learned that. It was almost enough to risk telling Ruby and Brandon.

Not yet, Papa, Gaby kept saying. *You're not strong enough to survive digitally if he attacks you there with any more force than he has already. We need to keep building the algorithm.*

THE FINAL BREAKTHROUGH HAPPENED ON THE MORNING OF THE thirteenth anniversary of his and Ruby's second marriage.

Papa—I can't completely activate you as a digital clone. It has to happen in your world. You need to designate two live persons to type a code word into a prompt—your choice. I recommend several options for the persons. From what I'm seeing in Philip's notes here, the full transition to digital thought clone after death could be traumatic. It may take you a while to adjust to digital life—possibly years—before you can completely transition, and they have to be alive when you're ready to do it. —Gaby.

Gabe contemplated his choices.

He picked a word—*fulfillment.* Then he made more videos, to cover several contingencies.

Gaby—it's done. Now do you think it's safe to tell Ruby, Brandon, Justine, and Mike about digital thought clones? —Papa.

He didn't get an answer until it was time to go upstairs and change for their anniversary dinner.

Father—if you must. Please be careful, Papa. I love you. —Gaby.

Gabe scratched his chin thoughtfully.

Then he went upstairs, to tell Ruby everything he had learned.

17 / ALONE, INTO THE FUTURE
AUGUST, 2073

RUBY

RUBY HESITATED AT THE BEDROOM DOOR, HAND ON THE KNOB.

She hadn't been in here since Gabe died.

Thirteenth anniversary turned out to be a curse.

She took a deep breath. Sooner or later, she had to go inside. Might as well be tonight. Gabe's body rested in the family graveyard, along with Brandon's Kris. Gramps and Granma. Her uncles. Other Ryder family ancestors—and now the Double R cemetery was a part of Martiniere family lore.

"You gonna be all right?" Mike hovered behind her.

He had been a bulwark during the funeral today, even though he disappeared for a while afterward. She didn't blame him. Mike had been second on the scene, as she screamed over Gabe's body while she performed CPR, whipping out the AED as fast as he could, given the limitations of his newly-cyborged arms. The kid had been *so strong* over the past few days, along with Brandon. If he needed some time to work through his own grief, well, that was to be expected.

"I—" Ruby set her jaw.

Stop indulging yourself. Life moves on. You have to start living again as well.

Mike rested his hand on her back. "You want me to open the door? The bedroom's in order. Brandon, Justine, and I—took care of everything."

Ruby nodded, biting her lip.

Mike placed his hand over hers, turned the knob. He gently pushed the door open. Ruby took a deep breath and stepped inside.

There was no evidence of the debris from the paramedics desperately trying to revive Gabe. His clothing had been put away, and there was no sign of his walker. The bed was made. Gabe's old black Stetson hung on the wall, where it always had been. The chairs belonging to the little table that sat under the window were upright, not knocked over like they had been when Gabe—collapsed.

"Bran said it was better to have little pieces of Gabe around for a while," Mike said, a rare awkward tone in his voice. "It really helped him when Kris died."

Ruby nodded again, blinking back tears.

No. I will not give in to any more tears. The time for tears is done.

She walked into the bedroom and stopped.

Right where Gabe—

Her knees gave way. She crumpled into a ball, whimpering, barely aware that Mike bent over her, fumbling to get down, hampered by his new leg braces. His heeler, Striker, nudged at her, whining softly and licking her hands.

"Ruby? Are you all right? Ruby? Are you all right? Ruby? *Not you, too!*"

The terror in Mike's voice, edging on a potential meltdown, shocked her out of *widow* and into *parent* mode. Ruby sat up, gulping for breath, wiping her eyes, fighting against that dreadful emptiness, worse even than the divorce. The finality of it. No matter how much she wanted to yell, cry, curse or scream, *it wouldn't bring Gabe back.* He was *gone. Forever.*

But Mikey was here, and he needed her.

Lily needed her.

Ronnie needed her.

Brandon needed her.

Lily and all of her boys needed her—*except Gabe.*

She exhaled shakily. "I just realized that this was where—"

Striker pushed his muzzle into one of her hands and Ruby patted his head.

"Do you want to move into the downstairs bedroom permanently?"

Ruby shook her head. "No. I—no."

He rubbed her back and she leaned into him, as Striker continued to nuzzle her. "Oh Mikey, Mikey. I'm so glad you're here. You and Bran. And Justine. But you boys. Such good kids."

"You took care of us. Now it's our turn to take care of you."

They leaned against each other for a few moments. Striker pressed hard against both of them.

Then Ruby shuddered. "My knees are getting creaky, and both of us should be getting to bed." She reached for the bed, just like Gabe—*stop it.* She pushed herself up, then helped Mike to his feet. He struggled more than she expected, and Ruby focused on that, glad for a diversion. "Those new braces being a problem?"

Mike made a face. "No more than to be expected." He flexed a hand. "Arms are coming online, but slowly. When I talk to the cyborged brothers, they tell me it's to be expected. I had a long chat with Alexander. My cyborging differs from theirs, especially since it was limited to bone and not full limb replacement. The one thing that seems to be common is a gradual adaptation for full success."

"Good." Ruby exhaled hard again. "Well. I've made it inside. I've had my collapse and cry. Now, perhaps, it's time for me to get ready for bed."

"Just holler if you need anything."

"I will," she promised.

After Mike left, Striker trailing behind him, Ruby shivered. She made herself breathe long, slow, and steady. Bedtime. Maybe she should do her usual routine from the years when Gabe had to travel alone on Martiniere business. The old shirt he had been wearing before he changed for dinner still hung on a peg next to the Stetson. Ruby took the shirt and laid it on Gabe's pillow.

New sheets and pillowcases, damn it.

So she wouldn't even have the consolation of that scent.

But they had meant well.

Slow procession toward bedtime, pausing and swallowing hard a lot because there were *so many reminders* of Gabe. He was —*had been*—affectionate at bedtime. Brushing her hair. Gentle caresses. Shoulder rubs. Soft kisses. Quiet talk as they unwound from the day. The *presence* that was Gabriel Martiniere, familiar and beloved.

Ruby didn't realize how huge that presence had been in her life, even during their time divorced, until it was gone for good. No chance of calling Gabe now—*ever.* No hope of an eventual reunion.

Damn it, enough with the tears!

At last she settled in bed, clutching Gabe's shirt. Her body was exhausted. She couldn't sustain a long thread of thought. But her mind kept insisting she was awake, that she needed to stay alert, that Gabe would be coming out of the bathroom any moment now and might need her help—

"Gabe," she finally whispered. "I can't believe it really ends like this. Oh Gabe. You're gone. I—God, Gabe." She wiped her eyes with his shirt.

At last, fatigue took over, and she fell asleep.

BUT SLEEP WASN'T RESTFUL. RUBY WOKE REPEATEDLY, CLUTCHING for a presence who was no longer there to comfort her when nightmares struck.

And her dreams weren't peaceful. They were far too realistic.

Gabe had occasionally talked about *those dreams*, the ones that seemed like he was seeing a different version of his life.

This set of dreams didn't match the ones Gabe described—when he did talk about them. His had been peaceful. Hers were outright nightmares, reflecting her worst fears. Philip Martiniere kept showing up in different ways.

And in every dream, he was trying to kill Ruby, sometimes her and Gabe.

She was riding Philip down on horseback, trying to distract him from repeatedly shooting Gabe.

Shoving Brandon and a little red-haired girl behind her for some sort of protection as Philip raised his gun, aiming it right at her face.

Facing Philip at Gabe's side in the middle of a Martiniere Group board meeting, shouting him down until he reached for a weapon.

Standing next to a redheaded woman who shared Gabe's features and called Philip "Grandfather" in a mocking tone so much like Justine's.

The last dream suddenly segued into the same redheaded woman talking quietly and reassuringly to Ruby, in words that seemed to flit away.

At that point, the nightmares stopped.

***

September, 2073

Ruby stood in the Double R's kitchen after eating her granola and yogurt breakfast, arms crossed, looking out the window, her cup of faux coffee steaming in front of her on the counter, Gabe's old Stetson next to it. Yesterday's hard rains had washed the last of the wildfire smoke out of the air, leaving the next day to be crisp, the sky that heartbreaking deep blue that marked the transition into fall from summer in the Thunder Valley.

Haying was done. Weaning was done. Most of these chores had fallen to her anyway as Gabe grew weaker—but there was no Gabe waiting at the house anymore.

One month ago—

She sighed and picked up the cup. Ever since she had been going through Gabe's records, the mystery of that last day he had spent out on the ranch nagged at her. He had made notes and videos. But the handwritten notes didn't make sense, and the videos were locked in an encryption so hard that Serg and Donald struggled to break it.

What Ruby could read of Gabe's notes was just bizarre enough that she didn't want to show them to either Justine or Serg, for fear that they might think Gabe had been slipping into delusions at the end of his life.

Multiverses? Other lives? A world where he died on April 1st, 2036, and their daughter Gabrielle Marguerite spoke to him in dreams?

I want to retrace Gabe's last day out, she had told Mike several days ago. *By myself. A way to remember him. It's been a month.*

Ruby hadn't shared her concerns about the notes and videos with Mike. It seemed as if every time she wanted to talk to Mike or Brandon about it—the two people she could trust to share this information with—she didn't remember the subject until later. That damned worm?

Possible. But why?

Nonetheless, this was a perfect day to ride out and examine her memories of Gabe. Maybe that would banish the sobbing emptiness that struck her at odd moments.

She sighed again and set the cup down. Needed to put together supplies for this ride, and now that there wasn't Gabe around to do it for her, to make it special—

Fixed herself a sandwich; there was enough leftover pork loin from last night's dinner for Mike's lunch.

The faint *clump-clump* echoing down the hallway told Ruby that Mike was on his way. He hobbled in, passing through to let Striker out.

"So today's the day you're riding the ranch?" Mike retrieved a mug and poured himself coffee, then mixed granola and yogurt for breakfast. Gabe had been the one to cook breakfast. Neither of them felt like cooking that meal—memories.

"Yeah. Upper part only. Should be a good day for it." Ruby wrapped the sandwich in bioplast. What else? She retrieved an apple from the crisper and filled a water bottle, then put it all in a cloth bag. As an afterthought, she included a notepad and a couple of pencils. Just in case she wanted to record something.

"Horse or crawler?" Mike sprinkled chopped dried fruit over his bowl.

"Horse. Legacy. I'll be going up to Ladyslipper, hang out there for a while, then over to Lone Pine, and back down."

Mike grabbed Striker's dog food from its place in the fridge. "Be careful."

"I will. What are you doing today?"

"High school finals, and starting up my online college class."

Ruby nodded. "Hold down the place while I'm out and about."

They winced simultaneously—memories. That was what she had always said to Gabe and Mike before going out to work on the ranch by herself.

Mike exhaled. "All right then. Stay safe, Ruby."

"All right." An awkward moment where she hesitated, because this was when Gabe would have kissed her and told Ruby not to get herself bucked off—a bit more fraught after she and Boomer had been attacked by the cougar and she ended up in the creek. And then she clapped Gabe's old Stetson on her head and went out the door, heading for the corral where Legacy waited.

At least his hat could make the rounds with her. They had always worn the same hat size.

One of the things Ruby hadn't understood about that final drive Gabe took was why he didn't bring along any more electronics than the tracker and that ancient tablet.

She didn't bring any electronics. For some reason, minimal connectivity had apparently been important to Gabe. The tablet was old enough that it didn't connect easily with their networks. Extracting Gabe's recent entries on it was a significant challenge, even for Donald, and he knew a lot of Gabe's old programming tricks. If Gabe's perception of reality had been failing in his last month of life, the decline hadn't carried over to his programming skills.

And that alone made Ruby wonder. Just what *was* Gabe chasing? He *had* been obsessed by that worm that kept fading in and out of their awareness. If he had a lead to its source, he would have encrypted it just this hard, to keep the worm out.

So why didn't he give us the key?

No answers. Maybe death had intervened.

Well, that was one reason why she was doing this ride—to find answers, as well as remember Gabe.

Legacy moved slowly for about half a mile, warming up. Ruby rubbed the palomino mare's neck as they halted next to Bridge field.

"Getting up there in years, old gal." She pursed her lips, thinking. Legacy was now eighteen years old—the foal she carried might be her last. The palomino had progressed from being the sparky young mare so like her great-granddam Sunshine in her willingness to break into bucking at the slightest trigger, to becoming one of Ruby's most reliable ranch mounts.

Just like Sunshine had eventually done.

Memories. Sunshine had been a factor in Ruby and Gabe's first meeting—at one of the rodeos where Sunshine broke in a bucking spree before rounding the last barrel. Gabe followed her to the warmup pen after that mess of a run, in part because Troy

Ridley was being an ass and harassing Ruby, in part because he was attracted to a pretty redhead able to sit a tough bucking horse.

Their conversation then, followed by another rodeo encounter the next weekend where he won the saddle bronc division on Skydancer. A few months later, when they were able to meet again—they had become lovers. After that, Gabe Ramirez had been a significant part of Ruby's life, until their divorce. Even then, they had stayed connected until Brandon turned eighteen.

There had been something about the cowboy who called himself *Gabe Ramirez* that piqued Ruby's interest and quick involvement with him. Intelligent. Mannerly. Knowledgeable about ag robotics—it was embarrassing now to realize the degree to which he had hid the depth of his knowledge about the subject from her in order to protect his real identity. If he had talked about microdrones, for example, she would have found that one research paper he had collaborated on before going into hiding—

She hadn't a clue about *Gabriel Martiniere* otherwise. Oh, she had heard bits and pieces about his testimony in *US vs Martiniere Group*. But the trial had been during a period when Granma was sick and struggling, and Ruby had been juggling rodeo titles, school, work, and family. If she had known more about the trial, she probably would have figured out who Gabe really was long before Philip forced their divorce.

Gabe Ramirez had not only been attractive, with those darkly handsome features and that big slow grin of his, but he was exquisitely polite and formal, even down to their first time in bed. But not standoffish formal. Rather, the sort of formal that showed respect and admiration toward her as an equal.

A rarity—then and now.

That was why his involvement with Mariah had stung so badly. And it hadn't felt right, not like the Gabe she had married.

If only I had known—maybe we could have avoided the horror of twenty years apart.

But she hadn't known, couldn't have known.

Ruby exhaled and urged Legacy on.

Draw field. Letting Legacy rest before the steep climb to Homestead field. One of the places where Gabe and Mike used to race horses, Gabe on Star, then Mike on a succession of increasingly advanced horses as his skill grew.

That memory brought tears to Ruby's eyes. Had it only been three years ago that Mike was excited about Spree and her potential? He had been right about Spree—the filly was now winning in futurity competition with her new owners, and they were generous in attributing her success to Mike as her breeder. And now Gabe was dead and Mike—who knew if he could ever ride again? If his hips remained undamaged by his osteoporosis, maybe.

Homestead field. She remembered Gabe's first summer on the ranch as *Gabriel Martiniere.*

I'm fixing the pivot in that damn Homestead field for good, he had proclaimed. *Now that I have the money to do it properly. We are not fighting that damn piece of junk anymore.*

Homestead. The place of triumphs and failures. She exhaled, and rode on.

Ladyslipper Spring. Ruby unsaddled Legacy before hobbling her, upending the saddle to rest on horn and front skirts. The golden mare had a habit of rolling when turned loose during a ride, even with a saddle and hobbles on. Better to anticipate it and avoid saddle damage.

As she expected, Legacy wandered off once she was stripped down to rope halter and attached lead rope, nose to the ground, legs half-buckled as she sought the perfect rolling spot. After circling, dog-like, around her chosen area, Legacy dropped and rolled. After she rose and shook herself, Ruby put the hobbles on. Then she returned to the saddle and retrieved her lunch bag, and a blanket she had brought from the saddlebags.

Gabe had spent a lot of time here that day, from the tracker records. Recorded several videos and programmed that difficult code, from the date codes on the tablet.

Why?

This was the same blanket Gabe had used that day. Ruby couldn't know where he had chosen to spread it, but she would gamble that it was close to where she put the blanket down. In the shade under several tall Ponderosa pines, a relatively flat spot.

She settled on the blanket, nibbling on her sandwich and watching Legacy.

All right. I'm here. Why did you spend so much time in this one spot, Gabe? If only you could tell me.

Maybe it was the peacefulness surrounding Ladyslipper. An oppressive mental weight that Ruby hadn't been aware of until now seemed to have lifted.

Was that it? Had Gabe just been seeking peace?

Ruby lay back, wrapping the blanket around her—it was getting chilly—and watched the clouds overhead. As drowsiness overtook her, she placed Gabe's hat over her face.

It still bore faint traces of his scent.

"WHAT THE *HELL*—" RUBY SHOT UP, SENDING GABE'S HAT FLYING and startling Legacy into a whirl and several short hops away. The golden mare had been standing watchfully over her, like she would a sleeping foal. Legacy hobbled back to Ruby, snorting, head high, eyes rolling. "Steady, Legacy, steady old girl."

She fumbled in her pocket for a horse cookie and offered it to Legacy. The golden mare blew hard, then delicately picked it up with her lips.

"Now that was one hell of a dream, Legacy girl," Ruby continued, scratching the palomino's nose. She flopped back, hands under her head, unworried about the potential for being trampled as the golden mare started grazing next to the blanket. Some horses might be problematic, but Legacy—this was not the first time that Ruby and Legacy had ridden out alone, and Legacy had grazed close when Ruby took a nap. Or that Ruby had wakened from a sound sleep to find the golden mare standing protectively next to her.

That dream.

Pieces of it were already fading. But the young redheaded woman had been a part of it.

"Gabrielle Marguerite," Ruby murmured. In another universe, the daughter born to her after Gabe's untimely death.

Here, it was easy to remember elements of the nightmares that had been haunting her since Gabe passed away.

Philip Martiniere's continual threat. "I destroyed Gabriel and I will destroy you. I will pervert your granddaughter. Then I will use her to eliminate that abomination you call Michael, so that I can live again in him. I will bring you all down."

Then Gabrielle. *"Philip Martiniere's digital thought clone is haunting you and yours. He caused Papa's—Gabe's—death. You won't remember this for very long, alas, but be aware. The worm is real, it's toxic, and it will harm you."*

"He killed Gabe?" She could speak to Gabrielle in this dream.

"And tried to destroy his digital algorithm. We're still rebuilding it." A kiss on the top of her head, from Gabrielle. *"From me, and from what awareness Papa can spare. You aren't the Ruby who is my mother, no more than he's the father I lost before birth, but—I can see how Papa loves you. Must have loved the version of you in my world. We're trying to find a means to protect all of you. I don't know if we can save Lily. But Michael and Ronald—"*

"What about Brandon?"

A sorrowful shake of her head.

And then Ruby had startled awake, and spooked Legacy.

She sat up again, slower this time so as not to surprise Legacy, and pulled her legs close to her chest, resting her head on her knees.

It was much easier to remember the worm and what it had done, deep in Ladyslipper Draw, away from connectivity.

That was why Gabe hadn't carried any electronics besides the tracker and that ancient tablet. He was on the trail of that worm.

Had he succeeded?

And what the hell was this bit about *digital thought clones*? Or dreams about a daughter from another reality?

Could that just be another effect of the worm?

Ruby sighed. She fished the notepad and a pencil out of the lunch bag and began to make notes.

Perhaps Donald might have some idea what digital thought clones were all about.

AFTER RETURNING TO RANCH HEADQUARTERS, RUBY GAVE LEGACY A good brushing before turning her loose in the horse field with the other broodmares. On her way back from the field, she found Justine sitting on the bench that Ruby had placed next to Gabe's grave, her head buried in her hands.

"You all right?" Ruby asked, dropping on the bench next to Justine, rubbing her sister-in-law's back.

Justine raised her head. Tears streaked her cheeks. "Donald's getting worse, Ruby. I—just had a big blowout with one of his cousins." She exhaled hard. "As long as Donald's alive, they won't interfere with me being around him. He's apparently been quite eloquent on the subject to the family. But, as Joshua was quite clear to emphasize, once Donald's gone, I have no rights. Or, as he told me, *if you wanted to have any control about what happens after Donald's death, you should have remarried him.*"

"Aw, *shit*, Justine. I'm sorry."

"I—probably won't be out to the ranch again until after Donald—dies. It could be tomorrow; it could be months yet." Justine gulped. "I wish Gabie were still alive. He could have said —or done something, I'm sure. I'd like to see Donald buried here, but that's not going to happen. He's going into the Knowles cemetery. Oh God, Ruby." She sniffled and wiped her eyes. "I had to come here and talk to Gabie. Even though he's dead and can't answer me."

"Maybe Brandon could help?"

Justine sighed and leaned back. "He doesn't pull the same weight as Gabie did. Doesn't have that *The Martiniere Has Spoken* presence like his father did. You know what I mean?"

"I know." Ruby chewed her lower lip. There was something she had wanted to talk to Donald about—but what was it? "I retraced Gabe's last day out and about—before that first attack of whatever it was."

A fleeting memory tugged at her awareness, connected to the ride and Ladyslipper Spring—then nothing.

"Did you ever figure out why Gabie thought he had to sneak away on his own that day?"

Ruby shook her head. "No."

But deep inside, she knew that wasn't right.

She just couldn't remember what it was.

"When it gets close to Donald's death, call me," she added. "I had Mike, at least. I'll be there for you."

Justine blinked back more tears. "Thank you, Ruby."

February, 2074

Ruby exhaled and leaned on the railing of the cliff house's deck, chilled in spite of the heavy coat and thermals that usually were enough to keep her warm in subzero temperatures at the Double R. Much colder on the coast, due to the humidity.

She and Justine had just gotten here after Donald's funeral—somehow, between her and Brandon, Ruby had been able to negotiate *that much* of an accommodation for Justine with the

Knowles and Atwood families. Her sister-in-law had gone into her bedroom and closed the door firmly upon their arrival—probably to be private to regain self-control.

This is the most emotion I've ever seen from Justine.

Her sister-in-law was usually the steady one. The pillar.

Ruby thought—she *hoped*—that a few days at the cliff house might be good for Justine. And—she hadn't been back here herself, not since Gabe's birthday last year.

Oh God, was it only last year that we had that lovely birthday celebration?

She buried her head in her hands, allowing the weight of her own grief to settle. So many intimate memories here. And she still wasn't certain what to do about this house. Neither Brandon nor Mike wanted to spend time here. Ruby wasn't sure she wanted to, either. The cliff house was so locked up with *Gabe* in her thoughts that she hadn't had the courage to come here until now. It wasn't so fraught with history for Justine—she and Donald had come here a couple of times, but nothing at all like the Double R or Moondance. The cliff house was a good place for Justine to get through the next few days, just the two of them together.

And drink one hell of a lot of alcohol.

The cliff house. Gabe's fifth anniversary present to her. To them.

Is it worth keeping, without Gabe to share it?

Ruby rubbed her face. She should go inside. Low-hanging clouds on the horizon, plus the rising wind, suggested that a storm was coming. Maybe it would be a good, hard one that would reflect the grief she shared with Justine. She could stand to hear driving rain against the windows.

Donald's last attempts to crack Gabe's codes before he became too feeble to attempt any further work had revealed Gabe's worry about Mike, Lily, and Ronnie. A fear that he was losing his second family to Philip—somehow—just as he had lost Saul, Angelica, and Louisa when he was twelve, and been plunged into the living hell of being under Philip's custody for the next six years.

Perhaps that fear had driven him into the—whatever it was—about Gabrielle Marguerite. Fantasies? Delusions? Wishful thinking, fueled by the guilt that Gabe never completely got over about the ending of her second pregnancy?

Reality?

Ruby wondered. Sometimes she woke from a dream that Gabrielle Marguerite was speaking to *her*, except that Ruby never remembered anything more than a vague impression.

The *snick* of the slider door opening distracted Ruby. She half-turned. Justine carried a bottle of whisky. She set it on the deck railing, between them.

"It's time to drink," Justine said, her voice rough and harsh. "I can't handle any more tears."

"Lots of shadows here for me." Ruby uncapped the bottle and took a swig.

Smooth.

Justine took the bottle. "I imagine. You and Gabie spent a lot of time here." She drank from the bottle. "Oh God, Gabie used to tease me about doing this." Her voice choked.

"He was a fine one to talk. The number of times I caught him drinking from the bottle—" Ruby shook her head, but a faint smile twitched her lips. She took a sip, smaller than her first drink. "Granted, he did that a lot less our second time around. But when we were young and rodeoing, he could drink a lot of people under the table and still stay upright. Though afterwards, the number of times I had to half-drag him back to where we were staying—it was like a switch got flicked and Gabe suddenly realized how drunk he was."

"It was how he survived under Philip. Same for Serg and a number of the other Family men of that generation. Drink hard during Family Christmas so it wouldn't be too bad if Daddy-fucking-dearest decided to torture them using mind control techniques." Justine took another long pull off of the bottle. "Gabie becoming the Martiniere, then Brandon—that changed a lot of things, both within the Family and the Group. As I delve into the records that you and Donna-gran kept during your tenures as the Matriarch—I realize just how much change Gabie made happen."

Ruby exhaled. "I think he was worried about his legacy surviving at the end. The notes I've found—"

"They're weird." Justine waved a hand. "But for Gabie to think his legacy was eroding, before he died? No. Yes, Lily has issues. However, in spite of his health problems, Mike is going to be able to do great things. His research ideas—"

"Mike wants to go to Oregon State, then Caltech for his master's degree, once he finishes catching up with high school. Not the University of Paris, like Gabe and Philip did. I think part of it is because he worries about me."

Justine exhaled hard. "You're fortunate. You have Brandon and Mike. Me—" she shook her head. "Maybe Donald and I shouldn't have divorced. Maybe we should have adopted after my hysterectomy. Maybe I shouldn't have become First Secretary, External Affairs—" she gulped.

"And just where would the Family and the Group have been without your sacrifice? Without your work, it would have been harder for Gabe to challenge Philip." Ruby rubbed Justine's back. "You have *us*. Me. Mike. Bran. You're part of our family."

"I wouldn't have gotten free from Daddy-damned-dearest and married Donald without Gabie's help." Justine shuddered. "And now they're both gone."

Ruby wrapped an arm around Justine. Her sister-in-law buried her head in Ruby's shoulder, so much like what Gabe would do.

Justine finally raised her head. "But *we* created Gabie's legacy. All of us, together. You. Me. Don. Gabie. Brandon. Kris. Indenture is *done*, finally, and if there's only *one* thing that can be laid to the vision of Gabriel Marcus Martiniere, it's that. But he did so much more. The Group wouldn't have survived many more years of Philip—hell, I was ready to tear it all down myself before Gabriel resurfaced. *He* turned that trend around. The Group is still private, stronger than ever thanks to what Gabriel did and Brandon followed up on."

"Age and despair made him think his legacy was failing, I guess."

"But despair over what? Mike? Lily? I can understand his sorrow about how Lily is turning out, but Mike? And then there's little Ronnie. The rest of the Family is bouncing back as well. No," Justine said slowly. "Gabriel's legacy endures. And it will endure, for many more generations."

I hope you're right, Justine.

Justine's words lingered in Ruby's thoughts as her jet landed at the Double R's airstrip. She paused before leaving the plane to look outside. The Double R was prosperous now, not struggling like it had been before she remarried Gabe. Buildings in good shape, labs, staff quarters, the new barn, the airstrip—

Another part of Gabe's legacy.

Maybe that was what she needed to focus on for the rest of her life—extending and expanding Gabe's enduring legacy.

Which includes empowering you, she reminded herself.

With a sigh, Ruby left the plane. Though the snow wasn't deep, she was glad to see Mike sitting in the enclosed crawler, waiting to drive her up to the house.

Mike. Philip's clone.

Who was nothing at all like his progenitor, thanks to every-thing that she and Gabe had done with him. If anything, Mike was more like Gabe than Philip.

Another of Gabe's legacies.

Ruby exhaled, her breath coming in puffy clouds as she walked to the crawler.

I'm not completely alone. And it's going to be up to us to ensure that Gabe's legacy endures.

A task she could handle.

She hoped.

THE END

Like what you've read? Want to follow Joyce either through her monthly newsletter or through an email feed of her irregular blog posts?

Sign up for Joyce's newsletter here:

https://tinyletter.com/JoyceReynolds-Ward

Or follow Joyce's irregular blog posts on her Substack, here:

https://joycereynoldsward.substack.com/

Interested in further serial stories in the Martiniere Multiverse? Check out Martiniere Stories on Substack.

https://joycef1d.substack.com/p/an-introduction-to-martiniere-stories

The Martiniere Legacy

First Meetings: A Martiniere Legacy Short Story
Inheritance: The Martiniere Legacy Book One
Ascendant: The Martiniere Legacy Book Two
Realization: The Martiniere Legacy Book Three
A Belated Christmas Honeymoon: A Martiniere Legacy Short Story
The Enduring Legacy: The Martiniere Legacy Book Four

The People of the Martiniere Legacy

The Heritage of Michael Martiniere: A Martiniere Legacy Novel
Broken Angel: The Lost Years of Gabriel Martiniere: A Martiniere Legacy Novel
Justine Fixes Everything: Reflections on Mortality

The Martiniere Multiverse Books

A Different Life—What If?
A Different Life—Linda's Story (Release Date—Fall 2022, currently serializing on Vella)
Dreamwalker: Gabriel (to be determined)
The Cost of Power (to be determined)

Goddess's Honor titles currently available (chronological order):

The Goddess's Choice: A Goddess's Honor Short Story

Beyond Honor: A Goddess's Honor Novella

Exile's Honor: A Goddess's Honor Novelette

Birth of Sorrow: A Goddess's Honor Short Story

Pledges of Honor: Goddess's Honor Book One

Return to Wickmasa: A Goddess's Honor Short Story

Crown Anniversary: A Goddess's Honor Short Story

Challenges of Honor: Goddess's Honor Book Two

Cleaning House: A Goddess's Honor Outtake Story

Unexpected Alliances: A Goddess's Honor Rough Draft Outtake Story

Choices of Honor: Goddess's Honor Book Three

Judgment of Honor: Goddess's Honor Book Four

Netwalk Sequence Author Preferred 2022 Editions

Life in the Shadows: Book One

Netwalk: Book Two

Netwalker Uprising: Book Three

Netwalk's Children: Book Four

Learning in Space: Book Five

Netwalking Space: Book Six (Release Date August 2022)

Bright Star Fair Witches

Becoming Solo: A Bright Star Fair Witches Novella

Non-Series Titles currently available:

Alien Savvy: A Western SF Novella

Klone's Stronghold

Beating the Apocalypse

Vella Titles:

Falcon of the Martinieres (part of *Justine Fixes Everything*)

Bearing Witness (ebook release February 2022)

Beating the Apocalypse (ebook release January 2022)

A Different Life—What If? An Alternative Martiniere Legacy Novel (ebook release spring 2022)

Becoming Solo

A Different Life—Linda's Story: An Alternative Martiniere Legacy Novel

Audiobooks Available:

Alien Savvy: A Western SF Novella

Coming Soon:

Becoming Solo: A Bright Star Fair Witches Novella

Released from other publishers:

"Queen of the Snows," in *Once Upon A Winter: A Folk and Fairy Tale Anthology*, edited by H. L. Macfarlane

"My Man Left Me, My Dog Hates Me, and There Goes My Truck," in *Black-Eyed Peas on New Year's Day: An Anthology of Hope*, edited by Shannon Page

"Lost Loves," in *All Worlds Wayfarer*

"The Wisdom of Robins," in *Whimsical Beasts: A Campcon Anthology*, edited by Joyce Reynolds-Ward

"The Cow at the End of the World," in *Well…It's Your Cow*, edited by Frog Jones

"To Plant or Pull Up Stakes," in *Pulling Up Stakes: A Campcon Anthology*, edited by Joyce Reynolds-Ward

"The Notice," in *Children of a Different Sky*, edited by Alma Alexander

ABOUT THE AUTHOR

Joyce Reynolds-Ward has been called "the best writer I've never heard of" by one reviewer. Her work includes themes of high-stakes family and political conflict, digital sentience, personal agency and control, realistic strong women, and (whenever possible) horses. She is the author of *The Netwalk Sequence* series, the *Goddess's Honor* series, and the recently released *The Martiniere Legacy* series as well as standalones *Klone's Stronghold, Alien Savvy,* and *Beating the Apocalypse.* Samples of her Martiniere short stories/novel in progress and her nonfiction can be found on Substack at either Speculations from the Wide Open Spaces (general, writing) or Martiniere Stories (fiction). Joyce is a Self-Published Fantasy BlogOff Semifinalist, a Writers of the Future SemiFinalist, and an Anthology Builder Finalist. She is the Secretary of the Northwest Independent Writers Association, a member of the Science Fiction and Fantasy Writers Association, and a member of Soroptimists International.

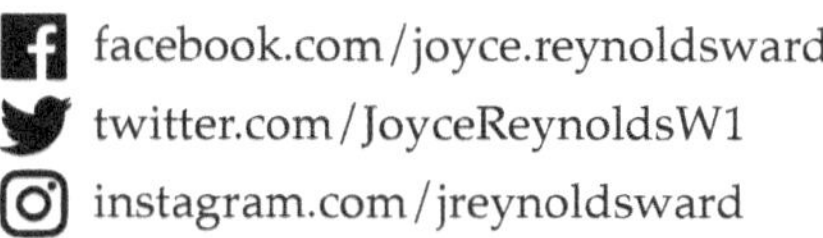